A BRUSH
WITH DEATH

Quintin Jardine
A BRUSH WITH DEATH

HEADLINE

First published in 2018 by
HEADLINE PUBLISHING GROUP

3

Cataloguing in Publication Data is available from the British Library

978 1 4722 3890 0 (Hardback)
978 1 4722 3889 4 (Trade paperback)

Typeset in Electra by Avon DataSet Ltd, Bidford-on-Avon, Warwickshire

Printed and bound in Great Britain by CPI Group (UK) Ltd,
Croydon, CR0 4YY

HEADLINE PUBLISHING GROUP
An Hachette UK Company
Carmelite House
50 Victoria Embankment
London EC4Y 0DZ

www.headline.co.uk
www.hachette.co.uk

Vast thanks to Dr Andrew Smith, Dr Miles Behan,
Mr Renzo Pessotto, Dr Ellis Simon, the staff of cardio-thoracic
ICU and Ward 102, and everyone else who played a
part in rebuilding my lovely wee wife's lovely wee heart,
thus giving us back our life.

Acknowledgements

My thanks go to my supremely talented friend Aine Divine, who helped me look at death in a different way.

One

'Where the hell is the wee toerag?' Detective Inspector Charlotte Mann muttered grimly, as the wide doors slid together behind a portly middle-aged man in a colourful shirt and shorts, pushing a laden trolley. 'How big is that bloody plane? There must have been three hundred people through by now. It can't be bigger than that, surely.'

'Excuse me, please.'

The passenger had manoeuvred his unstable vehicle around the retaining barrier. Lottie looked at him, and realised that she was blocking his progress.

'Sorry,' she said, stepping aside. 'Are you off the Dubai flight?' she asked as he made his way past her.

The traveller nodded.

'Are there many left in the baggage hall?' she asked.

'I'm the last one,' he replied mournfully. 'They've lost one of my wife's cases,' he added. 'It just had to be the one with all the family presents in it.'

'There's nobody else there? No one at all?'

'No, only a boy that got pulled up by Customs. They're giving him a hard time, silly bugger.'

'Maurice!' A shrill voice rang out from a few yards away. The

1

man looked across at its owner, a heavily tanned woman, shaking his head.

'Look, I've got to go,' he said.

'You didn't see a wee man, fifty-something, silver moustache, slightly scruffy?'

'Not in business class, no. Sorry I can't help you, but I've got troubles of my own.'

She nodded. 'Thanks anyway. Don't worry, they'll find your case. They always do, eventually.'

'Try telling her that,' he sighed, glancing at his glowering spouse, then went on his way.

She looked back at the international arrivals gateway, as if she was willing it to open again, then realised that she was alone; the friends, the families, the men in peaked caps holding up scrawled signs bearing passenger names, the last of them had gone. She turned, looking at the signage, picking through the symbols for toilets, taxis and buses, until she found a large stylised 'i' with an arrow pointing off to the right.

'Bugger,' she growled. 'What's happened to the little shite?'

She took her phone from her pocket and checked it for messages, but there were none. Detective Sergeant Dan Provan was missing, officially. I shouldn't have expected anything else, she thought. Apart from work, he's barely been out of Cambuslang in twenty years. What the hell made me believe he could get to Australia and back, no bother?

Lottie Mann and the man some observers called her leprechaun had worked together for most of the DI's career, and for all of her twelve years in CID. Under his tutelage she had risen from detective constable, while he had remained at sergeant rank, the height of his ambition, he said. Provan had achieved the status of an institution within the old Strathclyde police force, but when that was succeeded by the Scottish national police service, the general expectation had been that he would be pensioned off quietly, his experience counterbalanced by his irrepressible irreverence.

In fact, the opposite had happened. He had caught the eye of Bob Skinner, in the final few months of his police career as the last chief constable of Strathclyde, and Skinner in turn had marked the card of Deputy Chief Constable Mario McGuire, who had taken charge of CID across the country in the unified service.

McGuire had wanted to promote Provan, to put him in a position where he could teach others what he had taught Mann, but he had refused. 'Look, sir,' he had said when the DCC had made a futile attempt to insist, 'my pension's maxed out and it's under the old scheme, so I'd leave wi' two thirds of my final salary, and a lump sum in cash, tax-free. You try and put me somewhere I don't want to go, and I'll be out of here. You think I'm kidding? Ask Bob Skinner. He and I had much the same discussion. I'll no' be on a loser financially by retiring; what I'd have made in extra wages would have gone on train fares to work. Keep me with the big lass, sir, or I'm gone. She needs me,' he had added. 'Lottie's no' everybody's cup of tea; the one thing I haven't taught her is how to teach herself. She'd break more sergeants than she'd make.'

The Deputy Chief had given a great sigh. 'I did ask Bob Skinner,' he had confessed. 'He said you were an insubordinate wee bastard, and that you gave up taking orders on the day you gained full pension rights. But he also said you're fucking gold dust, and that I should hang on to you for as long as I can. So that's what I'm going to do . . . with one proviso. You've taken just two weeks' holiday in each of the last five years.

You're fifty-four, and you look every day of it, plus a few more. If I'm keeping you, I'm keeping you healthy, so you're going to use up that unused holiday entitlement. You're taking two months off, and no argument. It's the end of February, so piss off somewhere warm and sunny – the Canaries, maybe. Eat properly and get some exercise; it probably won't kill you. Don't try telling me DI Mann will miss you; she'll be too busy. While you're away, she'll be on a command course. Deal?'

'Deal. To tell you the truth,' Provan had confessed, 'I've been thinking I should go and see Lulu, my daughter. She went to Australia a couple of years ago, and she's been nagging me to visit her.'

'Where does she live?'

'Gold Coast City. She's a primary school teacher there.'

'Then go, Dan. Stay for the whole time, if she'll have you. The Commonwealth Games are on there in April.'

'Big fuckin' deal.'

He had gone nonetheless, astonishing Lottie when she had taken him to Glasgow International by checking in at the business-class counter. 'Ah got a deal,' he had insisted. 'I know folk.'

While he was away, she had indeed been too busy to miss him, much. She had spent most of the time at the Scottish Police College near East Kilbride, on the command course to which she had been ordered. She was not a natural in the classroom, but she had persevered, and had emerged with a greater understanding of staff management, and the realisation that she had been leaving all of that to Dan Provan. She did not share that with her tutors, for she had decided within the first three days of the course that Provan knew far more than they did about the subtle art of getting the best out of colleagues, be they subordinate or senior.

'Where the bloody hell are you?' she murmured as she turned to head for the information desk.

She had reached the escalators when she stopped, realising that there was one thing she had not done. She took out her phone again, found 'Dan' among her contacts and called his number.

She blinked as she heard a ringtone, confused as she realised that it was not sounding in her ear, but on another mobile, somewhere close. She spun round, eyes sweeping the area, until they fell on a man of medium height, standing at the entrance to WHSmith a few yards away, beside a laden trolley. He wore a light cotton jacket, cream coloured, and tan trousers. He was clean shaven and suntanned. His silver hair, which shone with vitality, was close cropped, and he was smiling, at her.

'Dan?' she whispered, into her unanswered mobile.

His smile widened. There was laughter in his eyes.

'Dan!' she shouted.

He silenced his phone and slipped it into a jacket pocket, then walked towards her pushing the trolley with one hand. She met him halfway, frowning as she gazed at him, shaking her head slowly from side to side, in something close to bewilderment.

'How did you . . .' she began. 'How long have you . . .'

'Ah walked right past ye,' Dan Provan replied; his accent had survived the transformation. He winked at her. 'We've known each other for twelve years, too. Ah don't know whether to be chuffed or insulted.'

'I know what *I* am,' she retorted. 'I'm bloody amazed. What's happened to you?'

'I'll tell ye in the car,' he said. 'Are you okay to go? Can I get you a coffee or anything?'

'No, I'm fine. Coffee would be wasted on me. I'm still in shock; talk about a metamorphosis!'

Lottie led the way from the concourse, heading for the pick-up area. It was a mild April day, but Provan shivered as they stepped out of the terminal building. She stopped at the payment machine; he snatched the ticket from her hand as she produced it and validated it using his own credit card. He glanced at the receipt, and winced. 'Nothin's changed,' he murmured.

She opened the boot of her car with a remote as they approached it. 'Are they new suitcases?' she asked, as he loaded his luggage. 'I don't remember those when you left.'

'Aye,' he confirmed. 'The old ones were condemned as well.' He grinned again as he closed the boot lid and moved towards the passenger door. 'Everything was condemned.'

The shock of his transformation was beginning to wear off. 'Come on, then,' she chuckled, as she started the car. 'Let's have the whole story.'

Provan settled into his seat and fastened his safety belt. 'You've met my Lulu, haven't you?'

'Yes, at her graduation party.'

'D'you remember she's a forthright lassie?'

'Not really. I didn't have much of a chance to talk to her.'

'Well she is; always has been. She's been able to put the fear of God in me since she was about six. And she's gettin' worse. When she met me at the airport, she took one look at me as Ah came through the arrivals door and said, "Father, what the hell have you been doing to yourself? You look like an old sofa with the stuffing coming out. You're fifty-four and you look ten years older. I'm not having it, do you hear me?"

'Ah heard her all right. The whole fuckin' airport heard her. The next morning she took me straight to this big shopping centre on the beach, and made me buy new gear.' He touched the jacket. 'Stuff like this, lightweight, bright. Even this fuckin' shirt.' Lottie glanced across, taking in a coconut motif. 'A complete wardrobe, underwear, shoes, the lot. She made me leave the shop wearing some of the things I'd bought there. The clothes I'd walked in wearing went in the bin.'

He paused, chuckling quietly. 'Was she done? Was she hell? From there she took me to this unisex hairdresser, the place she goes to, and handed me over to this bloke. He struck me as a bit of a mincer, but so what? To each his own.'

'Excuse me?' Lottie exclaimed. 'Did Dan Provan just say that? Dan the closet homophobe . . . with the closet door open?'

He nodded. 'You heard me right. Quite a few o' Lulu's friends in Australia bat for the other team. Ah talked to them, and let's just say Ah understand them better now.'

'Thank God for that!' she gasped. 'I've been wondering how to introduce you to my girlfriend. Joke!' she added loudly, as his eyes widened. 'I'm glad you've joined the twenty-first century, though.'

'It's a good place to be,' he admitted. 'Anyway, back to the barber's. "The moustache has to go," Lulu told him. "That's first. After that, turn him into something a little less unkempt." So,' he said, 'the wee 'tache wound up on the floor – cut-throat bloody razor, too – then he shampooed my hair, blew it dry, and left me looking like . . . this.' He tapped his head. 'And you know what? When he was done and I looked in the mirror . . .'

'You wondered where that respectable-looking bloke had been hiding for all these years,' she retorted.

'You're right,' he admitted. 'I really had let myself go, Lottie, had I no'?'

'I tried to tell you often enough,' she replied, 'but you weren't ready to listen. "Blending in", you called it, without realising that even in the pubs you went to, you actually stood out, because most people don't look like that any more. Just make sure you don't regress,' she warned.

'No chance of that. Lulu says she's going to Skype me at least once a week to make sure. Even if she doesn't, there's no worries. She did more than just dress me and groom me. The next stop was a sports shop, for runnin' shoes, shorts and a couple of vests. Then she took me to her gym, would you believe, and signed me up for a fitness course with one of their trainers.'

'Bloody hell! Does she want to inherit early?'

'That's what I asked her, but after the first couple of sessions, it was good. The lad gave me a circuit, using all their machines: treadmills, rowing, cycles, cross-trainers and this bastard of a thing called a Versaclimber.'

'You look none the worse for it,' she admitted.

'I *am* none the worse for it. I don't know if I ever told you, but in my young days, as well as playin' junior football, Ah was a runner. Roads and cross-country mostly; I did a couple of marathons, finished both of them just inside three hours.'

'No,' she said, surprised, 'you never told me that. Why did you stop?'

'Marriage, kids, job, lack of dedication, got to like the beer too much. Ah'm going to start again, though. There are plenty of guys my age still running decent times . . . not that it's about times, really. Just finishing's enough.'

'What else did Lulu fix up for you? Socially?'

Dan laughed. 'Women, you mean? Her pals are all at least twenty years younger than me. Mind you, there was a work colleague, a divorcee in her forties, that she introduced me to at the beach party she had for me . . .'

'Beach party,' Lottie repeated. 'A beach party for Dan Provan,' she said in tones of wonder. 'Absolutely surreal. So,' she continued, 'did you score?'

'If Ah had, it's been so long I wouldnae have remembered what to do. But no, she was a nice woman, sure, but no' the type for a quickie with someone who'll be on the other side of the world in a few weeks. Come to think of it,' he mused, 'neither am I.'

'But you're saying,' she suggested, 'that your interest in the opposite sex has been revived, now that you're . . . more marketable?'

It's never been missing, he thought, but declined to express it aloud. He was just about old enough to be her father, but his feelings for his colleague, boss and friend were complicated, and to be kept to himself.

'Nah,' he replied, 'still dormant.'

'Don't sell yourself short,' Lottie said.

'I won't; I'm five feet eight.'

'You know what I mean. You've scrubbed up very well, Dan.' She laughed. 'I tell you, if you were ten years younger . . .'

'Stop it, you're breaking my heart.' She had no idea of the truth that he spoke.

'So what's the Gold Coast like?' she asked.

'Pretty golden, Ah'll give them that. It's hot, that's the main thing. They could never have held the Commonwealth Games there at the height of their summer; people would have died.'

'And Lulu, is she happy there?'

'Mmm,' he murmured, a little sadly, Lottie thought. 'She'll never be back, I'm sure of that. She's tryin' to talk her brother into going out. I don't think he will, though; Jamie's doing well in Fire and Rescue, and he likes it. He's in line for promotion to

station manager in a couple of years. If he went to Australia, he'd
have to start at the foot of the ladder.'

'Literally?'

'Eh?'

She grinned. 'Ladder. Fireman. Get it?'

'Ah! The jet lag must be worse than I thought. Aye, very
funny.' He paused. 'Talking about kids, where's the wee man?
Where's wee Jakey? Ah thought he might have come with you.'

Even in profile, he saw her face cloud over. 'He's with his
dad today,' she said, quietly, 'until five, when he drops him off
with my Auntie Ann at my place.'

Provan frowned. 'And that's okay wi' you?' he asked her,
quietly.

'No, but it's okay with the sheriff, and that's what matters.
Scott went to court and asked for full visitation rights.'

'Even though he's still in jail?' he exclaimed.

'He's on home leave at weekends, and he'll be released on
parole within the next fortnight.'

'Even so. Visitation rights? Fuck! After what he did?'

'His dad got him a lawyer. Moss Lee; heard of him?'

'Who hasn't? He's a nasty piece of work.'

'Agreed, but he's flavour of the month, especially in family
law. The judges are wary of him because he always goes to
appeal if he loses, and in sheriff court cases he has a record of
judgements being overturned. He argued that supplying police
uniforms to criminals doesn't alter your parental rights. Scott
submitted a statement to the hearing; he claimed that I was
influencing Jakey against him and . . .'

Lottie's mounting anger and outrage were obvious. As she
stopped in mid sentence, her knuckles showed white on the
wheel.

'Go on,' Dan said, quietly. 'What else?'

'He claimed that you were too.'

'Me?' he exploded.

'I'm afraid so. He told the sheriff you were a drunk and a waster.' She hesitated for a moment before adding, 'And he implied that there was something between us.'

'Us?'

'You and me. Outside work. Jakey's grandpa heard him call you "Uncle Dan" one day. The bastard Lee went to town on that.'

'In open court?'

'No, it was what they call a child welfare hearing,' she explained.

'Did *you* have a lawyer?'

'I didn't think I'd need one. It was pitched to me as a simple discussion before a sheriff. I'd no idea Lee would be there until I turned up at the court.'

Dan whistled. 'When he said what he did, what did you say?'

'I told the sheriff that was bollocks, that you were a family friend as well as a colleague and that Jakey calls you that out of respect and nothing else. And don't worry, I also told him that you're a well-respected officer with a clean record, and absolutely no history of alcohol abuse. The sheriff didn't press the point. She asked me if I was firmly opposed to Scott having access. I couldn't say that I was absolutely against it, so the Sheriff said he could have him every other weekend, under the supervision of his own parents. But she also added that Scott's mother should be involved in his day-to-day care as well as my Auntie Ann. That I didn't like, but there wasn't much I could do about it.'

'I'm sorry, Lottie,' Provan growled. 'Ah should have been

there as a witness. Lee would never have said that if I'd been in the room.'

'Yes he would, Dan. But you couldn't have been there; the rules don't allow it. Suppose you had been, and gone off at Lee, it would have made things worse, not better.'

'Thanks a bundle. Ah'll get that shite of a lawyer, though, I promise.'

'No you won't. You'll forget it, and let it lie.'

'It's Scott that's the drunk waster,' he protested.

'Maybe prison will have sorted him out.'

'Sure, and a bright fuckin' light will have shone in his eyes on the road to Damascus. What about his girlfriend? Is she still inside?'

'Christine McGlashan was paroled three months ago. Her name was never mentioned at the hearing, and I never thought to ask. To be honest, I don't know if she's still in the picture.'

'Leave that to me,' he said. 'Ah'll find out.'

'No, Dan, please. Do nothing.'

'If that's what you want,' he murmured grudgingly. 'Let me ask you something, though. How do you feel about Scott now? I know it wasn't the ideal marriage, with his drinking himself out of the police service, but . . . is there still anything,' he tapped his chest, 'in here?'

She nodded. 'Yes, there is. Contempt. Maybe just a wee bit of pity that he's made so big a mess of his life, but nothing else, I promise you.'

'Do you want me to stop seeing the wee fella?' he asked bluntly.

'Absolutely not! Jakey likes you and he respects you. Dan, I need you around more than ever, now that Scott's parents have suddenly wakened up to the fact that they have a grandson.'

He nodded. 'Then Ah'm here for you. Now,' he said abruptly, his tone changing, 'what about the job? What have I missed there?'

'About the same as me. This is my first weekend on call since I got off the course.'

'How was it? Useful?'

'Time will tell. Most of the stuff I knew already.' She glanced across at him. 'Are you pleased to be back, or has this break made you think about cashing in your pension?'

'Yes and no,' he replied, 'in that order. What it has done is waken me up. I've been asleep at the wheel, being dragged along on your coat-tails.'

'There are people who'd say it was the other way around,' Lottie told him.

'Then they'd be wrong. My coat-tails arenae big enough for you.'

'Cheers, pal,' she chuckled.

'Metaphorically. You know what Ah mean. McGuire didnae send you on a course just to keep you occupied while I was away. You're bound for command rank; being in Serious Crimes is just a step on the way.' He put his hand to his mouth, stifling a yawn.

'Jet lag?' she asked, her eyes fixed on the overhead road signs that showed the exit from the M8 on to the M74.

'So they tell me. Lulu's advice is to ignore it and just stick to a normal routine wherever you are.'

'So we'll see you in the office on Monday as usual?'

'Bleary eyed and kangaroo tai—'

The blare of Mann's ringtone, magnified by the car's Bluetooth speakers, drowned out the rest of his Antipodean metaphor.

'I'd better take it,' she called out, then hit the receive button on the steering wheel. 'Yes?'

'DI Mann?' A woman's voice: one they both knew. Detective Chief Inspector Sandra Bulloch was their line manager in the Serious Crimes division.

'Two for the price of one, gaffer,' Provan called out.

'DS Provan? You're back?'

'Fresh off the plane. I brought you a boomerang. I thought it was appropriate, since everything winds up back on your desk.'

'Where are you, DI Mann?' Bulloch demanded, ignoring his wisecrack. The tension in her voice surprised them both.

'I'm on the motorway, on the way to drop Dan off in Cambuslang.'

'Then turn around, please, you're needed in Ayr. Sergeant, you'd best be involved from the start, so you should come too.'

'As long as you're ready for the coconut shirt, ma'am.'

'The crime-scene tunic will cover it up,' she replied curtly. 'It's a fatality, and it's landed on us rather than divisional CID.'

'High profile?' Mann asked.

'You could say. Remember the supermodel that was murdered in Edinburgh last year? This will be even bigger.'

Two

'Ah don't like that woman,' Dan Provan confessed, as Mann set her speed limiter to fifty on entering the average speed camera zone. He had been uncharacteristically silent for most of the journey; the DI suspected that he had been dozing.

'Which one?'

'The one we're going to meet, Bulloch.'

'Sandra's not here to make friends. That doesn't make her a bad boss.'

'Just as well, for she never will make any until she learns to smile. As for bein' a bad boss or a good one, popularity, motivation and success are interlinked. People will work harder for you if they like you than they will if they fear you; that's basic, and by that measure she fails.'

'That's also what they tell you on command courses,' the DI conceded. 'You'd make a better tutor than most of the people there. But don't be too hard on her; okay, she's serious, but it doesn't make her a bad cop. She can't be; she's made detective chief inspector. Bob Skinner took a shine to her, remember, when he came into the old Strathclyde force as the last chief constable pre-unification. He made her his exec.'

'So he did,' Provan agreed, 'but Ah always assumed that was

15

because he wanted a hatchet woman in his outer office. Max Allan, the old ACC, stuck her away in Special Branch, because there it didn't matter whether she pissed folk off or no'.'

'Maybe not,' Lottie countered, 'but Andy Martin put her in Serious Crimes when he was chief, and DCC McGuire's kept her there . . . the same perceptive man that sent you to Australia for two months.'

He grunted. 'We'll see. Does this car know where it's going?'

'The satnav does. Kirkhill Road, Sandra said; that's what I programmed into it. We're not far from Ayr now; it won't be much longer.'

'Ayr,' the refurbished DS murmured. 'When I joined the force, they used to say that the top gangsters in Glasgow lived down this way. I've got no idea whether that was true.'

'That would be before they all moved to the Costa del Sol,' Mann chuckled.

'Aye, but now we've got European arrest warrants, they might be movin' back.' He frowned. 'I wonder if this is a gang thing we're going to. It'll no' be a run-of-the-mill suspicious death if it's been passed straight on to our division.'

'Time will tell.' She grimaced. 'Bloody average speed cameras,' she grumbled.

'Lottie,' Provan sighed, 'we're the fuckin' polis. Blue lights and put the foot down.'

She smiled and took his advice.

Kirkhill Road was a narrow thoroughfare located in one of the most affluent parts of the prosperous burgh. The entrance from the larger approach thoroughfare was partly blocked by a police minibus, with two uniformed officers on duty. Mann showed her warrant card and they waved her through; as she made the turn, a man ran up to her car brandishing a mobile phone. Her suspicion that she was being filmed was confirmed when he shouted, 'Fergus Muirhouse, South Ayrshire TV; can you tell me anything about the incident, Detective Inspector?'

She braked, pushed a button to lower her window and gazed at him evenly. 'No,' she replied, 'because as you can see, we've only just arrived. How do you know me?' she asked.

'I saw you in Glasgow City Chambers, DI Mann,' he volunteered, 'when Chief Constable Field was shot. You were with Bob Skinner.'

'I'm sorry,' she said. 'I don't remember you.'

'No worries. The place was mobbed; I was right at the back.'

'You're quick off the mark today.'

'I live in Irvine,' the reporter explained. 'I won't be on my own for long, though. Can't you give me a head start on the rest? All my source told me was that paramedics had been called to an incident down the road there, at Leo's place.'

'Then you know as much as we do,' Mann lied. 'When we find out more, there might be a statement, but I can't make any promises. Now, if you'll excuse me . . .' She closed the window and slipped her car into gear.

The street was in shadow, beneath mature trees in gardens on either side; the houses had names, not numbers, but the detectives were guided to their destination by two parked patrol cars, and by a uniformed constable standing guard at a stone-pillared gateway.

Mann parked behind the first police car. 'Hold on,' Provan said as he unclipped his seat belt and climbed out, then opened the boot and rummaged in his cabin bag. 'Got it,' he muttered as he hung around his neck the lanyard that carried his warrant card.

'Did you take that to Australia?' the DI exclaimed.

'Of course,' he replied. 'Do you think I forgot about the job for a whole two months? I had a look at the force out there.'

'Tempted?'

'It would be a nice place tae work and the money's good. But like you said, I'm past it.'

'I never said that!' Lottie protested.

He smiled. 'If I was ten years younger, ye said.'

'I didn't mean that you were past it,' she exclaimed.

'Then what did you mean?'

She stopped in her tracks and stared at him. 'I don't know,' she answered quietly.

They moved on towards the crime scene. As they approached, they saw that the house had a name, emblazoned on a plaque on the wall beside one of the pillars 'Invincible,' Provan read aloud. 'That's a bit out of the ordinary.'

They identified themselves to the PC at the gateway and turned in to the driveway. It led to a two-storey mansion, built in red sandstone that had a look of the genuine article about it rather than a facing placed on brick. To its right there was a double garage, and on the left, set back and surrounded by tall trees, another large outbuilding. It was flat roofed, and its walls were mostly of glass, giving the detectives a clear view of the interior.

'It's a gym,' Mann murmured. 'And is that . . . ?'

Provan nodded. 'Aye. It's a boxing ring.' He frowned. 'Oh my,' he whispered. 'Leo's place, the boy said.'

'What are you thinking?' the DI asked.

His reply was forestalled by a cry from the doorway of the house: a female voice. 'DI Mann! DS Provan! This way.'

Detective Chief Inspector Sandra Bulloch stepped out of the vestibule into the dying evening sunshine, moving past a parked ambulance, and two other vehicles that stood beside it. One was a black Range Rover; it had a distinctive registration, a prefix, then 'MMG'. Provan raised an eyebrow, jogged Mann's arm with his elbow and nodded towards it. 'Serious enough tae bring DCC McGuire from Edinburgh on a Saturday,' he whispered.

'Good,' Bulloch said as they reached her. She wore a white crime-scene onesie; a few strands of dark hair had escaped from the hood. Despite the enveloping costume, tension seemed to come from her in waves. 'I'm pleased you could get here so fast. This is not one for the local CID for a couple of reasons, the main one being that most of them know the victim. I'm guessing you'll be senior investigating officer, DI Mann.'

'No' you, ma'am?' Provan exclaimed. Many years of experience had schooled him in signs of the buck being passed, and that was where his thoughts were heading.

'No, I won't be, Sergeant,' Bulloch snapped testily, as if she had read his mind. 'Not on this one.'

'And who would the victim be, ma'am?' Mann asked.

'Get yourself suited up, then come and see.'

She led them indoors, through a vestibule and into a large reception hall. A man stood there, and as they approached, he tossed each of them a packet containing the paper overalls they knew so well. None of his hair was on show, but they knew that it was red.

'Arthur Dorward,' the DS exclaimed. 'Do you attend every crime scene in Scotland?'

'The major ones, more or less,' the scientist replied, 'now that forensics is a central service. But I wouldn't have missed this one. Being a fan of the deceased, I wouldn't entrust it to anyone else.'

'No, I don't imagine you would,' Provan conceded.

'You know who it is?' Mann asked him, as she pulled the hood of the forensic suit over her head and adjusted it.

'Unless I'm very much mistaken. That gym's a giveaway; that and the name plate on the wall.'

'This way,' Bulloch said brusquely, once they were both clad. She's agitated, Mann thought. This is not like the DCI; something's up.

She led them out of the hall and through a corridor into a vast dining kitchen, made even bigger by a conservatory that had been added to the rear of the house. Four investigators were working there; a fifth person, a massive figure, stood apart, watching them from the kitchen area.

'Lottie, Dan,' DCC Mario McGuire exclaimed. 'Welcome to tomorrow's front pages.' He broke off, then looked again at Provan. 'What happened to the moustache?'

'I left it in Australia, sir.'

'Did you need an anaesthetic?'

'Aye, and paracetamol for a couple of weeks after.'

'And the shirt? What's with the shirt that I can see peeking out of that paper suit?'

'Blame ma daughter,' Provan replied. 'Alternatively, you could think of me as a caterpillar that's been cocooned in middle age for the last ten years.'

McGuire grinned. 'But you've shed it and now you're a butterfly.'

'Moth, more like it.'

'Where's the victim?' Mann asked, breaking into their man-chat. 'And who was he to have a place like this?'

'He's over there,' the DCC replied, serious in an instant, leading them towards the conservatory. They followed, and as they entered, they saw a right arm hanging down the side of a high-backed cane chair, the fingers touching the tiled floor, the back of the hand brushing against a cardboard carton that lay on its side.

'To answer your other question, Lottie, his name was Leo Speight, he turned thirty-seven years old last Tuesday, and until he retired last month he was the undefeated, undisputed middleweight champion of the world.'

The DI's eyes widened as she looked down at the lifeless form.

'You've heard of him then,' Provan observed, noting her reaction.

'Of course; the boxer. The world's other most famous Scottish sportsman, alongside the tennis player . . . but the pronunciation . . .'

'The DCC got it right,' Bulloch snapped. 'Speight . . .' she spelled the name letter by letter, 'pronounced "Spite" rather than the usual way, "Spate", like he was called until he turned pro. It was his promoter's idea, so that he wouldn't need a nickname, unlike most boxers.'

'Who found him?'

'His manager,' she replied. 'His name's Gino Butler; he called it in just after two o'clock. He's still on site; I told Inspector Grady, the senior uniform here, to put him in the gymnasium. You'll have seen that on your way in.'

Provan nodded. 'Time of death?'

'The early hours of the morning, that's the guesstimate. Between one and four o'clock.'

'What's that blue smear on his neck?' he asked. 'Ointment?'

Bulloch knelt and looked at it. 'Whatever it is, it isn't that,' she murmured absently.

'Do we have a cause?' Mann asked. Speight had been of

21

mixed race; in death, his skin looked yellowish. His head was supported by the chair's thick soft cushion, and angled slightly to the left. To the casual observer he might simply have been asleep. The giveaways were the blueness of his lips and the foam at the corners of his mouth.

The DCI made to reply, but faltered.

'The pathologist . . . Professor Bell from Glasgow,' DCC McGuire said, answering the question for her, 'wouldn't commit himself; he said there was a possibility of anaphylactic shock, from an undetected allergy, but he's looking at poisoning . . . non-accidental.'

'So it's a homicide?'

'Subject to confirmation, yes,' McGuire declared.

'The guy had forty-four professional fights,' Provan pointed out, 'plus God knows how many rounds of serious sparring. Could it have been a holdover, an undetected injury from his career?'

'It can't be ruled out yet, but that's not what Professor Bell thinks.'

'No history of ill-health, recent or further back?'

'None,' Sandra Bulloch said. Her tone was adamant.

'What makes you so sure?' the DS quizzed her.

'I'm sure, Sergeant, because Leo Speight was my brother-in-law.'

Three

'That's a bit of a bugger,' Chief Constable Margaret Rose Steele exclaimed.

'I couldn't have put it better myself,' McGuire agreed. In the background he could hear music, and high-pitched, excited sounds. 'Is this a bad time?' he asked.

'No, it's fine. Stephanie's watching *Chuggington* on Amazon. It's our pre-bed routine.'

'Are the two of you on your own?' he asked the woman who was his only superior in Scotland's police service, and also his former wife.

'Yes,' Maggie replied, 'my sister's out on the razzle. So,' she said, 'what do you propose to do about the situation?'

'It'll be your decision; this one's above even my pay grade. But . . .' he paused, 'we're both agreed that Bulloch can't possibly be the SIO, not with a family connection to the victim. DI Mann's the ranking inspector in the unit; she's here already with wee Dan Provan, straight off the plane from Australia, wearing the loudest shirt I've ever seen. In the normal course of events, Lottie would take charge, but this is far from normal.'

'Has it leaked to the media?'

'They know that there's been an incident, but none of the

23

detail yet. They're being contained at either end of the street. Lottie said there was only one guy there when she arrived, but I took a look out a minute ago; there must be close on a dozen of them already.'

'If we bring someone else in to take charge,' she said, 'who would it be? Detective Chief Superintendent Payne is national head of Serious Crimes; he's the obvious choice, I suppose.'

'Lowell Payne's in Madeira on holiday. This thing justifies an ACC in command, but that would be Sandra Strong, and frankly, she was not one of your predecessor's better appointments.'

'Which leaves you.'

'Precisely,' McGuire sighed.

'You sound as if you have a problem with that,' Steele observed.

'Don't you? I'm your designated deputy, the number two in the national police service. If I'm seen to be taking command of this investigation, what kind of a signal will that send to the media and the public? It'll either be seen as a lack of confidence in the criminal investigation division, or they'll say that we're prioritising, that Leo Speight's death is being given special treatment because of who he is . . . or was.'

He was left listening to the background sounds of *Chuggington*, and Stephanie's laughter, as the chief constable considered his analysis. He smiled, thinking of his own child, Eamon, who was rationed to fifteen daily minutes of *In the Night Garden*.

'Agreed,' she declared, interrupting his musing. 'That's how they'll present it, and damn it, Mario, they'll be right. DI Mann has to be the senior investigating officer. She is up to it, isn't she?' she asked, a little anxiously. 'You know her a lot better than I do.'

'Oh yes, she is.'

'And Provan?'

McGuire laughed quietly. 'Even more so, but he can't be allowed within a mile of the media.'

'If that's your main worry, exposing them to the press, then it's time for Perry Allsop to earn his corn. Yes, I know,' she added, 'my stated policy is that police officers rather than civilian PR staff should be our public face, but that's not set in stone. He's the communications director, so he can do some communicating. Get him down there, soonest.'

'Will do. I'll stay hands-on, but out of sight.'

'Not too hands-on,' Steele advised. 'You don't want to undermine the woman.'

'I know; I'll be careful.' He sighed. 'You know what I'd really like to do, Mags?'

If they had been on FaceTime, he would have seen her smile. 'I think I do, but we can't. It's impossible.'

'Legally, there's nothing to stop us. Perry Allsop and his people are civilian advisers. So why not another?'

'They're full-time, on the payroll,' she countered.

'There are plenty of areas where we use consultants.'

'But not this one, and you know it, Mario.'

'Yes, I do,' he admitted reluctantly. 'I'm thinking wishfully, that's all. Still, in an ideal world, bringing in Bob Skinner as an observer, adviser, counsellor, mentor, call him what you like, would be the obvious thing to do.'

'Even in that ideal world,' Steele said, 'he would probably tell us to piss off. His media job's using up all the time he can spare from helping Sarah out with the new baby, and getting to know Ignacio, the son he never knew he had until the boy was eighteen years old and needed his help.'

'Hah!' McGuire laughed. 'You say that, but this is the same man who took his boy James Andrew along with him on a stake-out when the kid was three years old. The first time I ever met Bob was at a murder scene. That same night, the first job he ever gave me was to look after his daughter; she was thirteen at the time and he'd brought her along.'

'That was then and this is now,' the chief constable said. 'Nostalgia time's over; you'd better go and brief your SIO.'

Four

'A poisoned chalice?' Lottie Mann murmured, as Deputy Chief Constable McGuire headed along the corridor, bound for his car and Edinburgh.

'What?' Dan Provan grunted, blinking hard, and fighting harder against an urge to yawn. 'A poisoned what? It's a carton – almond-flavoured soya milk – but we cannae be sure that's what poisoned him, no' until the scientists have run their tests.'

'I didn't mean that,' she retorted. 'I was being metaphorical. The boss has made me the SIO; that might look good on my CV, but it could be a curse.' She raised an eyebrow. 'Do you have the faintest idea what a metaphor is, Dan?'

'Aye, it's much the same as a simile, but what's a chalice when it's at home?'

'A drinking vessel.'

'There you are then,' he declared. 'Like I said, we cannae be sure.'

The DI shook her head. 'I give up,' she sighed. 'Come on, let's interview the guy who found the body.'

'We'll have to interview Sandra as well, won't we? Formally, I mean.'

Mann frowned. 'I hadn't thought about that,' she admitted,

'but you're right. She's family, so she might have relevant information about the deceased and his relationships.'

'If Speight was her brother-in-law, and she's single, as we know she is, he must have been married to her sister.'

'Wow! We'll make a detective of you yet, Bruce.'

'Bruce?' His face twisted into a bewildered grimace.

'I thought all Aussies are called Bruce,' she chuckled. 'And you've gone native, that's for sure.'

'I'll revert soon enough; is she still here, the DCI?'

'I don't know,' Lottie admitted as she stepped out of her tunic in the doorway of the dining kitchen. 'I—'

She was interrupted by a shout from the hall, at the other end of the corridor. 'DI Mann!'

'Question answered,' she said quietly. 'Yes, ma'am,' she called out as the two investigators walked towards their boss.

'Are you clear about your instructions?' Bulloch asked as they reached her.

'Crystal,' Mann replied. 'I'm leading the investigation, reporting to DCC McGuire.'

'Yes, he told me, and I'm in agreement with that call. You will keep me in the loop, though.'

'Was that a question?'

The DCI stared at Provan, her eyes like steel. 'It was a request,' she replied. 'One colleague to another. But it wasn't addressed to you, Detective Sergeant.'

'Ah want to know, though,' he insisted, standing his ground. 'Are you asking us or ordering us?'

'Whichever it takes,' Bulloch snapped. 'I don't react well to insubordination, Dan,' she warned.

'And I don't react well to intimidation, ma'am.' Mann laid a hand on his arm, but he shook it off. 'Sorry, Lottie, we need to deal wi' this. Our orders from the DCC were very clear and very specific. DI Mann is the lead investigator and she reports to him: directly, he said. That means, Sandra, that you're no' in the loop, and that we shouldnae share information with you. No,' he corrected himself, 'it's not that we shouldn't, it's that we can't.'

'Dan's right, ma'am,' the DI said. 'You must know that too. If you don't agree with it, you might catch DCC McGuire before he leaves, but honestly, I don't recommend it.'

Sandra Bulloch drew a deep breath and frowned. She glanced through the open front door in the direction of McGuire, who had stopped halfway to his Range Rover to talk with a uniformed inspector, as if she was ready to chase after him. Finally she sighed, and shook her head.

'I had hoped for a little professional courtesy,' she said, 'but if that's how you two see it, I can't argue with you. I'll let you get on with it.'

'Thanks,' Mann murmured. 'In that case, we might as well start with you.'

'Interview me, you mean?' Bulloch exclaimed.

'Of course. The victim's connected to a member of your family, and we both know the stats. Even with a male victim, a significant number of homicides are domestic.'

'Can we keep it informal?' the DCI asked.

'Up to a point,' her colleague conceded. 'I'm happy for you to prepare your own statement, sign it and let me have it, but it would help us if you could give us a run-down on the relationship between Speight and your sister. For openers, what's her name?'

'Faye; but,' she added, 'they're separated, and have been for a couple of years.'

'Still legally married, though?' Provan asked.

She shook her head. 'Actually, no, Sergeant; they never have been. But Faye regards herself as Leo's wife under Scottish common law. I called him my brother-in-law, but it's informal. Faye's got a court case running trying to establish her status as his wife, his widow now, I suppose. Leo was defending it; the lawyers have been sparring for a while, but the real fight was due in the Court of Session pretty soon.'

'Do they have any kids?'

'Two. My nephew Leonard, he's eight, and my niece Jolene, she's six.'

'What caused the break-up?'

Bulloch frowned. 'Since they were never formally a couple, there was never a formal separation either. Looking at it from Faye's position, I suppose you'd say infidelity: his. Leo would be away for long periods at a time before his fights, in Las Vegas with his trainer. There's this notion that fighters are celibate when they're in training camp, and that's why they train well away from home. That might be true for some, but it wasn't for Leo. Faye was wise to him from fairly early on in their relationship. Ach, the truth is that Leo never saw Faye and the kids as his family unit, even if he never admitted it. She lived with that for a while, but a couple of years ago, she found out that he'd fathered a child in America with a nightclub dancer called Rae Letts, and was maintaining a home for the two of them just like he did for her. That's when she started the legal action, to protect herself, as she put it. She'll be three now, the wee lass,' she added. 'They called her Raeleen. If you look in the kitchen, you'll see her photo on the fridge.'

'Your sister,' Mann said. 'Where does she live now?'

'Where she always has, since the kids came along; they're in a house that Leo bought for her in Barassie, near Troon. It's right on the beach.'

'Not far from here, then.'

'Not far at all.'

'How has their relationship been since the court case started? Acrimonious, I imagine.'

The DCI scratched her chin as she considered the question. When her assessment was complete, she replied.

'It was as civilised as they could keep it, that's the word I would use. They agreed to keep it that way for the kids' sake. But it was difficult too. Faye's lawyer took an aggressive line; he told her that she had to start calling herself Mrs Speight, so she did. She changed the kids' names at school too, from Bulloch to Speight, and the name on her bank account and her credit cards. If she hadn't done that, Leo might have offered her a financial settlement, but her lawyer told her he could get her half his wealth. That was a mistake. Leo was a lovely guy, with charisma coming out of his pores, but he was not a man you threatened. He was also nobody's fool; he made millions out of boxing and the promoters made millions out of him, but nobody ever ripped him off. You often hear of cases where big-time fighters wind up penniless and punch-drunk, but that was never going to happen to him. He was clever and he controlled his own affairs. When he retired, he was very wealthy, and healthy with it. You saw him; there was barely a mark on him after all those boxing wars.'

'Were you and Leo close?'

'Why should we have been, Sergeant?' she retorted. 'He was at odds with my sister, after all.'

'Have you contacted Faye since the body was found?' Mann asked.

'No. I've tried to be as professional as possible.' She flinched. 'Even when I saw him lying there, in that chair.'

'Then it's time you stopped, Sandra,' the DI told her. 'Your sister needs to know, and much better she hears it from you than from the telly or from a red-top reporter. Go and find her, tell her, and look after her.' She paused for a second. 'But please do not give her any details of the crime scene or anticipate any questions that Dan and I will be asking when we interview her.'

'You didn't need to tell me that, Lottie,' Bulloch protested.

Mann gazed down at her. 'Oh, but I did, boss. We both know I've got a big arse, and it takes a lot of covering. Give us her address and her contact details and tell her we'll want to talk to her, if not tonight, then tomorrow morning for sure.'

'What about formal identification? Will you want her for that? Leo's father's dead and his mother's in a care home with Alzheimer's. She's been there for years; she has no idea who Leo is.'

'That won't be necessary. I would say you were close enough for me to accept your identification, if Kirk Dougan, the procurator fiscal, agrees.'

'Okay.' The DCI took a notebook from her pocket, scribbled in it, tore out the page and handed it over. 'There: Faye's details.'

'Thanks.' The big detective's expression softened. 'By the way, Sandra,' she murmured, 'I'm sorry for your loss. I will tell you anything I can, as long as it goes no further.'

Bulloch nodded, then turned and left, breaking into a run as she headed for her car.

'Did you believe her?' Provan asked. 'That she and Leo weren't close?'

'Unless we find out otherwise, I think we have to. Why? Do you have doubts?'

'I've no reason to, not yet. But I do have an open mind on the question.' He walked back into the kitchen, beckoning Mann to

32

follow, leading her to its huge fridge freezer. At least twenty photographs were fixed to its doors by magnets. Some were places, some were people, but his eye settled on one, a black child with frizzy hair in the arms of a smiling woman. The Eiffel Tower rose behind them, but not the original.

'The Paris Casino, in Las Vegas,' Provan said. He slid the photograph out from behind its magnet and looked at the back. 'It says, "Love you Daddy, Raeleen". Sandra said the kid will be three years old, and she was at least two when this was taken. So it cannae have been there for any more than a year. Does that not make you wonder?'

'Wonder what?'

'How . . .' He stopped and shook his head. 'Naw, forget it. Nothin', just an attack of jet lag, that's all.'

Five

'This is bigger than my house,' Lottie Mann murmured as they stepped through the door into Leo Speight's private gymnasium.

'Mine too,' Provan agreed, surveying its equipment. 'It's got the lot. Free weights, Nautilus machine, leg press . . . you name it, it's here,' he said, then proceeded to astonish his colleague by launching a spinning kick with the outside of his moccasin that hit the heavy punch bag at shoulder height.

'Bloody hell,' she said. 'You'll rupture yourself.'

'Three months ago, I might have, but not any more. I told ye, I started working out when I was in Australia.'

'When did you learn that move?'

'About forty years ago,' he replied. 'I did all that stuff when I was a kid. It's amazin' what comes back to you.'

She shook her head. 'I don't know if I can take the new Dan Provan. It can't last; you're bound to regress.'

'No danger,' he assured her. 'I'll have to stay fit, if only to keep up wi' my grandson.'

'Grandson?' Mann exclaimed. 'Is your Lulu expecting?'

'No, Vanessa, Jamie's lassie, she is. They told me last week.'

'That's great. You'll be wanting to go and see them. Let's find this man Butler and interview him, then I can get you home. We can talk through a plan for the investigation on the way.'

Two doors were situated at the rear of the gym. Provan opened the one on the left to find himself looking at a steam room with changing, shower and toilet facilities beyond. Mann tried the other and stepped into a lounge. It was furnished with a huge U-shaped couch, on which a man sat gazing at a sixty-inch wall-mounted television. He was watching Sky News, which he silenced with a remote as the detectives entered.

'Mr Butler?'

He nodded, rising to his feet. His eyes were misty and he had the look of a person in physical pain.

'I'm Detective Inspector Mann; I'm in charge of the investigation into Mr Speight's death. This is Detective Sergeant Provan,' she added as her colleague joined her.

'CID?' Gino Butler exclaimed; he was frowning and looked confused. 'I could understand Sandra being here, but why are CID involved?'

'Because your client's death is regarded as suspicious. We can't be sure yet; other possibilities remain open, but an autopsy should tell us one way or another. We don't wait for that to start an investigation, though.'

'Jesus!' the man whispered, slumping back on to the couch. 'I just thought, well, heart attack, stroke, something like that.'

'You're Mr Speight's manager, we understand,' Provan said.

'That's what they call me,' Butler replied, 'and I suppose I am, but only in that I manage the business that he's already done; Leo took all his own decisions, and delegated nothing that he didn't have to. I'm his accountant more than anything else. If I manage, it's to look after the product endorsements, advertising deals, that sort of stuff. Other than to count the money, I don't get involved with the boxing side: that's Bryce Stoddart's job, or it was until Leo retired. Bryce was Leo's promoter,' he explained, reading Provan's unspoken question. 'He staged the fights, or co-staged the American and European ones, did the deals with TV and so on. My role there was to make sure everything was kosher, that all the pay-per-view money Leo was due found its way to him.'

'Didn't it always? Was Leo ever ripped off?'

'No, Sergeant, not with me looking out for him, but it has happened with other fighters.'

'How did Mr Stoddart feel about Leo Speight retiring?' Mann asked.

'It wasn't the best thing that ever happened to him,' the manager conceded, wryly, 'but he's a realist. He always knew the day would come. And Leo always said he would go out at the top; nobody was ever in any doubt about that. As soon as the Mario Fonsecco fight was made, he said that it would be his last. They could have taken it to Vegas, for Fonsecco was the great American hope, the up-and-comer, but Leo was the long-time undefeated lineal champ; he had all the belts and he was in control. He said it was going to be in Glasgow, and that was that. He even insisted on taking it to the Hydro. We could have waited until the summer, and had it in Ibrox or Celtic Park, with fifty thousand people there, but the champ said no, he wanted it indoors, in the heart of Glasgow, so it went ahead in January.'

'How did the other boxer's people take that?'

'They weren't bothered. They were on twenty per cent of the pay-per-view take, which was monster. They put a return clause in that said if Fonsecco won, the second fight would be in Madison Square Garden, but it was meaningless, because they knew that Leo would retire, win, lose or draw, and also because they realised that Fonsecco would most likely get chinned.'

'Which he duly did,' Provan said. 'Technical knockout, round number seven, sweet as a nut.'

'Were you there?'

The DS nodded. 'Leo's last fight? I wouldn't have missed it.'

'Me neither,' the DI murmured. 'How did you come to find the body, Mr Butler?'

'I came looking for him,' he replied sadly. 'He and I were supposed to be having lunch, in the Turnberry Hotel, with a publisher. Her name's Emily Raynor; she's managing director of Masthead, a London company. She wants to do a book with Leo, a ghosted autobiography. I said I would meet him there but he never showed. He wasn't answering his phones either, so I asked her to wait and came looking for him. You saw where I found him.'

'How did you get in? Do you have keys to the house?'

'Yes, I do, but the door wasn't locked. He wasn't big on locking doors; he was Leo Speight, for Christ's sake. Nobody was going to burgle him.'

'When you arrived,' Provan asked, 'were you aware of anyone else having been here? Was there anything in that room that struck you as unusual?'

'No, nothing. The place was neat as always; if there had been anything out of place, I'd have noticed it. Leo's a very tidy bloke. He had a touch of the OCD about him.'

'Did you call out, or search the house? Did you check to see whether there was anyone else here?'

Butler nodded. 'Yes,' he admitted. 'I did yell, and did I bomb up the stairs to Leo's room. I was half expecting to find a woman there; more than half, to tell you the truth. Leo was one for the ladies, no question. He had four children by three different women. I used to kid him on about being out to break Ray Charles's record.'

'Four,' Mann repeated. 'We knew about three. Who's the fourth?'

'Gordon; Gordon Pollock. Leo had him when he was eighteen, the age the boy is now. He and Trudi, the lad's mother, were just kids at the time, although even then Leo was a winner, in the amateurs: ABA super-welterweight champion.'

'Were they together, Leo and Trudi? A couple?'

'Hell, no; them going out was all a secret. Her dad, Big Shane, made out he was a bit heavy, a minor mobster; he threatened to have Leo kneecapped when he found out that Trudi was up the duff.'

The DS grunted. 'How did Leo react to that?'

'With a left hook and a straight right; he laid him as broad as he was long in his own kitchen. Then he put a carving knife to Big Shane's throat and explained the facts of the situation: that there wasn't a single man in Paisley who'd take that job on, and that if Shane ever threatened him again, he'd wind up in the river, regardless of whose dad he was.'

'You seem to know a lot about this, Gino,' Provan remarked.

'I was there,' he replied. 'I saw Big Shane go down, and I heard Leo mark his card. That was the only time I ever saw him threaten anyone, ever. We were all kids together back then, and Leo was my best mate. The truth is that we all grew up wide, all us kids, but Leo and I left that life behind us after he went to the Olympics, the very same year that Trudi got pregnant. He went to Sydney, won a silver medal . . . that was the only fight he ever lost,' Butler sighed, 'on points in the final to a Russian – fucking robbed he was too – and came back to sign a pro contract with old Benny Stoddart, Bryce's dad.

'Benny was a good bloke; he moved Leo away from Paisley, down to London, and got him a top trainer. He also enrolled him in the LSE. Even now that's pretty much unique for a fight promoter, but Benny said that he believed in training his boys for a life after boxing. We weren't stupid lads, Leo and me,' Butler added. 'We'd done our Highers, both of us. By the time Leo was twenty-two, he was British middleweight champion and he had a degree. So had I, only mine was from Strathclyde Uni.'

'What about Trudi? What happened with her?' Mann asked him.

'She had Gordon, but she stayed in Paisley. Big Shane and her mother insisted that he was brought up as Gordon Pollock. Trudi's still around; she works for me, in fact.'

'It wasn't her you expected to find in Leo's bed, was it?'

'Hell, no!' He laughed softly. 'Trudi's filled out a bit since then, to put it delicately. She's not Leo's type any longer.'

'Did you think you might find Faye there?'

'Definitely not. They're okay, they're as cordial with each other as they can be given the circumstances, and very good with their kids, but that's as far as it goes.'

'When was the last time you saw Mr Speight alive?' Mann asked.

'At the party last night.'

'Party?' she repeated.

'Leo's official retirement party; we held it back until all the money was in from the Fonsecco fight.'

'What was the venue?'

'A place called the Blacksmith; it's a bijou hotel in Newton Mearns, with a function suite attached. It's owned by one of Leo's companies. We used it because it was handy for everybody: the Glasgow crowd, the folk who flew in or came from a distance . . . celebrity friends of his like Joey Morocco, the actor, Aileen de Marco, the politician, Cameron McCullough, the businessman, and his wife . . . and of course Leo himself.'

'When did it begin?'

'Half six. We had champagne, then dinner and speeches. It was a bit like a wedding reception without a bride and groom. Bryce Stoddart said a few words, and wee Billy Swords, the TV guy, he was the MC for the night. He did the commentary on all Leo's biggest fights. After that Leo spoke; he thanked everybody who helped and supported him through his career, he swore on a stack of bibles that he really was done and there would be no comeback, and he finished by making an announcement. He said that he was thinking about launching his own boxing and MMA channel.'

Mann frowned. 'MMA?'

'Mixed martial arts; his plan was for a rival to the UFC promotion, but doing major boxing fights as well. It wasn't going to be on a satellite TV outlet; instead it was going to be streamed to subscribers, like Netflix, through a host platform. He was hoping that Bryce would agree to join him, and that Billy Swords would front it up. Maybe Bryce will take over the project, but I think probably not. I reckon the idea's as dead as Leo.'

'How would that have gone down with the existing promoters?' she asked.

'Like a lead balloon. It would have made a few people very annoyed, to put it mildly.'

'Sufficiently annoyed to . . .'

Butler finished her question. 'To take Leo out of the picture? I wouldn't have thought so. The Mafia doesn't run boxing any more.'

'He was at the party,' Dan Provan said, 'but he was found here. What time did he leave?'

'Around about midnight, give or take. There was music after the speeches; Joey Morocco did a couple of songs, then there was a disco. The thing went on till about two in the morning, but Leo wanted to be sharp for the lunch with Emily Raynor today, so he split early.'

'Was Faye Bulloch there?' the DS asked.

Butler nodded. 'So were the kids, until after dinner and the speeches. Gordon and Trudi were there too, of course. And Rae Letts, his Las Vegas girl, and their wee one, Raeleen. He insisted that they come.'

'Did he do that to wind up Faye?'

'No, he said that everybody that was important to him had to be there.'

'How about the publisher? Was she invited?'

'No,' the manager replied. 'There was no reason for her to be, was there? Leo had never met her before yesterday afternoon.'

'Where did they meet yesterday?'

'Here, at two o'clock, to let her outline the proposition to us. They were together for about an hour, in the conservatory.'

'Did you sit in?' Mann asked.

'No, I left them to get on with it; I knew what the headline terms were. After she arrived, I went up to the Blacksmith to check that everything was okay for the party.'

'Will Ms Raynor still be at the Turnberry Hotel?'

'She will be. She was booked in for last night and tonight. She's probably sitting there thinking she's been stood up.'

The detectives exchanged glances; Mann raised a questioning eyebrow, Provan nodded.

'Okay, we'll talk to her,' the DI said.

'She can't tell you anything,' Butler warned.

'Be that as it may, she had a private meeting with Mr Speight a few hours before he died. If he said anything to her that might have been relevant – even if she didn't know it – we have to interview her to find out.'

She extended a hand. 'Give me your business card please, Mr Butler, or your mobile number. You can go for now, but we may need to speak to you again.'

Six

'Are you okay with this, Dan?' Mann asked her colleague. 'You must be running on empty by now. If you like, I could call the woman at the Turnberry and make an arrangement to meet her tomorrow, before she flies back to London.'

He shook his head. 'I've hit the wall, Lottie, and climbed over it. My body thinks it's breakfast time right now. I can go on for a while . . . mind you, I'd like a bite to eat.'

'We'll pick something up on the way. Meantime, I'll contact Ms Raynor and ask her to be ready for us.'

'Will we no' have to stay here to talk to the press?'

'No,' she replied. 'The big bosses have decreed that the guy Allsop, the communications director, will do all that.'

'A civilian? I thought that was against policy.'

'Not any more. Hey, if you think I'm bothered, think again. I brief Allsop on what he can and can't say, but he has to stand there facing the cameras and the recorders. I've never been very comfortable doing that stuff.'

'You were all right last time,' Provan pointed out.

'Maybe, but Skinner was there. I knew I could rely on him if I got into deep water.'

'I wish he was still here. That guy Martin, the first chief of the new force; he was supposed to be the business, but he was a bloody disaster.'

'If you ask me,' Mann mused, 'he spent too much time trying to prove to the world that he wasn't Bob Skinner, instead of following his example.'

'His and the old fella who was chief before him,' the DS added. 'Sir James Proud, his name was. They called him Proud Jimmy, until he got his knighthood.'

'Past tense?'

'I think so. I'm sure I heard he had cancer.'

'Don't write him off, not till you read his name on a coffin plate. Come on, let's head for Turnberry.'

'What about Allsop? Shouldn't we wait for him if you have to brief him?'

'I have done. I spoke to him when you were in the toilet. I told him he can confirm the identity, but say that we're treating it as an unexplained death, pending post-mortem findings.' She opened her car door, and slid into the driving seat. 'We should get going. I'd like to meet Ms Raynor before she sees Allsop on telly.'

'Will they let me into the place wearing this shirt?' Provan muttered.

Heading out of Ayr, Mann spotted a McDonald's sign, and pulled in. Two hurried Big Macs and two coffees later, they were back on the road, but the rest of the journey went by in silence, mostly because the sergeant's head kept dropping on to his chest, only for him to snap awake, time and time again.

'I thought you said you were over the wall,' the DI laughed as she pulled up alongside the long white hotel, set on a crest overlooking the championship golf course.

'I'm wide awake now,' Provan promised. 'I wonder if the owner's in.'

'I imagine he's otherwise occupied.'

They walked for at least three hundred yards before reaching the main entrance. The DS whistled as they stepped into the reception area. 'How the other one per cent live, eh.'

'They're welcome to it,' Lottie murmured, with a hint of bitterness. 'My grandfather was a waiter in a hotel as posh as this. He needed the tips to survive because the wages were at starvation level.'

'That wouldnae happen now, though.'

'One can only hope,' she growled.

'One can,' he repeated, smiling. 'Did you learn that on your command course?'

As he spoke, he realised that he was being appraised by an attendant, a tall man in his twenties dressed in a tailored blue uniform, double-breasted, with epaulettes. His grin vanished and he reached for his warrant card on its lanyard. 'DS Provan and Detective Inspector Mann,' he said sharply. 'We're here to see one of your guests, a Ms Raynor.'

The man continued to stare down at him, focusing on his clothing.

'Incognito,' Provan declared. 'Ah'm disguised as a bloke who's just off a plane from Australia, which means handle me with care. Ms Raynor, please . . . that's assuming you can find her in a place this size.'

'Is she expecting you, sir, madam?' The accent was American.

'No, she isn't,' Mann told him, 'but it is important.'

'I'm not sure,' he murmured. 'We are very protective of our guests.'

'So are we,' the DI countered bluntly, 'and you will be one of ours if you obstruct us. Ms Raynor please, quick as you can. You can tell her it's in connection with her delayed business meeting.'

'Very well, if you insist. If you'll wait here, please.'

He walked across to the reception desk and spoke to the older of the women behind it. She glanced across at Mann and Provan, frowning, hesitating for a few seconds before turning her gaze to a monitor, then picking up a phone. The officers watched the scene for almost a minute, until their greeter approached them once again.

'Ms Raynor will see you,' he announced. 'If you'll follow me.'

They fell into step behind their escort as he led them from the reception area along a corridor that ran westwards and seemed to go on forever. Eventually he stopped, and opened a half-glazed door into what appeared to be a small conference room.

'Wait here, please, madam,' he said, ignoring Provan entirely.

'I think you were right, Dan,' Mann chuckled as the door closed on them. 'It was only your warrant card that got you in here.'

The DS scowled as he checked his watch. 'Cheeky prick.' He looked at his friend, suddenly anxious. 'Hey, never mind this being a long day for me, what about you? Should you no' be back for Jakey by now?'

'It's okay,' she assured him. 'I sent my Auntie Ann a text warning her I'd be late.'

As she spoke, the door opened, and a tall, dark-haired woman stepped into the room. She was younger than either had expected, younger than either of the detectives.

Managing director, the DI thought. She must be bright.

'You want to see me?' Emily Raynor began, with a mixture of curiosity and anxiety in her eyes. 'You're police officers?'

'Detective Inspector Charlotte Mann, and this is Detective Sergeant Dan Provan.'

'Reception said you want to see me about my meeting with Leo Speight. What's wrong? Has he been arrested for something?'

'No,' the DI replied. 'We're sorry to have to tell you that he's dead. His body was found in his house earlier today.'

'Dead?' the young publisher repeated. She was visibly shaken. 'But he looked so fit.'

'He was so fit. The official word at the moment is that his death is unexplained, but in fact it's suspicious.'

'That's police-speak,' Raynor exclaimed, her composure restored. 'Are you telling me he was murdered?'

'Not yet,' Provan said. 'Not until the pathologist says he was, but that's the way we're leaning.'

'That's terrible. Poor Leo. How can I help you?'

'We don't know if you can,' the DS admitted bluntly, 'but you met with him yesterday, and you talked with him for a while. So we need you to go over that conversation. Sit down, please, Ms Raynor.'

'That's Mrs.'

'Whatever, make yourself comfy.'

The trio settled into chairs at a small table beside a window that looked out on to the embers of the day as the setting sun gave a pink tinge to the expansive waters beyond the golf course. Is that the Firth of Clyde? Provan pondered. Or the Irish Sea? A wave of tiredness broke over him, taking him by surprise. Either way, who gives a fuck?

'Carry on,' he said. 'Tell us about your conversation with Mr Speight. We'd like you to recall as much as you can.'

'It was strictly business,' Emily Raynor began as soon as they were settled.

'Your business being book publishing?' Mann asked.

'That's right. I'm MD of Masthead Book Publishing; we're a small house, still independent, but what we do we do very well, and we are very profitable by contemporary standards. Mostly we publish genre fiction, crime and what we call chick lit these days.'

'Forgive me,' Provan intervened, 'but you look as if you've only known these days.'

'Touché, Sergeant,' she replied. 'And thank you. You're probably right, but publishing is a very fast-moving industry. I'm thirty-two, as it happens, but there are younger people than me in positions like mine. Masthead is profitable in difficult market conditions, and that's how I'm judged: by results, with no allowances made for age or anything else.'

'How do you do that? Beat the market conditions?'

'By taking no chances. I don't expect ever to publish a Man Booker short-lister; we stick to what we know makes money. As I said, that nearly always means genre fiction, TV tie-ins – cookbooks and the like – and celebrity biographies . . . if the celeb's big enough to be a sure winner.'

'Which you thought Leo Speight was?' the DI observed.

'Absolutely. He's been a huge name in British sport, yet he's still a mystery to many people. He's never done an authorised biography before. There have been a couple of unofficial attempts by journalists, but none of his inner circle would co-operate with the writers, so they were superficial and sank without trace.'

'What made you think he would have co-operated with you?'

She stared at Provan, wide-eyed, then smiled. 'One and three quarter million pounds, Sergeant. That was my opening offer when we met yesterday, although our owner, a hedge fund, had authorised me to go as high as two million. It's a massive advance for a sports book. It was for world rights to an autobiography, with a named co-author.'

'Who would that have been?'

'We hadn't got that far, but I've been in discussion with a Pulitzer Prize winner, an American novelist named Eroica Jonsen. You may have heard of her.'

Mann stifled a laugh. 'And then again he may not. Who started the ball rolling, Mrs Raynor?' she asked. 'Did you approach Mr Speight?'

'No, I approached Gino Butler about the project a few weeks ago.'

'Butler? Speight didn't have a specialist literary agent?'

'No, Inspector, he didn't. I hear what you're saying, but I didn't care who I dealt with if I got Leo's signature on a contract. Frankly, having Gino as the agent would have been easier for me.'

'And being on a percentage of the deal, he'd have been keen to sign up,' the DI suggested.

'Oh, Gino was, make no mistake about that. It was . . .' She stopped in mid sentence, a canine nipping at a corner of her mouth.

'Go on, please.'

Raynor sighed. 'Leo was the problem. As soon as we started to talk, it was clear to me that he'd been more or less dragged along to the meeting . . . figuratively, that is. Leo wasn't a man who'd have been dragged anywhere literally. He had an air about him, not of menace, but of complete physical self-confidence. I did a lot of reading about him before I came up here. One of the things that came across was his ability to win fights before he even stepped into the ring, by sheer, effortless intimidation of his opponents, without even saying a word. When we met, he seemed to fill the room. I couldn't imagine him ever being beaten, and I had the sense that he'd never imagined it either.'

'How did he react when you made your offer?' Provan asked.

'With what I'd describe as polite indifference. I pitched it as hard as I could, bigged up Eroica as the co-author; when I got to the advance, the headline figure, one and three quarter million, he didn't even blink. He smiled, paused for less than five seconds and then said, "Mrs Raynor, after tax and commission, that would increase my total wealth by about half of one per cent, near as damn it. In return for that, I would have to give you and your American lady full access to my life. I don't know if that's something I'm prepared to do." I have to say, that stopped me in my tracks. In my experience . . .' she grinned at Provan briefly, 'limited as it is, sports people are always about money, money, money, but not Leo Speight. That said, I knew he was wealthy, but not . . .' She paused. 'From what he said, he must have been worth over a hundred million. Who'll inherit that?'

The DS shrugged, and blinked hard to keep his eyes in focus. He had been asking himself the same question. 'That'll depend on his will,' he said, 'but I can see a few lawyers picking up six-figure fees arguing about it.'

Mann raised a hand, intervening. 'He couldn't have turned you down flat, though,' she pointed out, 'since you were due to meet again today.'

'That's true. He didn't. He said that he owed it to Gino Butler to consider it properly, so he'd think about the proposition overnight and give me an answer today.'

'It seems that you've had that, if not in the way you'd hoped.'

Emily Raynor nodded. Then her expressive eyes narrowed to match the smile that followed. 'And yet I haven't. Potentially, an authorised biography of Leo Speight is worth even more now he's dead. He has no privacy to protect, and if your suspicions are confirmed, the manner of his death gives it massive extra interest.'

'Maybe,' the DI conceded, 'but who does the authorising?'

'His estate will,' she replied instantly. 'His executor, when we know who that is. Who's the likeliest candidate, do you think?'

'We can't speculate.'

'I will. Gino Butler is the obvious. His manager and his childhood friend. And even when Leo was alive, Gino was obviously in favour of the project. I'm seeing a best-seller here, *Sunday Times* and *New York Times*. *The Life and Death of Leo Speight*, by Gino Butler with Eroica Jonsen. Oh yes, I need to speak with Gino again, as soon as possible.'

And so do we, Lottie Mann and Dan Provan thought, in mental harmony.

Seven

'Could it be that easy?' Lottie asked as they stood beside her car.

'It usually is, lass,' Provan replied, 'but let's no' get ahead of ourselves. We need Graeme Bell to tell us what killed Leo before we can think about interviews under caution.'

'That won't be till tomorrow morning, so we'd best get you home, and me.'

'Go straight to yours,' he said, as he reoccupied the passenger seat and strapped himself in. 'I'll get a taxi from there.'

'Sod that,' she answered. 'It's only an extra fifteen minutes for me to drop you. Auntie Ann won't mind.'

'She's a good woman, your auntie.' He yawned. 'She's single, isn't she? Mid fifties?'

'In your dreams, Dan,' she laughed.

Those dreams enveloped Provan before they had left the hotel grounds, but they involved Lottie, Australian beaches and a dead shape in a cane chair, conquered at last, rather than visions of a middle-aged Scottish spinster nurse. He slept all the way to Glasgow, oblivious to the sound of Radio Scotland, and to the news bulletin in which Peregrine Allsop's emotionless anglicised Edinburgh tones announced the death of Leo Speight, emphasising that the cause was at that time undetermined, but that further information would be released when it became available.

Not even the mention of Lottie Mann's name and his own, in a shouted question that Allsopp ignored, roused him from his slumber, nor did Fergus Muirhouse's televised description of how 'Glasgow's top detective duo' had been spotted at the scene.

He woke only when Lottie kissed him lightly, playfully, on the cheek and whispered, 'Wake up, Sleeping Beauty, and by the way, you need a shave,' into his ear.

Snapping back into wakefulness, he sat upright and stared at her. 'There's something I'm missing,' he said.

'Yes, your moustache,' she chuckled, 'but don't go growing it again.'

'No' that. Something at the crime scene.'

'It's not a crime scene till Graeme Bell says it is,' she pointed out.

'Don't be bloody pedantic, Lottie. It is, and we both know it. There's something there, something we've seen and it's wrong, but I'm buggered if I can put my finger on it.'

'You will, though,' she assured him. 'You always do. Now indoors with you and let me get home.'

Provan nodded. 'Aye, on ye go, lass. Thanks for this. I really would have got a taxi.'

'I know you would,' she agreed, adding, 'then you'd have gone to sleep again, and the driver would probably have taken you home via Hamilton to ramp up the meter, and you'd have been none the wiser.'

Provan winced at the thought as he retrieved his baggage from the boot. Standing on the pavement, he retrieved his keys from a pouch in the front of his cabin bag. 'What's the plan for tomorrow?' he asked.

'Light breakfast, then it's you and me for the Queen Elizabeth Hospital. Professor Bell's going to do the post-mortem on Speight at ten o'clock, and we'll need to witness it.'

'When was that arranged?'

'About fifteen minutes ago. Graeme called to let me know. You slept through that as well.'

'I'll drive,' he volunteered.

She shook her head. 'No, I'll pick you up. Your body clock will still be hours out of kilter.'

'Maybe.' He paused, frowning. 'Wait a minute, it's Sunday tomorrow. What about Jakey? Lottie, you don't need to be there. I'll dragoon a DC as corroborating witness and cover it.'

'No way. I cannot miss it. If this does become a murder investigation and we get to a trial, I have to be able to give evidence on every aspect. If I have to, I'll bring Jakey with me; there'll be a crèche at the hospital.'

Provan laughed. 'He'll love that, being nine.'

'I can park him in Graeme's office. But it won't come to that. Auntie Ann will do the needful again.'

'Or his granny?'

Her face grew thunderous. 'She's the very last resort.'

'Needs must,' he retorted. 'On you go now, get back to the wee lad.'

She left him standing on the pavement outside his terraced home. As she reached the junction with the main road, she glanced in her rear-view mirror and saw him gazing after her, keys dangling loosely in his fingers. A flush of unexpected pleasure surged through her, as she realised how much she had missed him.

She thought about him all the way home, wondering how it could be that she felt safer now that he was back, wondering why there was a smile on her face. 'Naw,' she murmured, still grinning.

The journey to her home in the East End took no more than fifteen minutes. She parked her car in its numbered bay. The smile vanished and her mood changed as she looked around; there was no sign of Auntie Ann's Mini. She checked her watch and saw that it was eight fifty.

'What's he been up to?' she murmured, as she ticked off possible reasons for her aunt's absence. The most likely, she decided, was that Jakey had persuaded his minder to take him to Frankie and Benny's for a Saturday-night pizza, a treat she herself had promised him that morning, when all had been calm and all that had been on her agenda was the collection of Dan Provan from Glasgow International.

She let herself into her little house. She loved the place; to her it was a mansion, representing independence, freedom from her waster ex-husband, and from a marriage that had started with crossed fingers and ended with clenched fists.

And yet it felt strangely empty. Jakey's green parka was gone from its hook on the hall stand, Ann's blue coat with it. She licked her lips, realising that she was thirsty; Dan had emptied the water bottle that she had taken to the airport, and then another. She hung up her own coat where Jakey's would have been earlier and moved into the kitchen. She was filling the kettle when she saw the yellow note, almost out of sight on the side of the fridge, in Ann's familiar scrawl: *Sorry, as text said, no option. A x*

She frowned, and then recalled a vibration on her phone just as Emily Raynor had come into the room in the Turnberry

Hotel. She dug it out of her trouser pocket and searched her messages. Sure enough, there was a text from her aunt: *Sorry, L. Bus crash on M8, major incident, all available staff called in. Mrs Mann's on her way to relieve me. Ouch, I know. Sorry again.*

The bus crash. Second item on the Radio Scotland news after the announcement of Leo Speight's death. She had still been focusing on Perry Allsop and it had washed over her, but it tied in with Aunt Ann's message. As an A&E sister at Monklands General Hospital, she would have been at the top of the list to be called.

So where the hell was Dorothy bloody Mann, and where was her son? No way his skinflint granny would have sprung for a pizza outing.

She scowled at her phone as she found her ex-mother-in-law's mobile number in her contacts directory and called it.

'I wondered how long it would take you,' a combative voice snapped. 'Just back, are we?'

She felt her eyes widen; she tried to control herself, with limited success. 'More to the point, Mrs Mann,' there had never been any informality between them, 'where are you? And where is my son?'

'I've brought him home. He belongs at his grandma's, not with someone whose commitment is as semi-detached as his mother's. I've just put him to bed.'

'At quarter to bloody nine,' Lottie exclaimed, 'on a Saturday night? What did he say to that?'

She heard a faint hesitation. 'We had a small disagreement,' Dorothy Mann replied. 'But I was firm with him. It's time someone was. Eight thirty is a proper bedtime for a child of his age.'

Lottie's temper gauge hit the red zone. 'Now you listen to

this, Mrs Mann,' she barked. 'When I want your parenting advice, I will ask for it, but don't hold your breath waiting for that to happen.'

There was a spluttering sound from the other end of the connection, finally forming into a cry of protest. 'Really, Charlotte, that is just too much. Have you no concern for your child's well-being? Not even a scrap?'

'Don't you dare say that to me!' she yelled. 'That stupid bloody hearing gave you access to Jakey, but it didn't give you the right to uproot him without my consent.' As she vented her anger, she was aware of an echo, and suspected that she had been switched on to speaker mode.

That fear was realised a few seconds later when a male voice broke into the conversation. 'Gimme that bloody phone, Dorothy,' Arnold Mann demanded in the background.

'Now you listen to me, woman,' he said, his voice louder and clearer as he commandeered his wife's mobile. 'We have a duty to ensure our grandson's well-being and we're damn well going to do that. My son—'

'Your adulterous, corrupt, alcoholic son,' she shot back.

'That's slander. Living with you drove Scott to distraction.'

'Scott drank himself out of the police force and he's doing time for resetting stolen police uniforms.'

'A mistake for which he has paid,' Arnold Mann replied, more calmly. 'He'll be released within the next few days, and he will move in with us. The governor described him to me, and to my lawyer, as a model prisoner, and believes that he'll leave jail a new man. I'm setting him up in business, and I give you notice that as soon as he's back on his feet, Moss Lee will ask the court to award Scott full custody of Jake.'

'Fat chance!' she scoffed.

'Every chance. Mr Lee's confident that his petition's going to succeed, especially when he tells the court about your continued association with that disreputable wee man who's old enough to be your father. Uncle Dan, indeed. Jake's been told never to call him that again, believe you me. By the way, if you were intending to pick Jake up tomorrow, forget it. He'll stay here, and on Monday morning I'll take him to school, but only after he's been for his interview.'

'Interview? What interview?'

'With the rector of Glasgow Academy. Dorothy and I believe it's time he went to a proper school, not that East End jungle.'

'That will not be happening! I'll pick him up at nine tomorrow, and you'd better have him ready.'

'Oh yes,' he exclaimed, with a note of triumph in his voice, 'and what are you going to do with him, being wrapped up in the Leo Speight investigation, according to the man I heard on the radio? There are twenty-nine casualties from that bus crash, fifteen of them serious. Somehow I doubt that your aunt's going to be available.'

Eight

It felt strange to Bob Skinner to be knocking on a closed door in his own house, but he did it nevertheless. It felt even stranger when that door was opened by a younger version of himself.

This is like a time-slip movie, he thought.

'*Hola, Padre,*' the youth said. 'Hi, Dad.' He grinned. 'Have you come for some tranquillity? Is my little sister still digging for her teeth?'

Bob nodded, returning his oldest son's smile. 'She surely is.' Dawn Costa Skinner, his sixth and, he swore, his final child, was five months old and ruling his household. 'But Sarah's just got her off to sleep.'

'Do you want me to sit with the others so that you can take Sarah out? Fine if you do.'

'Thanks, but your stepmother's pretty much nodding off herself. No, I wondered if you'd like to come out for a swift beer. There'll probably still be staff in the golf club; if not, we can go into Gullane, to the Mallard.'

'If you don't mind, Dad,' Ignacio Watson Skinner replied, 'I'd rather not. I have an important examination on Monday and that means a full day of study tomorrow. I need an absolutely clear head.'

'Have a soft drink?'

'No, really. We're fine here, if you want to talk. I have some Fanta in the fridge, and a couple of Saaz beers, the kind you like from Spain.'

Bob nodded. 'Whatever.' He followed his son into the small apartment that he had built above his garage. It had one bedroom, a shower room and a small living area, but it served the twin purposes for which it had been created: to make Ignacio feel like part of his family while allowing him a degree of independence.

Ignacio, the son whose existence had been kept secret from him until the boy was almost a man; the product of a one-night stand with a dangerous woman from a dangerous, violent and ultimately doomed family. By the time they did meet, the Watson curse had communicated itself to the next generation and Ignacio had been forced to spend a year in a young offenders' prison, a sentence that might have been longer without his father's influence and the skills of his half-sister, Alexis, who had organised his legal defence against a charge of culpable homicide, the Scottish equivalent of manslaughter.

'Heard from your mother lately?' he asked casually, as Ignacio uncapped a bottle of beer and handed it to him.

The young man grinned. 'Yes, I have, twice. She called me this morning, full of a story about a party she and Cameron went to last night in a place near Glasgow. Newting Marns? I think that's what she called it.'

'Close enough. Who was the host?'

'Leo Speight, the champion; *El Invencible*. It was to celebrate the end of his career as a boxer. Many famous people were there . . .' Ignacio seemed to hesitate, glancing sidelong at his father, 'including Joey Morocco, the actor, and . . .'

'Let me guess,' Bob laughed, 'Aileen de Marco, the Shadow Home Secretary and my former wife.'

'That doesn't upset you, to hear of her? With him?'

'Hell, no,' he exclaimed. 'I couldn't be happier for her. She's got what she really wanted in life, and she's on the way to being what she wants to be.'

'What is that?'

'Prime Minister. I'm not saying she'll get there, mind. She has to lead her party first, and the guy in the job isn't going anywhere in a hurry.'

'What about the actor? What do you feel about him? With her?'

Bob shrugged. 'Nothing. I don't know the man. Our paths have crossed only once, and very briefly, so I can't really say that we've met. The only thing I know for certain is that he'll never be more than second best to Aileen. Her career will always come first.' He paused. 'What did your mother think of him?' he asked.

'She thought he was vacuous.' He pronounced the word carefully. 'All show, no substance, she said. She called him Aileen's handbag, but I don't know what that means.'

'It means he's strictly for show,' his father explained. 'I probably was too, when we were married.'

'No!' Ignacio protested. 'You were a very important man. You were chief constable. You still are a very important man. You're a director of a big media group.'

'Only courtesy of the owner, my friend Xavi Aislado. That makes me useful, not important.'

'They wanted to make you a lord; Alex told me.'

'For the wrong reasons, so I turned them down. So,' he continued, 'Mia thinks that Joey Morocco's an empty vessel. What did she make of Leo Speight?'

'She said he was one of the most charismatic men she had ever met. In fact she said she put him in the top three, alongside you and Cameron. She was broken hearted when she called me again after it was on the news that he was dead.'

Skinner stared at his son. 'Leo Speight is dead?'

'Yes, didn't you hear? It was on TV earlier.'

'We didn't have it on. It hasn't been on all day, in fact. I took Mark and James Andrew to see Edinburgh City this afternoon, so I've missed out on news. What happened? How did he die?'

'From what the man said on TV, they don't know yet. He said they were looking for the explanation. But there were detectives at the house, filmed arriving in a car, a woman and a man with a very bright shirt.'

'Can you remember the name of the man who made the announcement?'

'Yes, it was funny; made me think of a bird, *peregrino* in Spanish.'

'Peregrine. Perry Allsop; that's who it must have been, the communications guy, but he isn't usually front of house.' He was frowning; his mind was in another place.

'You want to be there, don't you, Dad?' Ignacio said. 'You miss being a cop.'

'No,' Bob replied quietly. 'I'm done with that.'

'I don't believe you; you miss it. But this man, he may just have died. It may not even be a crime.'

'Trust me, son, Leo Speight did not die of natural causes; thirty years' experience as a cop tells me that. You said one of the detectives was a woman? Did they say who she was?'

'No. But she had dark hair, and strong eyes, if that helps.'

'It sounds like Lottie Mann, but the guy in the bright shirt puzzles me. Did he have a wee moustache?' He touched his top lip.

'No. No *bigote*.'

'Mmm. Dunno who that would have been, in which case the woman could have been Sandra Bulloch. Either way, neither one of them would have been there if the attending officers thought it was a natural death.'

'Your friend was there too. The big man, Mario.'

'In that case, it's a racing certainty they're looking at a homicide; the delay will be to establish the cause of death.' His frown deepened, and his expressive eyes showed a sign of regret. He might have called me, he thought.

His hand was halfway to his pocket, reaching for his phone, when it played a few bars of 'Tie a Yellow Ribbon', the song he had adopted as his ringtone following Dawn's birth. He peered at the caller identity, his eyes widening in surprise.

'Hello, Amanda,' he said as he took the call.

'Can you speak?' the director general of the Security Service asked him.

'Up to a point,' he replied, 'if this isn't a social call.'

'It isn't. You've heard of the death of Leo Speight, the boxer?'

'My son and I were just discussing it.'

'We have an interest in it,' she declared abruptly.

'In what way?'

'You know my service has an interest in serious organised crime?'

'Of course I do. Is that a factor here?'

'It might be. Mr Speight himself was as clean as a whistle, but we're not sure about his extended family.'

'What do you mean by that?' Skinner asked.

'His friend Mr Stoddart has associations that aren't quite so pristine. They're Russian, with friends in America and Germany, and they played a big part in Mr Speight retiring with the spectacular wealth that he did. Naturally they made even more than he did from his career, but with him apparently threatening to move into their area of operations after hanging up his gloves and his protective cup, we're wondering whether they might have had an interest in taking him out of play.'

'I can see all that,' he said, 'but what's it got to do with me?'

'I'm hoping you'll agree to keep an eye on the investigation for us,' she replied. 'The temporary accreditation I gave you a few months ago is still in place, as you are well aware. We can discuss the financial details at a later date. Were you impressed by the remuneration for your last involvement with us?'

'Very. I'm not daft enough to ask what budget it came from.'

'One that will never be scrutinised by a Commons Select Committee, that I promise you. So, Bob, what about it? I can even give you a leg man, if a situation arises where you need one. You know Clyde Houseman, my man in Scotland; I'll put him at your disposal.'

'I'm not sure my former colleagues will be too chuffed,' he pointed out.

'I've just spoken to the chief constable; she would be very pleased to have you around as an observer, but she asks that you try not to be spotted by the inquisitive media. There will be lots of them around, I imagine.'

'That'll be bloody near impossible; I'll need a cover story.'

'I agree. Mr Speight's insurers, I thought. In fact I've already made arrangements; officially you've been retained by them. That's what the chief constable believes. They do have an interest, in reality. Mr Speight had a policy to cover his boxing activity. It's still in place and will pay five million sterling in the event of his death through an outside agency; it envisaged a boxing fatality, but the way it's written, if he was murdered, his heirs will collect. It was due to lapse six months after his last fight. That was three months ago.' He heard her sigh. 'Come on, Bob, you are up for it, aren't you?'

He laughed out loud, aware that his son was staring at him with undisguised curiosity. 'You know me so well, Amanda. Who's the SIO?'

'Detective Inspector Charlotte Mann. Do you know her?'

'Lottie? Of course I do; which leads me back to an earlier question. Who was the clean-shaven bugger in the garish shirt?'

Nine

'Are you going to sit still for that, Lottie?' Dan Provan asked. 'Letting Scott's parents bully you?'

'The way they see it, they're just looking out for Jakey,' she replied lamely, as her colleague fastened his seat belt. He was dressed less garishly than the day before, but his lightweight blue suit was one she had never seen before.

'Come off it,' he scoffed. 'They're gettin' at you, and you know it. They can't do that, just kidnap your boy.'

'Mr Mann says that the outcome of the hearing means that they can; or rather, Moss fucking Lee says so.'

His eyebrows rose; Lottie rarely swore. The lapse showed the depth of her anxiety, and it fuelled his anger. 'Moss Lee's a shyster,' he snapped, 'and so's Arnold Mann. He had a street-corner garage in Maryhill – my uncle went to him once; his car was never the same again. Then he got lucky, landed a sales concession for a Korean car brand and built a chain of half a dozen dealerships that he sold to a bigger group.'

'For more money than you and I will earn between us in our lifetimes,' Lottie pointed out.

'Maybe, but he's still a shyster.'

'He's a rich bloody shyster! He can afford Moss Lee. He can

afford to send my son to the Glasgow Academy, whether he wants to go there or not. I can't. The only lawyer I've ever had helped me buy my house. She's a glorified estate agent, not someone who could go into court against the likes of Lee, but I can't afford a specialist.'

'Maybe I can,' Provan murmured.

She looked at him and felt something melt inside her. 'You are a lovely fella,' she whispered, 'and I don't deserve you as a friend. But I know that you've just blown at least half your life savings on your trip to Australia. I'm not going to let you blow the other half on me.'

'I'm not letting this bastard win,' he vowed.

'Me neither,' she concurred. 'They're such fucking hypocrites, the pair of them. You know, when Scott was on the piss and wrecking his police career, when he was giving me a hard time and virtually ignoring Jakey, they didn't want to know. But when he really hit the skids, got into criminal trouble and it went public, by God, it changed then. They were all over the media: it was all my fault, I was a terrible wife, I'd ignored his problems, hadn't cared about them. They'd never put a penny into our house, Scott's and mine, not a stick of furniture, but when I divorced him, they made sure that he got his share, more than his share considering he hadn't put a cent into the mortgage for about five years.

'They were all over Jakey, too. Suddenly they had a grandson and he was a victim. Did they help me put a new roof over his head? Well no, they didn't go that far. They just carped and made life as difficult for me as they possibly could.'

'What are you going to do about the wee man today?'

'There's nothing I can do, Dan. I had to back down. Mr Mann was right, Auntie Ann's still on duty at the hospital. If I picked him up and they found we'd taken him anywhere near Leo Speight's opening ceremony, Moss Lee would have a fucking interdict on me in a heartbeat, and they'd have temporary custody, pending Scott's release. I've got nobody else to help me, and I can't afford paid childcare, like I can't afford a decent lawyer.'

She was on the verge of tears, something he had never thought he would see. He reached across and squeezed her hand. 'There might be somebody else,' he told her. 'You leave it to Uncle Dan. Meanwhile, let's get on with our grim business. We cannae be late for Graeme Bell and his customer.'

She joined the motorway close to Cambuslang; the Sunday traffic was minimal and they reached the Govan turn-off in ten minutes. In half that time they were parked on a yellow line and heading for the mortuary suite in the vast Queen Elizabeth Hospital.

The building was still relatively new, but already the detective duo were familiar with its geography. As they turned the corner that led to the autopsy theatre, they saw Professor Graeme Bell standing at its door. He was not alone.

'Jesus Christ!' Mann murmured blasphemously.

'And General Jackson!' Provan added, completing one of his favourite phrases.

'Is that who I think it is?' the DI asked.

'There's only one of him,' the DS replied as Bob Skinner heard them approach and turned to face them.

'Good morning, both,' he exclaimed, beaming at the consternation on their faces. 'I asked the chief constable not to tell you I was coming, because I wanted to savour the moment.'

'Consider it savoured, sir,' Lottie Mann retorted. 'But aren't you retired? Am I missing something?'

'I must prepare,' Professor Bell muttered, beating the hastiest retreat possible, consistent with his dignity.

'I've got a reason to be here, Lottie,' Skinner said. 'Leo Speight's insurers have a substantial interest in the result of the post-mortem.'

'They're quick off the mark, aren't they?' she observed.

'You know insurance companies,' he retorted.

'Ah believe that,' Provan laughed, 'about as much as Ah believe in the tooth fairy. Have you turned into a spook, big fella?'

'Perish the thought,' he retorted, then grinned. 'But forgive me: can I see your warrant card, please, and then will you tell me what you've done with that decrepit round-heeled little scruff that used to hang on to DI Mann's coat-tails?'

'Blame Australia,' the DS replied, scowling but privately pleased.

'Blame his daughter,' the DI interposed.

'Ah,' Skinner laughed. 'If she's anything like my oldest one, that explains everything.'

'How much can you share with us?' Mann asked, ending the pleasantries. She had no more believed the cover story than had Provan.

'Without admitting to anything beyond my insurance connection,' he replied with half a smile, 'you share with me, I'll share with you. At the moment, my main focus is on Speight's associates.'

'You think one of them might have bumped him off?'

'I think nothing at the moment, and I won't start thinking until Graeme tells us that he was bumped. Shall we join him?'

Ten

'When my police career ended,' Skinner said, as they left the autopsy theatre, 'I assumed it would mean that I'd never have to attend another of these things. Wrong, as it's turned out.'

'You didn't have to attend this one,' Provan suggested. 'We could have briefed you.'

The former chief constable nodded. 'You probably could,' he conceded, 'but then I wouldn't have had the pleasure of seeing the look on your faces when you turned that corner.'

'Was that right about Speight's insurers taking a big hit?' the DS asked.

'So I'm told. Whoever wrote the policy framed the clause to cover accidental death, or death at the hands of a third party.'

'Suppose they have retained you directly, like you want us to believe: are you licensed for that sort of stuff?'

'Oh yes, DS Provan. I have all the available paperwork. I was even a member of the board of the Security Industry Authority, until I gave them some relocation advice.'

'Eh? You told them to move office?'

Skinner's eyes gleamed. 'No, Dan, I told them to stick the job up their arse . . . saving your presence, Lottie. It was just paper-shuffling. The Home Office wanted my name on the board, but not my positive input to its work.'

'Isn't your media directorship paper-shuffling?' Mann suggested.

'Not in the slightest. I have specific roles, and I even train people, young journalists, in investigative techniques, and in the proper way to approach the police.'

'What does that mean?'

'Among other things, it means respectfully, and always on the record. I have a standing instruction to our staff: if an officer won't consent to a conversation being recorded, walk away or hang up the phone. If possible, record the refusal and identify the person while you're doing so. Does any of that sound familiar?'

'No,' Provan said. 'Should it?'

'It would have if I'd been in the Strathclyde job for longer. It's the mirror image of a standing order I had in place for all ranks when I was chief in Edinburgh.'

'Did you ever break it yourself?'

'No.' Skinner smiled. 'Mind you, there were a few occasions when . . .'

He broke off as a door opened and the pathologist joined them in the corridor. He led the way to his office; it was small, and a tight fit for four, but they crammed in.

Skinner pointed at a coffee filter on a table in a corner. 'Does that work?' he asked.

'I thought you told me that Sarah had cut your ration,' Bell remarked.

He looked around the room, peering over Provan's head, and behind Mann. 'Do you see her here? I don't.'

The pathologist grinned. 'In that case . . . It'll have to be paper cups, mind.'

'Anything.'

Bell set to work over the machine. 'How is Sarah, by the way?' he asked.

'She's even more short of sleep then I am, but otherwise she's great. We both thought we'd drawn a line under the family with Seonaid.' He grinned. 'When you get to our ages, you take things for granted that you shouldn't. We're, lucky though; we have a nanny who's been with us for years. She's very happy; even if we packed the older ones off to boarding school tomorrow, Trish still has five years guaranteed employment. She'll be glad when Sarah goes back to work, I think; they're bumping into each other a wee bit just now.'

'Boarding school,' Provan growled.

'Not here, Dan,' Mann whispered brusquely. Skinner was intrigued by the exchange but said nothing, waiting in silence for the coffee to arrive.

'If we're all sitting comfortably . . .' Bell smiled as he perched on the edge of his desk. 'I'll submit my formal report in the usual way, Detective Inspector,' he began, 'within twenty-four hours, I promise, but I can give you the layperson's version now. Your man was poisoned, for sure. Death was caused by hypoxia, which is the end result of potassium cyanide poisoning. All this is subject to laboratory analysis of the stomach contents and of the container that was found beside the body, but that's how he died; there's no question in my mind.'

'Is there any possibility that it was self-administered?' Skinner asked.

'I can't rule that out, but why would he bother with the soya milk if he was going to off himself?'

'No' just that,' Provan added. 'Why would he want to do himself in? He was as rich as Croesus, and he'd just come from announcing a new business venture in his retirement.'

'All true, guys. So that possibility, having been considered, can be ruled out . . . which adds up to very bad news for the insurance company, Bob. One thing I will tell you,' the pathologist added. 'That was the fittest person I have ever autopsied. His musculature was perfect, and his cardiovascular system was phenomenal. Seriously, I would like to preserve his heart; it's the finest specimen I've ever seen. I'm going to approach his family to ask their permission.'

'What about his brain?' Mann asked.

'It was immaculate; no sign of any injury or past concussions. I hate boxing,' Bell said vehemently. 'I've done PMs on two people who died from injuries sustained in professional fights, so I know first-hand the damage that the sport can cause. Honestly, Lottie, if I hadn't known who that man was, and you'd tried to tell me he was a boxer, I would have laughed in your face. Externally there was barely a mark on him either; a couple of small scars round the eyes, but nothing else. He'd never had a nasal fracture either.'

'He was the best, Graeme,' Provan murmured. 'Ah've never seen boxing as an art, noble or otherwise, but watching Leo Speight made me think that way. He had reflexes like lightning, he moved like mercury and he had a way of knowing what the other guy was going to do before he did it. The man was an art form, literally one of a kind.'

'They found a donor card in his effects,' Bell sighed, 'but no organs could have been harvested in the circumstances. What a bloody waste! Imagine walking around with Leo Speight's heart and lungs.' He drained his coffee and stood. 'Now, lady and gents, if you'll excuse me, I have a report to write.'

The three investigators left him to it.

'What's your plan of action?' Skinner asked.

'I've called a team meeting at the crime scene,' Mann replied. 'For this one I have all the resources I need. There was only so much we could do yesterday, without knowing that we were actually dealing with a murder, but today the investigation moves into top gear.'

'Do you mind if I sit in?'

He sensed a moment's hesitancy in the DI before she responded. 'If you have the time, of course you can, sir.'

He smiled. 'I'll stand at the back, Lottie, I promise. The last thing I want to do is undermine your leadership. Besides, half your young guns won't know who the hell I am.'

'The other half'll tell them quick enough,' Provan grunted.

'You can be open with them. They can all be told that I've been retained by the victim's insurers and that I'm there at your discretion. Also, don't call me "sir", either of you; that would undermine your authority as cops. I'm a civilian, sort of; address me as either Mr Skinner, or just plain Bob, whichever you're more comfortable with.'

'Mr Skinner it'll be then,' Mann said.

The DS winked. 'Fine, Bob.'

'What have you established so far?' Skinner asked as they moved towards the exit.

The DI gave him a rundown of the previous day's events, from the time of their emergency summons to Ayr. He listened in silence, nodding occasionally, but not interrupting at any point.

'The book deal,' he said, when she was finished. 'The man Butler, the manager; what was his attitude to it? He was duty-bound to report the approach to his client, but do we know how he felt about it? Was he for it, agin it, or somewhere in the middle?'

'Definitely for it . . . Bob,' Provan declared. 'Mrs Raynor was quite clear about that.'

'And Speight himself?'

'Ambivalent at best, it seemed, although the publisher woman was still hopin' to talk him into it. That's what yesterday's meeting was for.'

'To be clear, now that Leo's dead, the book's an even better proposition for a publisher?'

'So Mrs Raynor said. She's hangin' around in Scotland. We've got no doubt she wants to tie up a deal with Leo's executor before another publisher cottons on to the potential.'

'Who'll she be dealing with?'

'Butler,' the DS replied. 'We think.'

The other man frowned. 'Would she be dealing with the estate, though,' he wondered, 'or would she be dealing directly with Butler as an individual? A biography has to have an author, and from what you're saying, there was nobody closer to Leo than him.'

'That's how she's thinking,' Mann conceded. 'We're not sure how much influence his adult son had with him, but he and Faye Bulloch had been separated for two years. The way Butler spoke . . .' She paused, then added, 'If we're right and he's the executor of the estate, either way Mrs Raynor would be dealing with him.'

'Would she now?' Skinner mused. 'But is he a significant beneficiary?'

Mann shrugged. 'No idea. Why?'

'Because of the added value of the book with Leo dead; if he's going to inherit, that's of lesser importance. But if he isn't, and he can do a separate book deal with this Masthead outfit, it makes him a person of interest, doesn't it?'

'Mr Skinner, as of this moment, everybody in this investigation is of interest. We've got a man poisoned in an empty house, with a cast list of mothers of his children, business associates, and general hangers-on.'

'And acting sisters-in-law,' Provan muttered.

'What do you mean?' Skinner asked.

'Our boss, Detective Chief Inspector Bulloch: Leo Speight's ex-partner, who was taking him to court trying to prove a common-law marriage, is her sister, Faye.'

He gasped. 'You're kidding me! I never knew that.'

'Neither did we. She kept it quiet.'

'She sure as hell did. When I was your chief in Strathclyde, she was my exec. I took her out of Special Branch and put her in that job. I've seen her full CV and her SB vetting report. There's no mention of her being connected to Leo Speight in any way.'

The DS peered at him. 'Who did the vetting?'

'ACC Allan signed off on it. Your old friend Max, currently doing time for perverting the course of justice.'

'Presumably whoever did the job on her was careless,' the DS argued, 'or just didn't think it was worth including.'

'With respect, Dan, that's not likely. Full family background and close associates is part of the vetting process.'

'I wouldnae know; I've never been involved with you spooks.'

'Trust me, it is; they reported to me, in Edinburgh and in Glasgow.'

'When was it done?' Mann asked.

Skinner frowned as he searched his memory and put dates in order. 'It would be around a year and a half ago. She'd been in SB for a bit over a year when I took her out of there.'

'Fair enough, but is it relevant to this inquiry?'

'Probably not, but anything out of the ordinary disturbs me in

76

a homicide investigation. Max Allan was known for doing favours for friends, and Sandra worked for him when she was a sergeant in uniform. Lottie, as I say, it's probably not relevant, but what if Max took her relationship with Speight out of that report? Okay, I'll grant you it needn't have been him; it could have been whoever did the vetting . . . but what if the relationship was excised because of something that was known about Leo that might have been embarrassing to Sandra and compromising to the force?'

'A lot of "what ifs" there, Bob,' Provan chuckled, clearly enjoying his new familiarity with his former commander.

'I know,' he conceded. 'I'm flagging it up, that's all. When did the relationship, if we can call it that, come to light?'

'Yesterday,' Mann replied. 'When the body was discovered, it was reported to Sandra; she called DCC McGuire and advised him. He benched her right away and told her to call us in.'

'She's isolated from the investigation? Completely out of the reporting chain?'

'Officially, yes. She asked if I'd keep her in touch with developments. I said officially no.'

'Unofficially?'

'When all this is over, we'll be working under her again; I don't want to be on her hit list.'

Skinner scratched his chin. 'If you tell her something you shouldn't and the chief constable finds out, or the DCC . . . Whose hit list would you like least to be on? Leave it with me, Lottie; I'll sort your dilemma.'

'How can you do that?' Provan asked.

'I can talk to Mario and tell him to give you a written order forbidding any disclosure. If she leans on either of you, you can wave it at her.'

The little detective sergeant grinned. 'That would do it. Why the fuck did you ever leave, big man?'

'Sometimes, Dan,' he confessed frankly, 'I'm not sure.'

They had reached the car park. Skinner pressed a button and the lights of a metallic-grey Mercedes came on. 'Are you going straight there?'

'Yes,' Mann told him. 'Do you have the address?'

'Yeah, I'll see you there. I'll give you a head start; it wouldn't do for me to arrive before you.'

'If you approach from the Buccleuch Avenue entrance to Kirkhill Road, you won't be seen by the media. They're all contained at the other end.'

He nodded and headed for his car.

'Just like old times,' Provan muttered as they watched him depart. 'How do you feel about it, Lottie?'

'Absolutely fine. He's on our side. And he's getting Sandra off our backs,' she added. 'Do you think he's right about her vetting report being doctored?'

'Oh aye. I've got half a mind to nip along to Shotts Prison and ask Max why he did it.'

'Don't engage the other half, not yet; it's probably not relevant. We have to get down to Ayr; I want to brief the whole team there, so that everyone's familiar with the crime scene.'

'Where will we be based after that?' the DS asked as he slid into the passenger seat. 'The nearest station, or get a mobile HQ van down there?'

'It depends on what progress we make,' she replied, engaging gear, 'but at the moment, I'm thinking neither. Obviously we'll do the routine stuff in Ayr, check CCTV coverage, such as it is, for cars in the vicinity around the time of Leo's death, talk to neighbours to see if there's a night owl who might have seen something, or someone leaving the house. If that gives us a result, fine; otherwise, once that's done, most of the people we'll want to talk to live nowhere near there. My thought is that we keep a presence on site, but the inquiry HQ will be in Glasgow. Would you have a problem with that?'

Provan shook his head. 'Not in the slightest. Ah don't fancy slogging up and down tae Ayr every day. Plus,' he added, 'it'll make it easier for you with Jakey.'

'Dan,' she sighed, 'my private life can't have a bearing on the way this investigation's run. If it does, I'm the wrong person for the job.'

'That's rubbish. Everybody's entitled to a private life. The chief constable herself's a single parent wi' a kid younger than Jakey.'

'She doesn't have a bastard of an ex-husband with a rich daddy who's threatening to take her child away from her, though, does she? My blood's boiling at the thought of having to leave him with those people overnight, let alone having him go for that interview tomorrow.'

'I thought you got a bit tetchy when boarding school was mentioned.'

She frowned. 'I called him back, you know, and expressly forbade him from taking Jakey to that place. He told me to get stuffed; his exact words.'

Provan's nostrils flared. 'I promise you this, Lottie; one way or another I'm going tae do that man. But in the meantime . . . I've got a temporary solution to your childcare problem.'

'Are you going to take time off?' she chuckled grimly. 'Not that Jakey wouldn't like that,' she added.

'I don't have to. Vanessa, my Jamie's lassie, they live near you and she can help, for the next four or five months, anyway. She's a home hairdresser, and now that she's pregnant, she's cutting back on her workload. I've spoken to her, and she'd be happy to look after Jakey when she's needed. She can arrange her jobs any way she likes.'

Lottie was staring at the road ahead. 'How old is she?'

'Twenty-eight.'

'Does she take shit?'

'No way. But she's a laugh. They'll get on great.'

'I'd pay her, Dan.'

'That's between the two of you.'

She glanced across at him and smiled. 'When we get to Ayr,' she said, 'you're getting kissed.'

'That could be construed as sexual harassment in the workplace.'

'So sue me.'

Eleven

'For a guy who's worth all that money, this is quite a modest layout,' Bob Skinner observed. 'Stereotypical Scot, not flashing the cash around.'

'See what's in the garage, though,' Provan told him. 'A Ferrari, a Bentley Mulsanne and a Ford Mustang. Oh aye, and a Harley-Davidson Low Rider . . . for nippin' down to Aldi, I suppose.'

'You know your motors.'

'A man can dream.'

They were standing in the main reception room of Leo Speight's house; it was the only space available to them on the lower level; Dorward's forensic team had finished there, but were still working in every other area.

Mann had decided that she would rather not have Skinner present during her team briefing in the gymnasium. Instead she had suggested that he and Provan might meet with Gino Butler, who had called to say he would arrive at two with the list of party guests and catering staff that she had requested from him.

'Does anybody really think that Speight could have fallen out wi' gangsters, Bob?' the DS asked.

'To be honest, Dan,' he replied, 'I have no idea. That's what's

81

been suggested to me, but no one is saying whether there's any evidence or where it came from. In the absence of facts, I'm going into it with an open mind. That's how it'll be. Why do you ask, anyway? Do you have a theory?'

'No' yet. I'm in the same boat as you: I don't know enough.'

'Excuse me, gentlemen.'

Both men glanced across to see a tall figure framed in the doorway. He had a naturally high forehead, emphasised by a receding hairline. He wore a tweed jacket and he was peering at them through a pair of round spectacles perched on the bridge of a long, hooked nose.

'This is a restricted area,' the newcomer said. 'Should you be here?'

Provan's lip curled; he tapped the warrant card that hung on its lanyard around his neck. 'This says I should.'

'I wasn't talking to you, Sergeant. I know who you are. It's your companion I'm concerned about.'

'Then don't be; he's not here, he's just a hologram.'

'Don't be flippant with me, Mr Provan,' the newcomer retorted, 'or you'll regret it. You're a serving police officer; this man is not.'

'How would you know that?' Skinner asked quietly.

'Because I know who you are. You're the man the previous chief constable explicitly banned from crime scenes.'

'Did he?' Skinner chuckled. 'He never told me that, and in the interest of fairness, I should have been the first to know. Since you seem to know who I am,' he continued, 'who are you, that he gave you that instruction?'

'Peregrine Allsop, director of communications.'

'Is that right? Well, Mr Allsop, my advice to you is that you put down your shovel.'

'What shovel?'

'The one you're using to dig yourself an ever-deeper hole. Whatever Andy Martin may have told you about me, I am not one to wander into a major criminal investigation without being invited, and without proper credentials.' He produced a laminated card from a pocket and held it up, forcing the communications director to move close enough to read it.

'I see,' he murmured. 'Nobody told me,' he complained.

'Well, in the immortal words of Freddie and the Dreamers, I'm telling you now. Have you got a function here?'

'I have to give the media an update on the investigation.'

'Then ye better go and talk to Lottie,' Provan suggested. 'You'll need to be properly briefed, but hear this from me. Don't say too much, and don't drop her in it.'

Allsop frowned. 'I know what I'm doing, Sergeant.' He looked at Skinner. 'Do you wish to attend, sir?'

The former chief gave a long whistle. 'Absolutely not. Dan's right. I'm a hologram; I'm not here.'

'As you wish.' He turned abruptly, and walked out of the room. As he left, Provan muttered something obscene.

'No, Dan,' Skinner said. 'If I had taken over the national force, I'd have appointed a media director too. Probably not that one, but it's a necessary function, one that needs a civilian specialist.'

'Maybe, but no' briefing the press on active investigations.'

'My guess is there's a reason for that: to protect Lottie. We both know it's not what she does best. And as for you . . .' he added, smiling.

'Fair enough,' Provan conceded. 'The lassie's got enough to worry about, apart from having to handle every aspect of this investigation.'

'What do you mean?'

The DS grimaced. 'Don't let on I told you this, but she's havin' major grief from Scott Mann's father and mother. The old guy's minted, and he's tryin' to get custody of Jakey for Scott.'

'Scott's in prison,' Skinner exclaimed.

'And totally rehabilitated as a result, they're sayin'. Whereas Lottie's in a job that means she cannae look after her kid probably. On top of that, of course, it was her that drove Scott to drink and intae bad company.'

'Who came up with that crap?'

'Ever heard of Moss Lee? High-priced, big-mouthed solicitor advocate?'

'Who hasn't?'

'Exactly. Arnold Mann's hired him. Lottie, she can't compete wi' that. There's a real chance that she's going to lose that kid, Bob. I've told her I'm not havin' it.'

'Me neither,' Skinner growled. 'Leave that one with me. I can do more about it than you.'

'Thanks. Now what did you show Allsop that had him standing to attention?'

'Never you mind.'

'That'll be —'

Provan's retort was interrupted by the appearance of another man in the doorway. 'Mr Butler,' the DS exclaimed. 'Right on time. Have you brought your list?'

'Yes,' the newcomer said. 'I'm sorry I couldn't have got here sooner, but I had to check with the security manager of the Blacksmith that everybody actually turned up. You wouldn't have thanked me if you'd had to chase people who weren't even there.'

'Not necessarily. If they hadn't been there we might have

wondered where they were instead. Were there any no-shows?'

'Damn few. It was pretty much a one-hundred-per-cent turnout, as expected.' He paused. 'Has the post-mortem been done?'

'Aye,' Provan replied. 'This morning; outcome as expected. Subject to lab analysis, he was poisoned.'

'So Leo was murdered?'

'Officially we'll call it a suspicious death, because we cannae rule out suicide one hundred per cent.'

'No chance,' Butler declared. 'Leo had everything to live for.' He frowned. 'The pathologist didn't find anything else, did he? No illness that we didn't know about?'

'Nothing at all. Given the business he was in, he was a phenomenon. But,' the DS tapped the side of his head, 'a pathologist can look at the brain and tell you if there was anything wrong with it. What he can't do is look at the mind. He can't tell you whether the deceased was happy or sad, whether his life was plain sailing or full of stress.'

'I can,' the manager insisted. 'Leo was a happy man. He was never going to have to risk his health or his life for money again. He had firm plans for the future and he was going to wake up every morning knowing that day was going to be a good one. He took a lot out of his sport and he was planning to give a lot back. Those aren't my words. They were his. It's what he said to me two nights ago when we had dinner here, after looking in at the arrangements for the party.'

'On your own? Just the two of you?' Butler nodded. 'Who did the cooking?'

'Leo did. He always did. He prepared nearly all of his own meals, and when he didn't, he supervised.'

'Even in restaurants?' Provan sounded sceptical.

'He very rarely ate in one. He never did when he was in training camp. He took responsibility for everything that went into his body. That's professional sport, Detective Sergeant. Drug testing in boxing was patchy at best, but Leo signed up to a voluntary code that was as stringent as any of them. He said that if a fight went over four or five rounds, he could tell whether the other guy had been doping or not. It happened a few times in his career.'

'How did he deal with it?'

Butler grinned. 'He hit them harder.'

'What about the soya milk?'

'That was part of his regime; he drank two cartons of the stuff every day, wherever he was. Always almond flavour; he didn't like the banana version.'

'Everybody close tae him would know that, would they?'

'Oh yes.'

Butler glanced at the detective's companion, weighing him up as if he was disturbed by his silence.

'Bob Skinner, don't mind me,' he said, extending a hand. 'I take it,' he continued as they shook, 'that as his manager, you're aware of the terms of Leo's life insurance policy, and the enhanced benefit in the event of unnatural death?'

'Of course. I negotiated it.'

'In that case, think of me as the insurers' insurance.'

'Does that mean your brief is to establish that Leo died of natural causes, if you can?'

'Or suicide: that would invalidate the policy altogether.'

'How much convincing will you need? If DS Provan can't rule out suicide completely, where does that leave you? How can you be persuaded that he didn't kill himself?'

Skinner beamed. 'The best way of proving that he was

unlawfully killed is by finding the person who did it. In that respect, I have every confidence in DI Mann and DS Provan, and so can you.'

'That's good,' Butler said. 'There's three million quid riding on it. If he was murdered, it pays out five mil; if not, only two. But you'd know that.'

Skinner nodded. 'I was told. But they didn't tell me how long the policy's been in place, or who the beneficiary is.'

'I set it up seven years ago. There is no named beneficiary as such. The benefit is part of the estate, so it goes to the heirs and successors.'

'Who would they be?' Provan asked casually.

'I don't know,' the manager replied bluntly. 'I believe I'm an executor, because Leo asked me if I would be, but he drew up his will alone, with his lawyer, Herbert Chesters, as his adviser.'

'Where can I find him?'

'It's not a him, it's the name of the legal practice he used. His handler there was the senior partner, Joy Herbert, Mrs. If you need detail, you'll have to talk to her. The office is in George Square. It's not a big outfit and they keep a very low profile, but their clients are all very high-value individuals. They're a law firm, but they do corporate structuring, taxation and inheritance planning as well. A lot of their clients are offshore.'

'Was Leo, officially?'

Butler glanced at Skinner as he responded to his question. 'No, not yet. It was something he intended to do, but he was waiting for the time to be right.'

'When would that have been?'

'When he had the settlement sorted out with Faye. His partner,' he added, anticipating the question. 'Estranged.'

'Was that proving difficult?'

'More difficult than it need have been. At the outset Faye didn't expect half of Leo's stash or anything like it; Leo offered her two million, cash, and she was okay with that. He'd already bought her the house where she's living. If it had been left to the two of them, they'd probably have worked it out over lunch, for Leo was very persuasive – but the lawyers got involved and all of a sudden the simple became complicated.'

'Bloody lawyers,' Provan grunted, not quite under his breath.

'Let me understand as clearly as I can,' Skinner said. 'He and Faye were never legally married.'

'No, never.'

'Did they ever actually cohabit? As in share the same permanent residence?'

'That's what the lawyer was trying to assert, but he was having trouble. He was trying to argue that Faye was Leo's common-law wife, but Joy Herbert didn't agree with that. She said that Faye's main residence was the Troon house that Leo bought for her when she first fell pregnant, and put in her name. She says that since Leo spent at least two thirds of every year in training camp in London or in Las Vegas, and since he had other homes, they didn't live together and certainly not long enough for her to be able to claim . . . what d' you call it?'

'Spousal rights?' Skinner suggested.

'That's it. Mrs Herbert said she should have bitten his hand off for the two million, but her lawyer promised her she'd get much more if she just hung in there, and stuck to her claim.'

'Who's her lawyer?' the DS asked.

'Moss Lee. Heard of him?'

'Ach!' Provan spat. 'I might have fucking guessed.'

'I know, he's an arsehole, but he was bloody persistent and Faye fell for it. Greed got the better of her. I think Lee was hoping Leo would just get tired of arguing and pay her off whatever the cost. Mistake. My friend was not a guy you could wear down. The longer the fight lasted, the tougher he got, in the ring and in life.'

'The fight's over, though,' Skinner pointed out, 'with the will being a substitute for the judges' scorecards. The investigation can't progress properly until its contents are known. Do you have a contact number for Mrs Herbert, Mr Butler?'

'Only the office, but I'm sure her mobile will be on Leo's phone.'

'Which is where, exactly?' he asked, glancing at Provan.

'At the lab in the crime campus at Gartcosh, for printing and DNA testing. It was on the floor beside the body; Arthur's folk took it. Lottie wants to know if anyone else handled it. If somebody else was here when he died, that might tell us.'

'I suggest you get it back. You need . . .'

'I know,' the DS sighed impatiently. 'Apart from the Herbert woman's number, we need a list of the calls he made before he died.'

'Sorry, Dan, I'm not trying to tell you what your job is.'

'You're managing nonetheless.'

'Excuse me,' Butler said, 'you don't need the phone to access Leo's contacts. They'll be on his computer; it's in his office. Unless they've taken that away too,' he added.

'They shouldnae have,' Provan replied. 'There was no reason. Where is his office?'

'I'll show you, come on.'

He led them out of the drawing room and upstairs to a small room overlooking the conservatory and the garden. There were signs of SOCO activity, but access had not been restricted. 'This is it,' the manager announced. 'This is where Leo did most of his business when he was here. We both did.' He paused. 'You need to understand that Leo was a bit of a nomad. It was hard to say where he lived. When he made his first big pay-TV score, he bought an apartment in Chelsea; he lived there a lot of the time. He bought a house on Lake Las Vegas, where his American girlfriend Rae and their daughter Raeleen live now. It's in Rae's name, just as the one in Barassie belongs to Faye. Also there's a place in the Bahamas, where a lot of sportspeople have property; that's where he was planning to live permanently after he retired. This place here was where he laid his head when he was in Scotland, nothing more.'

'With all those cars in the garage?' the DS exclaimed.

'His one extravagance. They were his only toys. The Mustang's got about a thousand miles on the clock; the Ferrari he bought from a golfer he knew. The Bentley was his main car; he drove that between here and London. He didn't mind flying but he wasn't a big fan of airports.'

'What did he use on Friday when he left the party?'

'The Harley. That was his real pride and joy.'

'It'd be mine too,' Provan said. 'Can you get into his computer?'

'Sure, I used it as much as Leo did, possibly more. There's no personal stuff on it. All that went on his laptop and his phone.'

'What laptop?'

'Leo separated his private life from his business life completely,' Butler explained. 'His business email was leo@speightinternational.com, with its own Cloud storage. Personally he was champ@ls.org, with a separate account for that, his music and everything else.'

'Nobody told me about a laptop. I'll need to check with

Gartcosh to see if it's at the lab. Did he take it with him everywhere?'

'Always.'

'If Gartcosh doesn't have it,' Skinner pointed out, 'that means he didn't die alone, or that someone else was here before you, Mr Butler . . . that's assuming you didn't trouser it yourself.'

The manager seemed to reel backwards, holding his hands as if fending him off. 'Wait a minute!' he protested.

'Well, did you?'

'No! Fuck's sake, man.'

'Fair enough, but the question had to be asked. Didn't it, Dan?'

He turned to see that Provan had withdrawn to a corner of the room, muttering into his mobile. 'You certain?' he heard him say. 'Aye, okay, Arthur; keep your ginger mop on.'

The DS frowned as he pocketed the phone. 'The laptop is at Gartcosh,' he announced. 'And a Samsung Edge. Mr Butler,' he continued, 'get us intae this thing, will ye, please.'

The manager nodded and moved past him to the desk, pressed a button behind the computer and waited for it to boot up. A minute elapsed, and then a menu appeared on screen. 'There you are,' he said. 'Do you like the screen saver?'

The background image was a still from a fight. Speight stood, gloved right fist held high and perfectly balanced, as his opponent fell forward; the photographer had captured the moment perfectly, even catching the glaze in the beaten man's eyes, and the look of detached professional satisfaction on the champion's face.

'Aaron Abbess,' Butler murmured. 'WBA champion, until that night four years ago in the MGM Grand in Vegas; he actually thought he had a chance, for about seven and a half minutes, until what you see there happened. That was Leo's signature fight, the one he'll be most remembered for.'

He moved the cursor on the screen, clicked the mouse, and a file appeared, a list of names and numbers. He scrolled down until he found 'H', then clicked again. 'There you are: Joy Herbert's mobile number.'

Both of his companions noted it down.

'We can look at the party list on screen if you like,' he continued. 'It's on here; I can print another copy too. I only brought the one.'

'Fine,' Skinner murmured. 'I'd like one if I may.'

Butler's hand moved the cursor once more, and clicked twice, opening a folder and then a file. Thirty seconds later a wireless printer on a desk in the corner hummed into action. He retrieved the two printed lists, clipped the sheets together with a stapler and handed them over.

'There you are, gents.'

'Thanks,' Provan replied. 'And thanks for helping us with the number. You can go now. Ye might want to avoid the media. Our PR guy will be announcing any minute now that it's a suspicious death.'

'Thanks for the advice, but I'm not quite done yet. I'm going to have a funeral to organise; nobody else is going to take that job on. Can you give me any idea, Mr Provan, of when you're going to release Leo's body?'

'I wish I could, but it's no' our call. That's down to the procurator fiscal, and in these circumstances there's no saying how long he'll take. It'll no' be before all the toxicology's done, that's for sure. Until there's little or no prospect of an arrest, he might hold on to it. And even if we are able to charge somebody fairly soon, his lawyers might want to do their own testing.'

Butler frowned. 'I see.'

'Was Leo religious?' Skinner asked.

'Church of Scotland. We both are . . . were, but he actually went on occasion. Out of respect for his mother, he said.'

'Did he ever express a preference for burial or cremation?'

'Not to me, but his father went up the chimney, so I suppose . . .'

'In that case, maybe you could think about a memorial service, with a private cremation when the PF does release the remains.'

'Mmm. Might do. I suppose I should talk to Joy Herbert, just in case he put an instruction in his will.'

'That would make sense,' Provan agreed, 'but we'll want to talk to her before anyone else does.'

'Another thing. Rae and Raeleen were at the party; Leo wanted everybody in his life to be there. They're due to go back to America on Wednesday. Can they do that?'

'I hope so, but I cannae say for sure. That'll be up to DI Mann once we've interviewed the mother. Where do we find her?'

'We put them up in the Blacksmith. Faye stayed there on Friday night too; it meant that all the kids could be bedded down and the mothers could enjoy themselves.'

'And did they?' Skinner asked quietly.

'As far as I could see. Faye doesn't have an issue with Rae. As far as she's concerned, she's from another world.'

'Then I hope she can get back to it soon,' the DS said, 'but if she tells us something that's relevant to the investigation, we might ask her to stay here for a while longer.'

Butler raised a questioning eyebrow. 'Could you force her to stay if she insisted on going back?'

'We could if she was locked up,' the DS retorted. 'But in practice she's free to fly back as planned. Sure, we'll want to talk to her, but she's no' even obliged to do that. It could get complicated, though, if she turned out to be a witness after she'd gone home. Would we have trouble getting her back?'

'If it helped convict someone of Leo's murder, she'd be on the first plane. She really loved him.'

'How did he feel about her?'

'Fond. He was fond of her; he told me he felt comfortable with her. Mind you, he said the same about Faye at the beginning. Leo didn't really do love; he never saw any at home when he was a kid. His dad, Leonard, was a quiet bloke who never smiled, and his mother developed Alzheimer's relatively young.'

'What effect did that have on Leo? Can you say?'

The other man sighed. 'I think,' he replied, 'that it was why he never got really close to anyone in his life, other than me, maybe. He was afraid that one day whatever had got into his mother's head might get into his.'

'Was that the real reason why he wasn't too keen on the book approach?' Provan asked.

'That may have been part of it. I explained to Mrs Raynor that he'd had a difficult family life. She wasn't bothered about that; she said she was prepared to skip over it. She told Leo that on Friday, but he didn't react to it. He said he'd mull it over and give her a final answer yesterday. I'm pretty sure it would have been "no thanks", though.'

'How would you have felt about that? It would have cost you money too, would it not?'

Butler's eyes narrowed; he peered at the DS. 'I've got money, Sergeant. Yes, my share of the advance as Leo's agent would have been just shy of a quarter of a million, but I wasn't relying on it to keep a roof over my head in my old age, I promise you. The Chancellor of the bloody Exchequer would have been more annoyed than me. He really does need the cash.'

'Fair enough,' Provan muttered. 'Although we may revisit that.' He glanced at the printout in his hand. 'Before you go, maybe you could help us wi' some of these names. Gene Alderney, for example. Who's he?'

'She; it's short for Genevieve. She's Bryce Stoddart's match-maker in the promotional company. She finds the opponents and negotiates with them. She's a holdover from old Benny's time; came on the scene about ten years ago. He always said she had bigger balls than him when it came to cutting a deal. When he retired, he insisted that Bryce keep her on.'

'Was she going to be involved in the new venture?'

'She might have been on the boxing side, yes, but not the MMA; that roster would all be fighters directly contracted by the company, so it wouldn't need a matchmaker.'

'Mmm.' He looked at the list again. 'Charles Baxter. What about him?'

'He's a chartered surveyor from Edinburgh; he's a partner in LJMcF. It's an international practice; it looked after all of Leo's property interests, personal and commercial, and he's the main man. His name's on the list, but he wasn't there.'

'Did Leo have a lot of property investments?' Skinner asked.

'Oh yes. Much of his wealth was invested in property.' Butler smiled. 'You've probably read estimates of Leo's net worth. Around sixty-five million, some papers say. Bollocks. He had to have been worth twice that in property alone; held in different companies in different countries. Last year, thanks to LJMcF, he bought an advertising agency in Kuala Lumpur, through a company called LS Asia, registered in the Bahamas. The agency was pretty much fucked; it hadn't made a profit in years. It was a distress sale really, but Charlie Baxter discovered something that everyone else had overlooked. It owned its own office block. Leo bought the company, inherited the debt, which was secured against the building, paid that off with a loan that he serviced through the rental income stream, and was left with an asset valued at forty million US dollars. If anyone deserved his party invitation, our Charlie did.'

'Augusta Cambridge,' Provan read. 'What about her?'

'She's an artist, painter. Have you ever heard of LeRoy Neiman?'

'Can't say I have.'

'He was an American, a legend; he specialised in impressionist paintings and screen prints of fighters, athletes, sporting events. They were wonderful, awash with colour. Augusta styles her work on his, although she's more conventional. She's done a few paintings of Leo in action; he commissioned them but she holds the copyright and the print income, which is worth having. She also did paintings of the crowds at a few of his fights. The originals are in public galleries in the countries where they were painted; the prints sell in the hundreds of thousands, and Augusta rakes it in.' He broke off, then added, 'That was one of the things about the champ. The people who hung around him tended to make a hell of a lot of money.'

'And Aldo Mosca,' Skinner said. 'Who's he?'

Butler gave a quick teeth-sucking intake of breath. 'That's a hell of a good question,' he replied. 'Of all the people on that list, he is the only one I didn't know, not until this week, and you have to go and pick him out. Turns out he's a movie director who wants to make a documentary about boxing. That's not his real name, though; the full version has nine or ten syllables.'

'If you didn't know him, how did he get on the list?'

'Leo added him, last week. I asked him who he was, but all he said was "a bloke I know". I asked if he really needed to be there, because the Blacksmith was going to be bung full by that time. He insisted. "It's not a request, Gino," he said. But he refused to tell me why. Truth be told, I was annoyed. He never kept secrets from me; as it turned out, it was the wrong time to start.'

'But Mosca was there on the night?'

'Oh yes. A little chap with greasy dark hair and black-framed specs: Italian, by his accent.'

'You spoke to him?' Provan intervened.

'As it turned out, I'd spoken to him before that, but I made a point of it on the night. I wanted to know how he was connected to Leo, but he didn't drop any hints.'

'Who else did he talk to that you know of?'

'I saw him chatting to Rae; I think she might have known him, or maybe she was just being friendly.'

'Did you arrange accommodation for him?'

'Yes, I put him up in a hotel in Glasgow. Leo didn't want him in the Blacksmith for some reason he didn't explain. He's still a bit of a mystery.'

'One that we'd better solve,' Skinner declared.

Twelve

'I've been expecting your call,' Joy Herbert said. 'Indeed, after the news alert that flashed up on my phone half an hour ago, I intended to call the police. Your spokesman described my client's death as "suspicious". Can you be more specific than that?'

'He was poisoned,' Lottie Mann replied. 'In theory we can't rule out its being self-administered, but we can't find a single reason in his personal circumstances for him to do that, so our presumption is that he was murdered. Mr Butler, his manager, told us that you handle Mr Speight's private legal affairs, and that you drew up his will. Is that the case?'

'Yes,' the solicitor confirmed, 'and I need to contact Mr Butler also. The will names him as an executor. The other is Mr Charles Baxter, who will have charge of all property matters.'

'Butler's just left us, heading home, but we need to see you soonest. I have to know the contents of the will. Do you have a problem with that?'

'Not at all. My client is dead; the will's of immediate importance. Also, as soon as I lodge it with the sheriff court, it'll be a public document. You'd better come to my office; it's in the Roberts Building in George Square. I'm just finishing lunch. I can be there in half an hour . . . that's assuming I can get a taxi, since I've had a glass of wine.'

'Make it an hour. We're still at Mr Speight's house in Ayr. Don't worry about a taxi. I'll send a police car for you.'

Mann heard the lawyer chuckle. 'As long as they don't put a hand on my head when I'm getting in, like they do on the telly.'

The DI noted her address, then ended the call. 'Amazing,' she remarked to Provan. 'A solicitor who wants to help the police.'

'Maybe she'll take your case,' her colleague said jokingly.

'If she was Leo Speight's lawyer, I couldn't afford her. Besides, she does private law, not family law; there's a difference.' She sighed. 'I wish she did, though; I feel so damn helpless. The thought of having to leave Jakey with those two overnight: it's so bloody frustrating.'

'Then don't,' he challenged. 'If you and Vanessa can get something agreed right away, you can take him home tonight and she can pick him up from school tomorrow.'

She frowned. 'Do you think we could?'

'I'll drive to Glasgow; you talk to her on the phone. If you can sort something out, we can pick up Jakey once we've seen the lawyer woman and dealt with whatever that throws up.'

'The in-laws won't like it. Arnold will yell about his appointment at the Academy.'

'Let him. What are they going to do? Refuse to hand the child over to his mother?' He grinned. 'If they tried that, we might have to get the polis.'

'Mmm. I don't like the idea of Jakey being caught in the middle, Dan.'

'He is in the middle. We . . . you have to get him out of there.

You cannae give in to these people, Lottie, otherwise they will take the laddie off you.' He held out his hand. 'Come on,' he said. 'Gimme the car keys, and you get on the phone.'

Thirteen

The Blacksmith proved easy to find. Skinner had programmed it into his satnav, but even as the helpful voice told him to bear left at the next exit, he saw it, isolated on the crest of a hill.

Half a dozen small bungalow-style units were arranged around the main hotel building, given extra privacy by several screens of trees. A larger plantation stood to the west of the complex, sheltering it from the prevailing wind that blew strongly across the surrounding moorland.

The car park seemed full, but as he approached, a car pulled out, leaving a space in the second row. 'Sunday,' he murmured as he parked. 'Lunch. Of course.'

As if to confirm his conclusion, he spotted four AA rosettes displayed proudly beneath the anvil logo on the signage above the main entrance. He strode into the reception area, to be greeted by a wave of noise from a large room to his left, a constant restaurant buzz given a hard edge by the strident voices of the inevitable few who believed that volume guaranteed attention.

'I'm afraid we're not seating anyone else for lunch, sir.'

Skinner glanced to his left at the speaker, a tall young man in a dark suit. He reminded him instantly of the star of a TV drama he had seen a few days before, but his lapel badge announced him as 'Matthew Quayle, Manager'. 'That will not ruin my day,' he replied. 'However good the food is, I value my hearing more. I'm looking for one of your hotel guests, Ms Letts, an American lady.'

'I'm not sure that Ms Letts is seeing anyone, sir,' Matthew Quayle said. 'She's had a terrible shock. As indeed have we all,' he added. 'Our owner has just passed away.'

Skinner nodded. 'I know. That's why I'm here.' He showed his plastic ID badge to the manager, watching as the man studied it, taking in his puzzlement.

'Security Service? Would that be private security?'

'Most people call us MI5.'

Confusion and panic were woven together in Quayle's expression. 'In that case . . .' he murmured. 'Can you wait here, sir? I believe Ms Letts and her daughter are in their bungalow. If you'll let me . . .'

'Sure,' Skinner agreed, 'you check, but I'll come with you.'

Deciding not to argue the point, the manager led the way out of the main hotel building, turning right, away from the car park, and heading for a group of bungalows that stood side by side on the most secluded part of the plot. He stopped at the second and pressed a buzzer on what appeared to be a video entry system. He spoke too quietly for his companion to hear clearly, but the word 'police' did float back to him. Eventually there was a click, and the door opened.

'I told her you were a cop,' Quayle said quietly. 'Less complicated that way. Will I come in with you?'

'Thank you, no, but I may want to speak with you again, so stick around, please.'

He stepped inside the bungalow, and came face to face with one of the most beautiful women he had ever seen. She wore no make-up, and her thick black hair was restrained by a headband, but her skin seemed to shimmer like bronze, and her brown eyes were wide open and mesmerising as she gazed at him. She wore a white shirt and close-cut black shorts, which emphasised the slimness of her long legs, even though her feet were encased in a pair of loud red rubber Crocs. Everything about her seemed perfect, and then she spoke.

'You're a police officer?' Her voice was her only imperfection; it was high and nasal, and tremulous.

'Of sorts.' He flashed his badge once more, but she barely looked at it. 'I'm looking at Leo's death from a specific angle.'

'What are they saying?' she twanged. 'Gino just called. They're sayin' it's suspicious? What the goddam does that mean?'

'It means he didn't die naturally. That's the official line, but he was murdered, Ms Letts. There's little or no doubt about that.'

'Murdered,' she repeated. 'You sayin' someone killed my Leo?'

'That's how it looks.'

The brown eyes were glazed with tears. She put her hands to her face. 'Jesus,' she mumbled. 'It's bad enough I've gotta tell my baby her daddy's dead, but this . . .'

'How old is your daughter, Ms Letts?' Skinner asked.

'Two,' she replied, wiping her eyes with the back of her left hand. 'Won't be three till August.'

'In that case, she's not going to understand death, and you don't need to introduce her to the concept, not yet. Tell her she's not going to see her daddy for a while, let her get used to the idea of him not coming back. My daughter was four when her mother died; she didn't get it straight away. That was a long time ago now. She told me she was eight or nine before she really accepted it.'

'How's she grown up, without a momma?'

'Pretty damn well.' He paused. 'Correct me if I'm wrong, and my apologies if I am, but you and Leo didn't actually live together, not full-time, did you?'

She shook her head. 'No.' She sighed, and her shoulders sagged. 'Come on through, Mr . . . er . . . What you say your name is?'

'I didn't, but it's Skinner, Bob Skinner.'

'Then come into the living room, sir. Raeleen's napping, and if we stay here talkin' we gonna wake her, and I don't want that.'

She led him into an apartment that was a smaller version of the area where Leo Speight had died, and through to the conservatory area. He was certain that the same architect had worked on both projects.

'You like a drink?' she asked.

He declined. 'Thanks, but I'm driving.'

'Yeah, but you're a cop.'

'All the more reason to take care. There are cops all over Scotland who'd love to bust me.'

'How did you piss them off?'

'That's a long story. What about you and Leo?'

She frowned; a wrinkle appeared above her nose, the only line on her face, he realised. 'That's a short one. I could say that we lived together when he was in Vegas. He bought us a house on the lake when I got pregnant . . .' She paused, as her mind went off on a slight tangent. 'Hell, I don't know how we can stay there now he's gone. Gonna have to move back into the city and get out my dancing shoes. He said he'd always look after us, but he didn't plan on bein' dead.'

'Wait and see,' Skinner said. 'He sounds like a man of his word, from what I've heard. You said "He bought us the house". Us being you and your daughter?'

'Yeah. It's in my name; so is my car. Leo had a condo, an apartment, when we first got together.'

'How did you meet?'

'I was a backing singer in a show at Caesar's; Leo was training for a marquee fight in the Grand, and one of the big wheels from the pay-TV company brought him along. Afterwards he brought him backstage, and we were introduced. It went from there. I knew there was someone in Scotland; he was open about that, and about the fact that he had kids there. Anyone else, I'd probably have told him to get lost, but I guessed that nobody would ever get a hundred per cent of Leo, so I decided to settle for my share. I moved into his apartment after six months, when he came back to train for his next fight, and lived there after he left. A year later, I got pregnant with Raeleen. He said our kid wasn't growing up in no apartment block; next thing I knew, he'd bought the house. You ever been to Vegas, Mr Skinner?'

He smiled. 'My wife's American. She made me go, before our first child was born. I've seen the lake, too; flew over it in a chopper on the way to the Grand Canyon. I imagine it's all changed since then.'

'It's always changing, and it always will. That's what Leo liked about it.'

'I get the impression that you two were really close.'

'We were, and I loved him. He loved Raeleen, and he said he loved our quiet time together . . . but never once did he tell me he loved me. I didn't expect that we'd be as we were forever. The last few months, I sensed a change was coming.'

'Did that upset you?'

The brown eyes widened very slightly. 'As in did it upset me enough to make me want to kill him, Mr Policeman? No, it didn't, because I always knew how things were. I know damn well that if he had told me he loved me, it would only have been because he knew I'd like to hear it. That wouldn't have been honest, and Leo was the most honest man I ever met. The business he was in, Jeez, there is some shadiness there, but he was above all that. There's a woman wants him to write his life story. Leo said to me, "She might not like what she got; a hell of a lot of people wouldn't like it and some of them are dangerous individuals." I don't care what Gino thought; Leo wouldn't have taken that book deal, whatever the money on offer. He told me he wasn't ready, and that's it.'

'I want to ask you about the party on Friday,' Skinner continued. 'I don't imagine that you knew many of the people there.'

'Maybe more than you'd think,' Rae Letts countered. 'Gino I knew, sure. And the fight guys: Bryce Stoddart, the promoter; Gene Alderney, the matchmaker. I met all of them in Las Vegas. They've all been to the house. The only guy I knew who wasn't there was Charlie Baxter, the property guy; he visited when Leo was training for the Fonsecco fight to get him to sign off on a property deal in the Bahamas. And Leo's other kids, of course; I knew the kids.'

'Leonard and Jolene?' Skinner exclaimed, surprised.

'Yes. Leo brought them over for Raeleen's birthday party. It was their school vacation. Gordon, too, the grown-up one; he came as well.'

'What about Faye?'

'The little ones' mother? No, I never met her before Friday night.'

'How did you get on?'

'Not well, with her bein' an abusive racist bitch. Imagine, her kids have Leo's blood in them and she's racist. But I can rise above that; what really annoys me about the woman is the fact that she calls herself Mrs Speight, when she isn't, never was and never would have been. This settlement she was hassling Leo about; damn thing was never necessary. I dunno why she hired that lawyer man, can't figure that out. Leo would always have looked after her. It's not as if he left her. He never lived with her full-time, no more than he did with me.'

'How did Leo feel about the legal action?' he asked.

'Amused. Yeah, that covers it. Leo didn't get angry. He wasn't stressed about it. He had his own lawyer, QC he called her, whatever the hell that stands for, and she said they were going straight to the top court, because Faye's guy didn't stand a chance. The only thing that Leo said, and he laughed, was that no way was he paying for her such-and-such lawyer, and that if his cost didn't leave Faye with too much, that was her lookout. The plan was that he was going to settle a ton of money on the kids, but not a hell of a lot on Faye.'

'Did she mention any of this to you?'

'Hell, no.' She smiled for a second. 'She and I didn't compare notes, sir.'

'There was a man there named—'

Skinner stopped in mid sentence as a door creaked ajar and a child toddled into the room, a tiny version of her mother. She was rubbing sleep out of her eyes. 'Mamma,' she cried. 'Hungry.'

'Okay, honey,' her mother exclaimed, gathering her up in her arms. 'Come 'n, I'll fix you something up. What you like? Got bananas here, and mango, and raspberries. How about I put them in the blender and we'll all have some?'

The toddler beamed and nodded. Skinner stood silent and watched as Rae peeled two mangoes and carved them off their stones, chopped bananas, and washed raspberries in a fine-mesh sieve, then put them all in a mixer, with most of a large carton of Greek yoghurt, before turning it on at full power and leaving it to run for a full minute as she dropped four slices of bread into a toaster.

When all was ready and the toast spread with syrup, he accepted a serving dutifully. The smoothie was perfect; mentally he noted the ingredients.

'Sorry about that interruption,' Rae murmured as they ate, 'but when this one wants fed, you best take care of it before all H E double L breaks loose.'

'I know,' he assured her. 'I have three daughters; there's thirty years between the oldest and the youngest. What you say is true, and it doesn't change with age.'

She stared at him. 'Sir, I am impressed. You must have led an interesting life.'

He nodded. 'I have. Just as well I didn't get home more often.'

'You were gonna ax me about a man,' she said, pouring coffee into two mugs.

'Yes, I was. His name is Aldo Mosca; he was a guest, but nobody seems to know a hell of a lot about him.'

She shook her head. 'No, not Aldo Mosca; that was what Leo called him on the guest list he showed me. His proper name is Aldorino Moscardinetto, and he was very touchy about anyone cutting it short, other than Leo. He's Italian. He visited in Vegas a little while back. I spent some time with him on Friday. He was, like, quizzin' me about Vegas and the people who hang out there, the fight people, the MMA crew.'

'Was it idle interest?' Skinner asked. 'Was he just making small talk? Chatting you up, as we say in Scotland?'

She laughed softly, a much gentler sound than her voice. 'I'm the wrong gender for him, Mr Skinner. He didn't say as much, but he's gay, I could tell. No, he was serious, a really intense little guy. He has piercing little eyes behind those big glasses that he wears. He was really interested; he even said he might call on me again in Vegas when he was there.'

'How did he get on the invitation list?'

'Leo put him there. I asked him why, but he didn't tell me much. He just winked at me and said, "Mischief", whatever the hell that meant.'

Fourteen

'When I was in Australia,' Dan Provan mused, 'a couple of my daughter's pals tried to sympathise with me about the hard times in Britain, wi' all this Brexit shite. They really think we're on our uppers, on the slippery slope to Third World status.' He smiled. 'I had to say to them, yes, things have been better, and we're no' a hundred per cent sure how it's going tae go when we do leave. But if it's that bad, how come our pubs and restaurants have so many young Aussies in them working as bar staff?'

He gazed down Buchanan Street as they stepped out of the Galleries shopping mall, down at the throng of Sunday shoppers listening to the mingling sounds of half a dozen and more street entertainers. 'Glasgow Sunday afternoon,' he said. 'There was hardly a space in the car park; now look at this. If we're keepin' poverty at bay, we're bloody good at it.'

He glanced to his left, at Lottie. 'Are you going to phone the in-laws tae tell them we'll be picking up Jakey?'

'No,' she replied. 'I'm not inclined to have a stand-up shouting match in public. I've just sent Nana Mann – that's what she makes him call her, Nana bloody Mann – a text saying I'll be there at six and to have him ready.'

'I'll enjoy that.' His smile gleamed.

'No, you won't,' she told him firmly. 'Sorry, Dan, but I'm going on my own. You'd be like a red rag to them.'

'Hey,' he protested. 'I've missed the wee guy.'

'Then miss him for a couple more days. It's got to be that way. Arnold would go off at you, and you're not one to stand there and take it.'

'What if they won't hand him over?'

Her eyebrows came together. 'It won't come to that. I know that Scott's on home leave all weekend. Arnold won't want a fuss with him there.'

'Today as well? You're bloody joking! What's the bloody jail coming to these days?'

'That's the way it is; he's nearly at the end of his custodial sentence. Suppose they said I wasn't having Jakey, I called for uniform support, and it got messy. No, they wouldn't want their precious son in the middle of that. There will be clenched teeth and muttered imprecations, but my boy will go home with his mother.' She trotted down the last three steps. 'Come on now, let's find this woman.'

The office of Herbert Chesters, Solicitors, was as discreet as the service it provided to its high-net-worth clients. It occupied part of the second storey of a sandstone building that gazed across George Square – which is actually rectangular, a truth unobserved by most of its denizens – at the opulent City Chambers, a memorial to the Victorian era, when Glasgow was the second city of both Scotland and the British Empire. The detectives noted that an orderly queue stretched from its entrance to the furthest corner of the Square and round into Cochrane Street.

Joy Herbert was waiting for them in the outer office of her

firm's suite. Provan had been expecting a thirty-something woman in a power suit. Instead he found himself facing a lady in her early sixties in a loose-fitting long-sleeved floral dress, bespectacled, her hair dyed a shade that was somewhere between red and auburn. 'Decent weather,' she observed as she greeted them. 'It's brought the crowds out.'

'What's happening in the City Chambers?' Mann asked, after introducing herself and her sergeant.

'The council's opened a book of condolence for Leo,' she replied. 'Nice of them, considering he wasn't actually from Glasgow, but from Paisley. Come on through to my room. I've looked out the document you're here to see.'

'How many people do you have in the firm?'

'I'm listed as the senior partner, but actually I'm the only one. Mr Chesters retired a year ago, and I'm taking time to consider his replacement. My choice will come from my three assistants. They're described as associates on their business cards, to give them a bit more status. I also have a paralegal clerk and a secretary. Since Mr Chesters left, we've been an all-woman firm. I don't find that's a hindrance at all.'

'How many clients do you service?' the DI continued as the three took seats around a small table. 'Or is that a secret?'

Mrs Herbert smiled. 'Not really, although the business editor of the *Herald* did describe the firm as "reclusive". I couldn't argue with that, even suppose I wanted to, which I don't since I regard it as a backhanded compliment. I don't advertise and I certainly do not have a website. Since Mr Chesters and I founded the firm twenty-eight years ago, we have always relied on word of mouth for new business development. Today we have thirty-eight full-time clients, all high net worth, and a turnover of just under three and a half million a year. I volunteer that because it's a public figure, although our clients' names are absolutely confidential.'

'I imagine Leo Speight was your biggest,' Provan ventured.

'Your imagination is too narrow,' the solicitor replied. 'We have several clients who are wealthier than Leo was at the last calculation. Our list extends beyond Scotland, and includes two billionaires.'

'We're hearing various estimates of Leo's wealth,' Mann said.

'Guesstimates, you should say. The estate's inheritance-tax liability will be difficult to calculate; much of it will depend on property valuations, and that'll be complicated by the fact that his holdings are in several different countries. I'll be relying heavily on his property adviser, Charles Baxter, to pull all of it together. Then there are the businesses that he owned, companies, where the shareholding might have been spread. The Blacksmith, the hotel on the outskirts of the city, is an example. It has two shareholders, Leo and his son Gordon Pollock; with his death, all of his equity passes to the boy, to be held in a trust administered by me, until he turns twenty-one in three years' time. That's what the will says.'

'The will,' the DI repeated. 'What does the rest of it say?'

Mrs Herbert picked up a document that lay on the table. 'It contains several specific bequests: there's a million pounds to Trudi Pollock, Gordon's mother, and three million dollars to Rae Letts. That's cash; the house on Lake Las Vegas is already in her name. Similarly, the house in Troon is in the name of Faye Bulloch.' She looked from one detective to the other. 'That may be important; Ms Bulloch styles herself as Mrs Speight, but the will doesn't. That title doesn't appear anywhere; it isn't bestowed upon her, Ms Pollock or Ms Letts. Ms Bulloch is trying to lay claim to it in court, but there's nothing in the will to help her . . . the opposite, in fact. Leo made a recent amendment leaving her one million sterling, provided that she drop her claim of spousal status, in the event of those proceedings not being concluded at the time of his death.'

'That sounds as if he was anticipating it,' Mann observed sharply.

'Leo was meticulous,' the lawyer replied. 'He covered as many contingencies as he could imagine. He made the adjustment before his last fight. He also has an insurance policy that covered him being fatally injured in the ring. Other bequests,' she continued, briskly. 'The cars in the garage of the house in Ayr go to Gino Butler, as does a bequest of half a million pounds. The house itself, that's interesting. When the will was drafted, it went to Gordon Pollock, but two weeks ago I had a letter from Leo telling me to remove that clause, pending a further instruction.'

'Was that instruction ever made?'

'Not that I know of, Detective Inspector.'

'Will that give you a problem in winding up the estate?'

'It shouldn't; if no instruction turns up, the value of the asset will be realised – I'll sell the place in other words – and it will be part of the final settlement. "What's that?" you're going to ask me. After all the bequests have been made and inheritance tax paid, the residue of the estate, including Leo's holdings in joint ventures with Mr Bryce Stoddart and others, and all property that isn't ordered to be sold or specifically bequeathed, goes to Leo's children as follows: ten per cent to Gordon, in addition to various hotel properties which become his by bequest, and thirty per cent each to his minor children, Leonard Bulloch, Jolene Bulloch, and Raeleen Letts. You see? Leo registered each of

A BRUSH WITH DEATH

those births, but he didn't afford his name to any of his offspring.'

'Why no', do you think?' Provan asked her.

The solicitor leaned back, gazing at the wall facing her. 'It may have been foresight, Detective Sergeant, a guess that Faye Bulloch might have used it in a future claim of informal marriage. But I don't believe so; Leo told me once that it was out of deference to Gordon and his mother. He had been denied the Speight name on his birth certificate – Leo wasn't even named as his father – so he didn't want to favour the others over him.'

'He really wasn't the marrying kind, was he?' Provan chuckled.

'No, he wasn't,' she agreed.

'And yet Sandra Bulloch, our boss, referred to him as her brother-in-law.'

'A show of loyalty towards her sister, perhaps. She needed it,' Joy Herbert continued. 'There was another late alteration, advised by letter. In the original will, Ms Rae Letts was appointed as her daughter's trustee, and Ms Faye Bulloch in the same capacity for her children. However, in a separate letter, not long after the beginning of the court action, Ms Bulloch was removed and I was named as trustee in her place.'

'What did Moss Lee make of that?' the DS wondered.

'Neither he nor his client have any idea that it happened.' She looked at Mann, and held up the document. 'I'll make copies of this for you, with the condition that nothing is released to the media before it's lodged with the court.' She grinned unexpectedly. 'Let's hope it's the final version.'

'Why shouldn't it be?' the DI asked.

'The way the will was drafted,' the lawyer explained, 'it allowed for what's known in Scots law as informal writings. That means it can be altered by a simple written, witnessed, declaration by the testator. The letters I mentioned were examples of that. I can only hope there are no others lying around in one of my late client's many properties.'

Fifteen

'The fee note comes to me,' Bob Skinner told his oldest daughter.

'We'll deal with that when we know the outcome,' Alex replied, smiling at him as the dying sun flooded the garden room of his seaside home. 'Now,' she continued briskly, 'what's this about you being involved with the Leo Speight situation? How did that come about?'

'How do you think?'

'I can only guess at insurance.'

He nodded. 'On the ball as always, kid,' he laughed. 'How about your workload? Are you busy this week?'

'I'm in the High Court on Tuesday, defending a client who's accused of incest.'

'Bloody hell! You're not going to trial, are you?'

'Absolutely not! She's as guilty as sin.'

'She?' he gasped.

'That's right. My twenty-year-old client had sex with her eighteen-year-old uncle. It's a very convoluted family . . . as is our own,' she added. 'I'm pleading her guilty then gambling that my plea in mitigation might keep her out of jail. Her story is that she met the lad at a club in Glasgow, spent the night with him and went back to Edinburgh. Uncle took a selfie of the two of them – fully clothed, nothing raunchy – and showed it to his mother. She hit the roof. Mum had him in her early twenties; meanwhile, *her* mum, the boy's granny, had divorced, remarried and had another child, at the age of forty-three. The half-sisters both looked remarkably like their mother, but the two never met, since the older sister severed all relations with her mother when she left her dad. You with me so far?'

'Struggling,' Bob admitted, 'but I think so.'

'Right. So the laddie's mum looked at the selfie and saw the spitting image not just of her own mother, but of herself when she was that age. Of course auntie had left nephew her mobile number, and her name, which meant nothing at all to him but confirmed the truth to his mother. She screamed bloody murder and went straight to the police.'

He gasped. 'The fiscal charged them?' he exclaimed.

'He charged *her*. The police found that her grandfather, the boy's great-grandfather, had a photo of him aged seventeen on his mantelpiece. She visited him a few times every month. She admitted that she'd seen it, but swore that she never made the connection when they met in a dark nightclub full of fake smoke and strobe lighting. The dyspeptic advocate depute, my old adversary Paula Benedict, didn't buy it and served the indictment.'

She shifted in her chair and drained the last of her sparkling water, straight from the bottle. 'So you see, Pops, I can't plead her not guilty, because according to the indictment she is, but I can do my damnedest to persuade Lady Ingram, the judge, that she's innocent nevertheless and get her an absolute discharge.'

'That's a belter,' he agreed. 'I must tell June Crampsey about it and make sure the *Saltire*'s legal editor's in court when the case is called.'

Alex laughed. 'When you joined the board of InterMedia, it must have been the best day of that woman's life,' she observed. 'You've turned into a newshound, a managing editor's dream.'

'No I haven't,' he protested. 'I have a responsibility as a director for the success of the paper, and if I can contribute to it by passing on information that comes my way, so be it.'

'Will that include the Leo Speight murder?' she asked.

'There I'm slightly compromised. I'm bound by confidentiality.'

'Who's binding you?'

'Theoretically, the insurers that I'm supposed to be representing.'

'Hey,' she said, 'this is Alex. I'm not really going to fall for that story. The information the insurance company needs it can get directly from the police or the prosecution. They're unlikely to settle a claim for the enhanced payout specified in the policy until there's a conviction for murder.'

'What if no arrest is made?' he countered.

'It could be tied up in the civil court for years, unless the Crown case is so strong that they're advised to settle. Either way, they didn't need to parachute you in there. Admit it, Maggie Steele and Mario have asked you to advise the CID team.'

'They wouldn't do that.'

'They would, given half a chance.'

'Then they couldn't do that.'

'They could, if they chose. They could bring in Sherlock; there's nothing in law to stop them.'

'But they didn't.'

She sat up in her chair, staring him down. 'Well somebody did. Come on, Pops, you're holding out on me. I'm an officer of the court, out with it.'

Skinner sighed, then reached inside his gilet and produced his wallet, from which he retrieved a laminated card. 'Client confidentiality, okay?' he murmured as he handed it over.

'Always,' she replied, then looked at it. 'Jesus!' she gasped, her eyes widening. 'Consultant director. When did this happen?'

'A few months ago. A situation arose that you really do not want to know about, and I was pulled in by Amanda Dennis, the head of the Security Service. As you know, she and I have been friends for years, as well as occasional colleagues. It was supposed to be a one-off, but it's evolved into . . . well, let's call it an informal association. If she really needs me, I'm there. Non-operational, though,' he added quickly. 'I don't wear a white tux and carry a Walther PPK.'

'Why is she interested in Leo Speight's death?' Alex asked.

'There's a suggestion that he – or the people around him – may have had links to criminal organisations.'

'I thought Speight was squeaky clean. That was his image, certainly.'

'He may well have been. I said only a suggestion, remember, but if people like that were around him, something he announced at his retirement party last Friday night might have upset them.'

'Do you really think so?' A sadness crept into her eyes. 'I hope not; I was a fan of his.'

'I have an open mind at the moment; I need to speak to a couple of people before I firm up my thinking. As for you being a fan of his, you were not alone among women. Leo had two families that I know of, two and a half if you count his teenage son.' He smiled as the door opened and Ignacio walked into the room. 'And speaking of teenage sons . . .'

'*Buenos noches, Papa y hermana,*' he said. '*Sarah dice que estará aquí tan pronto como Dawn se vaya a dormir.*'

'We're working on my Spanish,' Bob explained to Alex. 'It's the official language of InterMedia, and mine is crap. I might need to pick up some Italian as well. *Prego* and *grazie* are all I know.'

'Why do you need that?' Ignacio asked.

'I have to research and maybe locate an Italian guy with a wonderfully expressive name: Aldorino Moscardinetto.'

'The film director?'

Bob stared at his son. 'You know him?'

'Unless there are two of them; it is not a name you will forget. It's funny, too; I have a little Italian, and in rough translation his *apellido* means "little octopus". In Spain, his nickname is Pulpito. It means the same.'

'What else do you know about him?'

'Quite a lot; I am interested in film and I researched him for my Spanish school certificate, before I came to Scotland. He is very progressive as a film-maker. He does both drama and documentary, and his work is always controversial. Most of it has been in Italy, but he made one movie in Spanish, a history of the Blue Brigade – very bloody – and a couple of feature films in English for the American market. One was called *Lovechild*. There was a Scottish actor in it, Joey Morocco.'

Father and daughter exchanged glances. 'I remember it well,' Bob murmured. 'I was taken to the Scottish premiere. Far too intense for me, but the boy Morocco was okay. I had no idea who directed it, though; the screening was in Glasgow, so all the publicity was about Joey. Give me a moment, you two.' He pushed himself to his feet, picked up his mobile and walked outside into the garden.

Closing the door behind him, he scrolled through his contacts, going no further than 'A', then clicking on a number.

'Bob,' Aileen de Marco exclaimed, her surprise undisguised. 'What can I do for you? Or did you misdial?'

'No,' he told his former wife. 'I called the right number, but it's not you that I'm after. I need to speak to Pal Joey. Do you know how I can contact him?'

'That depends on why you want him. You haven't decided to settle scores, have you?'

'If I ever did,' he replied, 'you'd be the last person to know, but as I've told you before, I closed that account a long time ago. I don't care about the pair of you. There's something I need to ask him, that's all.'

'In that case . . .' she paused, 'he's here. We're in Glasgow. We came up for a party on Friday night and stayed over so that Joey could visit his parents. We're on the red-eye tomorrow.'

'Mmm,' he murmured. 'I know why you were in Glasgow, and whose party you were at. I saw your names on the guest list.'

'Were you invited too? You were well hidden if you were; I never saw you.'

'No, I wasn't part of the late Mr Speight's circle.'

'How did you come to see the guest list? Are you . . . ? You're not back on the force, are you? You haven't taken the chief constable up on the job offer you told me about?'

'Hell, no! Some people I'm associated with have a peripheral interest in the situation, that's all.'

'That sounds very spooky. I know you well enough not to ask any more. Here's Joey.'

The background noise stilled for a while, as she told her lover that the call was for him, he guessed.

When it resumed, there was a second's hesitancy. 'Mr Skinner?' Joey Morocco ventured cautiously.

'Bob, for fuck's sake,' he retorted. 'Given what we have in

common, I think we can be on first-name terms. I need to ask you about someone you know, someone I want to speak to, Aldorino Moscardinetto. I know he was at Leo Speight's bash at the Blacksmith on Friday, but I don't know where he is now, or how to get in touch with him.'

'I'm not sure of his whereabouts either,' the actor admitted. Skinner listened for traces of his origins in his off-screen accent but could detect none. 'I know the guy, yes, from one movie, but we're not buddies.'

'Do you know why he was there?'

'Not for sure, but I suspect that he was doing some sort of business with Leo. The champ was a very hot property, once he'd retired undefeated. There was a publisher after him, and at least three film production companies wanting to dramatise his life. Between the two of us, I've been sounded out about playing him, by Aldorino.'

'Is that why you were at the party?'

'No, no; Leo didn't even know about that. He and I were friends for years. We met at one of his fights, and I was a regular after that, whenever I could make it. I've visited him in London, and Las Vegas. I've even met Rae; she'll be broken hearted, poor girl.'

'She is.'

'Damn shame. She's a special girl, once you get past the voice. Leo really liked her. That said, he'd never have married her; I don't think he'd ever have married anyone, but he was very, very fond of her. Those were his own words.'

'Yes, I spoke to her today and got that impression myself. What about the Ayrshire end? Do you know how he felt about her?'

'Not really,' Morocco confessed. 'I only met her at the party.

He did say once that he respected her, but that he was wary of her.'

'I can guess why: Faye Bulloch called herself Mrs Speight, and she'd even hired a lawyer to try to make that official.'

'I didn't know that. How will his death affect it?'

'I've no idea. It could depend on the will. It'll be a problem for the executors; I'm told that probably means Gino Butler, his manager. Leaving that aside,' Skinner continued, 'do you know how Leo came into contact with Moscardinetto?'

'Oh yes,' the actor replied. 'It was through me. Leo asked me if I could put him in touch with Aldorino. He didn't say why and I didn't ask. If he'd wanted me to know, he'd have told me; that's the way he was.'

'I thought you said that you and the Italian weren't pals.'

'We're not. He's a humourless little shit and he was a bully on the set with most of the cast, especially the women. I do have his mobile number, though. I gave that to Leo and left him to it.'

'Would you give it to me?'

'Sure,' the actor said. 'It's in my contacts; I'll text it to you once we're done.'

'Which we are. Thanks for that.'

'My pleasure.' There was a pregnant hesitation. 'And Bob, I'm sorry, about . . . well, about things that happened in the past.'

Skinner chuckled. 'Like you shagging my wife, you mean? I appreciate that, but there's no need. Things have worked out well for everyone: I'm happy, Aileen's happy, and you've still got that classic profile. Cheers, Joey.'

Sixteen

'What's Mrs Herbert's next step?' Skinner asked, glancing around the room that Mann and Provan shared. The block-wide brick edifice in Pitt Street had been the headquarters of Strathclyde Police, the service that he had headed in the final months of his career. For years he had declared that he would never move to Glasgow, but circumstances had put him in a position where he had found it impossible to refuse.

The place was still in use, but in its last week of service, before the last of its staff transferred to a new building in Dalmarnock, on the east side of the city. Physically it was unchanged, but the energy that Skinner had felt every time he walked through its doorway had dissipated. There was no buzz to it; for all the excitement it generated it might as well have been a council office.

'She's going to meet with Gino Butler this morning,' Mann replied, 'and show him the contents of the will. Then, she said, she'll take his instructions on the parts that concern him, since he's an executor.'

'That was how she put it,' Provan added. 'In practice, she'll give him hers. All the beneficiaries will have to be advised. By letter, she said. Then it'll be a matter of dividing the spoils.'

'After tax,' Skinner pointed out. 'Who's going to make that calculation?'

'One of her associates is a tax specialist,' the DI told him, 'but the estate will be so complicated that she expects she'll have to bring in one of the big accountancy firms.'

'How is it distributed?'

'Most of it will go to his children. Gordon Pollock's share is adjusted because he gets the hotel businesses; the three young ones inherit equally.'

'How about his women?'

'Trudi Pollock gets some, Rae Letts gets a lot, but Faye Bulloch's share is dependent on her behaving herself. Not just that; she was removed as a trustee for her children and replaced by Mrs Herbert. She shouldn't have gone legal on him, that's for sure.'

'All this is provisional, of course,' Provan pointed out. 'The lawyer woman seemed to be saying that Leo could have altered the will without her knowing about it.'

'Informal writings,' Skinner said.

'You know about that?'

'Of course. It's a device that lets you adjust a will without having to go to a lawyer or redraft the whole thing. I used it myself a few months ago, after my new daughter was born. If Mrs Herbert volunteered that – is that what you're saying, Dan? – does she believe that he had?'

Mann frowned. It was the first sign of concern she had shown; to Skinner she appeared more focused than she had the day before. 'No,' she replied, 'she didn't say that for certain; she just flagged it up as a possibility. What she did say was that Leo had told her he was going to change the disposition of the house in Ayr, without saying how he was going to do it. Could that be significant?'

'It could give you a motive for murder,' Skinner suggested. 'If I were you two, first chance I got I'd have another look at Speight's house, and anywhere else he might have conducted personal business, and search for any documents that he might have left behind him. Not just that, I'd be looking for any notes he might have left, handwritten or on a computer, that indicated what change he was going to make. However,' he added, 'it's just as likely he hadn't done anything, as he had no thought of dying.'

'I'll do that,' the DI said, with a wry grin, 'soon as I have the manpower. I'll do anything, to be honest. I've never had any investigation like this before. Homicides in Glasgow are usually pretty straightforward. They're usually domestic, and the perpetrator's still at the scene, or occasionally they're gang related. With those, you've got a ready-made shortlist of three or four people, and all you have to do is pick the likeliest and prove it. With this one, we have a man who lived alone and died alone, apparently after drinking something he bought by the crate-load from the manufacturer.'

'You know that much already?'

'Yes. It seems that Leo didn't go to supermarkets, not in Scotland. My team have established that he shopped on line. The almond soya milk was a special item, purchased at source, and the barcode on the one we found beside him confirms that it was part of his last bulk order.'

'He bought it by the crate?'

'Apparently so.' She sighed. 'And it was public knowledge. About year ago, BBC telly did a feature on him when he was training in London. The reporter asked him if he had any rituals, and he volunteered that one.'

'Ouch! That doesn't exactly narrow the list of suspects. Have you ever had to deal with a poisoning before, Lottie?' Skinner asked.

'No,' she admitted. 'I never have.'

'I've investigated a couple, and they're nasty. They're also very difficult to solve, because a hell of a lot of premeditation goes into them. They're very well planned. While you might have an obvious suspect, proving that the poison wasn't self-administered is difficult, as is gathering enough evidence to bring a charge. I'm talking about cases, too, where there's a very short list of suspects.'

'How many people would have wanted to kill Leo Speight?' Provan challenged.

'That's for you to determine. At the moment, I'm focused on whether his death might have had any links to his business life, possibly to the new venture he announced at his party.'

'Suppose it did. Would folk like that be likely tae poison him?'

'Rule nothing out,' Skinner said.

'We never do,' Provan said dismissively. 'Now, what have you been doing and what's on your list? Come on, share and share alike, Bob. We don't want to be trippin' over each other.'

'No,' he conceded, 'or people might talk. Yesterday, I had a very useful chat with Rae Letts. I think we can agree she's unlikely to make the shortlist of suspects, since she only arrived on Thursday afternoon.'

'She could still have been in the house,' the DS suggested. 'Leo would want to see his wee lass, surely.'

'He did. He picked her up from Glasgow Airport in his Bentley and took them straight to the Blacksmith. I found that out from the duty manager after I'd talked to her. They never left the hotel on Friday. They had room service, breakfast at eight thirty, lunch at twelve thirty.'

'If that's all you found out, how was your chat useful?' Mann asked.

'She told me who Aldo Mosca is; his full name is Aldorino Moscardinetto.'

'The film director?' Provan exclaimed, taking both of his companions by surprise.

'I don't imagine there's two of them,' Skinner retorted. 'She didn't know why he was there, but she told me she'd met him before, when Leo brought him to her house. Thanks to a film-star friend of mine, I have a contact number for him. I have to see someone else this morning, but I can talk to him after that. Or you can if you'd prefer; it's your choice, Lottie.'

'I'd be happy if you did,' she replied. 'As it is, it's going to take Dan and me an age to get through that guest list and interview or eliminate everyone.' She glanced at the clock on her desk. 'In fact we should be going. We're seeing Faye Bulloch in an hour.'

'Will her sister be there?'

'She'd better not be!' the DI snorted.

'I'd take a bet that her lawyer will be, since she knows you're coming to interview her.'

An ear-to-ear grin lit up Provan's remodelled countenance. 'If he is,' he chuckled, 'that will make my day. It may ruin his, though.'

Seventeen

'You may have seen too many TV dramas, Mr Lee,' Lottie Mann said icily. 'Ms Bulloch isn't being interviewed under caution, nor is she a suspect in Mr Speight's death. Whatever you cost, it's a waste of her money.'

'Ask your father-in-law what I cost,' Moss Lee replied, grinning. 'Whatever that is, my clients always get value for it. And by the way, it's Mrs Speight, not Ms Bulloch, as I'm sure your senior officer, the detective chief inspector, would be quick to tell you if she was here.'

'I want Mr Lee here,' Faye Bulloch declared. If her lips had been any tighter, they could have been invisible. 'I'm a bereaved woman; I've lost my husband and I need all the support I can get.'

Provan gazed at her, trying to spot a resemblance to her sister but seeing very little. Where Sandra's hair was short, thick and well cut, Faye's was dyed, a pale blond shade, and it was so fine that even though it had been carefully arranged, strands flew wildly from the mass. He was sure that if he touched her he would feel the crackle of static electricity. She was dressed in black, trousers with a silken top; her eyes were red, her mascara smudged, and she held a clump of tissues in her right hand.

He turned his gaze to her solicitor. Lee, who was thirty-eight according to newspaper reports, gave the impression of someone who spent much of his time in the gym, but the sergeant suspected that was false, and that the width of his shoulders owed more to his tailor than to the weight he could press. His closely shaven face shone with moisturiser. Provan found it distasteful, but he had to concede that the man's black moustache, trimmed to the same width as his eyebrows, was impressive. He had spent thirty years of his life trying to achieve that effect, but had never come close.

'Okay,' Mann conceded, 'but he stays as a courtesy.' She looked Lee in the eye. 'That means you don't get to interrupt, or even open your mouth without my consent.'

'Do I have to put my hand up if I want to go to the bathroom?' he drawled.

She ignored him. 'First and foremost, Ms Bulloch,' she continued, 'I'm very sorry for your loss.'

'Thank you,' the woman replied, relaxing a little and dabbing at her eyes with the tissues. 'If you're not going to call me Mrs Speight, then call me Faye. I feel as if I know you anyway. My sister's talked about you. She likes you.' She glanced at the DS. 'She's talked about you too, Mr Provan, but you look nothing like the way she described you.'

He gave her a brief nod of acknowledgement. 'I'll take that as a compliment.'

Faye turned back to the DI. 'How did Leo die? I saw the man on TV yesterday and I read the papers today. "Suspicious death", they all said, but what does that mean?'

Hasn't your sister told you? Provan wondered silently.

'It means that indications are he didn't die of natural causes,' Mann replied. 'Until the autopsy findings are confirmed by lab analysis, we can only tell the media what we know for certain; we can't speculate.'

'Police-speak,' Moss Lee muttered. 'She's saying he was murdered, Mrs Speight.'

The DI flashed him a glare. 'No, I am not,' she countered. 'I can't be more specific than that.'

'If it's suspicious, what do you suspect?' Faye persisted.

Mann sighed. 'Ms Bulloch, we both know that you have a source in the police. You mentioned her already. Neither she nor I are allowed to give you confidential information from within the investigation. If I did that and it got back to her, or made its way to the media through other sources,' she glanced at Lee again, 'I'm in the shit. So let's stick with convention, where I ask the questions and you answer them if you can. Agreed?'

'This is Mrs Speight's husband's death we're discussing,' the solicitor blustered.

'Her marital status is between her and the civil court,' Provan snapped. 'Agreed, Ms Bulloch?'

She nodded, dabbing at her eyes once again. 'I suppose so.'

'Fine,' the DI said. 'Let's leave it there for the rest of this interview. When did you last see Leo?' she asked.

'At the party. Last Friday evening.'

'How did he seem?'

'He was fine, the same old Leo, calm, quiet, friendly.'

'Did you speak much?'

'Not much. He asked me how Jolene was getting on at school. She's not long started, and she's been having trouble with her numbers. I told him I'd been working on it at home and that Leonard's been helping her too. He's a very bright wee boy,' she added. 'He takes after his father. They stayed up for the meal and the speeches. After that, Leo took them to the bungalow where we were staying and we put them to bed together.'

It occurred to Provan that everything she said gave an air of settled domesticity to their relationship. Give it to Lee, he thought, he's coached her well. I can imagine him doing the same with Nana fucking Mann.

'You left them on their own?' he exclaimed.

'What are you suggesting?' Faye Bulloch protested. 'Every one of those bungalows has a baby-monitoring system built into it. There are alerts at hotel reception and all the parents are given speakers when they're in the dining room or the bar.'

'That's good to know,' Mann said. 'Before the party, when was the last time you saw your . . .' She stopped herself just in time from throwing Lee a bone that he might have gnawed on in court. 'Leo?'

'Last Tuesday. He came to see the children as always. Normally he'd come twice a week, Tuesdays and Thursdays, to see the kids and to have a family meal with us.'

'How did he seem then? Was he quiet and friendly then, with no strangers around?'

'Yes, of course.'

'He didn't have any problems that he mentioned to you, or that you might have heard of from anyone else?'

'What sort of problems?' Faye asked.

'Any sort,' the DI replied. 'Anything that might have distracted him and made him less friendly than usual.'

'No, none at all. He was always friendly; we had a good relationship, my husband and I.'

'In spite of the facts,' Provan growled, 'that he wasn't your husband, that he didnae live with you, that he never had done on a permanent basis and that you were suin' him for a financial settlement. By all accounts he was a nice fella, but he wasn't a saint. Nor was he giving in to your lawyer's demands. Far from it; he'd retained senior counsel to defend the action. You're not going to tell us, Ms Bulloch, that wi' that background everything was sweetness and light between you. Of course he had things on his mind; you were one of them. So please don't tell us your life was all rose petals and soft toilet paper!'

'Mr Provan!' Moss Lee protested. 'I must—'

'You must shut the hell up,' the DS snarled, 'or I'll march you out of here by the scruff of your neck and charge you with obstruction.'

'My sister will hear about this,' Faye Bulloch murmured.

Provan smiled. 'You must be confusing me with somebody who gives a toss.' As he spoke, he picked up in his peripheral vision a movement of the solicitor's head, a glance towards the coffee table, on which lay a mobile phone. He leaned across and snatched it up.

'Look at this, Lottie,' he said. 'The man's here on sufferance, and he's recording the meeting without our okay.'

'I don't need your okay,' Lee countered. 'And don't think about erasing it either. My phone, my property.'

Mann reached out a hand. 'Gimme, Dan. The man's right; he doesn't need our permission.'

Reluctantly the DS handed her the mobile. She peered at it, stopped the recording, clicked the dustbin icon in the corner of the screen and handed it back to Lee. 'Sue me,' she told him. 'Complain to the chief constable if you like. But do it quietly and do it somewhere else; otherwise we're going to start wondering why you're trying to disrupt this interview and whether your client has something to hide.'

'I don't,' Faye Bulloch exclaimed. 'Okay, if you insist, Leo and I have had very little to say to each other since I started my action for a property settlement.'

'Why did you do that?'

'I got worried about my situation. About a year ago, maybe a bit more than that, his attitude towards me seemed to change; he got withdrawn, he never spent any time alone with me, far less staying the night, which he used to do on the nights he visited the kids. I rely on him; I live on what he gives us. It was probably a drop in the ocean to him, but it was a lot to me given what I had before I met him. I was a chiropodist, DI Mann; I worked hard but I never liked the job. I didn't stop when I met Leo. I carried on working until I fell pregnant with Leonard; when I did, he insisted that I chuck the job. I've lived on an allowance from him, in this house, ever since. I never knew it was in my name until after Jolene was born. All that time we were fine. I really thought I was his one and only. I know now that whenever he was away, and he was a lot, he had other women. There were a couple in America before Rae,' she added.

'How do you know that?'

'That fucking old bat Gene Alderney told me. I dropped in on Leo one day at the house in Ayr, when he was just starting to train for a fight. I wanted to see as much as I could of him before he went off to camp, and I did it to surprise him. Alderney was there; she accused me of getting in the way of his training, of being a danger to his career. I told her that I was Leo's wife and that she should mind her own business. She laughed at me. She told me I was his concubine, and then she told me that he had home comforts in Las Vegas too. Leo heard it all; he told Gene to shut up, but he didn't deny it. When he got involved with Rae, he told me that straight away.'

'And you accepted it?'

'Don't answer that!' Moss Lee called out. 'It could come back to bite you in court.'

The DI shook her head. 'It won't, Ms Bulloch. I have no view about your legal action, and neither DS Provan nor I are potential witnesses against you . . . that's assuming the action can continue now that Leo's dead.'

'Fair enough,' she conceded. 'Yes, I accepted the situation, for the kids' sake as much as my own, and Leo and I went on being fine, until we weren't.'

'When was that?'

'At the time I told you, early last year; he visited the kids as usual, but he never stayed over. To be blunt, we didn't have sex any longer. Eventually, I asked him why. All he'd say was that it wasn't appropriate. I asked him if that meant he was committing himself to Rae, but he said that he wasn't. He said he had things on his mind that got in the way.'

'Did he go into any detail?'

'No, none at all. The more I pressed him, the more distant he got, and the more I began to worry about my own situation. The monthly allowance I lived on from Leo was very generous, but it was at his discretion.'

'There was no legal basis to it,' Lee volunteered.

'Thank you,' Mann retorted. 'I'd worked that out.'

'I decided that I needed to put things on a proper footing,' Faye Bulloch continued. 'That was when I hired Mr Lee. I'd heard Sandra mention him; she said he was the best court lawyer in Glasgow, so I went to him first.'

'And began your legal action.'

She nodded, chewing on her bottom lip.

'How did Leo react?'

'He didn't like it. He accused me of a breach of trust. He said

136

that if I'd talked it over with him, we'd have worked something out, but that he'd fight my claim for marital status all the way. He said that however good Mr Lee was, he'd hire someone better. He also threatened to ruin me financially.'

'How?' Provan asked.

'He said that when I lost the action, he wouldn't be covering Mr Lee's costs.'

'But he continued your allowance?'

'Yes, for the children's sake, he said.'

'Hold on, a few minutes ago, you said you and he had a good relationship.'

'We did,' she insisted. 'We agreed to disagree over the court action, but we were civil to each other. I loved my husband, Detective Sergeant, for all his faults.'

'If you say so. What is your financial position, Ms Bulloch?'

'I've salted away a few thousand over the years, but . . . well let's just say I'm like most women. I have expensive tastes.

'Lucky you,' Mann drawled. 'Faye,' she said, 'do you expect to benefit from Leo's will?'

'I would hope so. Mr Lee says that Leo's death will mean that my action will almost certainly succeed, and that I'll be awarded spousal rights.'

'You realise what that means, don't you?'

'It means I'll inherit a substantial share of the estate.'

'Time will tell on that one. More immediately, it gives you a damn good reason for killing him.'

Eighteen

'What have I done this time?' Cameron 'Grandpa' McCullough asked. 'You were fair mysterious on the phone.'

'Whatever you've done, I don't want to know,' Bob Skinner replied as he stepped into the villa in the Perthshire estate grounds. 'Unless you're going to tell me that you killed Leo Speight, in which case I'm all ears.'

'That's what happened, was it? The media seem to be scared to go that far, but that's what I read from the body language of the man Allsop on TV yesterday.' He held up a hand. 'I am innocent, so help me God.'

McCullough and Skinner had never clashed directly during the latter's police career, the main reason being that the latter's territory had never stretched as far as Tayside. The Dundonian was a very wealthy man, with a portfolio of successful businesses. For decades the local police had been convinced that many of them were covers for major organised crime, but they had never been able to build a case against him, and he had always protested his innocence.

Although their professional lives had rarely overlapped, a personal link had been forged between them when McCullough had married Mia Watson, a blast from Skinner's past and the mother of his son Ignacio.

'How's the boy, Bob?' McCullough asked, then called out, 'Mia, he's here!'

'He's doing fine,' the former cop replied. 'He has his own space in Gullane, and he's settled in at university; so far he seems to be sailing through the classes.'

'Does he still want to be a police officer?'

'Yes, he does. Alex is doing her best to talk him out of it and direct him towards the law, and Sarah's trying to point him at medicine.'

'And I'm determined that he does a postgraduate degree in business administration.' Mia's voice came from the living room as the two men stepped inside. 'I think you'll find that I still have more influence with him than anyone else.'

Skinner shrugged. 'I'd be surprised if you didn't; you brought him up, even if you did let him get into a shedload of trouble on your watch.'

Sensing an outraged response, he headed it off. 'Let's not rake over that, though. Ignacio will make his own mind up when he's ready. I'm not pressurising him in any way. If he asks me what I think about something, I'll tell him, but the worst thing any parent can do is impose their career choice on their offspring.' He pointed to a tray on a table by the window. 'Is that coffee hot?'

Mia ignored his question. 'But you do want him to be a cop?'

'As it happens, I don't. I'd be a hard act to follow, even if the selection process was flexible enough to admit someone with a culpable homicide conviction on his record. Now for fuck's sake. I'm gasping here.'

She relented and poured him a mug of coffee from the cafetière, then offered him a dark chocolate biscuit from a plate. He took two.

'Now we're all catered for,' McCullough said, filling a mug for himself, 'maybe you'll tell us what the hell you're doing investigating Leo Speight's death.'

'There's an insurance issue,' Skinner replied.

'That's bollocks for a start,' his host laughed. 'I know insurance companies. The bigger the stakes, the slower they move, and the mills of God grind faster than them at the best of times. They'd have sat on their hands until the post-mortem, then they'd have asked for a full report in writing, then they might have insisted on appointing their own pathologist to do a second examination. Once they'd done all that, they might have commissioned someone like you'

Skinner knew that every word of that scenario was true. 'Nevertheless,' he said, 'that's the story, and I'm sticking to it.' He looked at McCullough's wife, and as he did so, his mind took him back twenty years to the morning when he had awakened in her bed, surprised and disorientated, with an instant reaction that had had a catastrophic, and possibly life-changing, effect.

'Before I go any further,' he warned, 'I need you both to promise that this discussion won't leave this room. It can't be talked about across the table in your hotel, and it can't be a topic on your radio show, Mia.'

'Spoilsport,' she laughed, 'but okay. You needn't worry about Cameron,' she added. 'He never tells anyone anything.'

'Thank you both. The issue is . . . if Leo Speight died at the hands of a third party, his insurance policy has a big indemnity clause. It was written to cover him as a boxer and the premium was probably sky high, but its drafting is such that if it turns out he was murdered, the insurers will have to shell out. The way things stand, conspiracy theories will run wild on social media, and maybe mainstream too. It would be good to be able to knock them down as they arise. The police are looking at his family and close friends. My brief,' he said, 'is to look a little wider to see whether there's anyone else who might have had a motive to bump him off, and to eliminate them if I can.'

'That's still cobblers,' McCullough murmured, 'but go on.'

Skinner bit off half of a biscuit. 'To begin with, why were you at the party? How did you come to know Leo Speight?'

'Business. You know I have interests in Russia, yes?'

He nodded. 'Yes.'

'You also know of Bryce Stoddart, the promoter?'

'Mm-hm.' The confirmation was muffled by biscuit crumbs.

'Around twenty-five years ago, Bryce's old man, Benny Stoddart, was staging a fight card in Dundee, featuring one of our local heroes against one of his protégés. Benny wasn't an international operator at that stage,' McCullough explained. 'It was Leo Speight that took him to that level. For that bill, he needed council approval and business support, and he approached me, believing that I could help him.'

'And you could, of course.'

'Naturally. The bill was a success. The local hero got chinned, of course, but Benny made some money and I did too. We stayed in touch; I even invested in a couple of his projects and walked away happy. Benny retired and handed over to Bryce; by that time Leo Speight was the top man in his stable.' He paused, looking at Skinner. 'Are you a boxing man, Bob?'

'I watch fights. I even did a bit in my teens.'

'And some unofficially after that, I'll bet. Do you remember, about ten years ago, Leo Speight going over to Moscow to take on Brezinski, the guy who beat him in the Sydney Olympics, with their championship belts on the line?'

'Sure I do. I watched it on Sky. Speight won every round,

then he knocked him out; the Russian couldn't lay a glove on him.'

'That's right,' McCullough agreed. 'When that fight was in the making, Brezinski's promoter, Zirka, took the early initiative. Bryce was still getting used to being in charge and felt he was in a wee bit over his head, and so he came to me, asking if I'd use my influence over there to get him a fair deal. His worry was the usual: a home-town decision, that Leo would need to knock the guy out to get a draw. He was probably right about that, had I not been able to help him. I set up a Russian subsidiary company, through my associate Rogozin – you remember him for sure – and used that to get Bryce a Russian promoter's licence. By that time, though, Leo was the main man with the top US cable TV company, and called all the shots personally, so Zirka had to deal with him and Bryce. I helped Leo make a right few million that night; that's why I was on his party list.'

'I take it the Zirka people weren't.'

'No, they weren't. They couldn't have been pleased by Leo's announcement either, since Zirka's main activity is mixed martial arts. It's a shadow of what it used to be, and Leo's new operation will take it on directly. Okay, to get off the ground it might need a TV platform, at least until it builds up an internet subscriber base, but he has that.'

'Who are the people in Zirka? Tell me about them.'

'As far as I know, there was only ever one that counted; Yevgeny Brezinski, Speight's old rival. He retired after Leo beat him. He is Zirka, always was. He owns the company; he self-promoted his fights when he was active, but he never fought outside eastern Europe, so he never made any impact on the US market as a boxer.'

'What's your assessment of him?'

'I've never met him,' McCullough admitted. 'He's had a very low profile for the last ten years, since he stopped fighting. Rogozin did business with him, but only when he had to, while they were setting up that fight. He was wary of the man. He said he was scary, and very resentful towards Leo.'

'Does Brezinski have contacts in Britain?'

'None that I know of, but Zirka has used that announcer bloke, Billy Swords. I believe he's bilingual, and they needed an English-speaking MC.'

'Swords was at the party, wasn't he?' Skinner asked.

'Yes, he did his thing there, introduced the speakers.'

'Did you happen to notice when he left?'

'Yes.' It was Mia who replied. 'He went straight after the speeches, around eight o'clock. He said he had a job in London on the Saturday night and would need to be at the airport early next morning.'

'And Leo was still there?'

'Yes, he went at the same time as us, back of midnight. Why?'

'No reason.'

'With you there's always a reason. Bob, come clean. What happened to Leo? What are the police not saying? We have no interest in telling anyone else.'

'What makes you think I know?'

'You were probably at the autopsy!' she exclaimed. She caught the slightest tensing of his eyes. 'You bloody were! Weren't you?'

He grinned. 'I still have access, on occasion. Yes, I was. Speight was poisoned, but at the moment there's no way of saying with certainty how it was administered. There's a very obvious possibility, but it has to be proved. That's why the police are being reticent.'

'Of course,' McCullough agreed, his eyes narrowed. 'You'd better put Brezinski on your list of possible lethal enemies . . . to be ruled out,' he added, with an ironic laugh.

'How long is that list, Cameron? You're a man in the know. How many feathers would Leo Speight have ruffled with this new promotion company?'

'Quite a few, I imagine, in Britain and Europe. Not in America, though; Leo was too smart to have taken that market on directly – it's too well developed. Europe's the growth area for MMA, and all the boxing promoters are looking at it seriously. Not least among them Bryce Stoddart. I was watching him when Leo dropped his bombshell. Afterwards he claimed that he'd known about it all along, but that's not what his expression said.'

'I'd better have a word with him too,' Skinner said. 'Thanks for that.' He seemed to hesitate. 'Cameron, how bent is boxing? You and I are both old enough to remember the stories of our youth, about the US Mafia controlling the sport through front organisations. Has that gone away completely?'

McCullough frowned. Skinner wondered whether he was trying to frame an answer that would not be self-incriminating.

'The old dons,' he said when he was ready, 'they're all dead or in US federal prisons, but their organisations live on. They may have an appearance of legitimacy these days, but their driving force is still money, and they will protect their interests. Your list could be quite a long one; you might be able to eliminate most of them, but I'd still put money on those insurers having to pay out at the end of the day. Not that you really give a fuck about that. I can guess exactly what your interest is, and where it comes from. Your friends in Millbank? Am I right? God knows they've shown enough interest in me over the years.'

'No comment,' Skinner said quietly, reaching for the cafetière and warming up his mug.

'It's okay, I didn't expect any.' McCullough grinned. 'I saw your ex there as well, the Shadow Home Secretary, hanging on the arm of her actor friend. Maybe Leo would have gone into movies if he'd lived. He was quite the arty type, really. The painter woman, Augusta Cambridge, she was there too, with her easel set up in the corner.'

'Was she? I didn't know that. Her name wasn't on the guest list.'

'Oh yes,' Mia said. 'I spoke to her. Leo had commissioned her to paint the gathering. He was going to give prints to everyone who was there. I imagine Augusta will be in bits. I think that the two of them were close.'

'What? She volunteered that to you, or did you hear it from someone else?'

'She didn't volunteer it, but . . . We got chatting in the ladies' early in the evening. I said I knew her work and admired it very much. I asked her how she came to be there, and she told me. Then I asked if it was an unusual commission for her. She said that she wouldn't have done it for anyone else, only Leo, that he and she were . . . I told her I got the picture, and she smiled, a sad little smile. She said I didn't, not at all.'

'Did you fancy Leo?' he asked her, bluntly.

'Hey, wait a minute,' McCullough exclaimed. He smiled, but his eyes sent out a different message.

'I'm serious,' Skinner insisted. 'Everything I've heard about Speight tells me that he had something that women couldn't resist. I'm not asking if you wanted to have sex with him in the car park. All I want is a woman's-eye view of the guy.'

'You could always ask your ex,' she suggested.

'That wouldn't work; Aileen's not a reliable witness. Men always come second to her, after politics.'

'What?' Mia laughed. 'She's in a relationship with Joey Morocco, Bob.'

'Joey's a fucking handbag,' he retorted, 'a required accessory at posh events. So was I, until I figured it out. Come on, what did you think of Leo?'

'If you insist.' She winked at her husband. 'It's okay, Cameron, I won't shock you. I didn't "fancy" Leo as such, not least because he was a bit too young for me, but if I was in the market, I would have, no question. He was very attractive, obviously a he-man because of what he did, with an air of sheer invincibility about him. You could have bottled his sweat, called it "Charisma", and it would have outsold Chanel. That's what you saw from a distance, but when you met him there was something else more important and more alluring than all that. He was a very kind, caring man, and when you spoke to him, you felt . . . as if all your worries had disappeared, that nothing could touch you, and that you were utterly safe with him.' She reached across and squeezed McCullough's arm. 'You're the only other man who ever made me feel that way,' a smile flickered, 'and you are definitely not too young for me.' She looked at Skinner. 'You, on the other hand: yes, when I was much younger I fancied you . . . had you too . . . but you made me feel positively unsafe. You were scary.'

The two men gazed at each other in a silence that was eventually broken by Cameron McCullough. 'Now there's a thing,' he murmured. 'For all those years, your colleagues in the police came after me like I was the devil incarnate, and all along there he was, in plain sight.'

'That might be taking it a little far,' Mia laughed. 'You

didn't mean to scare me, Bob, but I did know some unsavoury people in those days, and you definitely made them shit their pants.'

He shuddered slightly. 'I wish now that I'd never asked you that question, but the first part of the answer was useful. It ties in with the impression that Rae Letts gave me when I spoke to her yesterday.'

'Rae Letts?'

'Leo's lady in Las Vegas, mother of a wee girl that you might have seen at the party. He looked after her, and from what she said, when he was with her he was very happy. And so was she, because she understood what you just said: that she was safe with him and that he'd always look after her.'

'As long as she looked after him? Wasn't he in court with another former partner?'

'That's true. I don't know whether she was greedy or just didn't trust him the way that Rae did.'

'It's all academic now,' McCullough observed. 'He's dead and the vultures are flying in circles over the estate.'

'They'll find it's all neatly apportioned,' Skinner told him. 'My police colleagues have a copy of the will. They won't all like what it says, but even Speight couldn't keep all the people happy all of the time.'

He finished his coffee and put the mug back on the tray. 'Thanks for that; the caffeine and the information.'

'No problem,' Mia replied as they rose to their feet. 'Nothing else?'

He nodded as one more question occurred to him. 'Yeah, while I'm here. Did either of you encounter a man called Moscardinetto at the party?'

'Yes,' McCullough exclaimed. 'As a matter of fact, I did. A

wee Italian geezer; bats for the other team, unless I'm much mistaken. I spoke to him when we were having drinks before the meal or, more accurately, he spoke to me. He came up and introduced himself. I had the impression that he expected me to know who he was, but I hadn't a clue. A peculiar little man, pushy too. He must have done some research on me, for he started asking me all sorts of questions about how the money was carved up after a fight promotion and how big a skim the Russian Mafia took. I told him that I wouldn't know, on account of I wasn't a boxing promoter and I wasn't a Russian mafioso. He looked down his nose at me and minced off.'

'I saw him later on,' Mia added. 'He was talking to Augusta Cambridge, and peering over her shoulder as she was working. He couldn't have been very complimentary; she didn't look too pleased. Why are you interested in him?'

'To be honest,' Skinner admitted, 'I don't know. He's an anomaly, that's all, and I don't like them. Thanks again.'

'Pleasure. Tell our son that his mum's expecting a weekend visit from him sometime soon.'

'I will, but don't push the career advice too hard. So long, both.'

Behind the wheel of his car, Skinner found that he was still thinking about Aldorino Moscardinetto, the party guest that nobody knew, the itch that wouldn't go away.

He decided to scratch it. He checked his incoming messages and found one from Joey Morocco, who had kept his promise. There was no text, only a mobile number with an Italian country code. He selected it and placed a call.

'Aldorino. Chi parla?' a voice responded aggressively.

'My name is Bob Skinner, Signor Moscardinetto. I have a role in the investigation into the death of Leo Speight. I know

you were at his retirement party on Friday, and I'd like to speak
to you about that.'

'This is important?'

Skinner was irked, by the question and by the man's dismissive
tone. 'A man is dead, *signore*; of course it's important. I'd like to
keep our discussion informal, but if that's not possible, we can
do it the other way.'

'Okay, okay,' the Italian sighed.

'Where are you? Can we meet?'

'I am in Glasgow, so yes, we can meet. There's a place near
my hotel, it's called Regina's, in San Vincenzo Street. It's quiet,
I see you there. Tonight, seven. Be there; I leave tomorrow.'

Nineteen

Dan Provan eyed the equipment in Max's Gymnasium, looking through a glass panel in the door from the reception area. 'No' bad,' he murmured. 'They've got a good range of gear in there, same stuff as they had in the Aussie gym. Ah'll mibbe ask about membership while I'm here. You never know, Lottie, they might have a special rate for polis.'

'Wherever you do join,' she said, 'I promise you I'll be there to see for myself. The thought of you on a treadmill still fills me with horror.' She turned to the manager, who was standing behind a small curved counter, and showed him her warrant card, as did Provan. He studied them both with the caution of someone who took no chances.

'We're looking for Gordon Pollock,' she continued, 'one of your members. We were told he was here.'

The man met her gaze calmly, with neither deference nor suspicion. He was black and bulky, with grizzled hair, long dreadlocks tied back by a band.

'Young Gordon? He's here.' He glanced at a monitor screen. 'Looks like he's taking what happened to his dad out on the cross-trainer. Damn shame, that; a tragedy.'

'Did Leo Speight ever come in here?' Provan asked.

'He wasn't a member himself, but he brought Gordon along here a couple of years ago and signed him up. Hell, he didn't need to be a member; the champ would have been welcome here any time. If you wait, I'll go tell Gordon you're here.'

'It's okay,' the DS said. 'We'll just go in. It doesnae look too busy.'

'I'd rather you didn't,' the manager told him. 'It is quiet, but there are some people in there, and a couple of them are likely to make you as cops. The kid doesn't need that.'

'No,' Mann conceded, 'you're right. We'll wait here.'

He pointed towards a door on the other side of the reception area. 'That's my office; you go on in there and I'll bring him.'

The room was small, remarkably so given the size of its occupant. The detectives stood as they waited; five minutes ticked by. Provan was on the point of going to look for their subject when the door opened and a young man was ushered in to join them. He was wearing a black tracksuit with white zigzag flashes on the chest and legs, his dark hair was damp and ruffled and he was barefoot.

'Gordon,' his escort said, 'these are Detective Inspector Mann and her colleague Detective Sergeant Provan. Sorry for the delay, officers; I thought he should towel down before meeting you. Even at that, you might want to open the window.'

'I played junior football in the nineteen eighties,' Provan snorted. 'I've smelt a bloody sight worse than him.'

'Maybe you have, Detective Sergeant,' the man replied, 'but this is my office, not a changing room.'

'Of course,' Mann said, as she released the upper section of the window and swung it open. 'Take a seat please, Gordon,' she murmured as the door closed on the manager.

'I'm fine as I am, thanks,' he retorted. There was a barely

suppressed rage in his voice, but the officers realised that it was not directed at them.

'First off,' the DI began, 'we are very sorry for your loss.'

'Aye, fine,' Gordon Pollock muttered, settling himself on a corner of the manager's desk.

Looking at him, she saw a facial resemblance to his father, but his build was different: squatter, more stocky. He was shorter, too. She knew from the autopsy that Leo Speight had been five feet ten inches tall. His son was no more than five eight.

'Were you close to your father?' she asked.

His eyes flared angrily. 'What do you mean? He was my dad.'

'She means did you see a lot of him?' Provan said quietly. 'We know that he and your mother were never married, never even lived together. So if you didn't, we'd understand.'

The boy gazed briefly at the DS and nodded. 'Aye, sorry.'

'How did you find out about his death?'

'Gino told my mother. Gino Butler, my dad's manager.'

'We know Mr Butler; he told us where we'd find you.'

'Ah. Gino's all right. My mother likes him; he was more than my dad's manager. He was his best pal too, from when they were kids.'

'And how about you and your dad?' Provan persisted gently. Sensing that Gordon empathised more with the sergeant, Mann leaned back against the wall of the cramped office and let him continue.

'We got on fine. He was great. Mind, I never saw him much until I was five or six; my Grandpa Pollock never got on with him. He wouldn't have him in the house, he wouldn't let my mum go near him, and he'd never let him see me. Once he died, though, it was okay.'

'What was your grandpa like?' Provan asked.

The young man winced. 'Fierce,' he replied grimly. 'He used to leather me if I did anything wrong. He gave my mum a slap or two as well, I remember. My granny was scared of him. I was only wee at the time, but I realise it now.'

'What happened to him?'

'He'd a heart attack. They found him in the River Cart, in Paisley.' A memory stirred in the DS but he let Gordon continue. 'After that, it was okay. My granny let my dad come and see me, and I got to know him. He'd made a few quid by then; we lived in a council house and he bought it. We all live there still; my granny and my mum don't want to move.'

'And you?'

'I'm fine there too. It suits. I'm at uni, and I can get the train in every morning. Some weekends I stay at the Blacksmith. It's got bungalows and I can use one when I'm there. It's my dad's hotel and I work there part-time.'

It's your hotel now, Mann thought.

'What are you doing at uni?' Provan asked.

'Hospitality and catering management. It was my dad's idea; it's good, I like it. He had plans for me, my dad did. He had all sorts of property; he had a plan to build a resort hotel in the Bahamas and he talked about me managing it once I got my degree and some experience.'

He shifted his position on the desk. 'You asked if I was close to my dad. Yes, I was. Did I see a lot of him? Yes, when he was here I did. Once or twice he took me with him, too. Two years ago, when he was training for a fight in America, he took me to Las Vegas. We stayed with his girlfriend Rae and my wee sister Raeleen – she was tiny then – in the big house on the lake just outside the city. I thought it was fantastic, but it was just another place to him, another piece of property. Nothing ever went to my dad's head. Everywhere I went with him folk were all over him, wanting autographs, wanting selfies. I thought they were fucking rude, a lot of them, but none of them ever pissed him off, and he never turned one of them down. I never once saw him refuse an autograph, or be too busy to stop and have a selfie taken.'

'If he was like that with strangers, how was he with people he knew?'

Gordon considered the DS's question for a few seconds before replying. 'Just the same. He always had time for everybody. He treated my mum like she was made out of china, even though she looks Clyde-built these days. Leonard and Jolene, he was all over them, same with Rae and Raeleen.'

'And Faye Bulloch?'

'Faye too, until she started that thing with the lawyer.'

'Did that make him angry?'

'My dad never got angry, not ever.'

'Not even when he was fighting?' Mann asked, intervening. 'I've done a bit of boxing, usually against men, and it was anger that fuelled me.'

'You couldn't have been very good then,' the young Pollock retorted. 'When my dad was in the ring, he'd look just as he did outside, calm, except he seemed to have this invisible, unbreakable shield around him. You couldn't see it, but it was there and nobody could ever break through it. That's why he never lost a professional fight, only that one in the Olympics where he was robbed by bent judges; that's why he was unbeatable. Did you ever see him fight, Mr Provan?'

'Aye, a few times, and I know exactly what you mean.'

'Right. If someone upset him, got on the wrong side of him, that's how he'd be. If you were the other person, you couldn't tell. He'd react to you in the usual way, but you wouldn't be able to reach him. I went to Faye's with him a few weeks ago, when he went to visit the kids – he wanted us all to know each other as brothers and sisters – and that's how he was. Perfectly pleasant, I never once heard him raise his voice, but he could have been a fucking hologram as far as she was concerned.'

'Suppose her lawyer had been there,' Provan said. 'How would he have reacted? We've met the gentleman. Let's just say he might have been provocative.'

'I can't imagine that. Dad's last fight, the guy Fonsecco tried to provoke him at the weigh-in, got right in his face, threatened him, swore at him, his spit flying in my dad's face. He never batted an eyelid, just stood there and took it. Fine, but I saw a few of his fights, and I tell you, I never saw him hit anyone as hard as he hit Fonsecco. The guy spent the night in hospital, under observation. You ask me what he'd have done to anyone who provoked him that badly outside the ring? I just don't know. I'm not talking about Faye, mind,' he added hurriedly. 'With her he was just sad it had got to that stage.'

'If he was such a calm guy, how could somebody get on the wrong side of him?

'By not doing it his way. I don't know how to put it, but he was used to people agreeing with him. If you didn't, he . . .' Gordon stopped, frustrated, rendered inarticulate by his youth and lack of experience of the subtlety of relationships.

The eyes blazed again, taking both detectives by surprise. 'But so fucking what?' he blurted out. 'He was my dad and someone fucking killed him! Gino saw him. It was him that found him. He told me what he looked like. So what are you lot going to do about it?'

'We're going to find the person who did it,' Mann replied

calmly. She had heard the same furious question upwards of a dozen times from the families of murder victims.

'Find him before me, then.' She had heard that retort almost as many times.

'You just leave it to us, son,' she admonished him quietly. 'On you go now, and thanks for your help.'

They stood silently even after the door closed, waiting until they were sure he had gone.

'Did any bells ring with you during that interview?' Provan asked.

'Should they have?' Mann countered.

'One did wi' me. Shane Pollock, the boy's grandpa. When he had his heart attack, they found him in the river. Remember what Gino Butler said?'

'By God, I do!' she exclaimed. 'When Leo flattened him, that's where he told him he'd wind up. Maybe we should ask for the file on his death. It was bound to have been reported to the fiscal.'

'And maybe we shouldnae bother,' the DS told her firmly. 'So we investigate and find that he did it? Leo's dead; we cannae charge him. Even an investigation, if it leaked – and it would – would leave a scar on his memory. Besides, from the sound of things, Big Shane belonged in the effin' river.'

Twenty

'You'd better be paying me mileage for this job,' Bob Skinner grumbled.

'That won't be a problem,' Amanda Dennis laughed, 'although you'll need to claim it on the official form. We are civil servants, don't forget. Where have you been?'

'You name it. Today started in Glasgow, then I went up to Perthshire. Now I'm sitting outside a swanky hotel overlooking Loch Lomond, where I'm about to meet Bryce Stoddart, Leo Speight's promoter. After that, I'm back to Glasgow to link up with an Italian film-maker, in the hope that he'll tell me what the hell he was doing at Leo's party. Nobody else seems to know.'

'How does it look from your side of the investigation? In terms of the brief I gave you, that is. I know perfectly well that you won't stick to it,' she added.

'At the moment, I might. I need to have a longer chat with Speight's manager about the American side of his career, but I've had some interesting information about the European end.'

'Interesting and relevant?'

'Time will tell on that, but a name's been put in the frame, a Russian who's already lost out to Speight and would have taken another hit if he'd lived to implement a new venture he announced at his farewell party on Friday. That's why I want to talk to Stoddart.'

'Do you suspect he might be in danger as well?'

'I won't know what to think about him until I've spoken to him. How about you? You've set me on possible infiltration of the boxing business by organised crime, and Bryce Stoddart is one of its big players. Does that imply that the Service has had him under surveillance?'

'I wouldn't put it that way,' the director general replied. 'We haven't had him under direct personal surveillance as such, but we do have a file on him, and we have looked into his financial affairs and his business relationships. His company, which is owned entirely by a family trust established by his father, has made substantial profits in the last several years, through the peak of Mr Speight's career. It employs big-firm accountants and it pays its corporation tax. The personal tax affairs of the Stoddarts, father and son, are impeccable too.'

'You've got nothing on him, in other words.'

'No, we haven't, but there is one small concern. The company makes an annual payment of one million sterling into a bank account in Switzerland; it's described as being in respect of consultancy services.'

In his car, Skinner frowned. 'Are HMRC okay with payments to a Swiss bank account?'

'They are, because they're backed up by invoices and because the owner of the account isn't a secret.'

'Are you going to tell me that it's held by a company called Zirka?'

He heard a sigh. 'I'm trying to remember the last time I surprised you, Bob,' she said. 'I have to admit that I can't.'

'I didn't know I was in a race,' he grunted. 'Got to go now; Stoddart was expecting me ten minutes ago.'

He left his car, a Mercedes E Class that seemed modest between a Porsche and a Maserati, locked it, and walked into the hilltop hotel. It had been a large country house, designed, he imagined for a Glaswegian industrialist who had wanted an escape from the grimy, disease-ridden city. Distinctive features in its facade suggested that it might have been the work of Charles Rennie Mackintosh. Its name, Beedham's, was displayed on a brass plate beside the door, but nowhere else, a touch of discretion that explained to Skinner why he had never heard of it. The signage of the Blacksmith seemed garish by comparison.

He paused in the entrance hall, looking for a reception desk but seeing nothing obvious. However, he was spared the need to announce himself, for a man stepped forward to greet him, casually dressed in a blue twill shirt and chinos, hand outstretched.

'Mr Skinner,' he exclaimed. 'Bryce Stoddart; I've been looking out for you.'

Skinner knew from an internet search that the promoter was forty-two years old, but he could have passed for five years younger. He was of medium height, broad shoulders, narrow waist, and his slightly crooked nose suggested that he might have been a member of a boxing stable rather than its manager.

'Come into the lounge,' Stoddart said. 'It's empty . . . not that it's full very often. The place has ten suites, and most of the guests tend to stick to them.'

He glanced around the hall, appraising its dark-wood fittings.

'Impressive, innit?' his companion remarked. 'A lot of people think it was designed by that bloke Mackintosh, but it weren't. It was a bloke called Roberts, one of his followers.'

The accent, he judged, was faux Cockney. The online biography had made no mention of Stoddart's education, but his cufflinks bore a crest that from the depths of his memory he recognised as Old Harrovian: the only thing the promoter had in common with Winston Churchill, Skinner guessed.

'It had me fooled,' he admitted. 'You're well informed. Do you use this place often?'

'Every time I come up. It's Leo's. His property fella, Charlie Baxter, found it for him; it wasn't quite derelict but he got it for a song, then spent three times as much restoring it. A suite here costs fifteen hundred a night, basic . . . not that I pay that, mind,' he laughed as he led the way out of the hall. 'The staff here speak seven languages among them, English included; Japanese, Mandarin, Spanish, German, French and Russian.'

'Where does the name come from?'

'It belongs to a mate of Charlie's; he thought it sounded distinguished, so he suggested it to Leo.'

The lounge could not have accommodated all the guests if the hotel were full. 'Mainly used for meetings,' Stoddart volunteered, reading his thoughts. 'Like this one. Where do you fit into the investigation, Mr Skinner?'

'Insurers. I'm representing their interests.'

That one-sentence reply seemed to satisfy the promoter. He nodded sagely. 'I guessed as much. You look too distinguished to be a cop. I helped Gino negotiate that policy for Leo, so I know its terms. I bet your clients are cacking themselves right now.'

Skinner smiled. 'You could say that.'

'I guess your job's to prove that he weren't murdered . . . although it's pretty obvious the police are sure he was, even if they haven't used the word. What do you want to ask me?'

'Who'd have wanted to murder him? That'll do for openers.'

'Nobody I can think of.' He chuckled. 'Other than that woman of his, maybe, if she thought she was going to lose her court case.'

'Mmm? Which woman? I gather Leo had several relationships.'

'Faye, her name is.' Stoddart winked. 'Mind you, if she did him in, it'll be covered up. Her sister's a cop. Joking!' he added. 'About Faye doing it, that is.'

Skinner raised an eyebrow as he nodded. 'Yes, let's take that as read. How about his professional life?'

'Boxing?'

'Yes. Your business is international, Mr Stoddart, and there are huge sums of money involved. You must deal with some fairly colourful people, to put it mildly.'

For the first time since the two men had met, the promoter frowned. 'Yes, okay,' he conceded, 'there are some hooligans out there, internationally, but what you've got to remember, sir, is – you said it yourself – there's shedloads of money to be made in boxing for the right match marketed in the right way, and put like that, Leo Speight was absolute bleedin' gold dust. He made everybody rich.'

'You mean *you* did, by promoting him.'

'No, I don't. I mean what I said: Leo did. I might have been his promoter, I might have made the matches for him, but he picked the opponents, he picked the venues and he dictated the terms, then he told me to get on with it. Same with Gino Butler. He and Gino were good mates, and Leo presented him as his manager, but in reality he was more of an assistant.'

'Is that your way of telling me that Leo Speight was a control freak?'

Stoddart frowned again as he considered the question. 'No,' he decided eventually, 'I wouldn't say that. There was no freakery about it. Basically, he delegated tasks and left Gino and me to get on with our jobs. Mine – Stoddart Promotions, that is – was making the matches and staging the fights. Gino's was, among other things, making sure that the training camps were set up and that the media were controlled. We did our stuff and he got on with his job: getting himself into perfect physical and mental shape, promoting the shows, and, finally, executing.'

Skinner nodded. 'He made money for everyone when he was active, Mr Stoddart, but last Friday's party, hours before he died, was held to celebrate his retirement. I'm told that at the party he announced a new business venture. He said he was going to become a promoter himself. Wouldn't the consequence of that have been him taking money from the people he had previously enriched, by becoming their competitor?'

'Ah, well . . .'

'Yes it bloody would!'

At the sound of the guttural outburst, both men turned and looked towards the doorway, which framed a middle-aged woman. She was short, with frizzy silver hair, and a perma-tanned face with glaring brown eyes.

'Oh dear,' Bryce Stoddart sighed. 'Mr Skinner, this is Genevieve Alderney. She's our matchmaker; she's also my father's other half. Gene, Mr Skinner's representing Leo's insurers.'

'Is your father here too?' Skinner asked.

'No, he and Gene live in Scottsdale, Arizona. He would have been at the party, but he's had a chest infection and decided not to travel.'

He looked at the woman, who had advanced into the room

and was standing in front of him. 'Do I take it you weren't too keen on Mr Speight's new venture?'

'Neither of us were, Bryce nor me. He, Leo, sprung it on us a month ago, no discussion. He was planning mixed shows, boxers and MMA, male and female, something that's never been done before, not in Britain at any rate. He was going to run one bill a month, on a new internet service.'

'Doesn't MMA use a cage rather than a ring? Isn't it a different shape?'

'It doesn't have to be,' Alderney snapped back at him. 'That's just a gimmick.'

'Yes, it is,' Stoddart intervened, 'but Leo was going to use a cage for everything, a circle rather than an octagon.' Skinner noticed that his Mockney accent had disappeared. 'We've all grown up thinking that boxing has to take place in a square enclosure, but it doesn't.'

'He was going to do this on his own?' Skinner asked. 'Without you?'

'That's how it was looking. But Gene's wrong; there was a discussion. She wasn't part of it, that's all. Leo offered to do it as a joint venture. He and I discussed it, but I argued that we'd be competing with ourselves on the boxing side. I felt that we should only do it if it was MMA exclusively, but Leo said that mixed-bill promotions were the whole point. He wanted to capture fans of both sports and bring them together. Eventually he was going to have crossover fights as well, putting fighters from one discipline up against the other.'

'I see. I can tell what you think of that, Ms Alderney.'

'Too damn right,' she hissed. 'I thought he was bloody ungrateful, too. Benny more or less took him in as a kid; he made him what he became.'

'Rubbish!' Stoddart exclaimed. 'Leo made himself. He'd a God-given talent when he was brought to Dad as an amateur, and he was well aware of it even then. Sure, the old man invested in his education, but over the years he's repaid that investment a hundred times.'

'Yeah?' Alderney fired back. 'Well we're fucked without him. Who else have we got in our stable that's remotely near his class? Nobody. We've got Afobe, the Ghanaian cruiserweight with one of the minor world championship belts; Giff Evans, the Welsh super-featherweight, who's got loads of potential but will never have the stamina to fulfil it; and Joe McBride from Edinburgh. A few decent fighters, but no superstars. Since your father retired, Bryce, you've been obsessed with Leo, and the rest of the business has gone to pigs and whistles. You think you'll hold on to your TV deal with what we've got? Only if you get your finger out right now, and even then only because Leo's dead and his new promotion with him. Fucking convenient that was,' she added sarcastically.

'Fuck off, Gene!' the promoter exploded.

'Hey, hey, hey,' Skinner exclaimed. 'Let's just calm down, okay. You're both rattled by what's happened, I understand that, but going off at each other will not help anyone.'

'I'll leave you to it then,' the woman announced. 'Fucking insurance companies,' she muttered as she headed for the door. 'Do anything to avoid paying, they will.'

'I'm sorry about that, Mr Skinner,' Stoddart said as the door closed on her. 'I'm sure she just stuck her nose in to see what was going on.'

'Yes, she's a proper ray of sunshine. You realise she just offered you up as a potential murder suspect?' He smiled. 'You didn't poison Leo, did you?'

'God forbid! No, I loved Leo; he was my mate, as well as my fighter. Between you and me, I was actually ready to go along with the new set-up, and take any of my stable in that wanted to sign up with us. Mind you, nobody else needs to know that.'

'Especially not Ms Alderney?'

'God, no!'

'What's your father's backstory?' Skinner asked.

'He did a bit of boxing in his youth. He won more than he lost but he knew he'd never be even British championship level, so he quit and became a licensed manager instead. It wasn't his main business at the time; my grandfather was a demolition contractor in south London, and Dad worked with him.'

'When did he become a promoter?'

'About thirty years ago. He did that for the boxers he managed rather than for himself. A very few people ran professional boxing in those days; they controlled it very tightly and most of the fighters got paid peanuts. My father rebelled against that. In the mid eighties he got a promoter's licence and started running his own small shows around London and the Midlands.'

'How did the regime take that?'

'Badly would be an understatement. Someone put a bomb in his car. No,' he added, 'it didn't go off. The police said it wasn't meant to, that it was just a warning. Either way it didn't work; Dad kept on going. The big breakthrough was his signing a deal with ITV for ten shows a year, each one with a championship fighter as top of the bill. I was at school by that time.' He held up his right hand, displaying his cufflink. 'I saw you clock these,' he said. 'Dad didn't send me there,' he added. 'My grandfather did. My mother had left by that time, and with my father's lifestyle, Grandad reckoned that the best thing for me was to go to boarding school. He picked the best and he was right. I know people from those days that I can still call on if I need a favour.'

'And do you?' Skinner asked.

'Every now and then. If you need approval to sell an extra few thousand tickets at a big outdoor venue in London, it helps if you know the Mayor's executive assistant.'

'And Gene?'

'I saw her at a few shows without knowing who she was; then about ten years ago, she moved in with my father. I've never liked the woman, but she does a fair job of looking after him.'

'She's been around for a few years, you said.' He smiled. 'She didn't have anything to do with the bomb in your father's car, did she? From what I've seen, I wouldn't put anything past her.'

'No,' Stoddart replied, his eyes hooded, 'but the old cow probably knew who ordered it.'

'And is that person still around?'

The eyes widened. 'As a matter of fact, he isn't. A few years after that incident, he drowned off the Costa Blanca when his jet ski overturned. Hey, Mr Skinner, if you're thinking what I think you are, you're letting your imagination run away with you.'

'Of course. That said, a friend of mine gave some thought a few years ago to starting a literary festival down there, but he gave it up when I suggested to him that most of his punters would be characters in true-crime books.'

The promoter laughed. 'I'm with you.'

'These days,' Skinner continued, 'most of them would be Russian. Not that I'm even hinting you'd deal with that sort.'

'Of course not.'

'As a matter of interest, who are Zirka?'

Bryce Stoddart's mouth opened; not quite a full jaw-drop, but close to it. He stared at his visitor. 'Who?' he exclaimed.

'You know who they are. I hope you do, since your company pays them a million a year.'

'Yes, I do know them,' Stoddart admitted, 'but I'm surprised that you do.'

Skinner shrugged. 'Really?' he said, ad-libbing. 'With the amount of money that Speight was insured for, and with the special clause in the policy, didn't you assume that the underwriters would instruct a complete investigation of everyone in the boxing business?'

The other man seemed to relax a little; he settled back into his chair. 'I suppose I should have,' he conceded. 'Zirka is a Russian promotion company; its principal is a retired fighter named Yevgeny Brezinski. He and Leo had history in the amateurs, and they were always bound to settle things as professionals. When they met, it was in Russia, but Leo insisted that his American cable TV backers should have the pay-per-view rights. It could have got nasty, but I forestalled that by cutting a deal with Brezinski that I would pay his company a million a year for as long as Leo was active. It's legit, I promise you. Our auditors declare it to HMRC every year.'

'I see. What does Zirka do now?'

'It's a promoter of mixed martial arts in eastern Europe and in Germany.'

Skinner scratched his chin, pausing more for effect than for thought. 'Mmm,' he murmured. 'That could have made Mr Brezinski a loser twice over, wouldn't it? Leo's retirement would put an end to his annual pay-off, plus the new venture, if it had gone ahead, might have made a big hole in his market.'

'Put that way, I have to agree, but how does it affect your clients?'

'It could make things very messy. The police may decide to

treat Brezinski as a suspect in Leo's death . . . once it's confirmed officially that he was murdered. Let's say they couldn't gather enough evidence to bring charges, but kept the file open so that it remained officially unsolved. My clients might find themselves on the end of a claim by the Speight estate for a payout in full of the special clause, relating to death at the hands of a third party.'

Stoddart smiled, and shook his head. 'I don't see that, Mr Skinner. Brezinski always knew that the payments would end one day, but he couldn't have known about the new venture. Nobody did, apart from me, Leo, Gino and Gene, and it wasn't announced until a few hours before he died. Suppose Yevgeny did decide to get rid of Leo before he became competition – and to be honest, I wouldn't put it past someone like him; he couldn't have done it within hours of its being announced for the first time, at a private party.'

'You're sure that nobody else knew? There's no crossover between your business and Zirka?'

'Crossover?'

'Business link; someone with a foot in both camps?'

'There's Billy Swords, I suppose. Our ring announcer,' he explained. 'He does stuff for Zirka. Leo knew that, though; even then he was happy to let him in on the project.'

'Good,' Skinner declared, rising to his feet. 'That covers some of the bases as far as my clients are concerned. From what you've told me, there seem to be no suspects in Leo Speight's business life. As for his private life, anyone who did claim for full payment of the special clause would immediately make themselves a suspect, so I don't see my clients having to pay out.'

'Not my business,' Stoddart said. As they moved towards the door, he glanced out of the window. 'Speak of the devil,' he murmured.

They stepped back into the reception hall just as a man came through the entrance door carrying a bundle under his arm. He was stocky, of middle age and middle height, and he seemed to bounce rather than walk.

'Hello, Billy,' the promoter greeted him. 'Mr Skinner, this is Billy Swords, our official master of ceremonies.'

'Indeed?' Skinner extended a hand. 'You're back?'

Swords stared at him, bewildered, as they shook. 'If you say so,' he retorted, and bounced on towards the stairs.

Twenty-One

'Toxicology will take longer than I'd hoped, Lottie,' Professor Graeme Bell reported. 'There's a backlog in the Crime Campus lab at Gartcosh and they refuse to prioritise. I've spoken to DCC McGuire, but he either can't or won't play favourites. The only thing they've been able to tell me to date is that the blue substance I found on Mr Speight's neck was oil paint. There was a single very fine hair adhering to it – not one of the victim's; it was synthetic. My guess is it was from a brush.'

'Thanks for nothing, Graeme,' the DI replied. 'Would it speed the process if the lab sent the results directly to me?'

'It might, but it would be against protocol. I work for the Crown Office, not the police, and I have to report on the basis of all the available facts. I need to consider the tox results in context before I can do that.'

'Fair enough,' she sighed. 'You're not changing your view that he was poisoned, though?'

'Hell, no, that's bloody obvious. Do you have any suspects yet?'

'There are a couple who'll benefit from his death, and one who maybe thought she would but might not, according to the will. Is there any way he could have been poisoned at the party but not died until he got home?'

'Not in my experience,' Bell declared firmly. 'Cyanide tends to kill you very quickly, plus . . . There is something that will be in my report but I can share it with you now. Not long before he died, Mr Speight had been sweating. You were in the house, at the crime scene, as was I. Will you agree with me that the temperature was not excessive?'

'The climate control for the area where he died was set at twenty-one degrees Celsius,' she told him. 'We checked. In the bedrooms it was eighteen.'

'Not enough to make you break out in a sweat, unless you were feverish, which he wasn't.'

'No, and he went home from the party on his motorbike; that was hardly going to heat him up.'

'He died wearing a tracksuit. Lottie, it appears that shortly before he died, Mr Speight engaged in some significant physical exercise. I didn't go over the whole place, but I saw that there was a gym in an annexe building. What I suggest to you is that when he got home from his party he was still wide awake. He probably still had adrenaline in his system from his big gathering and from the bike ride, so he went into the gym and ran, or cross-trained, or cycled a few miles to burn it off.'

'Fair enough,' Mann conceded, 'but is it significant?'

'If he'd been carrying a small but lethal dose of cyanide in his system, he wouldn't have been able to do that. He'd probably have died on whatever machine he was using. But he didn't. Instead he went into the house, drank his carton of almond-flavoured soya milk and expired in his chair, counted out by the celestial referee.'

On the screen of her tablet, he was beaming. 'Pleased with yourself, are you?' she said.

'Moderately,' he agreed.

'Then I'm pleased for you too, but only because I like to see a man who's happy in his work. It doesn't advance my investigation by one inch. You've told me what I knew already, but with knobs on. Whether he died in his trainers or his biker boots, same difference.'

Bell winked at the camera on whatever device he had used to take her Skype call. 'I'll enjoy telling the court as well, as soon as you catch your poisoner. So long.'

As her screen went blank, she looked up at Dan Provan, who had come into her room halfway through the call. 'Did you get that?' she asked.

'The gist of it. How about the toxicology?'

'Logjam at Gartcosh.'

'Can't we jump the queue?'

'The DCC says no. The only new information I have is that Speight had paint on his neck.'

'To be thorough, I suppose we better find out how it got there,' the DS said, 'although I have a fair idea. The artist woman, Cambridge, she was working at the party.' He checked his watch. 'Our next visitor should be able to confirm that, assuming she turns up.'

'Trudi Pollock? She's here already. I told them to hold her at reception until we were ready for her.'

'I'll go and get her.'

'Thanks. By the way,' Mann added, 'just before I spoke to Graeme, I had a call from Jakey. Vanessa picked him up from school, and she said he's happy as Larry.' She frowned. 'I wonder who he was?'

'Who?'

'The original Larry? The one people are as happy as.'

Provan smiled. 'He was an Australian boxer, or so one of my

Gold Coast friends told me. I'm glad the wee one's sorted.'

'Me too,' she agreed. 'The other side of the coin is that I had a call from Moss Lee.'

'Him? Don't tell me, Faye's going to confess but he wants a plea bargain?'

'We should be so lucky. No, he rang to tell me that Scott's being released on Wednesday, two days from now, and that he's going to press for an immediate custody hearing. As further evidence of my neglect, he said, he's going to cite my refusal to accept a generous offer to help with my child's education, against his father's wishes. Dan,' she confessed, 'I'm worried.'

'I'd be lying if I said I wasn't too,' he admitted, 'but I've got a feeling it's going to be all right. Ah'll go and get the Trudi woman.'

He left her and jogged down the staircase to the Pitt Street reception area. Three women were waiting there, but from the description he had been given he picked out their visitor without hesitation. She was short and almost square in build, but pretty, with an undefinable quality that made him want to smile.

Instead, he greeted her formally. 'Ms Pollock? DS Provan. Sorry to have kept you. If you'd like to come with me.'

He would have taken the lift, but she led the way, making for the stairs from which he had arrived, moving more nimbly than her build suggested she might. He took her into a small interview room on the first floor, where Mann was waiting. The visitor looked at the table as the DI offered her a seat. 'Is there no recorder?' she asked, in a clipped Glasgow accent. 'There always is on the telly.'

'You're no' under caution, so we don't need one,' Provan explained. 'We'll just take notes.' He smiled. 'That means I will; she's the boss.'

'Okay. How can I help you?'

'Just tell us what you know about Mr Speight,' Mann suggested. 'We need all the information we can get about him: who were his friends, who were his enemies, was anything worrying him. Of all the people on our interview list, you've known him longer than anyone else, save for Mr Butler.'

'For longer,' Trudi corrected her. 'Leo and I started primary school on the same day. We never met Gino until we went to the high school.'

'What was Leo like as a child?'

'Quiet. He was always quiet.'

'Was he always a fighter?' Provan asked.

'Not at first, until he had to be. His mum was a teacher; when we got to Primary Four, there were a couple of big boys used to pick on him because of it. He got beat up a couple of times, two on one. But one day one of them tried it on his own. Leo knocked two of his front teeth out; his second teeth they were too. I never thought he could fight. The other boy's mother kicked up a stink, but the headmaster knew what had happened. He told her that her son had only got what he'd been asking for. He told Leo's dad about it, though. He'd been a professional boxer himself, Mr Speight. I don't think he ever wanted that for Leo, but he must have given in to the inevitable, for he took him in hand and started to train him.'

'What happened to the boy with the missing teeth?'

She smiled sadly. 'Barlinnie happened to him, eventually. Last I heard he was still there. He never did learn his lesson.'

'Some never do,' Mann observed. 'Was Leo a loner as a youngster, or did he run with a gang when he got to the high school?'

'There weren't really any gangs in our school. But he wasn't a loner; he had plenty of pals. Gino was the best, though; he was the only boy that Leo was close to.'

'And you and him?'

'We were just . . . We hung around together. Leo had a bad time when we were both fourteen; his mother developed pre-senile dementia. She lost her mind, literally, and had to be put away. It was just him and his dad after that, until he was killed at work. Leo would be early twenties at the time.'

'What happened to him?' the DI asked.

'It was awful,' the woman replied. 'Mr Speight worked on the railways, in a freight yard. One day he got caught between two trucks and was crushed to death. Before that, though, he worked all hours when Mrs Speight took ill, making extra money for Leo's training expenses and his travel costs to amateur tournaments. When he was at work, Leo spent most of the time with me. Well, we were growing up, and after a while we started . . .' she paused for a second, 'you know.' She flushed, shyly and attractively, and Provan saw the pretty girl that she had been. 'Not until we were sixteen, mind,' she added. 'We were still too young, though, too young to be careful enough.'

'Mr Butler told us what happened when your father found out you were pregnant. He said that he threatened Leo, and that Leo flattened him.'

She nodded. 'That's what Gino told me, too. Leo never spoke to me about it.'

The DS paused his note-taking and looked at her. 'You weren't there?'

'I was upstairs in my room,' she told him, 'with make-up on the black eye my dad gave me. I had to stay away from Leo until it was better. I was afraid of what he might have done to my dad if he'd found out.'

'What do you think he might have done?'

'I didn't want to know that. Leo was the best amateur boxer in Britain. He had an aura about him even then. If you believe in those things, and I do, you'll understand when I say that his was huge. It was like a great big tree. My father's was like a scrubby wee bush. He made out that he was a gangster. He wasn't. He was just a big loudmouth in the pub and a big bully at home. I was glad when he died. I didn't even go to the funeral.'

'Do you think someone put him in the river?' Mann asked.

Trudi raised an eyebrow. 'You've been doing your homework. Frankly I don't care whether somebody did or whether he just had a heart attack and fell in like they said. Either way, my mother, Gordon and I were well rid of him. With him gone, Leo was able to help with Gordon.'

'Did you and he ever rekindle your old relationship?'

'No. We never even thought about it, to be honest. I was still a Paisley girl, but even by that time Leo was from somewhere else. Mind you, he did offer to adopt Gordon formally, so that he could use his name. My bastard of a father never filled in that part on the certificate when he registered the birth,' she added in explanation. 'He left it as "Unknown", even though it made me out to be a tramp. I said no, that Gordon would know who his dad was and that was enough for me. Leo said he understood, and that's why none of his other kids are called Speight either . . . whatever that woman Faye might write on their bloody lunch boxes.'

Her sudden venom took both officers by surprise.

'You and Ms Bulloch don't get on,' Provan observed.

'We don't have to, because our paths don't cross. That stupid legal action of hers: while Leo was alive it was a waste of time and money. I hope nothing comes of it now he's dead.'

'That'll be for the Court of Session, I'm afraid. Moving on,' Mann continued, 'there may be something you can clear up for us. During the party last Friday, we're told there was an artist at work.'

'That's right: Augusta Cambridge. I made the arrangements. You know I'm Gino's secretary?' Mann nodded. 'Leo wanted everyone to have a memento of the night, but something special, more than just a photograph. All the guests were going to get a print of her painting.'

'Did you notice the two of them talking that night?'

She smiled. 'Oh yes. She was sat up on a kind of dais with her easel, and he went and stood behind her, to see what she was doing. They knew each other quite well,' she volunteered. 'I heard Leo say to her, "Hey, Gus, are you never going to paint me?" She had her brush in her hand and she dabbed him with it, right there,' she touched the left side of her throat, 'and said, "There you are, an Augusta original." He said, "I'll never wash it off," and they both laughed.'

'As it turned out, he didn't,' Provan murmured grimly. 'It was an anomaly we had to clear up, so thank you.'

'Did you speak to Leo yourself at the party?' Mann asked.

'No, I was going to, to thank him for a great night, but he'd left when I went looking for him.'

'When was the last time you spoke?'

Trudi Pollock shifted in her seat, resting her thick forearms on the table. 'Last week. Let me see, what day was it? Yes, Tuesday. He came into Gino's wee office in Glasgow, where I work. It's an accommodation address as much as anything else. Gino spent most of his time with Leo, wherever he was.'

'Did you get the impression that anything was weighing on his mind?'

'Other than the party, no, and by then all the arrangements were made and we were able to go firm on the guest list. No, he was fine, the usual Leo. He wasn't there long. He did a bit of business, and when he left, he kissed me on the forehead, said, "You always were a wee treasure, Trudi," and he left. Those were the last words he ever spoke to me.'

Twenty-Two

Bob Skinner was not best pleased, but slightly more than Sarah had been when he had called her to say that he was going to be late for his son Mark's appearance on a television computer science programme that had been recorded a few weeks ago and was due to be screened that evening.

'Tell him I am sorry,' he had said. 'Record it and tell him we'll all watch it together as soon as we can.'

'Will that be tonight?'

'It depends how quickly I can get shot of this Italian that I have to see. I'd postpone him, but he says he's leaving tomorrow, and I need to talk to him before he goes.'

'Couldn't you stop him from leaving before you're ready to interview him?'

'A couple of years ago, when I was still a chief constable, I could have. I don't have the authority to do that any more.'

'What about DI Mann?' she had suggested.

'Lottie doesn't have the rank, and she doesn't have grounds either. She has no reason to regard him as a suspect. I hate it, babe, but it's best all round if I see the bugger at the time and place he specified.'

'Okay,' Sarah had sighed. 'I'll tell Mark you're on a secret mission. That'll keep him happy.'

'You're not wrong on this occasion.'

He was still fretting over Mark's potential disappointment as he nursed a mineral water in the dimly lit Regina's. It was quiet, as Moscardinetto had said, possibly because its prices were eye-wateringly high even by central Glasgow standards. To compound his annoyance, the Italian was late. To read his watch Skinner had to hold it in the single shaft of downlight that played on his corner booth. It showed ten past seven, and he had never been a man to let unpunctuality go unremarked upon.

He glowered at the door for three more minutes before the last thin shred of his patience snapped. He took out his phone, found the film-maker's number and called it. To his annoyance, it went to voicemail. He waited for two minutes then tried again, with the same result.

'Bastard thinks he can ignore me, does he?' he growled. 'We'll see about that.' He eased himself out of the narrow booth and walked across to the bar.

'Fizzy water not to your liking?' its uniformed minder asked him. 'I can do you a nice non-alcoholic cocktail if you like.'

'I'm sure you could, but I suspect I'd have to cash a fucking ISA to pay for it. I'm supposed to be meeting a guy here; he's Italian and he's been here before, because he knew about it and suggested it.'

'I think I know who you mean,' the barman said, a young man, a couple of years older than Ignacio, no more, with studs in his ears that Skinner suspected were gemstones pretending to be rubies. 'He was in here last Wednesday night with a young fella. I don't know what that was about. The Italian was an obvious three-pound note – this place isn't called Regina's for nothing, by the way – and the lad looked young. They sat in the far booth, over there,' he pointed, 'talking, and at one point the kid got quite agitated. I take it you're a cop. Is that why you're after him?'

'Wrong, but I am after him, if only for wasting my fucking time. What are the nearest hotels to this place? I know he's in one, but I don't know which.'

'My guess would be the Stadium. It's only about a hundred yards away, down the hill then round the corner in West Campbell Street. Not big, but posh and pricey; it belongs to a footballer. If it's not that, try the place up in Blythswood Square.'

Skinner nodded his thanks and left the cellar bar. He flinched as he reached pavement level, regretting that he had no overcoat. Getting old, he thought. The day had never been warm, and the evening was decidedly cold as he walked down St Vincent Street, passing his parked car before reaching West Campbell Street. The naming of Glasgow city centre always baffled him, even after the short period in his working life when he had been based there; he had never been able to work out why so many streets were prefixed 'West'. The one into which he turned appeared to be aligned from north to south, adding to his confusion.

The hotel was as close to Regina's as the barman had said, taking up half the block between St Vincent Street and West Campbell Street. Where Beedham's had spoken quietly of post-Victorian wealth and confidence, the Stadium yelled modernity, with stainless-steel embellishing – or desecrating, depending on the viewer's tastes – a yellow stone building, emphasised by plush synthetic carpeting and hard plastic fittings inside and a blue neon strip over the reception desk.

'I'm looking for one of your guests,' Skinner told the young woman who was positioned behind it, dressed in the manner of cabin crew on a Middle Eastern airline. Her badge named her as Raquel, and she was in the same age bracket as the barman in Regina's, but her ear studs were definitely diamond. 'A man by the name of Aldorino Moscardinetto. Is he in?'

She frowned at him, her dark, shaped eyebrows coming close together, then peered at something on a level below the desk. She looked up again, meeting his gaze. 'I'm sorry, sir,' she replied, in an accent imported from the south, 'Signor Moscardinetto gave us strict instructions that he only receives visitors by prior appointment, and there are no names on his list this evening.'

'Do you have a pen there, Raquel?'

The frown returned. 'Of course, sir.'

'That's good,' he said, smiling gently to put her at her ease. 'So many young people these days just make notes on their mobiles. In a couple of generations they'll have forgotten how to write, and they'll have long pointy thumbs. Take your pen please, Raquel, and your empty list, and write on it "Robert M Skinner, KBE, QPM", then call your guest and tell him that I'm here.'

The knighthood had been bestowed at the turn of the year, at the insistence of a grateful prime minister. It had been offered twice before and declined, until, mindful of the fate of Julius Caesar after three refusals, he had accepted, on the condition that it was not gazetted, or featured in any honours list. Within his circle only two people knew of its existence, Sarah and Alex. He was fairly sure that the secret was safe with Raquel, as she stared back at him, bewildered.

'Save some time,' he suggested. 'Forget his list, just call him.'

She capitulated, picked up a phone and pushed three buttons. He watched her waiting for the call to connect, but nothing happened. She listened for what seemed like an age but was little more than half a minute before shaking her head and declaring, 'I'm sorry, sir, He's not in.'

'No,' he corrected her. 'You mean there was no reply. You called him, so you must have believed he was in the hotel.'

'I did,' Raquel agreed. 'I've been on duty since four. Signor Moscardinetto came back in five minutes after I started. I've been here ever since then, apart from a couple of minutes just after six, when I . . . you know . . . and he hasn't gone out.'

'Could he be in any other part of the hotel? Dining room? Bar?'

'He'd have had to go past me to get there.' She pointed to her left, at an elevator door. 'That's the only lift.'

'Therefore the presumption is that he's in his room, but not answering the phone. He was alone when he came back, yes? He didn't bring a little friend with him?'

She nodded, then shook her head, in quick succession.

'In that case, you'd better take me up there,' Skinner said.

'Maybe he's asleep,' she suggested.

'If he is, we'll wake him, and he'll be able to tell me why he didn't turn up for our meeting in a bar up the road. Look,' he offered, 'maybe you'd prefer to call the manager if you're not comfortable with that.'

'I am the duty manager,' she replied. 'Hold on a sec.' She turned, opened a door behind her and called out, 'Jan, man the desk for a few minutes, please. Jan's our doorman and porter,' she explained as she lifted a flap and stepped out from behind the desk. 'He's on his break. This way.' She stepped up to the lift, pressed the 'ascend' button and the doors opened immediately.

183

Aldorino Moscardinetto's room was on the top floor of the hotel, the third. The corridor was as tasteless as the reception area had been, but better lit; the cheap garishness of the thick purple synthetic carpet was even more evident. Glancing down, he saw at least an inch of Raquel's heels sink into it.

She stopped at room three zero six. 'This is it,' she murmured, then knocked on the door and called out, '*Signore*, it's hotel management. Can I speak with you, please?'

The veneered door was as cheap as the rest of the decor; Skinner knew that if there had been movement behind it, he would have heard. A feeling of inevitability settled upon him, one that he had experienced all too often.

'Open it,' he ordered.

She looked at him, her eyes showing doubt, and something else: fear. 'Are you sure?'

'Yes.' He held out his right hand. 'Give me the pass key, kid, then back off a little. Just in case,' he added.

She did as he instructed, retreating all the way back to the lift. He slid the plastic key card into its slot, saw a green flash, then withdrew it.

The door was as light as he had suspected. As he opened it, using a handkerchief for want of a glove, and stepped into the room, the smell that greeted him confirmed that it was occupied.

A golden face stared back at him from the dressing table. A full head of hair fell across its forehead, but its right eye socket was empty. The left was there but saw nothing.

Fuck me, Skinner thought, he takes his BAFTA everywhere with him.

He realised that his tense was wrong as he advanced into the room, past the wardrobes, past the en suite bathroom. The room had a double bed and Aldorino Moscardinetto lay beyond it, on the floor, on his side, with a small pool of vomit beside him. A thick restraining cord from one of the curtains was wrapped loosely around his neck, on which a vivid purple circle was evident. His black cotton jacket had been discarded, thrown across the bed, leaving him clad in a white shirt, its high collar open, and pale blue trousers, which he had fouled in death.

He moved further forward into the narrow space where the body lay, between the bed and the wall. He leaned across it and placed two fingers against the carotid artery. It was a pointless gesture, for he had known he would feel no pulse. He rested the backs of the same two fingers for a few seconds against the dead man's forehead, trying not to look at his purple face, or into his eyes, knowing that if he did, the memory would stay with him for even longer.

By gauging the temperature against his own, he judged that the body was cooling but not cold. The room itself was not warm, indicating that the heating system was on a money-saving timer. He tried to guess what Sarah would deduce with her pathologist's skills, and concluded that she would suggest Moscardinetto had been dead for more than an hour.

Then he stood, and walked away, walked out of yet another crime scene, added to the hundreds he had viewed in his time.

As he closed the door behind him, Skinner saw Raquel standing by the lift, her hands covering her mouth and her eyes wide as she read his expression.

'Do you have any other guests on this floor?' he asked.

She nodded. 'Four,' she replied, her voice a little tremulous but under control.

'Check their rooms, please, now, and ask any who are in to go downstairs. Can you move them all to a lower floor?'

185

'Yes, we've got space.'

'Good. You need to do that sooner rather than later.'

She looked at him. 'We had a guest die on us last year,' she said, 'and we didn't have to do that.'

'This time you do. This floor will be very busy very soon.'

'You are police, then,' she murmured making the same erroneous assumption as had the barman in Regina's, a long twenty minutes before.

'Not any more,' he told her, 'but I know people who still are. You do what you have to do, and I'll call them.'

With his back to the door of room three zero six, he took out his phone, found Dan Provan's number among the hundreds he had gathered through the years, and called him.

'Aye?' The detective sergeant's gruff voice sounded in his ear. He assumed he had come up as 'Number unknown'.

'It's Bob Skinner, Dan. I'm calling you rather than Lottie because I'm guessing that by now she might be back home with her wee boy.'

'That's right, she is.'

'Then I'm not going to fuck that up for her, because I know how important it is. This is an executive decision that I no longer have the power to make, but I'm doing it anyway. I'm on the third floor of the Stadium Hotel in West Campbell Street, outside the room of Aldorino Moscardinetto. He's been strangled, probably shortly after five past four, when he was last seen. I need uniforms here right now, people who know or have been told who I am, I need a full crime-scene team as soon as possible, and I need you, DS Provan, because this links directly to the Leo Speight investigation. Don't worry about phoning your high heid yins; I'll do that. You call the rest and then get your arse along here. Until you arrive, I'm taking charge of the scene, so make sure that everyone you call knows that.'

He left Provan to his task, then took a deep breath. When he had gathered himself, he made another call. 'Love of my life,' he began as Sarah answered, 'let me ask you something. If a human body is four or five degrees below normal temperature in cool indoor surroundings, how long has it been dead?'

Twenty-Three

'Why are you no' wearing a sterile suit?' Dan Provan asked as he hopped from the lift into the third-floor corridor while trying to fit on a paper overshoe.

'I wasn't wearing one when I found the deceased,' Skinner replied, 'so there isn't a hell of a lot of point now. They'll find me in there, but I'm in the database so it won't be a problem.'

The DS wrinkled his nose. 'I don't need tae ask if he's still there,' he said. 'You should have telt them to close the door.'

'It is closed now, but it was open for long enough. I asked them to open the window, but they won't until it's been printed. That'll be a waste of time, of course, given that it's a hotel room. It'll yield dozens of untraceable prints that will have nothing to do with the investigation.'

'Aye. This corridor will be a forensic disaster too, wi' all the folk that have walked along it since it was last hoovered. How many rooms are there on this floor?'

'Twelve, but that's not important. In fact it's irrelevant. We know the perpetrator had to come this way, not through anyone's window. It's what's in the victim's room that counts.'

'I suppose Ah'd better take a look,' Provan sighed.

Skinner followed him along the corridor and into the murder

scene but did not advance beyond the door of the bathroom. Instead he waited as the DS approached Moscardinetto's body. As he was studying it, Skinner took the opportunity to appraise the scene more carefully than he had before.

'Has the pathologist been yet?' Provan asked from across the room.

'No, but I've got an informed guesstimate from my wife of the time of death, based on what I could tell her about body temperature. She puts it between five past four, when he got back to the hotel, and five o'clock.'

'How are we for CCTV coverage?'

'It's piss-poor, unfortunately,' Skinner conceded. 'This place was a cheap conversion from an office building, and they skimped on cameras. The entrance, the bar and the dining room are covered, and that's about it.'

'I see. Got any theories, big man?'

'Yes, but you're the SIO here, wee man, so let's hear yours first.'

'Fair enough,' the DS said. 'I'm thinking this might be a professional hit, dressed up to look like a random robbery gone wrong. The deceased walks in on the thief, he has a go, and the thief strangles him. That's what we're meant to think, except I don't buy it. Of all the rooms in this hotel, why pick this one? Okay, the drawers are half open, looking as if they've been gone through, but so what? Has anything actually been taken? The guy's wallet's still in his jacket with a mix of twenties and tenners in it. A real thief would have emptied that. Likely he'd have taken this thing too.'

With his gloved right hand Provan picked up the BAFTA statuette, then replaced it quickly. 'Fuck me, those buggers are heavier than they look!' he exclaimed. 'That would have made a good murder weapon.' He paused. 'That's how I see it anyway,' he concluded. 'You?'

'We're not a million miles apart,' Skinner replied. 'I agree with you that it's unlikely just to have been an unfortunate coincidence for Moscardinetto. However, I disagree on a few points. I believe it was a robbery, and I don't believe that the perpetrator came here to kill. Dan, I've visited the aftermath of quite a few professional hits, as opposed to premeditated murders; more than you have, I'm sure. But I have never seen one where the assassin came along unequipped for the job. Most of the victims I've seen were shot, a minority were stabbed. I can only recall one where the target was strangled, and that was done with a wire garrotte, almost to the point of decapitation. That weapon wasn't left at the scene, nor were any of the others; professional killers don't do that. This was spontaneous, bet on it.'

'I'm no' a betting man,' the DS retorted defensively.

'That's just as well for you, mate, and tough luck on the bookies. Any professional looks after the tools of his trade. This bloke came here for another purpose; he was disturbed and he improvised. He grabbed the nearest thing to hand, he overpowered Moscardinetto and he throttled him.' He paused, then added, 'Afterwards, I believe he took what he came for and he left.'

Provan frowned, his eyes narrowing. 'Okay with the rest, but how do you work the last part out?'

Skinner beckoned him with an upraised finger. 'Come here,' he said, 'and look at this.'

He led the DS to a platform beside the wardrobe, where a small four-wheeled suitcase stood, unzipped and lying ajar, displaying a pair of trousers folded over a hanger. 'What else do you see in there?' he asked.

Provan bent slightly from the waist and looked inside the case. 'It's got a compartment,' he murmured as his former commander's meaning dawned on him, 'a laptop compartment.'

'Exactly. It's empty, and trust me, there is no laptop or tablet, or any other form of computer, in this room. Nor is the victim's phone here; that's gone too. But there are chargers, for both, on the dressing table.'

'What about the safe?' the DS challenged. 'There's bound to be a safe.'

'There is,' Skinner conceded. 'In the wardrobe. It was closed, but I got the override code from Raquel, the duty manager, and opened it. I found an Italian passport, a Business Plus boarding card for Ryanair's flight from Prestwick to Rome Ciampino tomorrow, a small phial of what I believe to be amyl nitrite – although God knows how he'd have got that past an airport scanner – and three hundred and eighty-four euros in notes and change.'

'What's amyl nitrite?'

'Dan,' Skinner replied, 'I really don't think you'd want to know. Apart from those items, there was nothing else. Signor Moscardinetto's killer came for a specific purpose, and he found what he was looking for.'

Twenty-Four

'That was a pretty big call you made yesterday,' Lottie Mann murmured to Dan Provan as she stood in the doorway of room three zero six on Tuesday morning.

They would have been alone on the third floor of the Stadium had it not been for a single uniformed constable standing beside the lift to redirect any unauthorised arrivals, media or hotel guests. The crime-scene technicians had finished their work, and the remains of Aldorino Moscardinetto had been transferred to the mortuary to await the slicing and probing of Professor Graeme Bell, although a faint reminder of his former presence still lingered in the air, despite the fact that a window had been opened.

'I didn't make it,' he pointed out. 'Big Skinner slipped into full command mode, and he's no' a man you'd want to try to override. Besides, he was right. Your Auntie Ann's still on virtual lockdown at her hospital, and Jamie and Vanessa went out for a Mexican after you picked wee Jakey up. What would you have done with him if I had called you in? Ye'd have had to take him back to those two malevolent fuckers of grandparents. It would have been more ammunition for Moss bloody Lee but there would have been no other option.'

'Okay, I appreciate that, but how's it going to look to the bosses?'

'Have you had the chief constable biting your arse?'

'No,' she conceded. 'Not yet.'

'You may be the senior investigating officer on this case, Lottie, but you are not the only investigating officer.'

'Granted. Look, Dan, I'm not getting at you. I'm grateful for what you did. The only slight niggle I've got is that a civilian took my place. You're usually the first to point out that Bob Skinner isn't a police officer any longer.'

He laughed out loud. 'Aye, right. Then we're both wrong. Skinner will always be a polis. When he's on his deathbed and the priest sprinkles holy water on him, he'll try tae arrest him for assault. But when I got here,' he added, 'he made it clear to everyone that I was the ranking officer, without hardly having to say a word. He deferred to me, and everyone could see it. His guys in Edinburgh used to say that when he was chief he was usually there but never in the way. Oh aye, and speaking of Edinburgh . . .'

He reached into a side pocket of his jacket, produced a business card and handed it to her. 'Oh by the way,' he murmured, 'a big bird landed on my shoulder when nobody was looking and gave me that. You're to call that number, soon as you can.'

She peered at it. 'What the . . .'

'Later, later,' Provan said impatiently. 'First things first. Before I left last night, I had the young manager show me the footage from the few cameras they have in here. It shows the victim arriving just after four, as she said he did. In the three hours after that, until Skinner arrived, ten people came in. Six of them went to the bar and stayed there. The other four were hotel guests, and they were interviewed last night along with everyone else on the premises, staff and clients. None of them aroused any suspicion and nobody saw a fucking thing.'

'What about people leaving?' Mann asked.

'Half a dozen, but all of them are accounted for. One was a guest and five were bar customers. None of them,' he added, 'was carrying a laptop.'

'So our killer seems to have come and gone undetected. Any ideas on how he might have done that?'

'I think I know,' the DS replied. 'There's a fire escape, opening on to West George Lane. That's one way he could have got out, but the door's solid and can only be opened from the inside. He could have left that way, but how did he get in? That's the question. My best guess is through the roof. It's easy done. I had a look on Google Earth last night; it shows that right above us there's an access hatch that's probably been there for ever. This building's joined on to the one next door and that one has an external fire escape. Before you got here, I went up the fire-escape stairs and took a look. The hatch is old, and not secure. Not only that, I'm pretty certain it's been accessed recently. I'm goin' tae get the SOCOs up there to take a look. If I'm right, they'll find traces that'll match up wi' some from this room.'

'How about CCTV outside?' Mann was alert, excited. 'If you're right, with a bit of luck, we'll get an image of our perpetrator climbing up that escape.'

'I didnae see any public CCTV in West George Lane itself, but a couple of the buildings have got private coverage. I was planning to get a DC to visit them both, to see what we've got and if there's access. Failing that, there will probably be city public space coverage in West Campbell Street and Blythswood Street. Even if it doesnae cover the lane entrances, if we spot someone who disappears from sight between cameras, that'll be a start.'

'Progress!' The DI beamed. 'I should leave you on your own more often. Come to think of it,' she mused, 'when I was your DC and you were my DS, that's pretty much how it worked. So, boss,' she joked, 'what else have you got planned? What about the press? How do we handle them?'

'Don't push it. That's your shout, as usual.'

'I have been thinking about that. Subject to the DCC's approval, I think we should use Allsop again, or one of his deputies, and have a briefing at midday. I know, it's against policy, but this is a special situation. What we don't want to do is suggest any link between Moscardinetto's murder and Leo Speight. The media don't know he was at the party, and we ourselves don't know why. There may not be a link; his murder might relate to something else, and someone else.'

'Aye,' Provan drawled, 'and if Skinner had thought that, would he have called me, knowin' that you and I are up tae our oxters in the Speight case? Mibbe he was wrong, though. Mibbe someone just thought Moscardinetto's last film was shite.'

'Keep an open mind, Dan,' Mann replied. 'That's all I'm saying. Are there any other leads from last night that need to be followed up?'

'Just the one. Big Bob said that the barman in Regina's, the place in St Vincent Street where he was supposed to meet Moscardinetto, told him he'd seen him in there on Wednesday night, with a young lad. The story was they were talking and the boy got quite upset. That needs to be looked at.'

'Let's do it now,' Mann said. 'It's not far. Will it be open, d'you think?'

He drew her a long look. 'How should Ah know what time a

gay bar opens on a Tuesday morning? We can try it,' he conceded. 'If it's shut, then it's no' far from the office; we can come back later. By the way, you should talk to the manager downstairs before we go,' he suggested. 'He's crappin' himself. As soon as I arrived this mornin', he asked me when we'd be out of here. I told his assistant last night she had to find other accommodation for their guests, until we say they can open again.'

'If he had a CCTV system that showed us who went into this room,' the DI hit the door frame with the flat of her hand, 'it could have been a bloody sight sooner. The way it is, though, he's shut until the fiscal says otherwise. We have to preserve the scene, in case of an early arrest and the possible needs of the defence. Show me where his office is and I'll tell him that.'

They turned and headed for the lift. They were waiting for it to arrive, in polite conversation with the guardian constable, when the DI's ringtone sounded.

'Detective Inspector Mann?' She recognised the voice almost immediately. 'Joy Herbert speaking. I have just had a recorded delivery letter arrive in my office. It was posted last week, and only the Royal Mail can explain why it's taken so long to get to me. However, now that it has, I believe it's something that you might want to see. Can you get to my office, fairly quickly? I have a meeting in half an hour that I can't postpone.'

'I can be there in ten,' she said. 'I'm on my way now.'

'Where?' Provan asked as she returned her phone to her pocket.

'George Square. The lawyer has something she thinks I need to see. Talk to the manager for me, Dan; keep him as happy as you can. Then take a look into Regina's if it's open. I'll see you back at Pitt Street.'

'Fine,' he grunted. 'Oh, by the way,' he called after her as she left, 'what's amyl nitrite for?'

She paused, almost in mid stride, and stared back at him over her shoulder. 'Jesus!' she whispered, then kept on moving.

Twenty-Five

Keeping the manager of the Stadium Hotel happy proved to be a task beyond the outer limits of the diplomatic skills of the detective sergeant. Eventually he gave up on the task and reverted to his normal everyday bluntness.

'Mr Welch,' he said, 'I appreciate that every day you're closed you're losing money, and I promise you that we're no' doing it on purpose. But look at it this way. Would you rather have an unsolved murder hanging over this place indefinitely, or one that's wrapped up quickly then forgotten about?'

'Try telling that to Mr Mustard, my owner!' the manager shouted. 'He's got a lot of money wrapped up in this place. And he knows people,' he added. 'If you don't get us opened in the next couple of days, you'll hear about it, I promise you.'

'Is that right?' Provan retorted. 'Ah know people too. One of them's in the security business, putting systems into commercial buildings. If your owner had gone to somebody like him and spent a wee bit more money, we might have had a sight of whoever it was broke into one of your rooms with a credit card in the lock, and then throttled one of your guests with a curtain cord. So please don't waste your time moaning at me. You'd be better off talking to your insurers about covering your closure, and about how they're going to react when Mr Moscardinetto's family come after you for compensation for putting him at risk.' He kicked the cheap nylon carpet, wondering whether static electricity could ever be strong enough to start a fire. 'Or is your owner so tight that he doesnae have proper insurance either?'

He walked out, ignoring the man's continued protests as he called after the detective, and also the bellowed questions from the small group of journalists gathered outside, held back by two more uniforms. All they had been told by the press office was that there had been an incident in the hotel, but most of them knew who and what Mann and Provan were. Conclusions had been drawn, but there had been no morning speculation of a link to the Speight investigation.

Won't be long, though, he told himself.

As soon as he was clear of the building, he called the procurator fiscal's office and asked for D. C. Thomson, the deputy who was handling the Italian's murder. 'Beano,' he began as he was connected, 'I need more forensics on West Campbell Street, up on the roof. There's a dodgy hatch there I think our intruder used. As well as that, I need to access all the city TV footage of the block around the hotel between three yesterday afternoon and seven thirty, lookin' for a face that might fit. Finally, see if ye can get Fire and Rescue to do an inspection of the place. It looks to me like an insurance claim waiting tae happen.'

The public prosecutor laughed. 'Who's got up your nose, Dan? Management not best pleased, are they?'

'If my guess is right, you'll find that out for yourself as soon as we're finished wi' this call.'

'Thanks for the warning,' Thomson said. 'I'll attend to those matters right away . . . all three of them. Cheers.'

Provan was smiling with grim satisfaction as he turned the corner and walked lightly up St Vincent Street. He was looking forward to a gym session later, having negotiated a deal with dreadlocked Max, on the basis that having a cop on the premises was never bad for business.

As he approached Regina's, he was pleased to see that the neon sign above the cellar bar door was shining. He jogged down the steps and went inside.

There was little or no natural light and not much more of the artificial kind, but enough for him to see that the place was empty apart from a young man behind the bar, in a white shirt and a maroon waistcoat with a shiny back. As he approached, the custodian turned towards him and the DS saw that he was sporting a pair of decidedly dodgy ear studs.

He showed his warrant card and identified himself. 'Oh yes?' the barman said. 'Two in two days. There was a big bloke in here last night. He said he wasn't CID, but it was written all over him. Are you after the Italian bloke as well?'

Provan shook his head. 'No,' he replied. 'Ah'm after the bloke that killed him.'

Even in the gloom, he could see the colour leave the man's face. 'My God,' he gasped. 'When did that happen?'

'Yesterday afternoon, we think.'

'That explains the crowd outside the Stadium when I passed earlier on. What happened?'

'He died. That's all you need to know. What's your name, by the way?'

'Aidan Briggs.'

'Right, Aidan, you told my, er, colleague yesterday that the victim was in here on Wednesday evening with a younger man.'

'That's right, they were in the corner booth. Vodka martini, hold the olive, for the Italian, and a Malibu sunset, hold the rum, for the boy.'

'You said the kid appeared upset at one point. In what way?'

'I couldn't hear what was said,' Briggs confessed, 'but I could tell from his tone that he was bitching about something. The way it was, it was like the Italian was asking him stuff, and he was answering.'

'You mean like an interview?'

The barman nodded. 'That's what it was, I'm sure. The Italian set up an iPhone on a tripod, and I'm sure he was filming. You can record video on those things in practically no light at all.'

'How long were they here?' Provan asked.

'About an hour. Long enough for two drinks; the Italian bought both rounds.'

'Can you describe the lad for me in more detail?'

Aidan Briggs grinned, in the way someone does when he is very pleased with himself. 'I can do better than that,' he said. 'Given his age, I asked him for ID as soon as he stepped through the door. He showed me his driving licence; he'd just turned eighteen. I photocopied it in the back office in case he came back in here again without it. Hold on.'

He turned his back on the detective, opened a drawer below the cash register, then took out a box and rummaged through its contents.

'There you are,' he exclaimed, waving a sheet of paper, then slamming it on the bar for Provan's inspection. 'That's him: Pollock, Gordon Pollock.'

Twenty-Six

Without realising that she was rushing, Lottie Mann reached the solicitor's office in George Square six minutes after leaving the Stadium. She was out of breath as she climbed the stairs, and had to wait on the landing for a moment or two to compose herself.

When she was ready, she pushed the door open, reaching for her warrant card as she stepped into the public area, where a woman in her forties sat behind a desk. It was unnecessary.

'Detective Inspector Mann?' she asked. 'Please go straight in, Mrs Herbert's ready for you. It's the door facing you.'

She nodded and kept walking. Joy Herbert looked up as she knocked and entered, half rising from her chair as she indicated that the detective should take a seat at her desk. She checked her watch and smiled. 'You must have been close by,' she remarked.

'I was at a crime scene in West Campbell Street,' Mann replied. 'Before we begin, can I ask you something? Did Leo Speight ever mention the name Aldorino Moscardinetto to you?'

Mrs Herbert smiled. 'No, and you can be sure that if he had, I would have remembered a name like that. Who is he?'

'Who was he,' the DI corrected her. 'He was the victim at my crime scene, found dead in his hotel room yesterday afternoon.

He was an Italian film director, quite famous, and he was a guest at Leo's party last Friday evening. So now I have two mysteries on my hands. The first is, why was he there, and the second is who killed him?'

'Do you believe it was the same person who killed my client?'

'The law of averages alone, never mind my experience, suggests to me that two murders within three days, from the same group of people, are likely to be related.'

A gimlet eye fastened on her. 'That is the first time I've heard that word used in reference to my client's death. It's official, is it?'

'That's how I'm treating it. The lab people are taking their bloody time with the "I"s and the "T"s, but the pathologist has ruled out natural causes. There's absolutely no doubt about the second one; somebody garrotted him.'

'How very nasty! Do you have any, er, leads? In either case?'

'We have lines of enquiry, that's all I can say at the moment. The forensic trail in the second killing should be pretty clear. It's a matter of following it to an individual. To be honest, we've got a better chance of an early result with the Italian. His death was up close and personal. Leo's was at a distance. Now,' she exclaimed, 'we're both busy women, so what do you have for me?'

'A surprise,' Mrs Herbert replied. 'It seems that Mr Speight was about to break the habit of a lifetime. On Sunday, I told you that the will could be amended or overridden by very simple means, and that this had been done in a couple of instances. The letter I received this morning, signed and witnessed, advised me of further significant changes. Gordon Pollock is now to inherit his father's London dwelling and all of his hotel properties, in addition to the Blacksmith and his ten per cent of the residue. However, he will no longer inherit the house in Ayr. That, together with Leo's home in the Bahamas, his personal possessions, a bequest of five million pounds and thirty per cent of the residue, to be funded by a ten-per-cent diminution of the shares bequeathed to the three minor children . . . Are you with me so far?'

Intrigued, Mann nodded.

'In accordance with the letter, that apportionment goes to a lady whom Mr Speight described as his fiancée.'

'Eh? Who the hell's she?' the DI gasped. 'And where did she come from?'

'See for yourself.'

Herbert pushed the letter across to her. She picked it up, stared, blinked, stared again, then dropped it.

'Bloody hell fire!'

Twenty-Seven

Dan Provan was buzzing as he walked into the Pitt Street building. Its frontage may have been red brick, incongruous and ugly, but he loved it for its city-centre location, and he was dreading the fast-approaching day when he and Lottie would be relocated to Dalmarnock, even though that meant a shorter commute for him.

A uniformed woman behind the reception desk called out to him as he bustled past her. 'Hey, Dan, there's . . .' but his mind was still in Regina's and he did no more than wave to her in passing as he headed for the stairway.

He took the steps two at a time, pleased that he was able to do it at his age, and swung round the corner and into his bustling open-plan office . . . to see Bob Skinner seated beside his desk as three detective constables busied themselves around the room.

He hid his surprise as he walked towards him. 'Hello again,' he said casually. 'I thought you didnae like Glasgow.'

'That was then and this is now,' the visitor replied. 'I've got an interest in this investigation, remember.'

'With respect, Bob, your insurance company has got fuck-all interest in Moscardinetto.'

'No,' he agreed, 'but my other client might have.' He laid his plastic badge on the DS's desk.

'Robert M Skinner, QPM, Consultant Director, the Security Service,' he read. 'You're finally comin' clean. Come on then, what's your real interest?'

'Let's just say I've got an eye on the people who weren't invited to Speight's going-away party.'

'Specifically?'

'I'm not sure yet, but once I know what the deceased Italian was up to, I might have a better idea.'

'It wouldnae have anything to do wi' yon man McCullough, would it? My young DC, Willie Gowans, went up to Perthshire to see him yesterday afternoon, him and his wife. We've got people talking to everybody on the guest list,' Provan explained. 'The laddie said he's never been told fuck-all before in so many different ways.'

'No, it wouldn't,' Skinner replied firmly. 'I wish I'd known, I could have saved you a trip. I saw them myself yesterday morning. I have a personal connection with Mrs McCullough.'

The DS stared at him. 'What? Are you related, like?'

He raised both eyebrows dramatically. 'Define "related", Dan. Mia McCullough is the mother of my oldest son.'

'The boy that went to . . .'

'That's right, Ignacio did time. Basically for protecting his mother. Her husband isn't the sort to volunteer information; if I'd known, I'd have advised you against sending a young officer to see him.'

'Ah had nobody else. Oh, I've heard of McCullough all right; is he no' the biggest fucking hoodlum on Tayside?'

'That's what they used to say. I believed it for a while, but now I'm not so sure he did everything they thought he did. His sister Goldie, now she was very illegal, but she died a wee while back.'

'Are you saying he's legit?'

'Now, definitely he is. He has reason to be; apart from his link to me, his granddaughter . . .' He stopped in mid sentence. 'You know young Sauce Haddock, through in Edinburgh?'

'Aye, bright laddie. A future ACC, they say.'

'I'd say higher than that, but whatever, the granddaughter, also named Cameron, is his other half. So, Dan, if you had Grandpa McCullough's name in your long list of suspects, I would take it off if I were you.'

'Why did you visit him if he's that innocent?'

'Because he's been involved peripherally in the boxing business and because he has interests in Russia. He knows people. One of the entities he knows is called Zirka. It's a fight promotion company, owned by Yevgeny Brezinski, Leo's old rival, and it stood to lose if his new venture had come to fruition.'

'Are you saying this Brezinski might have done Leo in to stop it?'

'It's doubtful that he knew about it in advance of the party, but if he did, it might provide a motive. The time frame makes it unlikely, though. Bryce Stoddart has been bunging Zirka for years as part of a deal over Leo's big fight with Brezinski in Russia. His retirement meant that would stop, but killing Leo wouldn't start it up again.'

'You're still interested, though,' Provan declared. 'I can tell.'

'Yes,' Skinner admitted, 'I am, but I'm more interested in the Italian at the moment. What have you dug up on him since I saw you last?'

'I've found out who he was with in that bar: Gordon Pollock, no less, Leo Speight's grown-up son.'

'Your source being the barman, I assume?'

'That's right.'

'He told me the boy was agitated.'

'Me too, but I'm not sure he was necessarily upset at Moscardinetto himself. Briggs, the bartender, thought the Italian was videoing the kid on his phone.'

'The same phone that vanished from his hotel room along with his laptop,' Skinner moaned. 'That's a bit of a bugger. I'd love to see that recording.'

'The guy was a film-maker,' Provan reminded him. 'He may have videoed all his meetings as a matter of course. We're only the polis and we film quite a few of ours.'

'For evidential purposes. Was that what he was doing, and if so, why?'

'When we find the guy that killed him, we might know.' He clicked on his mouse to waken his computer. 'The lassie in the CCTV monitoring centre said she'd send me a link to the footage I'm after. Wi' a bit of luck, it'll be here. I'm sure I know how he got in and out, through the lane then up and over the roof.'

'Is there footage from the lane?' Skinner asked.

'No, worse luck. There's a couple of private cameras, and I got another DC to check them out. The focus on one of them was too tight to pick up passers-by, and the other one didnae work.' He checked his mailbox, and nodded with satisfaction. 'That's fine, the link's there. I asked for the footage from the street cameras near West Campbell Street and Blythswood Street between three p.m. and seven thirty.'

'What do you mean by "near"?'

'The cameras arenae actually in those two streets,' the DS explained. 'They're in West George Street and St Vincent Street, but they'll show us everybody that turned intae our target area off those streets. So if we find somebody that goes out of shot in one camera but doesnae reappear in the other, well, we want to know who they are.'

'I get that,' Skinner said. 'Let's have a look.'

'I wanted to wait for Lottie before doin' that.' He checked his watch. 'She went to see Speight's lawyer, but she's takin' her time.'

'We can run it again for her when she gets here. Get on with it, Dan.'

Provan held up a restraining hand. 'Wait a minute. Daisy's email asks me to call her before we access the links. Daisy Millar; she's the manager in the CCTV operations centre that I spoke to last night.'

He picked up the phone on his desk and dialled a number. 'Daisy,' he began, 'what did you want to tell me?'

As he listened, a smile formed on his face, and grew progressively wider. 'Ms Millar,' he exclaimed when the message had been delivered, 'you and that centre of yours are the best thing that's happened to the Glasgow polis since they invented truncheons. Thanks.'

He replaced his phone and turned to his companion. 'She's worked her socks off for me,' he said. 'She's had her staff look at the footage and analyse it. In our time frame she's only identified seven people that fit the criteria we gave her, either going into West Campbell Street and Blythswood Street and not reappearing at all, or coming back into shot a while after their original appearance. One of them was you. She knows you by sight, you bein' famous an' all, so she left you out.'

'She shouldn't have,' Skinner observed.

'I told her you found the body, so that's okay. Of the other six, four were middle-aged women, a group of three that turned into West Campbell Street from St Vincent Street and a woman on her own that turned off West George Street five minutes later. They arrived at quarter to four, twenty-five minutes before Moscardinetto, and they all left, heading in the opposite directions, at ten past five. Daisy says that they were all wearing their finery, and she has them down as a group of friends meeting up in the hotel for afternoon tea. She's right; they couldnae have been going anywhere else.'

'Yes, agreed. Go on.'

'The fifth person was Raquel, the hotel duty manager, who started her shift at four. I warned Daisy that she'd be on it and gave her a description, so she excluded her as well. That leaves only one person.'

He stopped, and clicked on the link that showed on screen. As Skinner watched, a new window appeared, a still frame of a thoroughfare that he recognised as West Campbell Street. There was a single man in shot, his back to the camera. Provan hit an arrow at the foot of the screen; traffic began to flow, and the figure began to move, walking with a strange bouncing gait, then turning into West Campbell Street, appearing momentarily in profile then disappearing from view.

'Daisy says he never reappears at all. There isnae another building you can access in that stretch of the street, other than the hotel. So either he's staff, which he's no' because they're all accounted for, or he's a guest, which he's no' because they've all been interviewed, or he went intae the hotel bar or the restaurant and stayed there.' He winked. 'But he didnae do that either, because Daisy had her folk run the cameras right up till quarter past eight, when I cleared the hotel of everybody but staff and guests. When you exclude all those alternatives, chances are he's our man. The only question I'm asking myself is where did he go after he killed the Itie and left the hotel.'

'That's easy,' Skinner said. 'He's a clever bugger, and he realised that he'd been clocked by CCTV on the way in, so he left the area using the lane, having checked that it had no public space coverage.'

Provan beamed. 'It's you that's the clever bugger, Bob. Ah suppose that now you're goin' tae tell me you know who he is?'

'Correct on both counts, Detective Sergeant,' he replied, without the faintest flicker of a smile.

Twenty-Eight

Mario McGuire had a problem. Boredom.

Those who had known him all his life would have agreed, had it been put to them, that he had never been driven by personal ambition. Instead he had defied consistently the hopes and expectations of others by doing things his way with such determination that his wife's private nickname for him was 'Sinatra'.

He had grown up with a range of business opportunities within his family, but had ignored them all and confounded his mother by joining the police service. 'Because I want to work for people, Ma, to make their lives better, not to have people working for me to give me even more of what I've got already.'

For the first few years of his service he had been a happy and contented beat cop, alongside his lifelong friend Neil McIlhenney. For a while Neil had borne the wrath of Mrs McGuire for 'leading my son astray', until she realised that she had never seen two such contented young men and resigned herself to the truth: that whatever else life held in store for Mario, it would not be lived out as a director of her recruitment consultancy, or as a builder like his late father, or even as a player in his grandfather's delicatessen, importing and property businesses.

If Mario had never stepped above the lowest run in the ladder of policing, he would have felt fulfilled, but after a few years in the force, he came to the attention of the newly appointed head of major crimes in Edinburgh, Detective Superintendent Bob Skinner, and was swept into his circle, once again with McIlhenney at his side.

Guided by his hard and ruthless boss, he had never looked back from that day on. Nor had he looked forward, very often. The job pitched him into a series of situations that left him few opportunities to focus on career planning, even if he had been interested in plotting his future course.

He had loved almost every day of his time as a front-line CID officer, the exception being an incident that ended for him with a gunshot wound to the chest that would probably have killed a man less robustly built than he was. That had made him take a longer view of life, and had probably contributed to his drifting into marriage with his girlfriend of the moment, his colleague Margaret Rose. Their short-lived union had fallen apart in stressful circumstances and under the weight of a secret that both of them, and McIlhenney, would take with them as they passed into the great white light.

And yet, in spite of himself, in spite of his indifference to his own position in the service, Mario McGuire had risen through the ranks, always a step behind his ex-wife, and usually a step ahead of McIlhenney, until the two were separated by the latter's move to London and a command post in the Met.

He had shared Bob Skinner's antipathy to the Scottish national police service from the moment of its inception, but unlike his mentor he had never been able to resist opening whatever closed door lay in his path – a tendency that had proved fatal to Maggie's second husband, Stevie Steele – and when it had come into being he had been one of its first assistant chief constables, under the command of Andy Martin, another graduate of the Skinner academy of take-no-prisoners crime-fighting.

'It's ironic,' he had said to Neil McIlhenney, on one of the rare evenings when they and their wives met for dinner, 'that out of all of us – you, me, Maggie, Brian Mackie, Stevie, even big Bob himself – the only one with a desperate, driving ambition to wear a chief constable's magic hat was Andy Martin, and out of all of us, he was the one that turned out to be fucking awful at the job.'

Sir Andrew's tenure had been cut short. He was gone, first to a short-term lecturing contract at an American university, then, it seemed, to obscurity, out of touch with all his former colleagues and friends. They assumed that Karen, his former wife and the mother of his two children, who had rejoined the police service after their break-up, knew where he was, but nobody cared to ask her.

In his place, Maggie, the widow Steele, had been appointed chief constable, with Mario McGuire as her designated deputy in the command team, increasingly confined to an office in central Scotland, shuffling paper, reviewing CID performance statistics from Shetland to Stranraer and yearning for the company and camaraderie of active service in a bustling major crimes unit.

Whenever he could, he seized the chance to go to a crime scene, following the example that Bob Skinner had set on reaching command rank. On occasion, he had to fight off the urge to take operational command; the Leo Speight investigation had been one of those times, as had the Moscardinetto murder that Dan Provan had reported to him just before nine on the evening gone by.

He smiled as he recalled the conversation.

'Who found the body?'

'You're no' going to believe this, sir. It was Bob Skinner.'

'Fuck me!' Paula, nursing Eamon, their teething infant, had thrown him a frown. 'Why shouldn't I believe it, Sergeant?' he countered. 'Does this mean there's a link to the Speight homicide?'

'Ah think that's why he rang me. Because he thinks there is.'

'With respect, why you? Why not DI Mann?'

'Because I'm no' a single parent who's been working for forty-eight hours non-stop. But you really mean why no' you, sir, don't you? That's between you and big Bob, but I guess it was because he knew we needed bodies on the ground right away and the crime scene established and protected.'

'Do you need me there?' He had struggled to keep a pleading tone out of his voice.

There had been a silence, which he realised in the light of the following day had actually been the sound of Dan Provan trying to remember what tact might be.

'Well, sir,' the reply had come at last, 'this is a fairly enclosed space, and you would probably fill more of it than we can spare. So with respect, ye're probably better where you are.'

And so, instead of jumping into his Range Rover, he had phoned Skinner. 'Why the hell were you there?' he asked, going straight to the point – and being met halfway.

'Word for word,' he had replied, 'that's what I was intending to ask Moscardinetto, had he not frustrated me by being fucking dead.'

'Fine, but your brief from Mrs Dennis and MI5 is to look for links to international organised crime. This guy was a film director, not a criminal.'

'The guy was an anomaly, Mario, the only person on Leo Speight's guest list with no obvious reason for being there. As for him being a film director, yes, that's true, but it's all I know about him. I'm going to ask Amanda tomorrow if she can find out what else he might have been.'

'Let me know what she comes up with. It could be convenient if he turned out to have been in someone else's gunsights, someone with nothing to do with Speight. I take it there's no chance of this being a bungled robbery?'

'None. Got to go now; I'm losing signal.'

McGuire sat at his desk, frowning as he replayed the conversations in his head, and even more frustrated that he was so far away from the action. Indeed, he had risen from his chair and was reaching for his jacket, his out-tray full and ready for removal, when his phone rang.

He snatched it up. 'Yes?' he snapped testily.

'Sorry, sir,' his assistant said. 'I've got Mr Dorward on the line from the Crime Campus. He says he needs to speak to the chief or you, and she's got the Police Authority meeting all morning.'

'Really? It's that important?'

'He says it is. I asked him what it was about, but he said it was confidential, chief officers only.'

'Ah, bugger it,' McGuire growled. Whatever else he might have been – and he had earned a few choice suggestions in his time – he knew that Arthur Dorward was not a drama queen. If he had gone directly to the top of the tree, and he had done so before, there would be a compelling reason for it. 'Put him through, Jane.'

He slumped back into his chair once more. 'Where's the national emergency?' he sighed as the senior SOCO came on the line.

'Right where you live,' his caller retorted. 'National emergency might be a bit strong, but it is fucking sensitive. It's to do with the Speight investigation.'

'Arthur,' McGuire exclaimed, 'I've told you already that I can't order the lab to drop everything else and focus on tox testing the Ayr samples. They're in the queue with everything else.'

'I know that and I understand it; so do Mann and Provan. This is different.'

'Go on then,' the DCC sighed.

'There was other testing to be done from the house,' Dorward continued. 'As usual, the investigation team need to put a name to everyone who's been in the place, using fingerprints and DNA analysis. My people collected samples from every room. We've processed them all, and identified almost all of them. Those that we haven't are prints we found on lavvy brushes, and they'll belong to the cleaners, as they usually do.

'Of the rest, there's one name that stands out. No, that's wrong. It isn't just standing out: it's jumping up and down and it's fucking screaming at me. What's it screaming? Detective Chief Inspector Sandra Bulloch, that's what.'

McGuire stared at the wall as he absorbed what he had been told, then he paused as he thought back to the previous Saturday afternoon.

'Jesus, Arthur,' he grumbled, 'what are you on about? Sandra was at the crime scene. Obviously you didn't see her.'

'Oh I saw her, Mario, no question about that. But there's more.'

Twenty-Nine

Skinner had to hold the line for three minutes and fifteen seconds, counted off on the display of his phone, before he was connected to the director general of MI5. 'Sorry, Bob,' she said, when she took his call. 'The Home Secretary takes precedence even over you.'

'That's okay,' he laughed. 'I know my place. Amanda, I need some digging done. We have a second body in this investigation; that is to say, I'm confident that the two are linked. It's that of a man named Aldorino Moscardinetto —'

'No!' she exclaimed, interrupting him. 'Don't tell me that. I'm a big fan of his work. He's one of the most provocative film-makers of his generation.'

'In that case, he provoked someone into cutting off his air supply with a ligature in his hotel room last night. I know that I could pull his biography off Wikipedia or IMDB in about a minute and a half, but I'm more interested in anything I might not find there. Can you help?'

'If there is anything,' she replied, 'then given time I'll find it for you – through colleagues in Europol and Italy if I have to. You say this killing is linked to Speight. Are you sure about that?'

'It has to be. When I work out how, I'll let you know.'

'Where's this going, Bob? Is there an organised crime connection, as we thought there might be?'

'In my opinion there could be, but that's all I want to say for now. I don't want to drip-feed you information that might or might not be important. When I'm ready to report, I will.'

'You're not getting personally exposed, Bob?' she asked, with a trace of anxiety.

He laughed her worries away. 'I'm less personally exposed now than I have been for the last thirty years. I spent a career chasing bad people who knew who I was and where I lived. You spooks work in the shadows where nobody can see you. Now,' he continued, 'before I go, I have another request. I would like to know everything there is to know about a man called Billy Swords. That's the name I know him by; it may be genuine, it may not. He's known to the public as a ring announcer in boxing and mixed martial arts. I want the rest. All about him, please, including phone activity and whether he took a flight from Scotland to anywhere on Saturday morning.'

'That's all? There is this myth, you know, that the Security Service can see everywhere and get to know everything, sometimes things that aren't even there. You'd be amazed how many people believe that.'

'I wouldn't be amazed at all,' he laughed, 'because I'm one of them.'

A 'call waiting' tone sounded on his phone; he held it out, looked at the screen and read the caller name. 'Amanda, I have to go,' he said. 'There aren't many people I'd cut you off for, but this is one of them. Think of it,' he chuckled, 'as me getting back at you for letting the Home Secretary keep me waiting.'

He thumbed two icons on the screen, then put the mobile back to his ear. 'Maggie,' he exclaimed, 'where's the fire? With your workload, you don't have time for social calls. Come to think of it,' he added, 'you never did.'

'That hasn't changed,' Scotland's chief constable replied. 'I've got a major situation, and I need your help.'

'I've retired!' he protested. 'Left the service. Been made redundant. However you frame it, I'm not a cop any longer. Plus, I'm rather busy, as you know, helping out somebody else.'

'All that stuff I know,' Margaret Steele agreed, 'but there's nobody else I'd trust with this. Also, if this isn't related to your remit from Amanda Dennis, it isn't a million miles away. Please, Bob?'

'Okay,' he conceded, 'you've got my attention. Tell me about it.'

'It's better that Mario does. He's with me; he brought the situation to me.'

If it's something he couldn't deal with on his own authority, Skinner thought, it must be serious.

'As you wish.'

'I'll put you on speaker.'

'Morning, Bob,' McGuire began, his voice reverberating. Skinner knew that his friend was not normally one for the basic pleasantries; there was tension in his tone.

'Same to you, big fella. Now what the fuck is it?'

'Trouble. Within the last hour I've had two phone calls, and deemed them serious enough to call the chief out of the Police Authority meeting. The first was from the legend that is Arthur Dorward, who's heading the forensic investigation of the Leo Speight murder. His people went all over the house, they combed everything, as they always do, to try to identify everyone who'd been there and left traces behind them. That search included the victim's bedroom.'

'You're going to tell me he wasn't a monk; we knew that already.'

'Correct. In his bed, on his sheets, they discovered pubic hair and bodily fluids, evidence of a recent sexual encounter. They also found a partial thumbprint on the switch of a bedside lamp, and other prints around it.'

'Any way of knowing how recent?' Skinner asked.

'Yes. Speight employed a cleaning company. Whether he was there or not, they went in every Monday. If his bed had been slept in, they changed the sheet, pillowcases, duvet cover.'

'How did they know for sure that it had been?'

'They put a paper seal on when they do it. If it's broken . . .'

'Monday night on, then; go on.'

'Dorward's lot profiled the samples, digitised the prints and ran everything against the database, and came up with a name.'

'Yes?' He sensed that McGuire was ramping up the tension deliberately.

'The second call,' the DCC continued, 'was from Lottie Mann, phoning from the office of Leo Speight's personal lawyer in Glasgow. She'd just received by post an amendment to his will, signed by him and properly witnessed by Trudi Pollock. That ties in with what Ms Pollock told Mann and Provan about her last meeting with Speight. The amendment brings in a new beneficiary, a substantial one at that, described in the letter as Leo Speight's fiancée.'

'You're not going to tell me it's a bloke?' Skinner grunted.

'No, I'm about to tell you it's Detective Chief Inspector Sandra Bulloch.'

'Ouch!' he gasped. 'I did not see that one coming.'

'Who could have?'

'What does she stand to inherit?'

'Millions. Squillions.'

'That changes everything. At the moment, I have a line of enquiry into the Moscardinetto murder that points me in the direction of the boxing business. I haven't fitted all the pieces together yet, but Dan Provan and I are pretty sure we know who killed the Italian. I've got MI5 looking into the suspect's background; I won't guess at what they're likely to come up with, but it's led us away from a domestic solution to the Speight murder. What you've just told me makes me think that the investigation has to look again at that option. More than that: if the team begin by looking at those who've most to gain from Leo Speight's death, it puts Sandra Bulloch right at the top of the list.'

'Exactly,' McGuire agreed. 'And that's why we're calling you. Fuck the niceties, we need you involved. Lottie Mann can't interview her own boss under caution . . . well she could, but we wouldn't put either of them in that situation. You can. You have the weight.'

'Can I caution her, legally?'

'You won't have to. We'll sit Brian Mackie alongside you at the interview. He doesn't know Sandra at all, and he's an ACC. He can administer the caution; in theory he'll be conducting the interview, but in practice you will.'

'My status being?'

'What does it say on the Security Service credentials you're carrying? Consultant director, something like that?'

'Yes.'

'On the record, that's how you'll be described.'

'And if it does go all the way and Sandra is charged with Speight's murder,' Skinner asked, 'and it goes to trial . . . how are you going to describe me in court when I have to give evidence?'

'We don't care about that,' Steele intervened. 'This is about more than criminality, Bob. The integrity of this force is on the line, too. We need someone there who won't go easy on her but with whom Bulloch can empathise. It might encourage her to be more open in her responses. She used to be your assistant; there's nobody better placed than you to take this on.'

'What does the fiscal say?'

'I don't care,' she replied. 'I learned that from you,' she added. 'It's my officer, my force and this has happened on my watch. It's my shout.'

He had taken the call in Lottie Mann's office. The door swung open; the DI stared at him as she entered, stopped, then stepped back out again.

'Okay,' he said, 'I'll do it, but here are my rules. One, before we get to an interview under caution, I see Sandra on my own. If I believe following our conversation that it's necessary to go formal, I will tell you. Two, my summary of that conversation and any subsequent statement that Sandra may choose to make will be reported to Lottie Mann, as SIO. I won't allow her to be sidelined. Three, if necessary I want to talk to Sandra's sister as well. Four, you say eff-all about this to the fiscal; I know him and I don't want him insisting that an advocate depute sits in on the interview because a police officer's involved. Does any of that give you a problem?'

'None of it,' the chief constable replied.

'Me neither,' McGuire grunted in the background.

'Tomorrow morning,' Skinner declared. 'Ten a.m., Wednesday. Mario, tell Sandra to report to your office but don't tell her why. I'll see her there. She won't be expecting me and I want to catch her raw.'

'She's not dumb,' the DCC pointed out. 'She may have

guessed that Dorward would put her in the house. She might bring a lawyer.'

'She won't. That would be a show of weakness, and she isn't weak. Let me know when it's set up.'

'What if she refuses to talk to you?'

'Then you will arrest her after all, and she will be cautioned. You're not short of reasons why you could. Let me know when time and place are confirmed. In the meantime, I've got to brief Lottie Mann on what's happening, and why. The big lass isn't as confident as you might think. She's got other stuff happening in her life just now; the last thing she needs is to feel that her bosses don't have total confidence in her.'

Thirty

'I'm slipping,' Dan Provan murmured. 'I should have known that something didn't fit.'

Mann peered at him. 'Did you leave your crystal ball in Australia?'

'I'm serious. Remember on Saturday, when we were all at the crime scene, when Sandra told us about her sister and Speight?'

'Yes. So?'

'She said there was a photo on the fridge of the wee lass, Raeleen. And there was, taken when she was two, less than a year ago. So how the hell did she know it was there? Faye and Leo were at odds for a couple of years. What reason could Sandra have had for being at his house and having seen that picture? How would she even have kent who it was?'

The DI nodded. 'You're right. You are slipping.'

He winked at her. 'It was probably just the jet lag. What's your excuse?'

'Are you happy with what's proposed, Lottie?' Skinner asked.

'Completely,' she replied. 'I'm relieved, to be honest. I was expecting a formal statement from her for the record. I'm glad I haven't had it.'

'I can guess why,' he said. 'If she'd given you a statement that didn't disclose the extent of her relationship with Speight, that would have been potentially criminal. She'd have withheld information from a police investigation of a serious crime.'

'What if we get one from her between the now and you seeing her the morrow?'

He looked the detective sergeant in the eye. 'If it's drafted by her or a lawyer, it'll be between you and her, until you choose to enter it into the record of the investigation. It won't have been made under oath, so you'll have a degree of flexibility. I'll say no more than that.'

'You don't have to,' Mann told him. 'I'll deal with it if it happens.' She glanced at her colleague, 'And when I say I will deal with it, that's what I mean, Dan. It'll be my decision and mine alone.'

'No it fuckin' won't,' he growled. 'If anything gets shredded by accident, it'll be me that does it. I've got thirty-five years' service and a full pension, and if I'm threatened with demotion, I walk out the door.' She made to react, but he held up a hand to stop her. 'This isnae a debate, Detective Inspector; it's me bein' insubordinate, and there's no bugger better at that than yours truly. Anyway, it's academic. She's had three days to give us that statement and she still hasnae done it. She could have handed it in here at any time, but she hasn't, and you can bet that as soon as she gets the summons from the DCC, the thought will go out of her mind. Sandra's a clever woman. She'll know she's not being called to Stirling for a job appraisal.'

'In a way, she is,' Skinner pointed out. 'She's already withheld information from the investigation.' He shrugged. 'But will she really give a fuck about that? She's about to inherit a fortune. Is she going to keep her job on? Will she be a police officer by the time they can put a disciplinary hearing together? Quite possibly not.'

Provan laughed, loudly enough for two detective constables on the far side of the room to turn to see what spectacle they were missing. 'You're a hell of a man to be sayin' that, Bob. Look at you! You must have the biggest pension in the history of the Scottish police service, you've got a part-time job wi' that newspaper group that probably pays you even more than that, and yet you're still here, up to your nuts in a double homicide investigation. Why? Because you can't fuckin' help it! What makes you think Sandra Bulloch will be any different?'

'Good point,' he conceded. 'Not that I'm confirming your wild allegations about my wealth. And even suppose you were right,' he added, 'how many kids have you got, Dan, school age or younger? None, the last I heard. I've got five, counting the one at university.' The smile left his face. 'But that's us, and it has nothing to do with Sandra. You are right, I won't take any preconceptions into our conversation. Yes, she was my assistant in the old Strathclyde force, but not for very long. I mustn't presume to know her. What I must do, initially at least, is show her the consideration that's due to someone who's recently bereaved. I've been there myself, so I know how it feels. It's over twenty-five years now,' he said softly, 'but the memory of that never fades, no matter what happens afterwards in your life.'

'Sorry,' the DS murmured. 'I'm a cheeky little bastard.'

'Don't worry about it. You're still in one piece, and I'm better prepared for my meeting tomorrow. Today, though; where do you go from here?'

'We haul in the man Billy Swords,' Provan replied. 'We've got him on CCTV,' he explained to Mann, 'approaching the

Stadium Hotel just before Moscardinetto was murdered.'

Skinner frowned. 'Can I make a suggestion about that?' he ventured. 'A request even, wearing my Security Service hat?'

'Of course.'

'I'd like you to let him run for a bit. Clearly there's more to the man than we know at this moment, and I'd like to fill in some of the blanks. I've already started the ball rolling on that, but there's more needs doing. Do you have the resources to keep him under permanent observation?'

'Yes,' the DI replied. 'On this one I can get whatever I ask for.'

'Then I suggest you do that. You'll find him at Leo's Loch Lomondside hotel, Beedham's; that's unless he's checked out. My guess is that he won't have. Bryce Stoddart is staying in Scotland until Speight's lawyer's ready to publish the will, and I suspect that Swords will stick with him.'

'Okay, we'll start there. If he has gone . . .'

'Let me know, and my friends in the south will find him for you.' Skinner paused. 'Then there's his phone,' he added. 'You'll want to know who he's spoken to since . . . how long? Let's say the last month at least. If you can identify all the calls made through the cell closest to Beedham's since Stoddart and his party checked in there, you should be able to identify his by a process of elimination.' He stopped and smiled. 'Or I could ask MI5 to do that too.'

'Yes please,' Mann said.

'Okay, I will. You should get on to BT and get a list of every call made from the Beedham's landline over that same period.'

'Wait a minute,' Provan exclaimed. 'All this cloak-and-dagger stuff might be fun, big fella, but Lottie's the one that's under pressure to get a result. We know, near as damn it for certain, who killed the Italian. Like as not he did Speight as well, so why the fuck should we play these games when we've got grounds to arrest him right now? Suppose we let him carry on and he kills someone else? We're the ones that'll be out front covered in ordure. You and your spook pal'll be nowhere to be seen.'

'I can't argue with that, Detective Sergeant,' Skinner conceded; then his eyes, and his voice, hardened as his tolerance expired, 'but I can offer you years of experience at command rank, taking decisions that were, with respect, way above your pay grade. What I'm suggesting to DI Mann is what I'd do if I was leading this investigation. It's also something I'd authorise if I was her chief constable and she came to me for permission. Since I mentored her present chief constable, I'm pretty confident that Mrs Steele would agree with me!'

'That's me put in my place then.' The DS sulked at the reproof.

'Well and truly,' Mann said. 'We do what Mr Skinner suggests. And that's not a debate either, by the way,' she added.

'Don't take it to heart,' his protagonist told him. 'Yes, you've got grounds to detain Swords for questioning in the Moscardinetto killing, and to take the fingerprints that will put him in the room, but you're nowhere close to having him for the Speight homicide as well, not without much more evidence than you have already.'

'I sense you're not convinced that he did that,' the DI ventured.

'I'm not,' Skinner admitted. 'It doesn't sit right with me. Swords – assuming we're right and his presence in that CCTV shot isn't just a massive coincidence – went to that hotel to steal something. The time shown on the public space camera, set alongside the time we know that the victim got back to the

Stadium, is proof enough for me that Moscardinetto found Swords searching his room. Clearly they struggled and Swords overpowered him, but it's unlikely he went there to kill him; more likely he went to steal the laptop.'

'How did he know which was Moscardinetto's room?' Provan asked, his interest renewed.

'Did Gino Butler say that he did all the bookings?'

'Aye.'

'Then speak to Trudi Pollock again. Ask her if Swords could have had access to the list of guest accommodation or if he just asked her straight out.'

'Maybe speak to Butler instead,' the DS suggested.

'Hell, no. You should pull his phone records as well, landline and mobile. Mr Butler needs further examination. As well as being Leo's best mate, he had access to everything. He knew where everybody was, and when.'

'Maybe we should do more,' Mann suggested. 'Now that we've seen the will and know who the beneficiaries are, we should treat all of the adults as suspects, pull everyone's phone records as far as we can.' She paused. 'Well, maybe not Rae Letts.'

'Maybe yes,' Skinner cautioned. 'She really loved Leo; if he told her he was going to marry someone else, you never know. Logistically, though,' he conceded, 'it would have been difficult for her to organise and carry out the killing.'

'Let's start with the Brits,' she decided. 'Thanks for that input, Mr Skinner. What's your agenda for the rest of the day?'

'I have an appointment in Edinburgh. Everyone we've spoken to seems to agree that Charles Baxter was the man behind Leo Speight's real wealth, his property empire. I thought I'd find out why he wasn't at the party on Friday. But before I go, I suggest you think about Augusta Cambridge, the host's painter friend. She was in a prime position while it was all happening, creating a record of the event. That means she was actively watching the crowd all night. It might be worth asking her what she saw.'

Thirty-One

Bob Skinner had been around Edinburgh for long enough to remember when the men who created the city's wealth, and their own, were based in the Georgian buildings of the New Town, in the two great squares, and George Street, which connected them. The age of information technology had transformed the city, replacing the old with modernity of questionable taste, but LJMcF, a global practice of property advisers, had bucked the trend by adapting its headquarters to meet modern needs and staying where it was, frowning across Charlotte Square at Bute House, the official residence of Scotland's first minister, with which the former chief constable was very familiar.

While the hidden infrastructure of the office was brand new, its fittings had kept faith with its origins, at the insistence of Historic Scotland. The drawing room remained as its architect had designed it, and it was there that tall, portly, three-piece-suited Charles Baxter greeted his visitor, gazing at him over the top of a pair of narrow gold-framed spectacles.

'This is something of an honour, Mr Skinner,' he declared in a cut-glass Edinburgh Academy accent as he offered his hand. 'It's amazing to me that in all the years you were top cop here, we never actually met.'

'Not that many years,' Skinner countered. 'For most of that time I was the second top cop, after Jimmy Proud.'

'Ah yes, Sir James. I'd heard he wasn't too well. Prostate cancer, is it?'

'That's right, but don't count him out. He's had surgery and follow-up treatment, a tough pathway, but it's leading him towards recovery. We live in the same village, so I see him regularly.'

'Do you miss it?' Baxter asked. 'Your old police force, I mean. I recall you being pretty vocal when this new creature was first mooted.'

'Too bad the politicians didn't listen,' Skinner grumbled. 'But that's all history; the police service is what it is, and after a shaky start it's in good hands. To answer your question, of course I miss it, but even if it was still there in its original form, with a chief constable based down at Fettes, that person wouldn't be me. I'd have moved on anyway. I never liked the role; I found it too constricting. When I was appointed, Jimmy, my predecessor, told me to forget convention and do it my own way. I tried, but there are things that can't be avoided; for example, keeping the city councillors happy.'

'I know that one,' the surveyor agreed. 'It's a big part of this firm's life too. That said, we can do it in ways you couldn't. I'm not talking brown envelopes, you understand, but we have other ways of making them feel important and maintaining their goodwill. Come,' he said, 'let's sit.'

The room was dominated by an oval dining table, but two high-backed chesterfield chairs were set on either side of a high fireplace in which logs burned in an iron basket, a welcoming contrast to the damp chill of the day outside. A Thermos coffee jug sat on a low trestle, with two cups. 'Yes?' Baxter asked, loosening the lid.

Skinner shook his head. 'I'd better not. I had some with lunch up in my office, and my wife has me on a ration.'

'Ah. Is the lady a dietician?'

'Worse, she's a pathologist,' he chuckled.

'You've put me off it now,' his host murmured, replacing the jug and settling back into his chair. 'Now, sir, why have you come to see me? Does InterMedia need some advice about the building up at Fountainbridge? I know you're a director of the group. Are you thinking about a sale and lease-back, perhaps, to raise some cash? Or restructuring existing borrowing?'

'We have no need. The group's in a very healthy cash position, so healthy that we took advantage of the slump in sterling to clear off a historic mortgage on Fountainbridge. The fact is, Mr Baxter, I haven't come to talk about my business, but yours. I'm involved – on the periphery, let's say – in the investigation into the death of Leo Speight. I understand he was a client of yours.'

Deep frown lines creased Baxter's forehead. 'He was more than a client. He was a friend, a very good friend. We got on like a house on fire, surprising I suppose, given the difference in our professions and our backgrounds.'

'And yet you weren't at his retirement party last Friday. Why was that?'

'There's a simple explanation. I was at a rival event, my parents' golden wedding anniversary, in Prestonfield House. You say you're involved on the periphery, Mr Skinner. Can I hazard a guess and suggest that you're representing the interests of Leo's insurers, given that there seems to be a degree of mystery about his death?'

Skinner grinned. 'I wouldn't discourage that speculation,' he said.

'I know about the policy,' Baxter confessed, 'the one that covered the outside possibility of his being killed in the boxing ring. He told me about it when it was set up. I've seen it and I know exactly what it says, so I'm going to assume that your brief is to establish that he died of natural causes, or if not, by accident or misadventure.' He gazed across the gap between the chairs. 'How did my friend die?' he asked. 'The police have described it as "unexplained". Are you able to tell me?'

'No, I'm not, but I'm not being obstructive or perverse. The police are waiting, impatiently I can tell you, for some lab work to be completed, hence that description.'

'What does that mean? Does it rule out any connection with his career?'

'The pathologist didn't find any; he's a top man, and believe me, he looked. My role in the investigation,' he continued, choosing his words carefully, 'requires me to assume that the autopsy is going to tell us stuff we won't like to hear. If that happens, I want to be prepared for it, so I'm looking into every aspect of Leo's life.'

'All I can tell you,' the surveyor replied, 'relates to his property portfolio. Leo never involved me with the part of his life that generated his wealth. He said I didn't need to know how it was earned, because that was tough and bloody. My job was to help him invest it and make it grow.'

'In that case, how did you come to see that insurance policy?'

'It had to be disclosed to a lender in a property deal, along with all his other policies. It was a very big deal.'

'How wealthy was Leo?' Skinner asked. 'I've heard all sorts of figures over the last few days, but nobody really seems to know.'

'No, because they couldn't,' Baxter agreed. 'The media estimates you read vary between fifty and seventy million, but they're all based on reports of the money he earned from his pay-per-view fights. They take no account of his property holdings, which were considerable and international. I've spent this week trying to work that out, and I'm nowhere near finished. Personally he owned homes in London, Ayr and the Bahamas.'

'Where was his tax base?'

'Monaco, although very few people knew that. Through his property company he owned a hotel there, near the football stadium. It was one of his first investments, and he kept an apartment on the top floor. Officially, that's where he lived, but he was on the move all the time. That said, in the last year of his life he spent more time in Scotland than he should have. I think there was a lady involved.'

'Did he mention a name?'

'No, but that wasn't unusual; he was discreet. I only found out about his American girlfriend, the mother of his youngest child, when he told me to find a family home near Las Vegas and put it in her name.' He smiled sadly. 'I did well by him. Our San Francisco office found the property and did the deal, and I visited after Rae and the baby had moved in. They made a nice little family, and Leo was clearly very comfortable with her. I'd hoped that it might become permanent, but Rae told me from the start that wouldn't happen.'

Skinner caught his eye. 'How did she feel about that? Did you sense any resentment?'

'None at all. She trusted Leo to look after her and the child, and that was enough for her.'

'What about Faye Bulloch?'

'For some reason she stopped trusting him, and demanded more than he was prepared to give her – specifically, his name. He was generous in all other respects, but that was a line he drew in the sand some time ago. She shouldn't have gone to that lawyer; it was a bad idea, or she was badly advised.'

'The property holdings you mentioned earlier; how extensive are they?'

'They're considerable. He owned ten hotels around the world, and had just begun construction on another site in the Bahamas. That included four in Scotland: the Blacksmith, where the party was; Beedham's by Loch Lomond; a place called Black Shield Lodge—'

'In Perthshire?' Skinner exclaimed.

'Yes, you know it?'

He nodded.

'He acquired that three months ago, from a man named McCullough. The chap has a certain reputation, so I was wary of him, but everything was kosher. The only condition was that he and his wife have a life rent on a villa on the estate. McCullough told me he intended to put the money into a trust fund for his granddaughter, since he knew she'd have no interest in running an hotel. It's already an impressive property; Leo's intention was to make it even more so, a rival to Gleneagles, but with a casino licence as well. He had friends in politics and entertainment, and was fairly confident of securing one.'

Aileen and Joey, Skinner thought, as a small smile flickered across his face. Everyone was at that party for a reason, it seemed.

'Four hotels in Scotland, you said?' he continued.

'That's correct. The fourth is a shoddy place in the middle of Glasgow called the Stadium. Leo bought it, on my recommendation, from the previous owner's administrator. We completed the deal last week and take possession on Friday. He got it for a song; our plan was to refurbish it to the same standard as Beedham's, hire a Michelin-star chef, and run it in the same way. He intended to close the place at the end of the month – which reminds me, as executor of that part of his estate, I must tell the staff.'

The surveyor smiled at his own cleverness. In his visitor's mind several pieces of a jigsaw clicked into place. 'Have you ever heard Leo mention a man called Aldorino Moscardinetto?' he asked.

'Never,' Baxter declared. 'If he had, I'd have remembered all those syllables. Who is he?'

'An Italian film-maker, also a guest at the Blacksmith party last Friday. As far as I'm aware, he was the only one to have been put up in the Stadium rather than in the venue or in Beedham's, as the boxing people were.'

'I suppose he was at the foot of the pecking order. Had I been able to go, I'd have been put up in the Blacksmith. Is it important?'

At the foot of the pecking order, Skinner thought; or Leo wanted to keep him apart from everyone else.

'Just wondered,' he replied casually. 'You were taking me through the property holdings.'

'Yes: ten hotels, four in Scotland, the one I mentioned in Monaco, one in Windsor, one in Cheshire, one just outside Toronto, one on Vancouver Island and one in Charleston, USA. Each of them I sourced for him, then handled all aspects of the deal. As his success grew in the ring, so his property empire grew outside. The Bahamian resort was going to be special; I'm not sure what'll happen with that. The funding's in place and the work's under way.' He frowned. 'That one's unstoppable; I'll have to think long and hard whether to find a buyer or to proceed. I'm expecting to be named as a trustee in Leo's will,' he explained, 'to administer the property holdings on behalf of the minor beneficiaries – his children, I imagine.'

'You imagine? When did he last discuss the will with you?'

'First half of last year; just after he signed the contracts for his retirement fight. He asked me to make as sure as I could that Faye couldn't get her hands on any of the property holdings, regardless of how the court case went. Those went beyond hotels,' he added. 'There were offices also, in Scotland, London, Toronto, New York; high-value premium rental properties. The building in which we are sitting, Mr Skinner, is owned by Leo Speight Holdings (Scotland) Limited, a subsidiary of the parent group, Leo Speight Commercial PLC, a company registered in the Bahamas.'

'Formidable,' Skinner said. 'What's it all worth?'

'As I said, that's what I'm trying to assess. What I can tell you is that the insurance policy you're interested in is just a drop in the ocean. Leo's business was highly geared; that is to say it was supported by borrowing from financial providers around the world. All that borrowing was underpinned by life insurance policies. Whatever Leo's net worth was when he was alive – I'd have put that at around a hundred and fifty million – his estate's not going to be valued at anything short of twice that amount.'

'Three hundred million?'

Baxter nodded. 'Gets your attention, doesn't it?'

'It does. It also makes me wonder who else could have been aware of those numbers.'

'That would depend on who knew the totality of Leo's property holdings, and I'm not sure that anyone did, other than me. His man Butler was never involved in that side of his life, and his corporate structure wasn't exactly designed for transparency. What are you getting at, Mr Skinner?'

'Nothing yet. I'm just lining things up in my mind. The deals he did, or that you did for him, were any of them confrontational?'

'None at all; they were all straightforward purchases: willing vendors, willing buyer. We never beat anyone down on price, never haggled. I only recommended a purchase if I was certain that it had medium- to long-term growth potential. There were only two exceptions to that: Beedham's was a country house, privately owned and in disrepair. We took a punt on it, because there was no certainty of planning consent to turn it into an hotel. That said, if we hadn't been given approval, Leo could still have restored it and sold it on at a substantial profit – or lived in it had he chosen.'

'The other exception?'

'That was the Stadium Hotel. The previous owner had gone bust. He thought his name as a footballer guaranteed him success, but as is usually the case, he was wrong. He was undercapitalised from the outset. He called in administrators, but that was only a delaying tactic to fend off liquidation. I made them an offer that would let him pay off his creditors, but no more than that. With no other bidders in sight, they accepted. The owner was hopping mad. He actually came here and threatened me; last Wednesday, it was. He told me that if I didn't improve the offer, all sorts of bad things would happen.'

'Police involved?'

'No need. A couple of my younger colleagues saw him off. Former rugby players; a few of those move into my profession. They may not be the best valuers, but they have their uses from time to time. For example, they're great at networking.'

'Is the deal complete?'

'Leo and I signed up and paid up last Thursday. The administrators are still in charge, but we're due to take possession on Friday after the staff have been paid off.'

'What's the previous owner's name?'

'Arthur Mustard. He's a Trinidadian, plays for a club called Merrytown. You may have heard of him.'

'I have. Did he know of Leo's involvement?'

'The administrators did, so I imagine he did too. Does that interest you?'

'Not much, but his threats might interest the police. He was right about one thing, though. A bad thing has happened, in addition to Leo's death.'

'What do you mean?'

Skinner reached across, plucked a copy of that morning's *Saltire* from the row of black-top newspapers on the oval table. The front page carried a report on Aldorino Moscardinetto's murder.

'You might want to read that,' he said. 'If you had, you'd have known what I mean. I hope you were planning to rip up the carpets, because they're awful, but there's one that does need replacing for sure.'

Thirty-Two

Augusta Cambridge had been hard to find. A call to the Blacksmith had ascertained that she had checked out of the hotel after breakfast on the previous Saturday morning, the day after the party, driving away in an old boxy Volvo estate. The manager remembered her departure, and the time, because he had shown her how to access the motorway south without hitting the Glasgow traffic.

'Through East Kilbride,' he told Provan. 'At that time of day you can save half an hour by going that way.'

She had given no address on checking in, as the booking had been made by Trudi Pollock, but the number of the Volvo was in the hotel records. The DS had hoped it would take him straight to her, but he was frustrated when a DVLA check revealed that the car was owned by a company, Cambridge Prints Limited, registered in the Isle of Man.

He had made three fruitless calls to numbers taken from the artist's Wikipedia page, but none of them had been accurate. He had managed to locate the publisher of the most recent coffee-table collection of her work, but she had referred him not to the artist herself but to her agent, a woman based in Bath, whose number went straight to voicemail.

Finally he had done the obvious. Trudi Pollock had picked up on the first ring. 'Miss Cambridge? Yes, I've got her contact details. She lives in Wiltshire. What do you need? I can give you her landline, her mobile and her email address . . . and her postal address if you need that too.'

He had noted them all down. Before trying to contact the artist, he had gone back to the online encyclopedia to learn a little of the woman he would be calling. He discovered that she was fifty-one years old, a Jamaican-born British citizen who had been an art director with a London advertising agency, and a part-time portrait painter, before finding an even more lucrative career. She had been commissioned to paint a series of studies of West Indian sprinters competing at the Athens Olympiad and had captured their movement so effectively that her work had won international attention. Within a year she had left the advertising industry behind, prints of her work were selling worldwide, and her lasting fame had been sealed by a follow-up series of images, created at Super Bowl XXXIX in Jacksonville, Florida, recording New England Patriots' victory over Philadelphia Eagles.

The Wikipedia entry noted that her rise to fame had been matched by that of Leo Speight, and that she had captured several of his fights, the last being his farewell performance in Glasgow against the American upstart Mario Fonsecco.

'Not quite up to date,' he murmured as he closed the entry, wondering as he did how much her final images of the doomed fighter would earn her in print form.

He tried the landline number first, to be greeted by a call-vetting system, the kind that always tried his patience. Nevertheless he waited for the tone, and when it sounded, announced himself in the most formal accent he could summon as 'Detective

Sergeant Provan of the Scottish Police Service, calling regarding the death of Leo Speight.'

He held the line, as the guardian requested, for a further twenty seconds, until finally a real human being answered.

'Mr Provan,' she said, 'I am Inge Bergvik, Augusta's partner. She is devastated by poor Leo's death. Is it really necessary for you to speak to her? There is nothing she can tell you.'

'That might be the case,' he agreed, 'but we still need to talk to her. We've been a wee bit guarded in what we've said to the press, because our lab's been dragging its feet, but we're treating the death as murder. Miss Cambridge was at the party the night before, and she was one of the last people to speak to Mr Speight. We need to know what they talked about, and more besides. If she can help us,' he cajoled, 'I'm sure she'd want to.'

'I am shocked, Detective,' the woman replied. He wondered what nationality she was, which Scandinavian country had issued her passport. Wikipedia had offered no personal information on the artist. 'Of course Augusta will help if she can. But please can she have time to compose herself?'

'Of course.'

'How do you wish to do this?' she asked.

'Normally we'd visit her,' the DS told her, 'but given the distance involved, could we use a video link, Skype or FaceTime, one of those.'

'We can do FaceTime. You will need an email address.'

'I have it. Look, my DI's away from her desk just now. Can I call you in fifteen minutes?'

'Yes,' Bergvik agreed. 'That will be acceptable. Until then.' She hung up with a click.

'Progress,' Provan sighed, replacing his handset and leaning back in his chair. Even as he did so, he heard the sound of another phone, coming from Lottie's office. With a muttered grumble, he jumped to his feet and headed off to answer it, hoping that the caller would hang up before he got there.

It rang on, determined as sometimes a phone can sound. He silenced it by snatching it up. 'DI Mann's phone,' he snapped, without meaning to.

'As customer-friendly as ever, eh, Dan,' a male voice laughed in his ear.

'I try my best,' he said icily. 'DI Mann's out of the office at the moment. Who is this?'

'Fuck me, have I been away that long?' the voice chuckled.

Provan felt his eyes narrow and his annoyance grow into anger. 'Scott? Scott Mann? Is that you?'

'Thank Christ for that, Dan, I was beginning to feel insulted. Yes, it's Scott, free and clear.'

'Not quite,' the DS barked. 'You're only released on parole; your sentence isnae served yet. So think about this, sunshine: harassing your ex-wife at her place of work, or anywhere else for that matter, will get you recalled faster than you can say Barlinnie.'

'I think you'll find that ringing my former wife to check on the safety of my son won't be called harassment by anybody.'

'Jakey's fine; he's got a proper carer out of school. You neednae worry yourself about him, Scott.'

'The day I take your word for anything, Dan, I'll go back to prison of my own accord, for I'll be past praying for. I'm not interested in talking to you; it's Lottie I want.'

'Be careful what you wish for, you whining shite,' Provan snarled.

'Lovely.' Mann chuckled once again. 'I hope they really are

recording this call for training porpoises, or whatever the fuck they do. Now, where's my wife?'

'Read the divorce decree, Scott; she's your ex-wife, and I repeat, she's no' here. Just leave her alone. Okay?'

'Why do I not believe you? I'll bet she's sat right there listening to this. She's under your spell, you evil little gnome. You won't be so fucking smug once my dad's finished with you, I promise you. We're taking Jakey away from her, and as for you—'

'Stop right there, son,' the DS said; the quietness of his voice was forced and ran counter to all his instincts. 'There'll never be a day I'm alive when you and your windbag of a father can scare me, but you harm Lottie and I promise you, I will put the fear of God into you, and him. If you really want what's best for your son, you will stop this nonsense right now and negotiate acceptable access arrangements with his mother.'

'We'll see her in court, Dan,' his adversary hissed, 'and you if you want to turn up, although when the sheriff sees you, it'll only help my case, you scruffy wee bastard. You tell her to take care of my son, do you hear me?'

'All I hear, Scott, is a bully, a spoiled coward who was as bad at bein' a husband and father as he was at bein' a police officer. You think she's helpless against you and your dad's creep Moss Lee. That's why you're so fuckin' smug.'

'Face facts, "Uncle",' Mann sneered. 'She is helpless; and friendless. A fat lot of good you'll be to her.'

'Time will tell on that, but for now, hear this. Whatever you think, that girl means a hell of a lot to me, so you come near her, or hurt her in any way, and this scruffy wee bastard will put you in your place.'

He slammed the phone into its cradle. As he let his fury go in a great tearing gasp, he heard a sound behind him, the creaking of a hinge. He turned to see Lottie standing in the doorway.

'How long have you been there?' he asked.

'Long enough, Dan, long enough. I'm glad I wasn't here to take that call. I doubt that I'd have stayed as calm as you.' Her mouth looked almost lipless. 'I'm going to crush those people,' she hissed. 'Whatever it takes.'

Provan nodded. 'That you will, love, that you will.'

'What did you call me?' she asked quietly.

He stared at her. 'Detective Inspector. What else? Now come on, ma'am. We have to speak to Augusta Cambridge on yon FaceTime thing, if I can get it to work.'

'Fire away,' she said, moving into her chair and drawing up another for him, facing the computer monitor. 'By the way,' she added, as she slid her keyboard across the desk. 'You mean a hell of a lot to me too.'

He smiled as he opened the FaceTime programme and keyed in the email address that Trudi Pollock had given him. As a dial tone rang out, they could only see themselves on screen, but after a few seconds the top of the screen showed a single word, 'Connecting', the image changed and their faces were replaced by that of a blond woman with a square face and round thick-framed spectacles.

'Detective Sergeant,' she said, 'I am Inge. Good to see you.'

'You too,' he replied. 'This is Detective Inspector Mann, my boss. She's the senior investigating officer into Leo's death.'

'Very good. I have Augusta for you.'

She moved out of shot and was replaced by another, her physical opposite, a black woman with delicate features and deep, clear brown eyes. She wore a heavy russet-coloured sweater and a scarf around her shoulders.

'How can I help you?' she began. 'From what Inge told me,

you believe that Leo was murdered, is that correct? The police announcements haven't been very enlightening. I've called Gino Butler several times but he hasn't come back to me. I guess that's because he's had nothing to tell me.'

'That's a fair assumption,' Lottie Mann agreed. 'We haven't shared anything with that gentleman. Nor with anyone else,' she added. 'The investigation is still gathering information, but to answer your question, yes, we are treating this as murder. We believe that Leo was poisoned, by a substance added to a drink in his fridge. Were you close enough to him, Miss Cambridge,' she ventured, 'to know anything of his personal habits, his foibles?'

She bridled, reading too much into the question. 'We were friends, Inspector, nothing else. As you'll have gathered, I'm gay, and even if I wasn't, there was the age difference. But I did see a lot of him, yes. I painted at all of his fights, with his permission, and I cut him in on the profits from the prints. Five per cent commission; he didn't want it, but I insisted. When he'd some down time, he'd visit me here, and we'd talk. You know his mother lost her marbles, poor woman, a long time back? I guess he needed a substitute; I'm proud that he chose me. He'd open up to me then, in a way that maybe he didn't with other people. The media kept saying he was reserved, but he wasn't with me. When I think about it now, I can see that Leo was more like a nephew to me than anything else. We had something in common, after all.'

'Explain that for me, please,' the DI asked.

The artist stared at her through the screen. 'Isn't that pretty obvious? Leo was black.'

'Mixed race.'

'Yes, with a light skin tone, but where he was brought up,

that made no difference. He was a black kid in Paisley, end of story.'

'That's interesting,' Provan said. 'He had no blood relatives we can interview, apart from Gordon, so we have no perspective on his early life, apart from what we can glean from Trudi Pollock and Butler, and we haven't really gone there with them. Did he talk to you about his ethnicity?'

'A little; he acknowledged it to me, which was something for him. He never tried to be white, but he never played on his blackness either. His father, Leonard senior, was Jamaican; a quiet guy, according to Leo. He'd been a boxer, but never won any titles. Leo said it was because he was too good; none of the guys with the belts would fight him, so he stayed on the outside. His ring name was Peter Jackson, taken from an old-time black fighter over a hundred years ago, another man that nobody wanted any part of in his prime. Leonard was Leo's first coach; he never talked about him much, but he told me that the things that made him special he had from his dad. That's where he got the Stoddart connection too. Leonard knew Benny Stoddart; he trusted him to look after his son, but he made sure he did. Leo going to LSE wasn't Benny being altruistic. It was a clause in the contract that his father insisted be put there.'

'He died in a workplace accident, didn't he?'

'That's right; when Leo was early twenties, just starting in the pros. The police decided it was an accident, but Leo never believed that. He told me it had been set up to happen, set up by his boy Gordon's granddad.'

'Leo told you that?' the DS exclaimed. 'Did he say whether he took that theory to the police?'

'It wasn't a theory. He knew for sure. He hired some people

to ask some questions, and he found the guy who'd been paid to set it up.'

'What happened to that man?'

'Nothing, but I doubt he slept easy for a while. As for Granddad Pollock, time and the river took care of him. Those were Leo's exact words, but if you were to tell me that time had a little help, you wouldn't surprise me.'

'We're not going to tell you that, Miss Cambridge,' Mann said. 'We have no plans to turn that stone over. We're interested in the present day, and in particular in anything unusual that might have happened at the party last Friday. We've spoken to a few guests already, but we believe you were best placed to see most of what happened.'

The artist pulled her scarf tighter around her shoulders. 'What are you hoping to find?'

'Any contact that Leo had with a guest that might have been less than friendly, but really any specific contact he had. For example, we know he spoke to you at one point.'

She smiled. 'Yes, we were fooling around. He came up to have a look at what I was doing; I told him he'd see it when it was done. Then we had a laugh. He'd been asking me for a while to paint his portrait, and I'd always said no, 'cos that's not something I do. I specialise in action scenes. He was standing behind me saying, "Come on, Gus, paint me," so I did; I turned and I dabbed a little paint on his neck. He grinned and said he'd never wash again, then he went back to his table.'

'Yes, Trudi Pollock told us about that.'

'She wasn't the only one who saw. There was another woman watching us. As Leo walked away, she kept on looking at me, and it was sheer venom she was radiating.'

'Who was it?' Provan asked, doing his best to sound casual.

'I never met the woman, but I believe it was the mother of Leo's middle two kids. She was pointed out to me on the night. What's her name again?'

'Faye Bulloch?'

'That's her. Leo told me she'd been giving him trouble. From her expression, I could see that he meant it.'

'Sheer venom, eh?' the DS murmured.

'Absolutely. A nasty piece of humanity altogether. I had an encounter with her later on. I arrived at the ladies' room just in time to hear her racially abuse Rae Letts. Specifically she called her "a fucking nigger tramp". If you'd care to prosecute her, I'll happily be a witness. The door was closed but I could still hear her.'

'What time did this happen?'

'About nine thirty.'

'How did the confrontation end?'

Their witness frowned. 'Mr Provan, this screen may not show it, but I am very large. I must have looked as angry as I felt, for the creature turned appropriately white, and left in a hurry. Ask the woman Trudi; she was there too. I know little Rae; one time when I was in Las Vegas for a fight, I visited her and Leo. She had gone into a booth by the time I got in there. When she came out, I asked if she was okay. She said she was, that people like that were to be pitied for they hate everything, even their own skin. I told her she was too kind for her own good, then we went back to the party. I didn't see the Faye woman for a while after that. I'd like to think I scared her off.'

'Are you saying she left?'

'I can't say that, but I didn't see her again for a while, not till after midnight, when the music was in full swing and I'd finished painting. She was back then, but she avoided me for the rest of the night.'

'Had Leo gone by that time?'

'Yes, a little while before. He came to say goodbye to me, in that big biker jacket he loved to wear. Last time I saw him, and he looked really happy. In fact I said to him, "You look as if you're in a really good place." He smiled, kissed me on the cheek and whispered, "I am, Gus; you'll know why soon." Then he was gone . . .' her eyes glazed over; a tear escaped and rolled down her cheek, 'and I never saw him again to ask him what he meant.'

Provan paused, allowing her time to recover her composure. 'Did you tell him about the thing with Faye?' he asked, when he judged that she was ready.

'No. Why ruin his night when he was so high?'

'Thanks,' the DS concluded. 'We'll follow up on some of that. If I need to speak to you further about it, I'll call you.'

'There's someone else we're interested in,' Mann added, before Cambridge could close the connection. 'The Italian guest, Moscardinetto.'

'The man who was murdered in Glasgow? Are you telling me he was there?'

'Yes. Didn't Leo point him out to you?'

'No, he didn't, and that surprises me. I know who Moscardinetto is, or was, and I'd have thought that Leo would have wanted him included in the finished work. Can you describe him?'

'I can do better than that,' Provan said. 'Wait a minute.'

He rose, walked into the main CID office and removed a blow-up of the Italian's passport photograph from a whiteboard on the far wall. Returning to the DI's office, he held it close to the monitor's inbuilt camera. 'Do you recognise him from that?' he asked.

'Yes, yes I do,' Augusta Cambridge replied firmly. 'And now that I do, I can tell you I did see him on Friday. I noticed him several times; he spoke to a lot of people, including me at one point, although I was too busy to be distracted when he did. I shooed him away when he tried to see what I was doing. I made a lot of sketches that will go towards the main work – I'll finish it anyway, as a tribute to Leo – and he's on some of them.'

'Can you remember who the people he spoke to were?'

'Yes, those that I knew. There was the white-haired man from Dundee, McCullough, him and his wife. They spoke for quite some time. The politician woman, the Shadow Cabinet woman, Aileen de Marco, they chatted for a while, and of course there was Joey, the lovely Joey Morocco. Moscardinetto looked pretty intense most of the time, but he was relaxed with him. I imagine they knew each other from the film world.'

'They did,' Mann confirmed. 'Anyone else?'

'Several people; young Gordon for one, Leo's son. They spoke for a while too. I can't guess what they had to talk about, but the boy looked very serious. Then there were the fight people, Bryce Stoddart and that dragon of a woman, Gene Alderney. Benny, Bryce's dad, wasn't there. They used ill-health as an excuse, but Leo told me that Benny's gone the same way as his mother; vascular dementia, he called it. He's out of it.'

'How did they all interact?'

'They looked pretty sombre, especially Alderney, but she does that to people.'

'Were you painting when Leo gave his retirement speech?'

'Of course, I was focused on him and as many people as I could.'

'When he got to the bit about the new promotional venture?'

'Alderney was the only person in the room who didn't clap when he announced it. No, she wasn't; neither did the Italian, but don't read anything into that. It isn't really his gig, is it?'

'So what is, and why was he there?'

'I don't know, but I can tell you this. Just before Leo left, the two of them spoke. They had a conversation away from everybody else, and I think . . . no, I'm certain that I saw Moscardinetto hand him something. I didn't see what it was, but something passed between them, something small enough for Leo to slip into the pocket of his biker jacket.' She paused momentarily. 'Then he came over to me,' she resumed, 'he said goodbye like I told you, and then he left.'

The scarf had fallen from her right shoulder. She pulled it across once again. 'That's it,' she said. 'That's all I can tell you, unless there's something specific you want to ask me.'

'No,' the DI replied. 'That's all, and that's fine.'

Cambridge frowned at her camera. 'Asking me about Moscardinetto; are you trying to tell me that his death and Leo's are connected?'

Mann chose to stonewall. 'We have no evidence of that, none at all.'

The painter smiled sadly. 'I don't think that's quite what I asked you, but never mind. So long.'

A second later, she vanished, and the two detectives were left staring at their own faces in the screen.

'Well,' Provan exclaimed, 'was that interesting or was it no'?'

Mann nodded. 'It leaves us with a very big question: what did Aldorino hand to Leo? But it tells us something too. If Faye disappeared between nine thirty and midnight, that gave her plenty of time to get to Ayr and back, and plenty of time to spike

Leo's drink. We need to talk to Dorward, to ask him what prints or DNA his people were able to recover from that fridge. If the answer is nothing, I'm going to ask him to send someone back to Ayr to check it again.'

'No' just that, Lottie,' the DS added. 'I don't recall seeing a biker jacket when we were at the scene on Saturday, but we didn't know about it then. We need to get back down there ourselves and take another look.'

Thirty-Three

Among the many things that Bob Skinner disliked about the Scottish national police service, one that he would have changed if he could, was its lack of a suitable headquarters building. Andy Martin, in his brief tenure, had chosen to base himself in Tulliallan Castle, where part of the Police College was located. His successor preferred to maintain her office in an undistinguished building in Stirling.

He would have had neither of them. Had he not walked away, and had he been appointed chief, as most observers had expected, he would have based himself in the seat of government, Edinburgh, with command teams in the cities of Glasgow, Dundee, Aberdeen and Inverness. He would have done everything in his power to prevent the sale of the Pitt Street building and the imminent move to the East End of the city.

Skinner saw this lack of a focal point as a sign of the politicians' failure to give any sort of direction to the creature they had made, beyond the creation of an appointed Police Authority, a supervisory body whose existence was unknown to most Scots and whose purpose and functions were a mystery to most of the rest.

As he sat in Mario McGuire's office, his mind drifting as his friend went through a folder page by page, he recognised his own failure. It had been a mistake not to concede that the new service would happen, and not to use the considerable influence he had, with the First Minister, Clive Graham, and with his then wife, Aileen, who was leader of the main opposition party but in favour of police unification. If he had done that, instead of sulking and glowering as he waited for the end of his career, he could have played a part in shaping the governance of the new force. He would have advised putting central services, including forensics and strategy, under the direct command of the chief constable, leaving the Authority as a largely advisory body, a bridge between police and politicians.

'If wishes were horses we'd a' get a hurl,' he recalled his grandfather telling him. He had done nothing, simply sat and watched the construction of a new level of bureaucracy that would swallow any cost savings that were made by rationalisation.

But he knew also that nothing that was made by government could not be unmade by its successor. A few months before, he had turned down an offer that would have given him real political power. As Mario McGuire closed the folder and pushed it across to him, he realised that he regretted that decision, as much as he regretted withholding his experience as the mess was being made.

'There you are,' the deputy chief constable said. 'Sandra Bulloch's HR file.'

Skinner shrugged. 'There won't be a hell of a lot in it that I haven't seen before,' he replied, leaving the folder where it lay. 'When's she due here?'

McGuire glanced up at the clock on the wall, to his right. 'Ten minutes, assuming she's on time.'

'Who's ever late for a summons to the Command Suite?'

'People who've never been here before,' the DCC retorted. 'That's quite a big pool. Welcome to modern policing, gaffer.'

'You can keep it.'

The DCC's dark eyes flashed and his smile dazzled. 'You really hate this, Bob, don't you?'

'This place? With every fibre of my being. Are you going to tell me that you like it here?'

'It is what it is. I prefer it to Tulliallan, where Andy Martin perched. They called his office "the Eyrie", would you believe?'

'He fell to earth, though,' Skinner muttered tersely. 'Fucking Icarus.'

'Do you ever hear from him?'

'Not a dicky bird. We'd stopped speaking even before he left.'

'How about Alex? Does she?'

'You are joking, Mario, aren't you? In a way, I'd like him to get in touch with her, so that he can see she's better off without him. Her new career is blossoming, as quite a few prosecuting counsels have found to their cost.'

McGuire scratched the dimple on his broad chin. 'There's an irony in that. You spent thirty years putting people in the dock, and now she's making a name for herself by getting them off. Look at that supermodel murder; she got a result there and no mistake. Her client was as guilty as sin; you know that as well as we do.'

'Blame it on the bossa nova,' Skinner chuckled. 'Better still, blame it on the Crown Office. If you want to be even more specific, blame it on the former solicitor general, Rocco de Matteo. He went into court with a hole in his case that was so big, Alexis used it as a gateway to the highway for her client.'

'Sammy Pye and Sauce Haddock weren't too pleased, though. Acquittals never reflect well on the investigating officers.'

'Nobody blamed them. They just gathered the evidence; de Matteo's people made the case. The co-accused was convicted, happily with a different defence advocate representing him. Lawyers like my daughter are actually good for the justice game,' he argued. 'They keep the prosecution on their toes.'

'Yeah,' the big DCC murmured. 'Just like we used to. You're right, by the way,' he added. 'I don't like this place. It's dull and it's drab and it's not where we should be. Worst of all, it's invisible. I had a major row with the communications people the other day. I had a look at our website and I tried to find myself. I couldn't. Neither the chief constable's office address nor mine is listed on it. There's a single reference to the senior officers working out of Tulliallan and here, but nothing to tell you who's where. It's as if we're hiding from the people we're supposed to protect. I tackled Perry Allsop about it; he muttered something about security. I told him to fuck off and fix it, but he told me it would have to be done through the Police Authority, his department being a central service. Utter bollocks.'

'Are you going to stay the course? You could walk into the next chief constable vacancy south of the border.'

'I won't be doing that,' McGuire retorted. 'Will I stay here? Honestly, I can't say for certain. As long as Maggie's in the room along the corridor, I suppose I will, but if she decides she's had enough of the bureaucracy . . . I don't see myself replacing her, that's all I'll say.'

The end of his confession coincided with a knock on the door; it opened and a young man in a black tunic leaned into the room. 'Sir, your ten o'clock is here.'

'Pretty good,' McGuire murmured with another glance at the clock. 'Only a couple of minutes late. Show her in.'

Both men stood and waited, watching the door until it

reopened and Sandra Bulloch stepped through it. She was dressed to impress, in a grey trouser suit, with black patent-leather shoes and a matching bag slung over her shoulder.

'Sir,' she began, then gasped slightly as the second presence registered.

'Chief Inspector,' the DCC said brusquely. 'Thanks for answering my mystery summons. Look, I have a meeting with ACC Mackie that I need to deal with now, so I'll leave you two to have a chat until I'm done.'

'As you wish, sir,' she replied quietly, with a slight frown that could have been either apprehension or curiosity.

McGuire swept out of the room by a side door.

'Take a seat, Sandra,' Skinner told her, resuming his own. He looked at her appraisingly; when she had been his assistant in Pitt Street, she had worn very little make-up to work, but she had prepared herself carefully for her Wednesday morning appointment with the DCC. Even so, her face looked drawn, and he wondered whether the cosmetics were there to hide tell-tale circles under her eyes.

'I will,' she replied, 'for now, until you've told me what the hell's going on here.'

'Let's call it a rescue mission.'

'What's being rescued?' she retorted.

'Possibly your career, that's if you're still interested in it. You can walk out of this room if you want, but not out of this building. You are going to speak to me, either here, one on one, or in another room, with someone alongside me and video and audio recorders running.'

'Why?' she asked quietly.

'They know you were sleeping with Leo Speight. That of itself isn't the problem. What is is your failure to disclose the fact to the officers investigating his death. That lays you open, potentially, to criminal charges, and it is absolutely a disciplinary issue, one that could be career-ending.' He paused. 'They're not guessing at this, Sandra. There is physical evidence that you had sex with Leo Speight in the week of his death. You may say that you had nothing useful to tell Lottie Mann because your mind wasn't on conversation at the time, but that wasn't your call. If Lottie was you and you were she, you'd be down on her like a lorry load of bricks; we both know that.'

'Lottie isn't Leo's type,' she whispered.

'You can cut that right out, Sandra,' he snapped. 'This isn't funny. The chief and the DCC aren't disposed to go easy on you. They asked me to interview you formally, under caution, with an ACC alongside me. We're only in this room alone because I insisted on it – as a first step. The rest of it hangs on what's said here . . . if we proceed. So, do we have a chat, or do I call Mario back, have you cautioned, switch on the recorders and make it adversarial?'

She gripped her bag, and for a moment he thought she was about to stand up and walk out, until she relaxed and settled against the padded back of her chair. 'On the basis that you're the devil I know, sir, let's do it the way you suggest. Where do you want to begin?'

'I want you to tell me all about your relationship with Leo Speight. How long have you known him?'

'We first met ten years ago,' she replied quietly. 'He had just started seeing Faye, and one day he picked her up from my flat. She introduced us, we said hello, and that was all, for a while. I didn't see him again until wee Leonard was born; I visited them at the maternity hospital and he was there.'

'How did he meet Faye?' Skinner asked.

'Through Gino Butler. The two of them had had a few dates, nothing serious. It cruised along until Leo had a big fight in London, a world championship unification against an American in the Millennium Dome, and Gino took her down with him. Naturally, Leo won, there was a party afterwards, they met and that's where it all started.'

'Leo moved in on his mate's girlfriend?'

'No he didn't, not just like that; they chatted the first time, that was all. At least that's what she told me. Faye did cool on Gino afterwards, though, no question. She never admitted it to me, but the impression I got from Leo was that when she was ready, she made the next move, not him. Have you met my sister?' she asked, unexpectedly.

'No, why should I have?'

'You're here, so I'm guessing you're involved in the investigation in some way. Did they call you in to mentor Lottie, is that it?'

'No, because Lottie doesn't need mentoring; she's as good a detective as you are – and wee Provan's better than the pair of you,' he added. 'However, you are right: I do have an involvement, from another angle. I haven't met your sister, though. Why did you ask me if I had?'

'I'd have been interested to know what you thought of her.'

'What do *you* think of her?' Skinner countered.

'I think she's a greedy, conniving woman,' Bulloch replied bluntly. 'Leonard was no accident, sir. She set Leo up. She's a couple of years older than he was, three years older than me. She was thirty when she fell pregnant and she'd been on the pill since she was eighteen.'

'Whether she set him up or not, it worked for her. They had two kids together, and he bought her a house.'

'It wasn't enough, though. You know she took him to court?'

He nodded. 'Yes, I'm aware of that. I have to ask, was it prompted by your relationship with Leo?'

'Hell, no! She doesn't know about that.'

'How long were you and he together, Sandra?'

She looked him in the eye and smiled softly, revealing a side of herself that he had never seen. 'It only started seriously about nine months ago. I didn't actually see much of him until then. He flitted in and out of Faye's life, and I was in a long-term relationship of my own.'

'I know,' he said. 'I saw your vetting report before you came to work for me in Pitt Street. Your other half was called Craig Goram, and he was an English teacher in a secondary school in Clydebank. You lived together in a flat in North Kelvinside.'

'Mmm. Did it also say that he was having it off with one of his pupils? A pretty young thing; she was sixteen when it started, and he left me for her as soon as she started uni.'

'No, that detail wasn't there. If it had been, I would have remembered it; I'd probably have done something about it as well.'

'Too bad it wasn't,' she retorted, 'for I bear Craig nothing but ill will. We were a couple for seven years, and for almost half of that time he was shagging someone else on the side. Don't be thinking, though, that I went to Leo on the rebound. I was single for a few months after Craig went off. I joined a dating website pretty much straight away, and got him well and truly out of my hair. I was quite happy, then one Saturday, early January last year, Faye left the kids with me early doors because she was flying off to the fucking Canaries, as she did whenever she felt like it, and asked me to run them down to Ayr, 'cos Leo was having them until she got back. I did that; he asked me to stay for lunch, and I did. In the afternoon, he was taking Leonard and Jolene to a play park, and he asked me if I'd like to come with them, so I did. I went home after that.

'Three days later, when Faye was back, he called me and asked me if I'd like to have dinner with him. He picked me up in his Bentley and took me to Beedham's. I'd never heard of it, so I had no idea it was his. Okay, the staff were deferential, but he was Leo Speight, so of course they were bloody deferential. It was only when I asked him whether it was part of a hotel group that he smiled and said, "You could call it that," and explained. I told him that Faye had never mentioned it, and he said, "No, she wouldn't have, because she doesn't know about it." I asked him if he was hiding assets from her because of the court case, but he said no, that nothing was hidden from anyone with the brains to look for it, which clearly he said her lawyer didn't have, because it had never been mentioned in any of the legal papers. Then I asked him if it was all a big pissing contest between them, and whether he'd give her what she wanted if she just said "please", and gave up all the legal crap, and he said, "No way", and he explained that he'd known from the start she'd got pregnant to trap him, and that she'd seen Jolene as extra leverage, nothing more, but it wasn't going to work because he would never give her precedence over Trudi or Rae.

'We were really getting down to it by then. I'd had a few bubbles too many; I asked him flat out what he was all about, whether he was a closet Muslim, with a stable of concubines. He smiled at me and said he'd once scared the shite out of a *Sun* reporter who'd done some digging and had the nerve to ask him that same question. I thought I'd gone too far, but he took my hand and he said, "Sandra, I don't know what the fuck I am yet." I remember the rest of it word for word. He said, "With Trudi I was careless with my dick as young people are, but we both knew that getting married would just have been plain stupid. With your sister, we both know I was set up, but I should have seen that coming. It was never on the cards that I would marry her, but I gave her a comfortable lifestyle that she's taken completely for granted and always wanted more. Then I met Rae, and she's just lovely, the antithesis of Faye in that she's good to me and asks nothing of me, nothing at all. She is absolutely the best friend I have, and will ever have, and I am the same to her. She understands, we both understand, that if we ever married it would change that perfect dynamic between us, and we're happy that it will never happen. We have a beautiful child, and I will be around to raise her to adulthood, as I will be for Leonard and Jolene and as I was and still am for Gordon, from the time I was able to take on that role. Trudi I treat with respect and give what she wants, which has always been to feel good about herself, something that ape of a father of hers denied her. Faye? Materially I would give her anything she asked for apart from the thing she's demanding, my name. So yes, I suppose that's what I am right enough," he told me "a wealthy man in circumstances that were completely unplanned, but which do not define me in any way. I'm not that potentate, I'm a man who's still looking for his perfect partner, that one person that makes me burn inside with a flame I never want to put out. Faye? Frankly she was never more to me than a light from a book of matches, so there's no way back for her, which," he said, "is probably just as well in the circumstances," and we looked each other in the eye and I realised, without the thought ever having crossed my mind for a second before, that all I wanted to do was go somewhere very private with him and eat him alive.

'So I told him, "Leo, what the hell is the point of owning a place like this if you can't get a room?" And that is what we did, the best suite in the place overlooking Loch Lomond, and I knew right then that he was where I wanted to be. I didn't tell him, though, not then, not until a while later, at the end of January, back in that suite in Beedham's after he'd gone to train for Fonsecco and come back and beaten him, back there when he promised me that he was finished with fighting for good, and spoke my own thoughts out loud. "You're the one," he said. "You really are the one. We'll probably never have kids, for we will never need them, but Sandra, will you have me and me alone?" And I said to him "Are you crazy? Of course I will." We were in no rush to tell anyone; we enjoyed having our secret so much that we wanted to keep it for as long as we could. We agreed that I wouldn't go to his retirement party, because people, my sister most of all, would wonder about my presence there, and it would be a distraction from the main business of the night: so I stayed at home, my home, alone. Our plan was that on Monday morning, last Monday, I was going to see the chief to hand in my resignation and take accrued leave – I have enough – in lieu of notice. Then we were going to fly to the Bahamas, get married, and not come back until we were good and bloody ready, whenever that was. We had all the rest of our lives in front of us; it was just perfection. I'd never imagined being so happy and I don't believe Leo had either.

'And then on Saturday morning, while I'm packing my bloody suitcase would you believe, I get a call from a uniformed inspector, a man I will hate forever through no fault of his own, telling me po-faced – if you can fucking sound po-faced, he managed it – that there's a major incident in a house at Ayr and protocol says I'm needed there, and he gives me the address and it's Leo's. I wet myself, literally. I was terrified, shaking. It took me ten minutes to get myself together and to get dressed, but I did and I drove down there. All the way I was telling myself, "It's all right, Sandra, it's all right; there's been a burglary and that stupid cunt's overreacted because of whose house it is." Then I got there and I saw the ambulance, and I saw Arthur bloody Dorward looking like an undertaker in a paper suit. I got out of my car and he handed me a tunic like his and said, "Through there" – that was all. I was shaking like a leaf but I behaved like a professional should; I put it on and walked in there still hoping that all I would find would be a housebreaker with a broken jaw, but of course I didn't. Instead I found Leo sitting in his chair, and he was . . . dead!'

As she spoke the last word, she stiffened in her chair, grasping its sides, her jaw clenched, her face chalk white even under the make-up.

Had Skinner been more self-aware, he would have known that his own face was contorted, twisted into a mask of tension. For several seconds he stared at her, then he blinked, shook himself and murmured, 'Let it go, kid. You need to let it out.'

She did, in great ripping sobs; the tears flowed uncontrollably; she folded in on herself, her arms clutching as if she was trying to make herself disappear. He wanted to go to her, to hold her, but he knew that would have been the wrong thing to do. Instead, he stood, walked across to a table in the corner of the room, switched on a kettle that sat there and made two mugs of tea from Mario McGuire's private stash of Scottish Blend.

By the time they were infused, Sandra Bulloch had begun to regain control. He pressed a mug into her hands; she accepted it with a nod of thanks. She took a sip, then dabbed at her face, smearing her fingers with a mix of Revlon and black mascara. He went back to where the kettle was, picked up a kitchen roll and handed it to her, looking away as she ripped off half a dozen sheets and went to work on the wreckage, not stopping until all of it was gone, and there was nothing to hide the hollowness of her cheeks and the redness of her eyes.

'Thank you,' she whispered. 'I'm sorry, sir. I lost it, but . . . I've been holding all that inside me since Saturday. I haven't been able to cry, not even at home. Once I started to talk, I just couldn't stop. I think I was finally conceding that it wasn't all just a bad dream, that he really is dead.'

'Don't be sorry,' Skinner insisted. 'I should apologise. I should have been much more sensitive.'

'No,' she insisted, 'you were fine. I'm glad it was you that talked to me. I know you, I've worked for you. I barely know the DCC and I don't know the chief at all.'

'We can stop this if you like, Sandra,' he offered. 'I've still got clout with those two. If I say that we resume tomorrow somewhere else, that's what will happen.'

'Thanks, sir, but I'm ready to continue; I need to continue.'

He nodded and sat down once more. 'If you're sure; finish your tea first, though. I'm sorry there's no milk; Mario thinks that's for wimps. Christ, I'm surprised he's even got tea. His wife's family business sells the best coffee in Edinburgh.'

'She's a Starbuck, is she?' Bulloch said with a noise that was a mix of chuckle and hiccup.

Skinner shook his head, smiling. 'No, Paula's a Viareggio, all the way.'

He took a mouthful of his tea, winced at its blandness, then put his mug on a corner of McGuire's desk.

'When I was half the age I am now,' he said quietly, 'Myra, my first wife, died in an accident, a crash. She always drove too fast, but still, it was a road she used every day and it should never have happened. I was at the scene; I saw the wreckage of her car, barely recognisable it was, then I had to identify her at the mortuary, after they'd cleaned her up as best they could. I blanked out part of it for years after that, stuff I'd seen and refused to admit was true. Going through her things, I found that all her life she'd kept a diary, a secret diary that I never saw and never knew about. I was too fucking busy to notice or even be interested, truth be told. She did though: I found them all in a suitcase in the loft, along with a dress and a pair of shoes that I didn't remember ever seeing before.

'I closed it again, locked it tight. It took me years to read them; I reasoned – I know this now – that her life was in that case, and subconsciously I feared that if I let it out, I would extinguish it altogether. Eventually, though, I did, and in there, I found a woman I'd never known at all. Maybe she was bipolar, a word that wasn't in common use then; maybe she was, but I doubt it. I liked to believe she was always a single entity but chose only to share a part of herself with me, the good, chaste, wifely side, and express the rest of herself elsewhere. But I knew I was overthinking that; I know damn well I just bored her rigid from the start.

'Myra nearly had two funerals. I came very close to cremating her other life, those diaries, in the garden incinerator, but I held myself back from that because I decided that I didn't have the right. Instead I made the worst decision of my life. Alex, our daughter, had grown up with only vague infant memories of her mother, backed up by the Christmas tree fairy images I'd described for her. I decided that she had the right to know all of it, so I gave her the suitcase. It fucked her up for years; I'm not sure she's over it yet, not a hundred per cent. The dress fitted her, and the shoes. She told me, not that long ago, that she used to put them on and go out on the pull; she insisted that she never went all the way, but if she did, that's not the sort of thing a girl would tell her old man, is it? I do believe, though, that Myra was the reason she and Andy Martin broke up the first time, because looking at him through her mother's eyes, she found him as boring as Myra must have found me.'

He stopped, realising that he was staring at the ceiling, and that Sandra Bulloch was staring at him. He shook his head, quickly, vigorously. 'Why am I telling you this?' he asked himself aloud, then turned his face towards her.

'I'm telling you,' he said, 'because from my own life I understand completely why you didn't tell Lottie and Dan, or Mario, when you had the chance last Saturday, about your relationship with Leo, and I can even see why you called him your brother-in-law, as they told me you did. It was your secret, yours alone, and it was precious to you, so in your grief you made an instant decision to protect it, to shut it away like Myra's other life was hidden in that suitcase. It wasn't relevant to the investigation, so why should it ever have happened? That's what you did, Sandra, and I am here to tell you that I will defend your right to do it before any tribunal, or any court. As far as this interview's concerned, you can go home right now, on a couple of weeks' compassionate leave – use up some of that accrued leave if you need longer; the chief constable will allow that, I promise you. She's had her own tragedies; she'll understand yours.'

'Thank you, sir,' Bulloch replied, leaning forward, her elbows on her knees, her hands shredding a sheet of kitchen paper. 'In that case, please, can Leo and me stay secret? Not because it would make my sister my enemy for ever; I've always been prepared to accept that. Just for my sake and his?'

Skinner frowned. 'Sandra, if it was just a matter of keeping some irrelevant forensic findings out of the report that goes to the fiscal, that would not be a problem. As for your story of your relationship with Leo, I've no doubt that could be corroborated by the staff at Beedham's, and anywhere else you went together. But it isn't as simple as that.'

'Why not?' she asked, puzzled. 'What is the problem?'

'Leo is,' he replied. 'Thanks to him, your secret won't be a secret for much longer. As soon as his solicitor reveals the content of Leo's will to all the beneficiaries, it'll be out of the bag. When she lodges it with the Sheriff Court – although God alone knows how long that'll take given the property valuations and tax calculations that are needed – it'll become public knowledge.'

He reached inside his jacket, produced an envelope and handed it over. 'This is a copy of an amendment to his existing will that Leo made last week. It's properly drawn up and meets the requirements of Scots Law. You'll find that he's left you a lot more than a memory.'

Her hands trembled slightly as she picked at the adhesive seal of the envelope, before abandoning any attempt at neatness and ripping it open. She extracted the copy and began to read. As she progressed, her eyebrows rose and her eyes widened, then became misty. 'He did that . . .' she whispered.

She stared at the document, blinking hard. 'Faye will contest this,' she declared.

'She'll be wasting her time,' Skinner told her. 'That's not just my opinion, it's my lawyer daughter's; I asked her about it, hypothetically. She was quite clear in her opinion, that the Moss Lee action is bound to fail. She'd have to prove they lived together as man and wife, and from everything I've been told, they never did. Faye's best course of action is to be nice to you.'

'That'll stick in her throat.' She took a deep breath, then blew it out. 'Leo, my love,' she murmured, then glanced across at her companion. 'He did that for me. Given the timing, it's almost as if he knew he was doing to die.'

'Indeed,' he said. 'That takes us into an area that's properly for Lottie and Dan, but I'll go there anyway. Did Leo ever say anything to suggest he might have felt threatened?'

'Nothing,' she replied. 'But would he have? Being threatened was part of his professional life. He went up against people who were out to do him serious physical harm. In the build-up to the biggest fights, the promotional stages where they were selling tickets and TV pay-per-view buys, the part that he did but never liked, most of them were very specific about what they were going to do to him. He never rose to it, he kept silent, then on the night, he showed them the error of their ways. That was a line he used a few times in interviews after fights. If anyone had threatened him outside of boxing, he'd have acted in the same way: ignored it until the time was right, then switched on his other brain and dealt with it.'

'His other brain?'

'Yes, he said he had two. The normal one, the one he walked around with, and the one he switched on when he did his business. He was like you in that respect.'

'Me?' Skinner exclaimed.

She nodded. 'Yes, you. There are two sides to you, and I've seen them both. There's the sympathetic personality, a big soft nelly at times, and there's the guy who shot that terrorist in Glasgow without batting an eyelid, and probably without losing any sleep over it.'

'Mmm,' he grunted. 'You might be right about the eyelid, but not about the sleep. How did Leo feel about the other side

272

of the boxing business,' he asked, moving on, 'and about some of the people in it?'

'He didn't talk about it much, maybe because I never asked. It was the source of his wealth, he did say once, but that didn't mean he had to like it. He liked the older Stoddart, I do know that. He told me that his father had respected him and that was enough for Leo. I think he was wary of the younger one.'

'Bryce? Why?'

'How did he put it? "Bryce has no idea of the future," he told me. "When I'm gone from boxing," he said, "my business life really starts. Bryce will struggle to hold on to his, because he's been too reliant on me for too long." I never met Bryce, but my assessment was that Leo was a lot brighter than him.'

'His business life, you said. Was that the new mixed martial arts thing he spoke about at his party?'

Sandra laughed. 'He had no intention of following through with that,' she exclaimed. 'I helped him work on what he was going to say, so I know. "It's a good idea in principle," he told me. "I've done the groundwork, including bringing Billy Swords in on it as the frontman, but no fucking way will I actually do it myself. Having created the blueprint, I'll hand it over to Stoddart Promotions as a farewell gift if Bryce wants it. It'll be interesting to see how they react . . . especially the old bat." The old bat was a woman called Alderney. She had something to do with the Stoddarts, and she was one of only two people I know he ever actively disliked, the other being Trudi Pollock's father. His real business? That was property; he had big, big plans for that. The hotels, the offices, the Bahamas; that was just the story so far. When I asked him what he was going to do, he laughed and said, "Keep on growing, ethically. Maybe I'll run for president one day." He'd have made a damn good one.'

She held up the photocopy. 'My brain's not working yet, sir. What does this mean, bottom line?'

'It means,' Skinner replied, 'that after specified bequests have been met and inheritance duty paid, you and Leo's kids inherit the residue of his estate, in the way that he lays down.'

'What about the property?'

The way I read it, Gordon gets the hotels, and the rest's shared among the five of you.'

'Three of them are children and Gordon's not much more. I can't look after all that!'

'You won't have to. There's a man in Edinburgh, Charles Baxter.'

She nodded. 'Leo mentioned him; he said he was the key man on his property side. In fact he said that if Bryce Stoddart had his brains, he'd be running all the big shows in Las Vegas, not hanging on in Britain, relying on him for the big paydays.'

'He wasn't kidding. Baxter's an executor and he'll be trustee for the children. If you want my advice, go to him and ask him to manage your interest in the portfolio as he did for Leo. That shouldn't be a problem for him.'

'It might if it means I have to deal with my sister.'

Skinner shook his head. 'As I understand it, you won't. Leo took her out of play altogether.'

'I don't know whether that's good news or bad. She's a dangerous woman.' Her mouth gaped as the implications of what she had said came home to her. 'You don't suppose . . .' she gasped.

'I don't suppose anything, nor should you, until the Gartcosh lab finally unplugs its finger and completes the analysis that Mann and Provan are waiting on.'

'If you say so, but it'll be difficult.'

274

'Then get yourself out of it, Sandra, as far away as you can. If I were you, I'd take that leave, I'd go and see the lawyer and Baxter, get the keys to the house you will own in the Bahamas, and bugger off there as you and Leo intended. While you're there, do some life planning. You may prove me wrong, but I don't see you coming back to the police service, not with the sort of wealth you're going to have. That kind of money needs managing, and it's not the sort of job you want to delegate too far.'

'I think you're right,' she conceded, 'but how can I go with the investigation under way? You realise, don't you, that the will makes me a person of interest. Nobody had more to gain than me from Leo's death, sir.'

'Somebody did, or thought they did, but not necessarily in material terms. If you'd done more time as a homicide detective, you'd realise that only a small minority of murders are about money.'

He stood, almost jumping to his feet. 'Get out of here,' he said, an order, not a suggestion. 'Go now. I'll square everything with Maggie and Mario.'

'Thanks,' she replied. 'I will, if only to escape Faye. Do you know when the will's going to be read, or whatever it is they do with wills in Scotland?'

'Ask the lawyer. Her contact details were in the envelope. 'Oh,' he exclaimed. 'One more question before you leave. Did Leo ever mention a man named Aldorino Moscardinetto?'

'The murdered Italian? No, he didn't, not by name, but now you ask, something comes back to me. A couple of weeks ago, he stayed over at my place. He had gone to the toilet, and left his phone on the bedside table. It rang so I picked it up and answered it. The voice on the other end said, "Who are you?" with no pretence at being polite, but just then Leo came back and I handed the phone over. When he was done, I asked him who that rude bugger was. He laughed and said, "Sorry, that was him being his normal self. He's a guy I'm involved in a project with; you could say it's a public service." I'd forgotten about it, and until now I didn't make any connection, but the caller name on the phone was Aldo.' She stared at Skinner. 'That was him, and now he's dead too?'

'That's right,' he said. 'Which makes me even more curious: what the hell was that project?'

Thirty-Four

'Yes, sir, I hear you. I'm not happy but I hear you . . . Yes, sir. Can I have a formal statement from her, for the record? . . . Aw, come on, sir! Let us be the judges of that . . . No. No. No, sir, I do not want to be replaced. I'll live without her statement, if that's what you and the chief constable are ordering. Can I have that order in writing, for the file? . . . She is? . . . I am? . . . I am. Yes, sir, thank you, sir.'

Lottie Mann pocketed her phone and leaned back against her car. It was parked alongside a van with police markings, in front of the house in which Leo Speight had died. She was aware that Provan had been watching her throughout the exchange, but it had shaken her and she chose not to return his gaze, not until she had absorbed what she had just been told, and recovered from its impact. For his part, the detective sergeant understood that he was not being shut out. The concern that showed on his face was for her and her alone.

A cold wind was blowing off the Firth of Clyde, under grey skies, and neither officer was dressed to resist it, but they ignored its bite.

Eventually the DI stood to her full height and turned towards her colleague. 'How much of that did you get?' she asked him.

'The phrase "I'm not happy" struck a chord,' he told her, 'but I'd be guessing at the rest.'

'Then this is it, Dan. In the context of this investigation, Detective Chief Inspector Sandra Bulloch does not exist; there is to be no mention of her in the record, or in the report to the procurator fiscal. We are not to approach her directly. If we need her input on anything that might arise from now on, we have to tell the DCC and he'll do what's necessary. We don't need to interview her because it's been done already, at a higher level. Chief Constable Steele and the DCC are happy that she didn't set out to hamper the inquiry, and that she has no knowledge that's relevant to it.'

'Are we no' supposed to make that call?' Provan retorted.

'They're the masters, Daniel, we're the servants. That's how it is.'

'So next time we see her, be it in Pitt Street or at the new glass palace in Dalmarnock, we just forget all about her shagging the victim in a murder investigation and pretend that it never happened?'

'No, because that isn't going to happen either, not in the foreseeable future, and if I read the DCC right, probably not ever. He's just told me that Sandra's gone on compassionate leave, and that I'm to stand in for her as acting head of Serious Crimes, Western Area.'

The DS smiled. 'Suddenly my day's got a lot brighter,' he said. Then he shivered theatrically. 'Still fuckin' freezing out here, though. Will we go and see if Dorward's folk have finished in the kitchen?'

Mann nodded. 'Good idea.'

They headed for the villa, where crime-scene tape still hung from one side of the entrance door. Provan brushed it aside and opened it, leading the way inside.

They were confronted in the hall by a familiar figure, red haired, bushy eyebrows bristling as he tore off his sterile tunic.

'Arthur,' Mann exclaimed. 'I didn't expect you to be here. I was expecting one of those wee yellow things with one eye; you know, a minion.'

'You want a job doing right,' Dorward retorted sharply, 'sometimes you've got to do it yourself. I don't like it when my unit's asked a question that we're supposed to be able to answer but can't, as someone found out this morning.'

'Can you answer it now?'

'Maybe. I've found something that was missed before, a hair wedged inside the fridge door's rubber seal. Nothing else, just that hair, but it should have been found first time round. It's got a follicle, so I'll be able to create a DNA profile of the owner. But you know as well as me, that'll be the easy part. Matching it's the tricky bit, if there's nothing on the database.'

'Is it male or female?' Provan asked.

'Going by the length, it could be either, and that's all I've got to go on at this stage. I'll let you know, soon as I can. Here,' he said as he handed the keys of the property to Mann, 'you'll need these to lock up when you're finished whatever it is you're here to do.' He picked up a small case, fished a car fob from his pocket and made for the door.

'What if it's Sandra's?' Provan murmured as it closed on them, leaving them alone. 'They've already got her DNA on the database, so they'll match it quick enough if it is hers.'

'I'm wondering the same thing,' Mann admitted. 'If it is, I'm bouncing it straight back to Stirling. "Hands off", that's the order. If she needs to be hauled back off leave, DCC McGuire can do it. But that's another issue,' she continued. 'Let's do what we came for. Where do you want to start?'

'I'll do downstairs, you do upstairs?'

'Fair enough, but we'd better wear crime-scene gloves since we'll be handling stuff. If Arthur has to come back here again and we've compromised anything, we'll never hear the end of it.'

'I take it you brought some.' Her face fell; he smiled. 'But you know I always carry them anyway, so it doesnae matter.'

Suitably gloved, the DI headed for the staircase, her low heels snagging occasionally in the thick carpet. As she climbed, her mind went back to her conversation with the DCC. She liked McGuire and had always found him amiable. She had never doubted that there was another side to him, but the gulf between them in rank had led her to imagine that she would never experience it.

When she had called him to ask permission to haul Sandra Bulloch in for interview, in the light of what she and Provan had learned about her relationship with the dead man, not forgetting her failure to provide the written statement she had promised, she had met the other McGuire full on. He had been abrupt, not quite to the point of rudeness but not far short of it.

'Under no circumstances do you have permission to interview DCI Bulloch, DI Mann. She has been seen already in this office and we are satisfied that she has no part to play in your inquiry.'

His formality had taken her by surprise, but she had stood her ground, initially. 'Sir, she's a person of interest. She's the major beneficiary in Leo Speight's new will. He signed it, and a couple of days later he was dead. If you were leading this investigation you'd want to talk to her, at the very least to put this new information to her.'

'Come into the real world for a minute, Mann. I *am* leading this investigation. The only reason I'm not front and centre is because the chief and I agreed that we didn't want anyone to think we didn't have confidence in you. We were aware of the forensic evidence before you were, and we decided to act upon it at our level. That's happened, and a decision was taken, on evidential grounds, that there should be no further investigation of DCI Bulloch. Do you hear what I'm saying to you?'

'Yes, sir, I hear you. I'm not happy but I hear you.'

'Your happiness is not my immediate concern, Detective Inspector. Are you in a position to proceed with your investigation?'

'Yes, sir. Can I have a formal statement from her, for the record?'

'There will be no formal statement because she has nothing to say that is relevant to your inquiry.'

'Aw, come on, sir! Let us be the judges of that.'

'Are you questioning my orders, Lottie? Don't you understand them? There will be no statement. Look, do you want me to replace you as SIO? I can have DCI Pye and DS Haddock across from Edinburgh inside two hours.'

'No. No. No, sir, I do not want to be replaced. I'll live without her statement, if that's what you and the chief constable are ordering. Can I have that order in writing, for the file?'

'No you bloody can't! Let me spell something out for you. If this leaks, if Sandra Bulloch's involvement with Speight leaks, before your investigation is over, or before the will becomes public – and it's been agreed with the lawyer that no other beneficiaries will be advised before it's lodged in the sheriff court – someone's career will end. Make sure it isn't yours or Provan's. Now be quiet and listen to me. DCI Bulloch is going on leave.'

'She is?'

'Yes, on compassionate leave; consider that word, Lottie, compassionate. I don't know when she'll return, so I will need to address that situation. You're her temporary replacement.'

'I am?'

'Yes, you are, Acting DCI, and that awkward wee bastard you work with is acting DI, whether he likes it or not. It's up to you whether you share that with him before he sees his next salary advice, because he's been acting like a DI for years. Are you on side with that, and are you ready to carry on, DCI Mann?'

'I am. Yes, sir, thank you, sir.'

Her head was still buzzing, marvelling that confrontation had turned into affirmation in a matter of seconds. She smiled in anticipation of Dan Provan's reaction when she told him of his temporary promotion. His first instinct would be to reject it, but she knew that he would realise that if he did that, they would be separated, and that was something he would not allow.

She was under no illusion that either step-up would be made permanent. She was too new to DI rank, too low in the pecking order to be a serious candidate, just as Dan was too old. She would enjoy it for as long as it lasted, though, and so would he, whether he liked it or not.

Yet there was something else that had stayed with her from that discussion, something about McGuire's manner, his formality, the brusqueness of his voice and even of his choice of words.

. . . a decision was taken, on evidential grounds, that there should be no further investigation of DCI Bulloch. Do you hear what I'm saying to you?

She had heard, but had she heard it all?

. . . a decision was taken . . .

Was it possible that he had disagreed with it? Was that what she was supposed to hear?

'Fuck it,' she whispered as she walked into Speight's bedroom. 'Let the high heid yins play their games.'

Thirty-Five

'Are you happy?' Mario McGuire asked his former wife.

'Personally or professionally?' Maggie Steele countered. 'At home I have a lovely wee girl, and a sister who can combine her work with looking after her when I'm not there. Every day that passes is another day of Stevie being dead, but it is what it is. I can call that happiness.' She glanced around her room. 'Professionally, I'd like to be in more salubrious surroundings, but I enjoy the work I do, and don't find it unbearably stressful.'

'Don't play games with me, Mags,' he said. 'Are you happy with the way the situation with Bulloch was resolved? Has Big Bob run rings round us yet again?'

'What do you mean?'

'I mean that it started with us asking him to do a specific job for us, one that could have been handled entirely in-house, but we decided would be better tackled by someone outside the disciplinary chain.'

'Yes,' she agreed, 'and I still think that was right.'

'But did we ask the right person? Look what happened. Bob made the rules; it wasn't going to be formal, not under caution, just a one-on-one chat, with him to make the judgement on how to proceed after that. We did it his way, and next thing we know,

Sandra's on her way back to Glasgow and you're told to rubber-stamp a request for indefinite leave that you never heard her make.'

'What was the alternative?' the chief constable challenged. 'That we take a grieving woman who's committed a technical sin of omission but hasn't actually hampered the investigation, put her through the whole disciplinary process, and formally suspend her? We couldn't have done that privately; we'd have been required to grant her representation. Her name would have got out, she'd have been cast as a suspect by the media, and our force's reputation would have taken yet another kick in the genitalia, one which it seriously does not need.'

'Yes, okay,' her deputy conceded, 'but don't you think we'd have worked that out for ourselves?'

'Mmm. Yes, I think we probably would have . . . but how much damage would we have done to Bulloch in the process? The sympathetic approach was the right one, and to come back to your question, yes, I do believe we asked the right man. In fact I can only think of one other person I'd trust to take the job on . . . and that is me.'

'*Tu? Perché?*'

She laughed. 'Stick your Italian up your arse, McGuire. I had enough of that when we were married. Yes, me. Why? Because I've got something in common with Sandra Bulloch, and so has Bob. All three of us have lost partners in violent circumstances. What did we need to know from that interview, first and foremost? Tell me.'

He sighed. 'Oh I get it, don't worry. My concern is for our integrity as serving police offers. We needed to establish her good faith, I agree. Did she take Leo for a ride, literally, worm her way into his bed and into his will? Is she a potential poisoner, or an innocent victim?'

'Just so. Bob said that after a few minutes with her he was in absolutely no doubt. That being the case, he did what he did out of regard for her grief, just as we would do as police officers with any other person in that situation.'

'But telling her to get out of here,' McGuire argued, 'was that not a step too far?'

'He did more than that. He told her to get out of the country. Look, she's a DCI, she has resources, she knows the people around Speight. Suppose she worked out for herself who killed the man she was in love with? Can anyone predict how she'd react? Remember when we were married,' she said, 'and that dickhead cut my arm to the bone? What did you do? You went into the cells at St Leonards, on your own, and you battered seven colours of shite out of the guy without leaving a mark on him. Don't try to deny it, because I know you did, and although I shouldn't, I still love you for it. What's Bob done for Sandra by railroading her out of the picture? Possibly he's got her out of harm's way.'

Thirty-Six

'Bugger,' Acting Detective Inspector Dan Provan muttered, just as Acting DCI Mann trotted downstairs to rejoin him in the hall.

'What?'

'That was our DC Gowans,' he replied, 'winning himself no bloody medals. He's come up with hee-haw on Billy bloody Swords. He cannae even find a mobile account in his name with any of the providers.'

'Maybe he's a Luddite and doesn't have one; or he has a pay-as-you-go that he tops up in Tesco.'

'Mibbe, but this is a man on the move; we know he works for other folk than Stoddart. He's no' going to risk running out of credit in some foreign country.' He smiled. 'But that was the bad news. This is the good; Willie Gowans could find no record of him catching a flight out of any Scottish airport on Saturday. We should probably lift him now, but I've told Willie to get on to Trudi Pollock to find out what hotel he was booked in at. He must have had a car; if we can get the make and number from his hotel, get him on camera driving towards Ayr on Friday evening, and match up that hair on the fridge, then we've nailed him for both murders.'

'What if he drove to his Saturday gig in London?' Mann asked.

Provan frowned at her. 'I'm cookin' by effin' gas here, Lottie, don't spoil it.'

'I know,' she laughed. 'Let's see what Gowans comes up with . . . Detective Inspector.'

'Whit!' He stared at her.

She told him of her heavy discussion with the deputy chief and the full terms of its conclusion.

'Can he do that?' he exclaimed. 'Make me an acting DI without asking me?'

'Looks like he can. I'll still call you Sergeant if it makes you happy. It'll not be for long. They'll parachute someone in as a permanent replacement. I hear there's a guy in Shetland who's hot stuff.'

'Sandra'll definitely no' be coming back, then?'

'I don't see how she could,' Mann said. '*Not* to CID. Uniform if she wants to, once the smoke's clear, but not to her old job.'

'I'm not sure I like her being off limits to us,' her colleague observed.

'Me neither, but that's the way it is. Dan, we may be officers to our team, but to the people at command level, we're other ranks. We've had our orders, set in stone. You know, the longer I have to think about it, the more I sense the heavy hand of Bob Skinner behind them. If I'm right and he's given Sandra a clean bill of health, I'm okay with that.'

'Aye, mibbe. Did you find that jacket upstairs? There's no sign of it down here.'

'No. I went through the wardrobes in every room. There's some stuff there that looks like Sandra's . . . unless the champ wore a size fourteen ladies' suit, a thirty-six C-cup bra, and a thong that was more afterthought than underwear. His is all Jermyn Street and Savile Row; no Marks or Ralph Slater there . . . and definitely no biker jacket.'

'It must be somewhere,' Provan said. 'If we've been through the whole house, and we have, that just leaves the gym. Graeme Bell did say he'd been sweating shortly before he died.'

They left the house and walked round to the gymnasium. Its heating system was running, and so it was pleasantly warm. 'Where do we start?' Mann pondered.

The DS looked around. 'Nae coat-hangers in here,' he replied, 'but the changing room's through there. That's the likeliest.'

He wandered towards the rear of the training area and the two doors they had encountered on their previous visit, opening the one on the right. A wave of heat washed over him. 'My God,' he called out to Mann, 'the steam room's still on. Do ye fancy a Turkish bath while we're here, Lottie?'

'I prefer a sauna,' she replied tersely, 'but only on ladies' night.' She walked on, into the changing space. 'There's a cabinet here, Dan,' she exclaimed. 'It looks as if it's self-locking, though. Wait a minute.' She took the key ring from her pocket and looked at it, comparing brand names with the one on the door. 'Here it is,' she said. The lock was waist high; the key slid in easily, and the door swung open. 'And there we are.' A motorcycle jacket, light brown with gold flashes, hung inside, above a pair of high biker boots with Velcro fastenings.

As she took it out, her eyebrows rose in a look of surprise. 'Heavy, is it?' Provan asked.

'No, it's not. It's surprisingly light, top-quality leather. I doubt if you're expected to fall off wearing this.' She held it up with her left hand and felt in the side pocket with her right. 'Empty,' she grunted. She explored the inside and found two pockets; one held a small black LED torch, the other a tube of pastilles. 'Sod it. I doubt the Italian passed him either of these.'

'Just a minute,' Provan intervened, holding out a hand. 'Let me see it. I had something like this once.'

He took it from her and closed the collar, securing it with two studs. As the lapels came together, an outer pocket was revealed, secured by a zip. He opened it, plunged in his hand, then drew it out again with a look of triumph on his face as he brandished a small black plastic object no more than three inches long.

'What is it?' Mann asked.

'It's a memory stick,' he replied. 'The next question is "What's on it?" We'll need a computer or a laptop to find that out. A laptop,' he repeated, 'like the one we think Billy Swords stole from Moscardinetto.'

'There's a computer in Leo's office, isn't here? We can use that, if it isn't password-protected.'

'We'll find that out when we try,' the DS said, closing the cabinet and slinging the jacket over his shoulder.'

'What about the steam room?'

He grinned at her wickedly. 'We can come back once we've had a look at the memory stick.'

Leaving and locking the gym, they returned to the house, and to Leo Speight's office. When they booted up his computer, they found that, as Mann had suggested, it did ask for a log-in password. Provan shrugged, keyed in 'champion' and the desktop opened, displaying an image that they recognised as an Augusta Cambridge painting.

'See?' He grinned in self-satisfaction. 'It's always something easy.'

'What's yours?' she asked.

He mumbled a reply.

'What?'

'It's Lottie,' he repeated, more clearly, 'okay? What's yours?' He glanced up at her and saw that her face was slightly pink; a relic from the steam room.

'It's "cheekyweebastard". All one word,' she added.

He swung round in the swivel chair. 'Would that be a statement of fact, or a term of endearment?'

The flush on her cheeks grew deeper. 'Both.'

He was about to insert the memory stick into a USB slot when Lottie's phone sounded. 'A minute,' she said as she took the call. 'Mr Skinner,' he heard her say. He sighed without quite knowing why.

'Actually, we're about to look at a memory stick that we found in the jacket Leo Speight wore to go home last Friday night slash Saturday morning. The painter woman said she saw Moscardinetto hand him something just as he was leaving.' She paused, and in the silence Provan's own ringtone, 'Down Under', rang out.

'Okay, if you'd like, we can do that,' he heard her say as he turned his attention to his incoming call.

'Willie, what have you got?'

Young DC Gowans had an enthusiasm about him that Dan Provan had no wish to curb; indeed he hoped he would never lose it.

'I checked on the man Swords, Sarge,' he began. 'Like you said, he's registered at a wee hotel overlooking Loch Lomond. He's driving a hire car, an Audi, registration Sierra Mike sixty-six Mike Whisky Golf. When I checked, the company told me that Ms Pollock booked it for him. I spoke to her and she told me that the boxing people are staying in Scotland for a while to be on hand if we need to speak to them again.'

'Good lad. Now you get on to the CCTV folk and see if you can find him on the road to Ayr last Friday evening.'

As he ended the call, Mann was finishing hers. 'You first,' he said. 'Skinner?'

'Yes. He says he wants to view the memory stick with us. He also says he has the answers to some questions. I've said we'll meet him in Pitt Street, as soon as we can get back there.'

'Will that be before or after the steam room?'

'God,' Lottie exclaimed. 'My password was well chosen.'

Thirty-Seven

'The impossible we do at once,' Amanda Dennis said. 'Miracles tend to take a little longer.'

Skinner's phone interrupted his music as he cruised past the Gyle shopping centre, heading along the West Approach Road away from central Edinburgh and his office in Fountainbridge. It broke into his thoughts also; for most of the time since he had left Stirling he had been replaying the events of the morning, their outcome and the implications for professional and personal friendships stretching back for more than twenty years.

When he had told the chief constable and her deputy that he had sent Sandra Bulloch on her way, McGuire had been barely able to contain his anger, and had made little or no attempt to conceal it.

'You're telling us, Bob, that you let a person of interest in a homicide investigation leave this office without consulting either the chief constable or me?'

'No, Mario. I'm telling you that I was invited to conduct an interview that would determine whether she was a person of interest. I agreed on the basis that I would do it my way, and use my own judgement. That was, and still is, that Sandra Bulloch didn't kill her fiancé, and had no information at all that could be

293

helpful to the investigation, other than the matter I mentioned: the phone call to Speight that she and I presumed, in hindsight, was from Aldorino Moscardinetto – a presumption, that's all, still to be proved. I saw her reaction to questioning, you didn't. I decided that a further more formal interview was unnecessary, and more, that it would be both cruel, and discourteous to a senior police officer. So yes, I told her to go, and yes, I told her to go as far away as she could manage. A judgement call, yes, and frankly, it was one of the easiest I've ever had. What would you have done?'

'Minimum? Ask for her passport. Confirm her whereabouts during the time Speight was being poisoned.'

'By asking her neighbours whether her lights were on, and whether any of them saw her leave the house. Aye, sure. You know what, Mario? If you don't understand why I made that decision, then I'm happy for you. If you never do, I'll be even happier.'

A phone call would be made in the near future to mend damaged fences; that he knew, but he was less certain whether it would be McGuire or himself who made it.

When his ringtone cut in on Donald Fagen, he thought that question had been answered, but it was the head of the Security Service, her mood a welcome change from those he had left behind him.

'Does that mean you have something on Swords?' he asked.

'Oh yes. For openers, his real name isn't Billy Swords; that's the name he adopted when he became a British citizen. He did that because there are parts of the world where a Russian might be made less than welcome. He admitted that to the Home Office person who interviewed him when he made his application twelve years ago.'

'Billy Swords is a Russian?' Skinner exclaimed.

'He was, and he still is; he has dual nationality. That name's a rough translation of the one he's had since birth forty-seven years ago, Uilyam Mechikov.'

'Do the Stoddarts know about this?'

'The older one does, certainly,' Dennis said. 'He was one of Mechikov's referees on his naturalisation form.'

'As a matter of interest, who was the other?'

'A man named Gino Butler. He's described as an accountant; one referee must be a person of professional standing. Does that ring any bells . . . if I can use that boxing analogy?'

'It does. Butler was Leo Speight's best pal, his manager by name but his assistant in reality. I've met him; and Swords too, for that matter.'

'You sounded surprised earlier, when I told you of his origins.'

'I was,' he admitted. 'Still am. His English is impeccable.'

'It should be. He worked for the Russian diplomatic service in the late nineties, well after the end of the Soviet era. He was posted to the London embassy. He was a second secretary in the commercial department.'

'You know what I'm going to ask you,' Skinner said.

'I do, and the answer is yes. Quite early in his London posting, Uilyam Mechikov was identified as a member of the Federal Security Service, what we call the FSB. That's why I was able to pin him down so easily. He owned up to that part of his past on his application form.'

'I imagine that was because he guessed it would be run past your service and you'd probably pick him out.'

'Probably,' she agreed. 'However, finding out other things about him wasn't so easy. As I said, he didn't give up his Russian passport, and much of his business is still conducted under the name Uilyam Mechikov. But not all of it. He pays his UK income tax as Billy Swords but his local taxes as Mechikov. His telephone landline and his TV licence are held as Swords, but his Vodafone contract is Mechikov. That's why we didn't find him straight away.'

'Have you got access to his mobile records?'

'We're getting them within the hour,' Dennis replied.

'When you do, they should be checked for calls to a Russian called Brezinski, and a company named Zirka. In particular your people should look for any calls made from four o'clock on Monday afternoon for the rest of the day. I think you might find one made around five to a Russian number.'

'Calling about what?'

'You're aware of the murder in Glasgow of Aldorino Moscardinetto, the film director?' Skinner asked her.

'Of course. The London media don't ignore everything that happens in Scotland. What's the connection to Mechikov?'

'Mechikov killed him.'

'What? Are you sure of that?'

'Pretty much. We can place him in the vicinity of the murder, and by now I'm sure the Gartcosh SOCOs will have picked up evidence that will put him in the room. At my request the police have been letting him run for now, to see where he took them. Do something for me, please, Amanda – or rather do it for Detective Inspector Charlotte Mann. Put a stop-and-detain order on Swords, or Uilyam Mechikov, whichever passport he uses, at all ports and airports. Also, can you have someone check as soon as possible whether he was on any flight to London late Friday night or Saturday morning, and if so, when he flew back to Scotland.'

'Will do. Does this relate to the murder of Speight, Bob?'

'There is a connection between the two men,' he replied, 'and obviously it suggests a connection between their deaths.'

'You don't sound convinced.'

'I still need to be. I don't believe the Italian's murder was planned; it looks to me like a burglary interrupted. In fact I'm slightly surprised that a chubby mid-forties guy like Swords was able to do it. Aldorino was ten years younger than him and didn't look out of shape.'

'Don't discount him. When the Soviet Union collapsed, and Yeltsin climbed on board that tank and asked its crew whose side they were on, if our Uilyam wasn't driving it, he was in one very like it in the same city. Those tank corps people were elite.'

'Noted. You'd get a laugh for that in Scotland, by the way.'

'What?' she asked, puzzled.

'Our Uilyam. Translates as Oor Wullie, our most famous wee boy.'

'I'm always amazed by the breadth of your Scottish culture,' she replied.

Thirty-Eight

'Swords has gone,' Dan Provan announced as he strode into Mann's office. 'When DC Gowans checked back with Beedham's, they told him that he'd left yesterday morning. He didnae check out or anythin', just stuck a bag in his motor and drove away. I've sent the nearest available uniforms in there to seal off his room, and Gowans is on the way too, tae see what he's left behind him, if anything. I've put an advisory out for his car, UK-wide.'

'That won't do you much good,' Skinner told him. 'From what I've learned about this man's history, he'll have dumped it very quickly. My guess will be that it's within a mile of where we're sat now, either picking up tickets on a meter or in a car park, where it'll be less easy to find. It'll be somewhere near the Central station, and he'll have caught a train last night.'

'Magic,' Lottie Mann sighed. 'And we can't even say which name he's using.'

'You should assume he's travelling as Mechikov. He doesn't know his second identity has been uncovered. He thinks you're looking for Billy Swords, or rather the man who used to be Billy Swords. That name's no more than a National Insurance number now, as far as he's concerned.'

298

'Won't he be using bank cards?' the DI suggested, glancing at Skinner then at Provan.

'And leavin' a trail?' the DS countered. 'If you want me to guess, whatever cards he has as Swords, he'll have pulled as much cash as he can with them as soon as he could, and that's what he'll be travelling on. How much could that be, Bob? You're the rich man in the room.'

'It depends how many credit cards he has and what their cash limits are; potentially thousands. He won't be bothered about maxing out, since he'll have no intention of repaying anyone. If your guess is right, Dan, and I'm sure it is, Billy Swords has disappeared, until he chooses to resurface as Mechikov.'

'If,' Mann said mournfully. 'For all we know, he has a third passport.'

'He can have as many passports as he likes,' Skinner said, 'but he only has one face, and by now that's on site at every point of departure from this country. The Security Service has made sure of that, and pretty soon it'll have accessed his phone records. Meantime, let's have a look at this memory stick. That's what we're all here for. Sandra said Leo and Moscardinetto had a project going. Hopefully this will tell us what it was.'

'Sandra said?' Provan exclaimed, glaring at the DI. 'You were right, Lottie.'

She smiled. 'I usually am, but let it lie.'

She slid the stick into an empty slot on her computer, then waited as its contents were displayed on screen. One file was labelled 'Rough Cut', the other was untitled. 'What are those?' she asked.

'The Rough Cut one's a movie file,' Skinner told her. 'The other's a Word document. Unless the software's been changed since my day, you should be able to open them both. Here, let me.' He reached for her mouse and clicked on the nameless file.

It had no heading, it was single spaced and it had been created in a font so small and dense that it was almost unreadable. 'Bugger that,' he murmured, selecting the entire document and changing it to Times New Roman, fourteen point, double spaced, big enough for him to make out without resorting to his hated spectacles. 'There you go,' he murmured, and began to read, silently, as did his companions.

'Here you are, my friend, a rough edit of our documentary. As we agreed, none of the people you will see have any idea that you are involved. They think I am interviewing for a new drama series of Netflix; I have used this deception before and I find that with that encouragement people want to please me. It is the fascinating story that you promised it would be. I am suspecting that some of it will be unknown even to you. We have two ways of going forward as I vision it. It can be the documentary that we set out to produce. We do it this way, my target is to enter it in the Panorama series in the Berlin Festival, with the hope also that your name will attract a BAFTA nomination, where I have won before, and if we are brave maybe an Oscar too, where I have not but I have the ambition. But there is another way. I have a friend, an American lady who is a screenwriter, a genius. She is of the left wing, which means that she is popular with her colleagues, but not with the people who control the money in cinema. What I like to do is show it, what we have, to her and invite her to extend her creativity to produce a script for a feature film, a drama. We maybe change names, make it appear to be a work of complete fiction, a drama not based on boxing, for there have been too many of them, but on what happens behind boxing as we began to talk about, a fight film with no fight scenes. We do this, it has more impact, especially if we have a star who is committed to play the part that is you under another name. I already spoke, with no detail, no secrecy broken, with Joey Morocco. He told me after we work together before that he wants to do it again, and this would be his chance. He would be executive producer, which is no more than a title; you would be producer, I would be director and producer. We would not need to spend big money on this. The budget could be a maximum of five million euros, if Joey agrees to cut his pay and take points of the gross instead. I can find two million, if you can find three, and maybe Joey will kick in a million of his own if we ask him nice. He do that, he can be a producer too instead of just executive. Anyway, you watch what I have shot already, and if you say we go ahead as we said at first, I agree. But as you watch, try to think of actors speaking the words, and a screenplay that shows what happens rather than tells. If my vision can be your vision, then we are heading for Cannes, not Berlin.'

Skinner leaned back in his chair, finished before either of the two detectives. 'I'm righteously angry already,' he said when they had caught up with him. 'I'd have liked to see that movie made, and now I never will.'

'Let's see how far he got,' Mann murmured as she clicked on 'Rough Cut'.

The monitor darkened for a few seconds, then flashed brightly, until the setting stabilised and an image came into focus. It was Leo Speight, bright eyed, smiling, clean shaven, his dark hair lustrous, his skin tone a shade or two darker than it had been in death. The contrast to their last sight of him was dramatic. Skinner thought he had never seen a man look so full of vitality; he leaned across the DI once more and paused the image.

'Where is that?' Provan wondered aloud. The location was outdoors, a busy square, bathed in watery sunshine. Speight, who was seated at what appeared to be a café table, was wearing a high-collared white shirt and the same biker jacket that lay on a chair in the corner of Mann's office, or its twin. In the background, the people, frozen in mid stride, were dressed for winter.

Skinner leaned forward and peered at the screen, then reached out a pointing finger. 'See that fella there, that big white statue? His name's David; he's a copy of the original by Michelangelo. The building behind him is the Palazzo Vecchio, and the square's called the Piazza della Signoria. He's in Florence. I took my daughter there on holiday when she was fourteen. Bored out of her skull, she was.'

He restarted the video, just as Speight settled back in his chair, laid down his glass and switched his gaze to the camera from the person behind it.

'So here we are,' he began. 'School is out. It's all over. I am now officially an ex-champion, having relinquished all my belts yesterday, and now the story can be told. Why? Because I was smart enough and good enough to be a winner all the way, but I was lucky too, or I might have become a victim. Now the time has come for me to share my experiences, so that no one else gets taken.'

His voice was quiet, but deep enough to transcend the background noise. There were very few traces left of a Paisley accent.

'I was naïve when it all began,' he continued. 'I should have known better. My father warned me often enough. "They will offer you the world," he told me, "but they'll never actually hand it over. You've got to take it for yourself, son." My dad never could, because he was never on the inside. When he was Peter Jackson, he knocked out two British champions and a former champion of France in his first twelve fights, but the London establishment froze him out because he wouldn't leave Benny Stoddart and sign up with them. So he went to Vegas, late seventies it was, a couple of years before I was born, and took a fight there on the undercard of a heavyweight championship fight, against the big American hope, a young guy called Kid Soledad, a Latino.

'He battered him all over the ring in the first round, then went back to his corner and took a swig from a water bottle that had been doctored. Fuck knows what they put in it, but when he went out for round two, he was a target, and the Kid did not miss. The bandages under his gloves must have been loaded too, for he hit my old man upside the head and caused a slight bleed on the brain. He survived, with only a wee bit of long-term damage, but his career was over, and all the money he ever earned, and a good chunk of Benny Stoddart's too, went on medical care.'

The recording paused for an instant; when it restarted, Speight was holding his glass. 'How do you load gloves? Easy, you put the bandages on, then once the witness from the other side has gone, you soak them in plaster of Paris and let it dry. Turns your fists into fucking boulders.' He smiled gently. 'I got them back, though. The first time I fought in the States, Kid Soledad was still around, making a comeback. He was the age I am now, and I was the age he was, twenty-two, when he hurt my dad. That was another undercard fight, in Atlantic City, but they let me pick my opponent, and I chose him.'

There was another minuscule break in the video; Skinner realised that Moscardinetto had edited out his questions. 'His gloves were probably loaded that night too,' Speight chuckled, 'but they did him no good, because I never let him hit me. I spent five rounds making him look bad, but not so bad that the ref would stop the fight. Then in the sixth, I got him in a clinch and whispered in his ear, "What happens next is for my dad." I set him up with a feinted jab, then threw a big uppercut. It wasn't a punch I usually threw, because it was too showy, and left you open to a counter if you missed, but I wanted the crowd to see it and to remember. It was a showreel punch; it lifted him up on his toes, and then he fell forward. There's an old saying in boxing: "When they fall face down, you can go and collect your winnings." It's true; the ref knew it as well, for he never bothered to count.'

The screen froze on him. When movement restarted, the watchers could see that some time had elapsed by a sudden shift in the shadows, and by the plate that blinked into being on the table, with knife and fork together besides the relics of a meal.

'After the Olympics, Yevgeny Brezinski and me always had to happen. I won that final, but he got the decision. A video review showed that I outscored him by three to one; I knocked him down in the last round but the ref called it a slip. That's how bent the officials were. He had my gold medal, so I was having his world championship belt, to hang alongside mine. The only question was where it would happen. He had his own promotion company, Zirka. I was with the Stoddarts – Benny was still around at the time, but beginning to show the signs I'd seen in my mother – but I made my own decisions. I told Bryce to propose Las Vegas as the venue, because that's where the biggest bucks are always, but they turned it down flat. We proposed the Emirates Stadium, sixty thousand capacity, they said no.' The champion laughed. 'We even suggested the Stade de France in

Paris, but no, Yevgeny would only get in the ring with me in Russia.

'He and I spoke once during the negotiations. "I want it to be like *Rocky Four*," he said. I told him he should remember how that one finished, but he said, "This time be different." It was all ritual dancing, really. He was never going to fight anywhere else; the simple fact was he didn't want any part of me, only the money I brought with me. For I did; Brezinski against anyone else always made peanuts, but against me, Spotlight, the US cable network, got involved, along with the British pay-per-view market as well. So we did the deal; it was complicated but we managed it, even though I had to give him fifty per cent of the TV money, which he'd never have earned on his own.'

He reached for his glass, which had been refilled with something that looked like bitter lemon, and took a long drink. 'Then he offered me some of it back. Bryce had a message, directly from Yevgeny, he said, guaranteeing me ten million euros in cash, Swiss bank account, the lot, if I canned the fight. I could do it any way I liked, quit on my stool between rounds with a fake injury, take a dive, up to me.'

The picture blinked once again, resuming with Speight staring not at the camera but above it. 'I agreed, of course. What else was I going to do; it was the only way I'd ever have got the fucker inside the ring. If I hadn't, he'd have injured himself training and the fight would never have happened. I couldn't allow that. He owed me for the Olympics, just as Kid Soledad owed my father, and I always collect what's due me.

'When we went into the ring that night, Brezinski thought he was going to win, his trainer thought he was going to win, Bryce Stoddart thought he was going to win, and so did a few punters, because there was a late rush of betting on him. It took poor old

Yevgeny five or six rounds before he began to realise what was going to happen. I was never better than that night. Everything he was, I was double that. I hurt a different bit of him every round. I was never a sadistic fighter, usually. I didn't inflict unnecessary pain, not even on Kid Soledad, but I did serious damage to Brezinski. I broke a couple of his ribs in the fourth, I hit him on the right shoulder in the seventh, dislocated it a wee bit, but he carried on, hoping against hope that I'd go down or pretend I'd broken my hand. I carried him a round for each of those ten million euros, which had never gone near any Swiss bank, by the way, and then I tucked him in for the night and went home with his belt. After that, the boxing game was mine. I owned it and anyone who wanted to play did it by my rules.'

The screen went dark again, save for a clock icon, ticking down ten seconds to zero. When it had run its course, the scene was different, as was the person before the camera. A young man with a facial resemblance to Leo Speight but a shorter neck and a more serious expression. His skin tone seemed lighter, but the gloomy surroundings might have contributed to that.

Provan hit the pause icon. 'I know who that is, and where. How about you, big fella?'

'It's Regina's,' Skinner replied. 'I'm guessing that's Gordon Pollock, although I've never met him.'

'That's right. Let's hear what he's got to say.' He set the screen in motion.

'. . . love my dad,' the youth began. 'I do everything he says and I know he only wants what's best for me, but he's a fucking control freak. Also he's got it totally wrong about boxing. He says to me that no way am I going anywhere near a boxing gym, yet he sent me to a school that plays rugby, where you can get hurt far worse.'

'Glasgow High,' Provan mouthed to Skinner as the video ran on.

'I only met my Grandpa Speight the once. I wasn't supposed to, just like I wasn't supposed to see my dad, but my mum sneaked me round to his house one day, when I was three, or maybe just four. I have a vague memory of this big jolly black man, with a shaved head and an old scar alongside it. He told me all sort of stories that I was too young to understand at the time. My mother told me later, though; they were about fighting, about it being the poor man's way out of being poor, and how my dad was on the way to taking the whole family out of poverty with his fists. I told my dad that story when he kicked up a fuss about me wanting to box. He told me that if Grandpa Speight had been treated right he'd have made millions, and he'd never have had to step inside a ring himself. He said I'd no idea what went on in professional boxing and that I was never going to find out.

'My Grandpa Pollock found out, though, about me seeing Grandpa Speight. I mentioned it in the house one night and he went berserk, as usual. He battered my mother, he battered me, and he even hit my granny when she tried to stop him. I said to him, "You wouldn't do that if Grandpa Speight was here, or my dad," and he hit me again. I was going to run and get Grandpa Speight, but he locked me in the stair cupboard, the bastard, and didn't let me out for a whole day, then belted me again for peeing in there. I wish I had gone for Grandpa Speight, for a few weeks later he died, in some sort of accident at work.'

There was a flicker, another question excised.

'Grandpa Pollock died himself, thank Christ, not long after that. Years afterwards they told me he had a heart attack and fell in the Cart, but I found out later that nobody in Paisley believed that. I was told he had so many enemies in the town, there was a queue to toss him in there. The same people believed that he paid somebody to kill Grandpa Speight in the railway yard. Years afterwards I asked my dad what he thought. He looked at me, more seriously than I ever saw him, and he said, "If he did, then things went full circle, didn't they. Never mention that man's name to me again, please, Gordon." I never did, not because I was afraid of my father, I never was that, but because I feared that if I did, I might find out how the old bastard really went in the water.'

Unlike that of his father, Gordon Pollock's monologue was delivered without him once looking at the camera.

'Not that any of us cared,' he continued. 'My mum was glad he was dead, and she and my granny didn't even go to his funeral. Nobody did, apart from my dad and me. Later on, when I was older, my dad said that he only went to watch the crematorium curtains close. He said he'd have had him buried, because it was cheaper, but he didn't want to poison the worms.' He laughed. 'The world thinks my dad's a gent, and he is, but that's the side of him they'll never see: how he is when somebody crosses him.'

He looked above the camera as Moscardinetto asked a question that was inaudible on the soundtrack. 'Me, no, I'd never cross him. I disagree with him one hundred per cent about him not letting me box, even though I know he's right. If I did, I'd have a big sign round my neck, saying "Leo Speight's son: knock him cross eyed and boast about it to your mates." But it wouldn't stop me giving it my best shot. I said to him, "Maybe I'd surprise you if you let me try." He said no, that I wouldn't, because I'm too nice a lad. I said to him, "But you're a nice lad." He gave me that serious look again and he said, "No I'm fucking not. Ask anyone I fought." Anyway, I've stopped arguing with him about it. He says he's developing a chain of hotels and that he wants me to get my degree in hospitality management so that I can be ready to run them. He's given me a place of my own to live as well, at the Blacksmith; so my mother can get a life, he says. Fact is, she's happy with the one she's got. I wish he would let me box, though, just to find out.'

The young man faded to black, and the DI paused the recording. 'Very interesting, but where does it take us?' she asked, looking at Skinner for a response.

'It's telling us why Swords was sent to steal that laptop,' he suggested. 'Nobody knew about the copy that Aldorino gave Leo at the party. But who knew about the project itself?'

'The people who were in it, obviously.'

'Not necessarily. They agreed to be interviewed by Moscardinetto, but did they know about Leo's involvement, and did they know what the end product was going to be? That's not clear yet, not at all. What is, though, is this: Leo's story about Brezinski trying to bribe him to throw their fight provides a potential motive for his murder. If that leaked – and some of it must have, for Swords to have been sent to steal the laptop and the phone – it would be very dangerous, and possibly fatal for Leo. But we're not done yet. That line at the foot of the screen tells me we're not much more than halfway through. We should watch the rest before making any judgement.'

Mann nodded and pressed the arrow icon. The action resumed with a man on screen in an office location that could have been anywhere.

'Who's that?' Provan asked.

'Bryce Stoddart,' Skinner told him, 'and I'm very interested to hear what he's got to say, now we know about that bribe.'

'One might say,' the promoter began, 'that Leo is the acceptable face of boxing. What I will say is that the day his father brought him to see my father was the best that Stoddart Promotions ever had. He was a driven man, Peter Jackson – that was the name he used in the ring when he fought for my father. That came to an end when he was injured in a fight in Vegas. Dad told me that he overmatched himself, that he insisted on taking that fight, against his advice. They said he recovered from the brain blood clot, but I'm not sure about that. He was a bit peculiar, obsessive about that Vegas fight, making all sorts of claims about it that Dad said couldn't have happened. Despite that experience, he had a lot of time for Dad, and that's why he brought Leo to him once he'd made a name for himself in the amateurs.

'Dad wasn't sure about him, to be honest. A lot of good amateurs don't make the transition to professional. The deal we did with him was contingent on him coming back from the Olympics with a medal. Dad didn't think he would, that's why he agreed to send him to the LSE, but he got a couple of lucky breaks and only lost to Brezinski in the final. There were complaints about the judges, but you always have those at the Olympics. Bottom line, take a look at Leo's medal and you'll see that it's silver, not gold. There are misconceptions that Leo Speight made Stoddart Promotions; they're bollocks. He made us bigger, yes, but we'd have got there anyway.'

Stoddart fell silent; for a moment or two the watchers thought that the recording had frozen, but he resumed. 'Look,' he said, 'the truth is that Leo Speight cost us money. The fight he had in Russia with Yevgeny Brezinski; there were, say, certain agreements made in relation to that. On the night, Leo broke them, without consulting me or anyone else. Our co-promoter,

Zirka, let's just say they were not pleased, and when these people are pissed off with you, you've got trouble. Leo doesn't know this, but he's lucky to be alive. He thinks he knows all about the business side of boxing.'

Stoddart gave a sudden harsh, startling laugh. 'Actually he knows fuck-all about it. Oh, sure, he's a clever guy with a university degree that my father paid for, and there's nobody better at number-crunching with the TV companies, but that's the bit of the iceberg you can see. The rest of it, that's the dangerous part and it drags the shiny bit along with it. I'll be frank with you: if you look at the accounts we have to file with the taxman every year – and you can; they're public property with a company our size – you'll find that every year since that fight we've paid Zirka a million. It goes though the books as a consultancy fee; actually it's a fucking bounty, it's compensation for Leo reneging on the deal he made. Zirka's still in business, but it's a pissy little eastern European operation these days. It makes hardly any money. Without our contribution it would probably have sunk long ago, but we're tied to them, thanks to Leo. Not just the pay-off; there's more, but I really don't want to go into that.'

The screen blinked once more. 'Don't be fucking daft,' Stoddart continued. 'No, Leo never knew about the pay-off, or that Zirka had made physical threats against him. He never saw our accounts because he wasn't a shareholder in the company; he knew he made money for us, but as long as he made enough for himself, he was happy. He's a fucking innocent, Leo, that's the truth. He bounced something off me the other day, something he's thinking about doing now he's finished in the ring. Some pan-European MMA and boxing operation he wants me to get involved in; he can't be serious. If there was nobody else out

311

there doing that sort of stuff, maybe, but there is, and you don't want to mess with them.'

Abruptly, Bryce Stoddart faded, to be replaced by Gino Butler. The location was another café, but indoors at a window table, with a view across water to an island. 'Largs,' Provan muttered, as the narrative began.

'I've never seen myself as a boxing manager,' Butler said. 'You're asking me about my experience of the fight game, but all I can tell you is what I've seen through Leo Speight's eyes, more or less. I don't have a stable of fighters, just one client, and if we hadn't been mates since we were kids, I wouldn't have him. Even then I don't think it would have happened if it hadn't been for Mr Speight, Leo's dad. He was a nice bloke, and I liked him, but I can imagine that if you didn't know him he could have been a bit scary. He had a big scar on the left side of his head,' Butler tapped himself just above the temple, 'right there, and you could see it, 'cos he shaved his head. His eyes stood out too, and it was as if he was always staring at you. He shuffled when he walked rather than taking big strides. I almost said that apart from that you wouldn't know he'd been carried out of the ring at Caesar's Palace on a stretcher, but that's not true. You knew that he'd suffered a head injury, and there were other signs that he'd been a fighter.

'How good was he? Depends who you ask. Leo swears that he was drugged and slugged in that American fight, and that if it hadn't happened he'd have been a world champion and retired a rich man. Ask Bryce Stoddart and he'll tell you different. I've heard him say that Mr Speight was average at best and that his father only got him the Las Vegas fight because he was a cheap option who was going to make the other guy look good. Mind you,' he added, 'I've never heard him say that when Leo was in the room. I asked his dad – Benny Stoddart, that is, not Leo's dad – about him being drugged. "Things happen, son, that you don't want to know about: never forget that." That was all he said, but I never have forgotten it.

'I don't know the truth of it on either side, but I do know this: you don't get on those Las Vegas fight cards if you're a bum. You might not always be there to win, but you are there to look good, and unless you're the champion, to make the other guy look even better. Leo, he never needed that; he was always the best. Like I said, he's been my career, and I've got his dad to thank. When Leo went off to London to train, Mr Speight made me go down there as often as I could; then when I graduated he got Benny to fix it for me to be down there full-time. Nice man, Benny; it's a pity about the dementia. At first I got bunged a small salary as Leo's assistant while I completed my accountancy training, When I qualified, Leo declared that I was his manager, full-time.'

There was another edit, then Butler resumed. 'You said I could be frank, Mr Moscardinetto, so I'll answer your question, but edit this out, okay? I liked Benny, like I said, but I can't say the same about his son. Leo's always been the boss in their relationship, but still I've never trusted Bryce Stoddart as far as I could chuck him, and he's a chubby bastard. By the time Benny had to give up, because he couldn't remember by lunchtime what he'd had for breakfast, Leo's career was established and he was working to a programme that he drew up himself. That was simple: win all the belts, defend all the belts against all comers, make as much money as possible, then move on. Bryce tried to manipulate that, he tried to match Leo with people that I could have beaten, possibly because he wanted to protect him as an asset, but most likely because he'd been promised a backhander.

He pays a backhander himself, every year, to Brezinski's company Zirka. He thinks Leo doesn't know about it, but he does. I asked Leo about it, but he told me to ignore it. "It's his money he's paying out, not mine," he said, then he laughed and said, "Mafia stuff, in Bryce's head. He knows fuck-all, Gino." What did he mean? I don't know, honestly.'

The picture froze, then restarted once more. 'Leo's my entire boxing experience, as you'll have gathered. Now that he's quitting, I have to find a new career. Being the guy he is, he's working up a new business plan for a new fight channel, multi-discipline, with its own TV outlet. He'll float it as his own project, but he won't actually do it; he says it's for me, a terminal bonus, and for Bryce if he wants part of it, although Leo says he won't because he's too chicken, too scared of upsetting his imaginary mafiosi. I probably do know enough to run it on my own, but I don't know if I will. Leo and I have a personal conflict of interest of sorts; he might not be so keen when he finds out, as he's bound to.'

The screen went to black once more; Mann paused the replay. 'What did he mean by that?' she asked. 'A personal conflict of interest?'

'I have no idea,' Skinner said. 'Maybe you should try to find out from other sources before you put it to him directly. But let's see this through to the end.'

'I don't really know why you want to talk to me,' Trudi Pollock told Moscardinetto's camera. 'I know I work for Gino Butler, and he works for Leo Speight, but that doesn't make me part of the boxing business. To be honest, I hate the sport. My Gordon wants to box, he has done ever since he was wee, but he'll get no encouragement from me. Nor from Leo, thank God. He's forbidden him, point blank, from ever getting in a boxing ring, although Gordon's pushing twenty. How do you forbid an adult from anything? I suppose you can if you're Leo Speight.'

A dreamy smile crossed her face. 'Leo's like a brother to me now,' she continued. 'That sounds a wee bit incestuous, given that we've got a son together, but it's the truth. We went to school together, and when we got old enough, we went out on dates, pictures, youth club discos, and we did the sex thing because it was part of growing up. I'm Catholic and I thought I knew all about when it was safe and when it wasn't, but as it turned out, I didn't. Why am I telling you all this? You've got a kind face, that must be it. Still, I don't want any of this getting on to Netflix.

'My mum, she thought that I saw Leo as an escape route. She reckoned I must have reckoned that if I had a baby with Leo I'd get away, get out of the house I was brought up in. My father was a horrible man, you see. Just a beast; he never abused me sexually, but he did in every other way. No, I don't want to talk about him, really I don't. He has nothing to do with boxing anyway. But he did split me and Leo up. I should be ashamed to say this, but I'm not. I was glad when my father died. When he did, it was too late for Leo and me, but it always was really. He was with that Faye woman by then; she had her anchor sunk into him big-time . . . or she thought she had. She has to have it in someone, that one. I . . .' Suddenly her pretty face was distorted by bitterness. 'No,' she declared, 'I'm not going there. It's his business, more fool him.'

She smiled again, and the screen seemed to be brighter. 'So, back to business, what do I know about boxing? Next to bugger-all, but I do know this. Of all the people I've met that are connected with it, there's only one I'd ever trust, and that's Leo. I suppose you'd expect me to say Gino as well. I wish I could.'

'That's a statement,' Provan observed as her contribution

ended. 'And she works for the guy, too. Do ye think we should talk to her again?'

'My gut says no,' Mann replied. 'I don't want to be asking anyone direct questions from this recording. At the moment, nobody knows we have it and that's an advantage. I propose that we re-interview Gino Butler and see what we can squeeze out of him. Is that the video finished?'

'According to the screen, there's another couple of minutes left,' Skinner said. 'Let's see what's in them.' He clicked the play symbol, then froze it again as another face appeared, older, scowling. She was seated; there was a window behind her through which the dome of St Paul's Cathedral could be seen.

'Who the hell is that?' the DS exclaimed. 'I'd hate to be looking at her over the cornflakes every morning.'

'By some accounts the guy who does barely knows she's there,' Skinner retorted. 'That is Genevieve Alderney, matchmaker of Stoddart Promotions and Benny's bidey-in, as we say in Edinburgh. Let's hear what she's got to contribute.'

'You're making a TV series, *signore*?' she began. 'You want it to be as realistic as possible? Then I hope you don't want it to be a comedy, because there's no fucking laughs in the business. There's tragedy in plenty, but no brighter side. I only ever heard of one man who walked away reasonably unscathed from a serious head injury in the ring. That was Leo Speight's father, who fought as Peter Jackson, and look what happened to him. Got crushed by a truck in a railway yard before his son could earn enough money to get him out of there. I've been in this business for much of my life, and I've never met a happy old fighter. They all retire with problems. Leo Speight maybe not, but he's different. Speight never inhabited the boxing business, not really. From the moment he turned pro, he floated above it.

He was maybe the best fighter who ever pulled on a glove, and for sure he's made more money out of boxing than any other European. But he's not the real face of boxing; the real face is ugly, it's fifty-something if it lives that long, it's battered out of shape and its owner can't stick three syllables together without tripping over them. Or he's younger and he's in a wheelchair and he can't fucking speak at all, or he's in a bed being fed through a tube and having his ass wiped by a nurse, until he runs out of money to pay for his care and they switch off his life support. You want to make your TV movies, you make them about people like them, not about some Hollywood hero like Leo Speight, goddam him. He's fucking lucky to be alive, but nobody's luck lasts forever.'

The screen went black.

'There's a cracking last line, if ever I heard one,' Skinner murmured. 'You might want to have a chat with her.'

'Aye,' Provan shot back at him, 'but we might want to do a bit of research first. Did nothing strike you about her, Big Bob? The accent, it's just no' right. Genevieve Alderney: ye expect something cut-glass, no' something that sounds like a concentration camp guard that's been to night school. Sorry, naebody called Genevieve Alderney was meant tae talk like that.'

He nodded, hunched in his chair, lips pursed, eyebrows together in a frown. 'I hadn't noticed, Dan; I was too busy studying her body language to listen to how she sounded. But you're right: something's off about her. Tell you what,' he said, straightening up, 'leave the research to my side of the house. We'll get results faster than you.'

Thirty-Nine

'So what have we got here?' Skinner asked, eyeing the tall glass on the table with a degree of suspicion.

With the Pitt Street police building in its final few days, the canteen had closed, driving the trio to the nearest coffee shop, in Sauchiehall Street, opposite the Dental Hospital, an eyesore of a building whose brutalist style had been inflicted on the famous old thoroughfare half a century before.

'They call that a macchiato,' Provan told him.

'Not the fucking coffee, you hobbit!' the former chief barked. 'What have we learned from the video we've just watched? First off, none of the people we saw knew that Leo was behind the project. Why? Why did he keep his involvement secret?'

'Isn't the answer in the Italian's covering note?' Mann suggested. 'Leo saw it as a documentary on boxing, warts and all, so he wanted people to speak frankly, about him rather than to him. Once he'd done those interviews, Moscardinetto saw it as even more than that. He may have seen it as a piece of art; Leo probably saw it as his boxing legacy. The only thing that's certain is that nobody's going to tell us. Because they're both dead.'

'Yes, and by whose hand? That's the issue. We're one finger-print match away from proving Billy Swords killed Moscardinetto,

318

but many miles away from nailing him for Leo. We don't even have a motive, and unless he carried a cyanide capsule around with him, and a key to Leo's house, we don't have means or opportunity either. So I repeat, what have we learned from what we've just seen?'

'Speight took a bribe to lie down to Brezinski,' Provan replied, 'then reneged on it. We've learned that. Stoddart's been paying it back ever since, at a million a year, to keep the Russians from getting even with him.'

'Leo said the bribe was never paid,' Skinner pointed out. 'According to Butler, he knew that Stoddart was paying out the so-called bounty. He laughed it off as a fantasy, but is it? Is the money for something else? There's other questions from the film. Stoddart said there's more than the bribe, but he wouldn't go into detail. He and Gene Alderney both said Leo was lucky to be alive, but to me . . . it's difficult to explain, but I heard each of them in a different way. Then there's what Butler said about a personal conflict of interest with Leo, and also the fact that Trudi Pollock, who works for him, doesn't trust him. And Alderney, what about her, where did that bitterness come from? For that matter, where the hell did *she* come from? Hopefully the call I made before we came along here will give us a clue to that. Lots of questions, lots of people to re-interview, but nothing that points to Leo and Aldorino having the same killer. I'm sorry, Lottie, Dan, but there are two of them out there.'

He took a mouthful of macchiato, and was wincing at the taste when his phone sounded. The detectives watched him as he answered, 'Yes?' without naming his caller; saw him listen, smile, nod once, twice, make notes on a paper napkin, then end the call and grin at them across the table.

'Which piece of good news do you want first?' he asked.

'You choose,' Mann replied.

'Very well. That was my friend, my principal, my boss, if you like, in London. The first gem is this. Uilyam Mechikov was arrested twenty minutes ago at Newcastle airport, trying to board a flight for Dubai, having just bought a ticket for cash at the Emirates desk. She's arranged for two officers of what we used to call Special Branch to bring him to Glasgow and hand him over to you, at Pitt Street, at midday tomorrow. When he gets here, you can ask him about the second diamond that's fallen into our laps, something that was actually known before his arrest. At quarter past five on Monday afternoon, at which time we may assume Moscardinetto was dead, Mechikov made a phone call. Not to Brezinski, or Zirka, or anyone in Russia, but to someone close to home: Gene Alderney. Two minutes after that, our Genevieve sent a text message saying, "Got it. Complication. Dealt with." The recipient was Bryce Stoddart.'

Provan beamed. 'You lot have your uses right enough,' he laughed.

Skinner looked at Mann. 'I suggest that you have those two arrested on suspicion of murder, and detained overnight. We can tackle them in the morning, when we're fresh and they're not. By that time, we might know where the hell Alderney comes from.'

Forty

'You're something of a mystery, Ms Alderney. I've had people check on you. They tell me that you've been a part of the Stoddart Promotions team for ten years, but before that, you're pretty much invisible. In fact, you're a very special person. You have a passport that says you're a British citizen, but you don't appear to have a National Insurance number, you've never paid any income tax in the UK, and the NHS haven't heard of you either. Are you going to tell us how you managed that?'

The little eyes narrowed beneath the heavy forehead. 'I'm not going to tell you anything, Mr Skinner,' the woman replied. 'My business is my business and if you want to know it you have to find out from someone else. These clever people of yours are going to have to work harder.'

He smiled. 'They did. And they got back to me this morning, just as I arrived here. They tell me that the only trace on official records of a Genevieve Alderney was a birth registered in London in nineteen fifty-two, to a single mother whose address was given as a home for girls run by the Church of England. Father unknown, I'm afraid. There's nothing on the registers after that, no marriage, no children, no death, and only the original of her birth certificate is known to exist.

321

No copies were ever requested or issued. Dead end, it seemed.'

'Tough shit,' she growled. 'I am who I am.'

'Yes, but who the hell is that?' he countered. 'That's what we want to know. You see, my clever people didn't give up. Oh no, they went to the only possible source of information on baby Alderney: the Church. They discovered from its records that the child was adopted when she was only two months old, by a couple with the biblical-sounding names of Joseph and Mary Stoddart, to be a little sister for their son, Benjamin, whom they'd adopted two years previously. The child was renamed Adelaide Stoddart; a second certificate was issued in that name and an NHS number also. The medical history recorded under that number reveals that poor wee Adelaide, God bless her, was a sickly child. She had a heart defect that could be repaired very easily today, but that wasn't the case in nineteen sixty-one, when she died in Great Ormond Street Hospital.

'Joseph Stoddart, who was a demolition contractor, died of mesothelioma in nineteen eighty-nine. Mary, Benjamin Stoddart's adoptive mother, died in two thousand and six. In February the following year, Genevieve Alderney's birth certificate was presented to the UK Passport Office. The form and the photos with it were countersigned by Gino Butler, chartered accountant. Passport interviews hadn't been introduced at that time in that part of the country, and so it was issued without you having to explain who you'd been for the previous fifty-five years. That's what we'd like to know now.'

'I'm Gene Alderney,' she replied. 'I've always been Gene Alderney.'

'And I've always been Frankie Valli,' Dan Provan scoffed, following with a reasonable rendition of the chorus of 'Big Girls Don't Cry'.

'Yes,' Alderney hissed. 'You should stick to that.'

'Moving on from the acting detective inspector's second career as a Jersey boy,' Lottie Mann said, 'and temporarily from the passport issue, we'd like to ask you about a phone call you received on your mobile just after five last Monday from Uilyam Mechikov.'

Watching her closely, Skinner saw a very slight tightening of the woman's eyes at the mention of the name, and possibly the first tiny crack in her formidable armour.

'Who is he?' she blustered. 'Never heard of him.'

'You also know him as Billy Swords. He works for Stoddart Promotions, among others, as a master of ceremonies.'

'Ah, Billy,' she exclaimed, with a flash of a smile. 'You should have said. Yes, I probably had a call from him.'

'Probably?' Skinner repeated. 'Yes or no?'

'Okay, yes, but I don't remember the time.'

'Why did he call you?' Mann asked.

'He wanted to ask me if I knew how much longer we'd be stuck in Scotland. I told him, how the hell should I know?'

'Why do you think he wanted to know that?' the DI pressed.

Alderney shrugged. 'Same answer, dear. How the fuck should I know?'

Provan raised a hand. 'Were you no' concerned about that yourself? Your business is in London, mostly; you came up for Leo Speight's farewell party, and okay he's deid, and it's sad, but the funeral's no' going to be for a while, and we havenae asked you to stay here. So? Why did ye, you and Stoddart? Beedham's is a very nice hotel in a very nice spot, when the midgies aren't biting lumps out of you, and you're probably still on Leo's tab, since it was his place. Even so, I don't get it.'

She stared at him, head tilted back, lip curling slightly. 'Like

I give a fuck about that also,' she sneered.

'What was the complication?' Mann snapped.

Once more their subject's confidence seemed to waver, but only for a moment. 'What complication?'

'Immediately after you took the call from Mechikov – I'll use that name since it's the one on his mobile phone account – you sent Bryce Stoddart a text.'

'You've been reading my texts?' Alderney blustered.

'We're the police,' the DI answered coolly. 'We have access as part of a homicide investigation.'

'But you have not said yet that Leo was murdered.'

'Not Leo,' Skinner said quietly. 'The inquiry is into the death of Aldorino Moscardinetto, in Glasgow on Monday. Your associate Swords, or Mechikov, the guy who phoned you immediately after he was killed, has been arrested in Newcastle and is being brought back to Glasgow this morning. What do you think he's going to say when he's questioned?'

'I should care? I know nothing about it. Who was he anyway, this Moscardinetto?' She sneered dismissively.

'We think,' Mann replied 'that he was the complication mentioned in your text to Bryce Stoddart. "Got it. Complication. Dealt with." That's what it said: we believe that "it" was the dead man's laptop, which was stolen from his hotel room, along with his phone.'

'The phone was important,' Skinner added, 'because he used that to record his interviews. You can shoot a movie with a mobile these days. Some people do.'

'Is that so? Again, I should care. Who are you anyway, mister? You're not the insurance investigator that Gino Butler said you were, that's for sure.'

He smiled. 'You got me. No, I'm not; actually I'm a sometime member of the Security Service, and believe me, I will find out who you really are.'

'I'm Genevieve Alderney,' she retorted. 'Check my passport.'

'We're checking more than that, believe me. Now, challenge us with an explanation of what your text to Stoddart meant, if it wasn't what all three of us believe it was.'

'It was to do with our next fight promotion, in London, next month, with McBride the Edinburgh lad heading the bill. We needed a contract signed by an American fighter we're bringing over. It arrived, but the complication was that a drug-test report was missing. I dealt with by having it faxed to our office. Some people still use fax.'

Skinner nodded. 'Pretty good, off the top of your head, so it's probably true. But I doubt that it happened on Monday. Now tell us something else. Why did you tell Moscardinetto, the man you say you've never heard of, let alone met, that Leo Speight was lucky to be alive, but that his luck wasn't going to last forever?'

She stared at him for several seconds before replying. 'Why should I say that?' she asked softly.

'No,' he countered. 'Not why should; why *did* you, Gene? I don't know what you found on the laptop, if you were able to access its contents, but that doesn't matter. There was another copy of the interviews that Moscardinetto recorded. He slipped it to Leo last Friday night. We have it, and we've viewed it. You feature, prominently. You really shouldn't have killed him, you know. He was going to make you all movie stars.'

Alderney's face was impassive. 'You have me on camera,' she said, 'talking to a man whose name I can't even remember, who just turned up at my office saying he wanted to make a movie about boxing and boxers. I told him some truths, some tough

325

home truths, and I said something about Leo Speight. He was the most famous fighter on the planet, so why would I not use his name? You have to do better than that, mister.'

'No, we don't, we really don't,' he told her. 'That interview tells us a lot, but there's one word you use that tells me most of all. During it you refer – passionately, if I may say so – to the victims of boxing, citing the example of a young man, vegetative, having, and I quote, "his ass wiped by a nurse".'

'Yes,' Alderney barked. 'It happens, no joke.'

'I know, I know,' Skinner agreed. He smiled and glanced towards Mann. 'Apologies, Lottie, for the indelicacy, but a London-born lady in her sixties and given to vulgarity would never say that. To her he'd be having his arse wiped, poor lad, as I'm sure he is. I don't know where you learned your English, madam, but it wasn't in this country. I will find out where.'

'Theories, theories, all fucking theories,' she sighed. 'I have had enough of them. I am leaving; I'm going back to London.'

'Oh no,' Dan Provan said heavily. 'That you are not. I don't care whether we charge you with conspiracy to murder, or Bob here holds you under the Terrorism Act, but either way, you are staying in custody.'

Forty-One

'Gene is my father's partner,' Bryce Stoddart insisted. 'He's retired and lives in Arizona. I told him all this.' He nodded towards Skinner, seated beyond the two detectives. 'What's he doing here anyway? He told me he worked for an insurance company.'

'He's helping us with our inquiries,' Provan replied, with a mischievous grin that seemed to unsettle the promoter. 'Look, chum,' he continued, 'we've checked that out. You lied to Bob here. Your dad lives in a care home in Dulwich, wherever that is, and he has done for seven years. As well as having dementia, he's in the final stages of motor neurone disease, poor bugger. You tell people that he's still involved in your business, because most of them don't trust you. You lied to Bob about Gene Alderney, too. She was never anywhere near your business until about ten years ago, when she appeared out of the blue and your father got her a passport using a birth certificate that he found when his mother died. It belonged originally to his adopted sister, who never made it to ten years old.'

The promoter paled. 'How did you find all that out?' he murmured.

Provan glanced round at Skinner. 'Insurance companies know everything.'

'Look, Mr Stoddart,' Mann continued, 'we're not here to play games, and I'm done sparring with you people. I'm going to give you one opportunity to put yourself on the side of the angels, by telling us about the laptop and phone that were stolen from Aldorino Moscardinetto's hotel room on Monday, after he was murdered, by your associate Billy Swords. When I say one opportunity, I mean it.'

'She does,' Skinner added quietly. 'Cough up, Bryce.'

Stoddart returned his gaze. 'I don't know what you're talking about,' he said.

Provan shook his head. 'That was really, really stupid. You went to Harrow School, Bob says. I thought you lads were supposed to be cleverer than ordinary folk.'

The DI drew a document from her bag and opened it for inspection. 'This is a warrant,' she announced, 'signed by a sheriff in accordance with the Criminal Procedure Scotland Act. It allowed us to search Beedham's hotel for property we believe to be stolen. His lordship took very little persuasion, because we were able to show him that the property really was there. Are you familiar with a facility called "Find my iPhone" and "Find my Mac"? No? That's a pity for you. It works through the iCloud. When a phone or a laptop is stolen, you can use it to show you exactly where it is. Our clever friends in the insurance industry were able to trace Moscardinetto's mobile provider. They agreed to help us as soon as they heard what had happened to their client, who was something of a hero in his own country. Yesterday afternoon, my officers searched your hotel on guidance received through the Cloud. It's not very big, so it didn't take them long.'

Stoddart looked at Skinner. If he had hoped to find a friendly face, he was disappointed. 'We told you,' he murmured.

'Okay!' the promoter exclaimed. 'I'll tell you. They're in the safe in my room.'

'You're too late,' Mann told him. 'We've got them. You had your chance and you turned it down. As DS Provan said, you'll have a few years to reflect on how stupid that was. For now I'm suspending this interview, but you and Ms Alderney will be charged, after you've been given the opportunity of a consultation with a solicitor.'

'I had nothing to do with it!' Stoddart protested.

'Stop!' Skinner called out. 'I'm going to give you another piece of advice, and this time take it. You have rights; take advantage of them and keep your mouth tight shut from now on until you've seen a lawyer.'

'Do you know one?' he asked.

'As it happens, I do, but it wouldn't be ethical for her to represent you as I might be a witness in a future trial. The big noise in Glasgow is a man called Moss Lee; I'm sure he'll take you on. We'll give you his number and leave you alone so you can call him from this room, but don't do anything stupid. There'll be a cop outside.'

The trio headed for the door. When they were outside, Provan turned on Skinner. 'What the fuck did you do that for, tellin' him to keep quiet?'

'You know as well as I do,' he fired back, 'or you bloody should. As soon as Lottie told him he was being charged, you passed the point where you could question him.'

The DS sniffed. 'Mibbe,' he conceded. 'But why did you tell him to call Moss Lee?'

'Two reasons. If he'd asked around, chances are that's the name he'd have been given anyway. Also, Lee's not half as clever as he thinks he is. I had a call from my daughter last night, of which more in due course.'

'Let's hope you're right, for lots of reasons,' the DS sighed.

'What's all this about, Bob? Any ideas?'

'Not all of it, but I have about this part of the inquiry. I have a gut feeling that it all goes back to . . . Bugger!' he exclaimed as his phone sounded. 'I meant to put that on flight mode.'

He looked at the screen; it read 'Alex'. He took the call. 'Yes, kid?'

'Bad time?' she asked. 'You sound a shade testy.'

'Sorry. No, not really. The crisis is over. What's up?'

'I've just had a call from a cop in Newcastle, Detective Chief Superintendent Ciaran McFaul. He says he knows you from way back.'

Yes, Skinner knew him. Their paths had crossed twenty years before during a murder investigation, from which many things had flowed, including his son Ignacio. The victim had been Mia's brother, and a relationship had developed, very brief but long enough.

'He phoned me,' Alex continued, 'about a man who's been arrested in Newcastle, on suspicion of murder. He's being brought north to Glasgow, but before he and his escort left, he was advised of his rights to legal advice. He asked DCS McFaul if he knew any lawyers in Scotland. He must have heard of me, somehow, for he dropped my name. The call was made at the suspect's request, asking if I would represent him. His name is Uilyam Mechikov, but according to DCS McFaul he's also known as Billy Swords. Pops, this thing you've been working on in Glasgow and been all mysterious about, is it connected?'

'Very,' he replied. 'I found the victim, and was involved in identifying your potential client. You shouldn't do it, but your associate could, if you don't discuss the case with her at all . . . and if you think she's up to it.'

'Cecily? She's been straining at the leash waiting for

something like this. I take it that her client speaks English?'

'As well as she does,' he assured her. 'He's a TV personality of sorts. And for your ears, not hers, as she has to come to it fresh, he is also as guilty as sin.'

Forty-Two

In Skinner's working lifetime, Scottish lawyers, like cops, had become younger as a group, bright young things, with an increasing proportion of them being female. Cecily Marsden was not one of that generation; she was in her late forties, and had returned to practice after an extended career break to raise her children.

She had joined Alexis Skinner's growing practice to handle most of the sheriff court work that came its way, Legal Aid summary cases that mostly required two pleas, 'Guilty, my lord,' followed by mitigating circumstances. Alex had taken her on as an associate because she had seemed to be a safe pair of hands, but had realised quickly that she was more than that and had come to value her opinion.

She was all business as she stepped out of the Pitt Street interview room to face Mann and Provan, dark suited, ash-blond hair perfectly arranged, cut short to fit under a wig whenever an old-style sheriff required it to be worn. She and Swords/Mechikov had been closeted for twenty minutes.

'My client is ready for you, officers,' she said. 'One thing before we begin. He wishes to be addressed as Mr Swords; that's the name under which he was naturalised.'

'We'll call him Ishmael if it gets his co-operation,' the DS grunted. Both the DI and the lawyer stared at him. 'What?' he exclaimed. 'Have ye never read *Moby Dick*, or are you surprised that Ah have?'

'I'll never stop being surprised by you, Dan,' Mann said. 'Sorry, Mrs Marsden; my colleague's an acquired taste. Your man will be charged under both names, so what we call him on the record doesn't matter to us. Before we go in there, is there anything you want to ask us?'

'Will Mr Skinner be here?' the solicitor responded. 'I understand that he's involved in the investigation in some way.'

'He'll be a Crown witness when this goes to trial, so it wouldn't be appropriate for him to be in there.'

'What's his locus, exactly? He's not a police officer any longer. My client seems to think he's working for an insurer.'

'That's not something we can discuss. When we get to the stage of formal disclosure to the defence, you'll see the extent of his involvement. Are we ready?'

'Almost,' Marsden said. 'Can you tell me whether the fiscal is immovable about the charge? Is he wedded to prosecuting for murder?'

'The only betting there'll be on this one,' Provan told her, 'will be on how long the jury takes to convict. I'll have fifty quid on forty minutes maximum, and it'll be unanimous. I've been in CID for a quarter of a century and I've never taken a stronger case tae court. That's me being frank,' he added, 'because you're connected tae Big Bob's daughter.'

'Thanks for that courtesy, Detective Sergeant,' she replied, looking from him to Mann. 'I asked the question because there are circumstances in which my client might be prepared to plead guilty. He has certain information that might be of interest to you in a broader context, even if it relates only indirectly to your case.'

'Plead guilty to what?' the DI countered.

'To a charge of culpable homicide as opposed to murder.'

'The problem with that is, we believe he was surprised by the victim returning to his room and catching your client in the act of stealing his computer. He killed him after a struggle. You can argue it wasn't premeditated, but it happened in the course of a crime, and that's premeditation.'

'I could argue that my client was only defending himself against a younger, fitter man.'

'We have information about your client's early career, before he left Russia. You might not want to go there. Look, to save time, I'll tell you that we also have him on CCTV, approaching the hotel, and we've matched fingerprints taken in Newcastle by the arresting officers with those found in the room and on an entrance hatch on the roof of the building. In addition, yesterday evening we recovered the victim's computer and phone in the hotel where your client was staying. We have his prints on those too. That's how done he is, Mrs Marsden.

'Look, you know we can't make a deal,' Mann concluded, 'only the fiscal can do that. But we can make a recommendation, depending on what your client has to say. That's the best I can offer at this stage. If you want, you can go back in there and put it to Swords, if that's what he wants us to call him. He doesn't want to piss us about, though; there could be a difference of ten years' jail time in the outcome. Make sure he knows that.'

The lawyer sighed, then nodded. 'Give me a minute.'

The minute stretched into three, until Marsden reappeared and gave another nod. The detectives followed her into the interview room, where their suspect was waiting. It was difficult for them to judge his height, as he was seated, but the forearms that protruded from the rolled-up sleeves of his white shirt suggested that his stocky build was more muscle than fat. As he peered at them, his eyes were so puffy that Provan was momentarily suspicious that his Geordie colleagues might have given him a slap, until the paleness of his face brought him to realise that the man was showing the effects of lack of sleep. He had a grizzled stubble on his chin that was at least two days old, and as they seated themselves across the table from him, the detectives realised that he was as badly in need of a wash as he was of a shave.

'Welcome back to Scotland, Mr Swords,' the DI said. 'We haven't met before, but we know who you are . . . both of you. To complete the formalities for the recorders, I am Detective Inspector, Acting DCI, Charlotte Mann, and my colleague is Detective Sergeant, Acting DI, Daniel Provan. I believe you were cautioned and advised of your rights when you were arrested at Newcastle airport, is that correct?'

'Yes,' the prisoner replied, his mouth tight.

'You were told also that you were being detained in connection with the unlawful killing on Monday of Aldorino Moscardinetto, in a hotel called the Stadium in West Campbell Street, Glasgow. We believe that you strangled Mr Moscardinetto with a curtain tie-back. Do you wish to make any statement about that accusation?'

Swords glanced to his right, at Cecily Marsden. She spoke for him. 'My client will offer no comment at this time on the killing. However, he does wish to make a voluntary statement about the break-in and the theft.'

'He's aware it may be seen as an admission of guilt?'

'As an admission to those charges, yes.'

335

'Very good.' Mann gazed across the table. 'But before we go there, I'd like to ask him a couple of questions about a matter separate to this investigation. He hasn't been charged with that, but we'd like to give him the chance to eliminate himself as a suspect. He hasn't been cautioned so technically I'm free to do that anyway, but in these circumstances I'd like your approval on the record.'

'You have it,' Marsden agreed, 'on the basis that I will intervene if I think you've crossed over.'

'We won't,' Provan said, looking directly at the prisoner and seeing nothing but curiosity. 'Mr Swords, last Friday evening, you attended a social gathering in a place called the Blacksmith, right?'

'Right,' he agreed. 'It was Leo Speight's official retirement party for his friends and family. He asked me to be master of ceremonies.'

'Ye know that a few hours afterwards Mr Speight was found dead in his house in Ayr?'

'Yes, I know, God keep him.'

'I'm sure he will. When did you leave the party?'

Swords frowned, but otherwise looked unconcerned. 'It must have been not long after eight,' he replied. 'I told Gino Butler, Leo's guy, that I'd have to leave early as I had a gig in London at a darts tournament next day. You can check. I was there; it started at two thirty.'

'Aye, we know, but our clever young DC Gowans can place you at Beedham's hotel at half past midnight. What we don't know is where you were during that four-hour gap, or how you got to London, 'cos you didnae fly out of Glasgow.'

'No,' he shook his head, 'I didn't. I flew through Edinburgh, eight o'clock flight Saturday morning, but I booked as Mechikov, because the card I used to pay was in that name. I am naturalised British, but I am Russian too, by birth. I have dual nationality. As for that three hours that you're worried about, I don't like the chef at the Blacksmith. Last time I ate there I was sick, and with my flight next morning I couldn't take the chance of it happening again. So I didn't eat there. Instead I stopped in Glasgow on the way back to Beedham's and I had a curry in a restaurant called Shish Mahal. You can check; I'm known there so they'll remember me. Also I paid with a card, another one, a Billy Swords card.'

Provan grunted. He leaned towards Mann and whispered, 'Looks like that big bugger might be right. The two murders arenae connected.'

Her face impassive, she looked straight ahead. 'Thank you for that,' she said. 'That was helpful. Feel free to make your statement now, in your own time.'

Swords nodded. 'First of all,' he began, 'I don't know why this thing was wanted, this laptop. I don't know and I didn't ask, because I thought it might be better if I didn't know, just in case something went wrong . . . as it has done. I was told to go and get it, that was all.'

'By whom?' the DI asked. 'For the record,' she added, with a nod to Marsden.

'By a man named Bryce Stoddart; he's the head of Stoddart Promotions, the crew who promoted all of Leo Speight's fights. Even the one in Russia against Yevgeny Brezinski. The co-promoter there was a Russian outfit called Zirka, but it was the Brits who called the shots, specifically Leo Speight himself. As I said, I don't know why Bryce wanted it, but he did, and he said it was urgent. He gave me the man's name, his hotel and his room number, and told me that he wouldn't be there for a couple of hours in the afternoon, because he had a meeting with Gino Butler. I didn't want to use the front entrance of the hotel in case there was a camera, and so I studied it from the lane and saw that I could get in across the roof. I recovered the laptop from the safe – these things are easy to crack – and also obtained the target's phone as a bonus. Then I returned to Beedham's and handed them over to Bryce. I stayed there overnight, but when I heard that the man was dead, I thought I had better make myself scarce. I left my car in a car park near the Central station, took a train to Manchester, and then another to Newcastle, where I was arrested. That is it; Bryce Stoddart is the man you want.'

'We have him, Billy,' Provan told him. 'He's being held in this building after we found the laptop and phone in his safe. We also have Gene Alderney under arrest. She's being held on suspicion of passport fraud, for starters. We'd be interested to hear anything you know about her.'

Swords surprised them by laughing. 'You have her?' he exclaimed. 'If I tell you about her, will it help me?'

'We can't make that promise,' the DS replied, 'but if you don't tell us everything you know . . . You're a smart man, work it out.'

He looked at his solicitor once more; she nodded.

'Gene came to Britain after the Brezinski fight. She ran Zirka; Yevgeny was a simple guy, only a puppet. When Leo knocked him out, Zirka was in trouble, financially and I think in other ways I never knew about. The Stoddarts – father and son it was before Benny retired – encouraged her to get out of there and move to London; they even arranged a new identity for her. She didn't keep her old name like I did; she became Gene all the way.'

'Hold on,' Mann called out. 'Zirka's still active in a small way. Who runs it now? Yevgeny?'

'I do,' Swords replied. 'You're right, it isn't much, but I keep the name alive for Gene. I can go back and forward to Moscow as I choose. I'm Mechikov there, Swords here.'

'And when she was there, who was Gene Alderney?'

'Her name was Lyudmila Brezinskova. She's Yevgeny's mother.'

Forty-Three

'Where's Detective Inspector Mann?' Moss Lee demanded. 'She's the SIO in this case; we should be speaking to her, not you.'

'She's recused herself from this interview. Cracking word that, isn't it,' Provan observed. 'Sounds very American. She's sittin' it out because she feels that it wouldn't be appropriate with the two of you being on opposite sides in another matter. You're stuck with me and Detective Constable Gowans, whether you like it or not. To be frank, I don't like it myself, Mr Lee, but it's my job and I'll do it.'

'You realise that was recorded,' the lawyer said. 'Your superiors will hear that remark.'

The DS chuckled. 'A shit I could not give; they'll hear that as well, I'm sure. You can leave if you like, but your client stays.' His gaze left Lee and moved to the man by his side. 'Now, do we get down to business, Mr Stoddart? You should understand, this conversation is between you and me, not us and him.'

The promoter nodded. 'I know that, but I'm still going to take his advice, which is that I should make no comment at all.'

'Your choice,' the DS conceded. 'I don't care whether you do or don't. Either way, you're going to be charged with conspiracy to steal a laptop computer and an iPhone from Aldorino Moscardinetto, and you're also going to be charged with his murder.'

'His murder?' Stoddart squealed.

'Of course. Billy Swords will be charged with that, and so will you.'

'I never told him to kill the guy!' Lee tugged at his client's sleeve but he shook him off.

'It doesn't matter,' Provan told him, not bothering to conceal his smug satisfaction. 'You sent him out on a criminal enterprise. The Crown will argue that makes you as guilty as him; art and part, as Scottish law puts it. Isn't that right, Mr Lee? You're lucky you're no' in England; we cannae charge you with being an accessory after the fact as well, because we don't have them up here. What we have will do fine, though.'

'Okay, I'll co-operate,' Stoddart sighed.

'It's a few hours too late for that. You were given every chance to come clean earlier on today, but you didn't. Mr Swords got in first, and that's how it works.'

'You mean he gets off for grassing on me?'

'Was "grassing" common parlance at Harrow?' the DS chuckled. 'Oh no, he gets charged as well. It might get interesting, though, if the Crown decides to accept his guilty plea to culpable homicide; that's manslaughter to you English folk. That usually carries a fixed-term sentence, not life. You could be tried separately from him and be convicted of murder even though you were nowhere near the place.'

'That's unlikely, Mr Provan,' Lee protested. 'You're trying to intimidate my client.'

'And succeeding, from the smell in here,' he replied cheerfully.

Stoddart was trembling. 'I'll tell you everything and take my chances,' he said.

'I really don't think—' his lawyer began.

'I don't care what you think or otherwise,' the promoter shouted. 'In fact, you can leave now.'

'No!' Provan snapped, surprising himself and astonishing DC Gowans at his side. 'He stays. I'm not having this blown on some technicality. Get on with it, Mr Stoddart; say what you have to.'

The man drew a deep breath, then he began. 'You've seen a copy of the video we found on the laptop. You've seen me on it, you've seen Butler, Trudi, Gordon and also Gene's intemperate outburst. We were all asked separately if we'd contribute to research for what Moscardinetto told us was a boxing documentary. We didn't know that Leo was involved, and we sure as hell didn't know that he'd been interviewed. Our first clue to that came when Moscardinetto asked me about the offer made to Leo to throw the Brezinski fight. That was only known to three people other than me: my dad, who is beyond any memories these days; Gene Alderney, who made the fucking offer . . .' He broke off. 'Her real name—' he began, but Provan stopped him.

'We know who she is; Swords told us that.'

'Yeah,' the promoter sighed, 'he would, wouldn't he. The third person was Leo himself. That was when the alarm bells started to ring.'

'Did Gino Butler not know?'

'No, never. Leo warned me that he never should; when he felt the need to warn you about something, you heeded it. Anyway, when Moscardinetto turned up at the farewell event, those alarm bells turned into a full-volume siren. Then when Leo died . . . fuck's sake, we were bricking it that everything would come out. Gene and I decided that we needed to get hold of the laptop Moscardinetto had with him on Friday. He never put it down all night; even when he ate, he secured it to himself. We knew those interviews had to be on it, so we told Billy to steal it for us. Billy has previous on that sort of thing, as you probably know by now. When the Italian interviewed us, he'd given us his card with a mobile number on it. I cleared the way for Billy – or thought I had – by sending the guy a text that was supposed to be from Gino, asking him to meet Gino at his office at half past four. Moscardinetto texted me back, saying he would. I don't know what happened to stop him; whatever it was, he walked in on Billy opening his hotel safe. There was a fight; Billy told me he subdued him, that was all.'

'It sure was for the Italian,' Moss Lee grunted, unable to keep silent even as a spectator.

'All that you'll have worked out,' Stoddart continued. 'This will be new to you, though, I think. Gene – I'll keep calling her that – had to offer Leo that bribe. She needed him to go down because she had a secret that only she and my father knew about. Yevgeny Brezinski had a contusion on his brain from a previous bout. He won it, but afterwards he complained of headaches, and had a private scan done that showed up the injury. He was at huge risk going into any fight, but with Leo, well, it was suicidal. So the offer was made and Leo said okay. You know what happened: he fought a straight fight, and he won by a knockout. An hour later, Yevgeny went into a coma, on the way home with Gene. She took him to a private hospital, where they operated, but the damage was too great.'

'He died?' Provan asked.

'Worse, he didn't die. He's in a permanent vegetative state, in a private clinic in Switzerland. My father was only too aware of our part in the business. He knew, Gene knew, that even with Leo going into the tank, taking a dive, there would be a risk, but the money involved was too great. They let it go ahead. Ever since, I've been paying Zirka a million a year in so-called consultancy fees. That money's actually gone to Yevgeny's hospital costs.'

'Did Leo know the whole story?'

'God, no. If he had ever found out he'd have put us all in jail, even if he'd gone down too for not reporting the bribe.'

'But with Moscardinetto turned loose on his warts-and-all film, were you no' afraid that he would find out?'

'Our first priority was to get that laptop. Leo dying was fortuitous. It gave us a chance to bury the film for good.'

'Especially if Aldorino was dead as well.'

'That was not the instruction,' Stoddart protested.

'You'll forgive me,' Provan murmured slowly, 'and maybe the jury for thinking it looks that way. And Leo,' he added, 'did he walk in on somebody too?'

Moss Lee stirred, but the DS stalled him with a single pointing finger.

Stoddart gazed at him. 'Are you asking if we killed him? No, absolutely not. For a start, I wouldn't have been brave enough to try, and don't bother suggesting Billy either. He idolised Leo; he'd have killed me before he'd have harmed him. Anyway, our first suspicions didn't arise until I was interviewed by the Italian, and that didn't happen until last Friday morning, before I flew up here. I assure you, DS Provan, if Leo was murdered – and nobody's said definitively that he was – you are looking for someone else.'

Forty-Four

'Congratulations, you two. You closed the book on a complex murder investigation. I wish I could have been in the room, instead of watching a video feed.'

'We got by with a little help from our friend,' Provan sang, in a fit of magnanimity, but softly, so that his voice did not carry beyond their table in the Sauchiehall Street coffee shop.

'Thank you, Joe Cocker,' Skinner laughed, 'but you did the hard graft. You broke down the suspects. I just made a few phone calls.'

The DS nodded. 'Put that way, you're right. We did get a result, didn't we, Lottie, and we might have saved the nation the cost of a trial too, if the Crown accepts Swords's plea to culpable homicide.'

'Which it will,' his former chief said, as he picked up his flat white. 'The decision will go all the way up to the boss, the Lord Advocate, and he always takes the cheaper option. I know this,' he added. 'I have dinner with him fairly often.'

'What about Stoddart?' Mann asked. 'Will the Advocate go all the way with him?'

'I know you implied he would, but I don't see how he can. Theoretically the court could accept Swords's guilty plea to culp hom and impose a ban on reporting until after Stoddart's murder trial. They might even get a conviction, although I doubt it, but it would never be upheld at appeal, no way. True, Dan did beautifully in getting him to cough all that up under the threat of a murder conviction. However, when Moss Lee gets his act together, if Stoddart keeps him on, he'll offer a guilty plea to the theft charge. I suspect that the Crown will take that too. Even the lesser homicide charge will be hard to prove.'

'How much time will they be looking at?'

'Come on, Lottie,' Skinner said, 'you know how that goes. It'll depend on who the judge is, and how tough he or she decides to be. It'll also depend on how good the pleas in mitigation are. Cecily Marsden can't appear in the High Court; she isn't qualified for that, not yet. Alex could, but she won't. She'll retain the best QC available. Force me to guess, I reckon Swords gets eight to ten years, and Stoddart gets at least six, because he was the principal; he ordered the theft and the theft led to the killing.'

'If ye believe that,' Provan observed. 'If you accept that they never meant tae kill Moscardinetto.'

'The fake text sending him to Butler's office kind of proves that, doesn't it, Dan?'

'I suppose,' the DS conceded. 'I wonder why he came back early.'

'I know,' Mann volunteered. 'While you and Gowans were congratulating each other, I phoned Gino. I thought the guy might have called his office to verify the time, or something like that. But no, it turns out that by sheer chance, Butler was walking along Gordon Street, on his way to Joy Herbert's office to discuss Leo's estate, when he encountered Moscardinetto waiting for a taxi. The Italian asked him what he was doing there when they had a meeting in fifteen minutes. Gino said, "What meeting?" and kept on moving, since he was late for the lawyer.'

'Jesus,' Skinner whispered. 'By such a random encounter a life was ended.'

'Aye,' Provan said, 'if you accept that Swords wasnae told to wait for him and kill him when he got back.'

'Sure, but you've just sat across the table from Stoddart, Dan, and looked him in the eye, as have I. Is he a man who would order a killing? I don't believe so. Do you, really?'

Slowly the DS shook his head. 'No. No, Ah don't,' he admitted. 'What about Gene Alderney?' he asked. 'What are we goin' tae do about her?'

'You're going to do nothing,' Skinner replied. 'She's already given you an explanation for Swords' text message; it may be a lie, but to a jury it's her word against his. There's no other evidence that she knew of the theft of the laptop and phone, we have no statement that was ever made in her presence, and nothing's been said by Swords or Stoddart to incriminate her in any way.'

He smiled. 'We, on the other hand – by that I mean the service of which I am a sometime member – we are going to turn her over to the CPS in England for prosecution for passport fraud, and to the Home Office for deportation as an illegal immigrant. The passport charge, if it's laid, could be unfortunate in theory for Gino Butler, since he countersigned her application and her photographs, as a member of a suitable profession. But . . . the CPS would have to prove that he actually knew she wasn't who she purported to be. That's not going to happen, so he'll get out from under.'

'What about her son?' Mann suggested. 'She covered up his existing brain trauma, she tried to bribe Leo Speight, and she kept his collapse secret.'

'If those are crimes in Russia, Lottie, that's where they'll be dealt with.'

'Suits me,' Provan observed cheerfully. 'One less case to process, one fewer report to the procurator fucking fiscal.'

Skinner gazed at him. 'You sound like a man who's beginning to realise that there are other things to life than pursuing bad bastards and locking them up.'

'You could be right there, Chief. Australia's done wonders for me. Mind you,' he added, 'so's this case. I havenae had time tae bother about jet lag.'

'And you're not finished yet, Dan. One down, one to go.'

Instantly the DS's countenance became mournful. 'Thanks for remindin' us. One tae go, you say, but we're goin' bloody nowhere. You were right, though: Speight's murder has bugger-all to do with the Moscardinetto killing. Why were you so sure of that?'

'Stoddart told you. The time frame was wrong, in a couple of ways. They only tumbled to the film project a day or so before Leo died. If someone had broken into his house and shot him while he slept, okay, that would have been feasible, but poisoning usually takes planning; they hadn't had the time.'

Skinner drained his questionable coffee. 'Whatever,' he said, 'that's me out of it.'

'How come? What about the insurance company? Ye're no nearer solving their problem.'

He grinned. 'That will not keep me awake. That policy is real, but any insurer reckless enough to write it for a boxer deserves to pay out in full. My real brief was to establish whether Leo Speight's death could be traced back to international organised crime. With your considerable help, I've established that it can't; I don't have a locus any longer. I can go back to my

348

real jobs now: InterMedia and looking after my family. For that, I thank you both.'

'With our considerable help,' Mann paraphrased, taking him by surprise. 'That being the case, how about returning the favour? You've been involved from the start, you know the whole story. It makes sense for you to stick around, if only as a sounding board.'

'I'd be happy to, Lottie,' he said, 'but I'm not sure how Stirling will feel about that. I don't think I'm flavour of the month with the DCC.'

She showed him an uncharacteristic smile. 'We won't tell him if you don't.'

'In that case,' Skinner replied, 'remember what Gino Butler said in his interview? "Leo and I have a personal conflict of interest of sorts." That's where I'd go next, if I was still involved . . .'

'Let's ask him what he meant,' the DI declared, cutting across him.

'. . . but not necessarily directly,' he concluded. 'Go back to the first principle of cross-examination, Lottie. You know what that is: before you ask the question, it's best to know the answer. Let me speak to someone else first, to see if I can find out.'

Forty-Five

'Good evening, sir,' Sandra Bulloch said. 'I didn't expect to hear from you again; not that I mind you calling.'

'How's it working out?' Skinner asked. 'I left Stirling not long after you did.'

'It's good,' his former assistant replied. 'I've spoken with Leo's lawyer; she confirms that the new will, as adjusted by his letter, is the final version. She expects it to be challenged, and she advised me to retain my own lawyer since she and the two executors have to stay neutral.'

'Who does she expect to challenge it?'

'My sister, on behalf of her children, who lost out slightly when I was added. Strangely, it doesn't worry me. I don't have children and I never will have, so Leonard and Jolene will be my heirs. Long-term they'll be better off. Faye will want something for herself, of course . . . she and her solicitor.'

'All she'll get is what you choose to give her. What about the job front?'

'I had a call from the chief constable the evening I saw you,' Sandra told him. 'I won't say she was warm; no, she was formal, but she was broadly sympathetic. As of now, I'm on compassionate leave, for a month. When that's up, we speak again. However, the possibility of disciplinary action will still be on the table. She said that was the consensus view, without revealing who else was involved in the decision.'

'I think that would be DCC McGuire; Mario can be a hardliner. If you do go back to the job, it won't be in CID, I'm afraid.'

'No, I didn't think so,' she confessed. 'I have a sergeant's uniform that still fits. I might need it . . . if I go back,' she added, 'but I can't think that far ahead. I'm still coming to terms with Leo being dead, and waiting for the outcome of Mann's investigation. Do you know how it's progressing? Has the lab finally reported?'

'Not yet,' Skinner said. 'That's one of many things I should have warned the justice minister about, but didn't, when the great new era was being put together. In my time, arses would have been kicked by now, but Maggie doesn't have the power to do that, since forensic services aren't directly under her control. Bloody nonsense!' he grumbled. 'The inquiry does go on, though. You'll read tomorrow of arrests in the Moscardinetto case. Mann and Provan were hoping that the two deaths were linked, but they're out of luck. Leo's investigation continues; they're still following up existing leads and looking for new ones, which is why I'm calling you.'

'I'm sure I've told you everything I know that's relevant, sir.'

'Probably,' he agreed, 'but there's one thing I'd like to ask you.'

'Err . . .' she murmured, and he laughed.

'Purely unofficially, and if Mario should ever quiz you, it was Dan Provan that called you. I've seen a recorded interview with Gino Butler. It was part of the project Leo had going with Moscardinetto; we know all about that now. In it, Gino says that he and Leo had a conflict of interests, on a personal level. Do you have any idea what that might have been?'

'I can't think of anything . . .' Bulloch stopped, frowned, then continued, 'other than the fact that my sister's been sleeping with him for the past several months, probably longer. That's your personal conflict of interest. Mr Skinner, did Gino know that Leo was involved in this project with Moscardinetto?'

'As far as we can tell, nobody did, apart from you; and from what you said to me, not even you knew the details.'

'Then he's an idiot for not figuring it out.'

'How did you know about the relationship between Butler and Faye?'

'From my eight-year-old nephew. He called him "Uncle Gino" one day; I asked him where that came from and he said that was what Mummy said they should call him. He added that he stayed at their house some nights but that Mummy said Daddy wasn't to know. I didn't tell him, but I did square Gino up about it a few months ago. He fired right back; he said he knew about Leo and me.'

'How?'

'It might have been from Gordon. We were at the Blacksmith for dinner one night and we stayed over in one of the bungalows rather than go back to Ayr, or go to mine. The next morning Gordon was there, and he saw us together. He didn't know who I was; Leo introduced me by my full name, Alexandra, but that was all. He was a very private person, so I was impressed that he did even that much. Don't underestimate how close those two were, sir, father and grown-up son.'

'They were conflicted over Gordon's dream of being a boxer,' Skinner told her. 'That's on Moscardinetto's tape too.'

'It wasn't a conflict, just frustration. Leo told me that the only way he'd let him go into the ring would be if he thought he was better than him. As good as, that wouldn't have been enough; he'd have had to be even better. So he schooled him, to find out, as his own father did with him. They trained together down at Ayr and they sparred. Leo said he didn't have it; he was too gentle a lad, there was no danger in his eyes.'

'I see. So you think that Gordon let your secret slip and Gino came out with it?'

'Absolutely, Mexican stand-off. If I told Leo about him, he'd tell Faye about me. As it happens, I don't think Leo would have been bothered about him screwing her, but if she'd found out about me sleeping with Leo, well, cue Hurricane Faye.'

'And if she'd found out you were going to marry him?'

'But she didn't,' Sandra insisted. 'She couldn't have. Even if Gino had known, which he didn't, he's not that stupid!'

Forty-Six

'No fucking way!' Gino Butler shouted. 'Suppose I had known they were going off to get married, which I didn't, I'd never have done that to Leo. He was my mate.'

'Come on,' Mann said. 'You were having a relationship in front of his kids, one that they were told by their mother had to stay secret. You were quite happy to do that to him.'

'She wasn't his business any more.'

'So why weren't you frank with him? You referenced it in your interview with the Italian. We have a copy, we've seen it. You see your relationship with Faye as a conflict of interest. How would that have been?'

'That was just a casual remark,' he protested.

'Naw,' Dan Provan barked. 'It was full of meaning. There was more to it than just you and she watchin' the sunrise together. That's what folk do, and I doubt Leo would have cared a toss about it. But if he'd known that you put Faye up to settin' Moss Lee on him, as the two of us reckon ye did, I doubt he'd have taken kindly to that. It would have been the end of a lifelong friendship, and you'd have been kicked right off the gravy train.'

Butler's face flushed, and the DS knew that his inspired guess had been right on the button. 'Why did you do it?' he asked.

354

The other man sighed. 'I could see the gravy train was pulling into the station anyway. Leo was done with fighting, and his new career in property development wouldn't have had a role for me. He told me as much; that business plan he had for a new fight promotion, he told me about it a while back. It was meant for Bryce and for me, he said, once he was finished with boxing. He warned me that he was moving to the Bahamas and we wouldn't be seeing much of him in the future. I thought that would leave Faye vulnerable once the kids were grown and he stopped supporting them. The house was hers, but fuck-all else, so I told her to go to court to get some.'

Mann tapped the top of Butler's desk. 'Excuse me, but did it ever occur to you just to ask Leo to make provision for her?'

'If I'd done that, and he'd known about us all along – that was the thing with Leo, not much got past him – he'd have said, "Pal, you've made enough out of me over the years, you look after her." And he'd have been right.'

'But that wouldn't have suited you at all, would it, Mr Butler?' the DI challenged. 'Faye might have been all right for a bit of horizontal jogging, but you didn't want anything more than that, did you?'

'Frankly, no. But look, Leo never did know about us, or I'd have heard about it.'

'And Faye never did know about Leo and Sandra having a relationship?'

'Christ, no, or the whole world would have heard.'

'How did you find out?' Mann asked.

'The manager of the Blacksmith told me; he's a bit of a gossip. I warned him that if he breathed a word to anyone else, he'd be out of a job and unemployable.'

'When did you learn they were engaged?'

'Same time as you lot did, I suppose. When the lawyer called and told me about Leo's letter, me being an executor.'

'You didn't know earlier, and you didn't let it slip?'

He shook his head and looked at the DI. 'No, absolutely not, I swear.'

'Was there anything else you kept from Leo apart from you and Faye?' Provan asked.

'Nothing; just that one thing.'

'What about Gene Alderney's passport application?'

'That? It was ten years ago. No, he never knew about that. How's it relevant today?'

'You'll find out quite soon,' the DS chuckled, 'when the folk frae the Passport Office ring your doorbell.'

Forty-Seven

'You're sure?' Skinner asked the faces on screen.

'Yes,' Lottie Mann answered. 'Butler knew they were together, but he didn't know about the two of them being engaged. If Leo didn't tell his oldest friend, we can't see him having told anyone else. Could Sandra have let it slip?'

'No way. She was dead set on keeping the secret until they were long gone.'

'Are we fixating on Faye as the prime suspect here?' she ventured. 'Should we be looking at someone else?'

'Don't rule anybody out,' he said, 'but if she didn't know, she had little or no motive. Have you spoken to the hotel manager?'

'As soon as we were finished with Gino. He swears, on pain of prosecution, that he didn't tell anyone else about Leo and Sandra.'

'What about Gordon?'

'We've seen him too; we caught up with him at the uni this morning, between classes. He's still heartbroken over his father's death, but he was genuinely astonished when we told him that the Alexandra he met was Faye's sister, and that his dad was going to marry her.'

'We can rule him out, Bob,' Provan insisted, 'as a suspect and as a leak. The kid was genuine. Other than him, I cannae see anyone else who'd have known about the relationship.'

'I can,' Skinner countered.

'Who?'

'Let me follow that up. I have another suggestion for you two. Gino Butler styles himself as Leo's best friend, but I'm not sure that he was.'

'If not him, who?' the DS challenged.

'Rae Letts. Sandra said I shouldn't underestimate the bond between Leo and Gordon. Likewise, her relationship with Leo was very strong. I had that impression when I spoke to her, and it was confirmed by Charlie Baxter, who stayed with them in Las Vegas.'

'Do you know where we'll find her?'

'At the Blacksmith, I think. She told me she wanted to stay for Leo's funeral, and that Gino had said she could. While you interview her, I'll make a call to check out my suspicion.'

'Fair enough,' Mann said.

She was about to cut the video connection when Provan stopped her. 'Where are you just now, Bob?' he asked.

'I'm in my office in Edinburgh,' Skinner replied. 'Why do you want to know?'

'Just wondering. How do you find the life? After the polis, I mean.'

'Honestly? I love it, I love the freedom, I love the variety of work I have, I love being able to apply skills to my media work that I never even knew I had, and I love being able to use the old ones when I'm asked, and at my discretion. Do I miss being a cop? Not for a single second. Is that enough for you, Dan?'

'That's fine. Thanks very much. Cheerio the now.' He hit the disconnect button.

'What was that about?' Lottie asked, as the boring police-service wallpaper reappeared on her computer screen.

'Life, kid,' he murmured, 'and about a growing realisation that there may be more to it than I've acknowledged for the last ten years or so.'

'Going to Australia has opened your eyes, hasn't it?' she laughed.

'More than Australia, my lovely lass, more than Australia.' He pushed himself to his feet. 'I'll go and check that Rae Letts is still at the Blacksmith.'

She looked after him as he left her office, gazing at the back of the neat, well-groomed, articulate, caring man that she had known for all her police career, and yet not known at all, not properly. Strange, unexpected thoughts were forming in her mind as her mobile sounded.

'Tsha!' Irked by the interruption, she snatched it from her desk. Her face darkened as she read the caller display.

'Scott,' she snapped. 'What do you want?'

'I want my son back,' he retorted, 'and next Thursday I'm getting him back. The hearing date's set, and I am so looking forward to it. I'll enjoy watching you hurt when the sheriff takes Jakey off you. You will rue the day that you crossed me and my dad.'

She snapped. 'You know what?' Heads turned in the outer office as she shouted. 'You and your vicious shite of a father can both go and fuck yourselves. I am going to fucking have you both, and boy, will I revel in your pain!'

Forty-Eight

As she walked into the Blacksmith, Lottie Mann was still thinking about her explosive exchange with her former husband – as was Dan Provan, by her side, although she did not know it. Their first sight of Rae Letts brought them back to the job in hand.

She was waiting for them in the hotel's small lobby, standing with her child held on her left hip, dressed in black from head to foot. It was her serenity, even more than her unquestionable beauty, that impressed them both. She had the bearing of a woman who treated life's blessings and its curses with equal equanimity, being neither raised too high nor brought too low.

She lowered Raeleen to the ground and extended her hand as they approached. Provan reached her first and took it, wondering for a moment whether he should shake it or kiss it.

'You be the detectives?' she began. 'Detective Mann, Detective Provan?'

'That's us,' the DI said. 'Lottie Mann. Detective inspector, to be precise.'

'I'm sorry,' Rae exclaimed. 'I'm not used to British ways.'

'Dinna you worry,' Provan told her. 'We get called that all the time these days. American TV's changing everything; Ah'm a

360

Blue Bloods fan myself.'

She smiled, and the lobby seemed to grow a little lighter. 'I don't think I quite fit the typical viewer profile of that show. Do you want to go somewhere private?' she asked. 'We can go to my bungalow.'

'Here will be fine,' Mann assured her, heading towards a small waiting area, where four chairs were grouped around a low table. 'I don't think this is going to get busy any time soon.'

'No, it's not; we have a party in this evening, but nothing till then. I should explain: I'm going to be here for a while, and I didn't want to sit on my hands, so I asked the manager if I could help out as a receptionist. He was happy I should, especially as I don't need to be paid.'

'How's business?' Provan asked, as they sat, the toddler Raeleen on the floor beside her mother, playing with an ageless Barbie doll.

'Since Monday, it's gone crazy. Fridays through Sundays, we don't have a spare room or table for the next four weeks. Ghouls, I guess, coming to see where Leo ate his last meal.' She looked at Mann. 'Can you guys give me any idea yet when the funeral might be?'

'Sorry,' the DI replied. 'That's not our call. We have a person called the procurator fiscal; in the US that would be the district attorney. Indirectly, he's our boss and he makes that decision.'

'Not the coroner?'

'We don't have one of them, not in Scotland. The fiscal fills that role. I can't even make a guess about your question, as we don't have a definitive cause of death yet.'

'But you are treating it as a homicide, yes, like Aldorino?'

'Yes, we are. Did you know Signor Moscardinetto?'

'Yeah, I did. He came to visit in Vegas six weeks ago, then I saw him again last Friday. He and Leo went out on the lake in the boat when he was there. They had something cooking between them, but I didn't ask and Leo didn't volunteer. The newspapers are saying this morning you got a suspect in custody. They say it was a robbery gone wrong. Is that so?'

'More or less,' Provan admitted. 'There's no link to Leo's death, though; we're satisfied about that.'

'Then who did kill him?' She raised her chin and looked the DS in the eye. 'Not me,' she declared. 'Don't you ask me that, now. That man was golden, he was precious. If I could ever kill anyone, it would be the man did that to him.'

'You're not a suspect, Ms Letts,' Mann promised her. 'Staff and other witnesses place you here all night, so you had no opportunity. You could have had a motive, though. Did you know that Leo was intending to leave Scotland and the US, to base himself in the Bahamas full time, and also that he was planning to be married?'

'Yes, I did.' She glanced down at Raeleen, who was twisting Barbie's leg in an unnatural direction. 'Don't do that, honey,' she whispered.

'When did you learn? Who told you?'

'Last Friday evening. Leo did. Once the dinner and all the speeching was over, he took me to one side and said he wanted to see Raeleen. So we went out to the bungalow. She was asleep; he just stood there looking at her for a while. Then he said to me, "Rae, I have something to tell you that I want you to keep to yourself for a day or two. Things are going to be different. I've found the woman I want to marry, and we're going away together. Her name's Sandra, she's serious but she's nice, and I love her. You and Raeleen will always be family, and you can come to visit us in the Bahamas any time you like, but that's the way it's going to be." The way he looked at me, I've never seen anybody look so sorry.'

'How did you react?'

'Did I blow my stack, you mean? No, I didn't, because I'd been expecting it. The last few times he stayed in Vegas, all through last year in fact, he slept in another room and we never had sex at all. He didn't say anything, but there was something about him that had never been there before. When he told me, I was sad, but I was happy for him too. He never promised me a thing, but he always treated me like a princess, and our daughter like a little queen. I knew that would never change, so I was . . . content. I said that to him, kissed him on the forehead and we went back to the party. A little after that, he left on his Harley. When I heard he was dead, my first thought was that he'd crashed the thing in the dark, but he didn't, did he?'

'No, he was poisoned.'

Her face contorted as if she was sharing his pain. 'Shit, that's awful.'

'Rae,' Provan said, 'when you spoke to Mr Skinner, you never told him this.'

'He never axed,' she countered. 'I was in shock; maybes I still am. I didn't feel then that I should be sharing a secret Leo had entrusted to me.'

'Understood,' Mann murmured. 'Do you know if he shared it with anyone else?'

'I know he didn't, because he told me he hadn't and he never lied to me.'

'The other women in his life, the mothers of his other children; did you speak to them during the dinner?'

'No. Faye I wouldn't 'cos that one always hated me. Trudi was sat on the other side of the auditorium. Mind you,' she added, 'I did hear them talking to each other. Yelling, more like. I went to the ladies' room one time, as they were serving coffee, and I hadn't even got the door open 'fore I heard them going at it. One of them said Leo's name, not sure which, but next I hear Trudi shout, "That's all you fuckin' know." Then I walked in, and Faye turned on me, called me something horrible. I ignored her, walked past her. I don't know what it was about, but that Faye, the way she looked; I thought I might have saved Trudi's life by opening that door.'

Forty-Nine

'The same Bob Skinner who was briefly our chief constable in the good old days?' Joy Herbert asked.

'The same, and I'm so glad you feel that way,' he replied.

'How can I help you, Mr Skinner? I'd like to think you're after my professional services, but I suspect that a man of your age and status has decent advice already.'

'I do,' he acknowledged, 'but I have friends, and my people have a full dance card at the moment. I know you've just sustained a loss from yours, and that's why I'm calling.'

In the silence that followed, he could sense caution and a change of attitude. 'As I'm sure you're aware,' the solicitor said eventually, 'I can't discuss my clients' affairs, not even those who are inconveniently dead. I assume that you're referring to Leo, Leo Speight the boxer.'

'Also Leo Speight the property developer and father of the decade. I wish I'd met him while he was alive. He seems to have been quite a guy.'

'He was all that; he made his fortune in the most brutal business, but meet him and you'd think he was a writer, or an academic. There was nothing threatening about him at all, and nothing ostentatious. Your choice of words suggests that you only met him after he was dead. Am I right about that?'

'I'm afraid so. I won't bore you with the story of how I came to be involved with the investigation of his death, but I am, for my sins . . . or should I say for someone else's. I don't need to discuss his business with you, Mrs Herbert. I've already spoken to people on both sides of it and to members of his extended family, so I know about it. I'm aware that his estate is far more valuable than any of the sports-page estimates. As for the contents of his will, I know what they are because the investigating officers gave me the main details. I also passed a copy of the late addition on to Sandra Bulloch, but I didn't look at it. If I had, I wouldn't need to ask you this question. Who witnessed his signature?'

He heard an exclamation that might have been a sigh of relief. 'Yes,' she said. 'I can tell you that without bringing the wrath of the Law Society down on my head. The signature on the main document, the primary will, which was drafted by my office, was witnessed by a member of my staff; that's the norm, as I'm sure you know from personal experience. However, the letter that I received on Tuesday, amending the original – the informal writing, as Scots law describes it – was signed by Leo in another location. That was witnessed, complete with an attestation as to his state of mind, by another individual. That person is a beneficiary in the original will, but is not mentioned in or affected by the alteration: it was Trudi Pollock.'

Fifty

'How can I help, DI Mann?' she asked, facing them in the cramped little office. 'I told you everything I know last time.'

'Not necessarily, Ms Pollock,' Mann countered. 'You answered all our questions. We have a couple more that we need to put to you.'

She shrugged. 'I'll help if I can.'

'Thanks. I want to go back to last week, to the time when Leo came into the office here. You told us before that he did a bit of business. We'd like to know what that was.'

She sighed and looked at her desk. 'He went onto the computer and he wrote a document, a letter, then he asked me to do an address label for an envelope. The address was his lawyer's, Herbert Chesters, in George Square. While I was doing that, he printed out the thing, then he signed it and asked me to witness his signature; so I did. It was kind of formal, attesting that it was his signature and that he was of sound mind.'

'Did he show you the letter?'

'No, he didn't; he put it straight in the envelope and sealed it. I was going to give him a stamp but he said it had to go recorded delivery and had to go to the post office.' She looked away, and her cheeks went a tell-tale pink.

367

'Go on, hen,' Provan said quietly.

'I shouldn't have,' Trudi Pollock continued, 'but I couldn't help myself. As he was leaving, Leo turned in the doorway and said, "Trudi, make sure you empty the trashcan on that computer. I forgot to do it." I went to do that, but to access it, you have to open it up. When I did, there was only the one document there, the one he'd created. It was headed "Will amendment". I really, really shouldn't have but I was too curious; I opened it and I read it.' She looked at the detectives. 'Do you know what it was?'

'Yes,' Mann said. 'It was what it said. It changed his will to include Sandra Bulloch, the woman he intended to marry. They were going off together.'

She nodded. 'That's right, although I never knew they were going away.'

'Did you know who Sandra was?'

'I was pretty sure. I knew that Faye had a sister and I thought that was her name. Gino mentioned her once; he said she was a police officer. Is that right?'

'Aye, that's right,' Provan confirmed. 'Detective chief inspector. In fact she was our boss. She was called to the scene when Leo's body was found.'

Trudi's hands flew to her mouth. 'Oh the poor cow,' she murmured. 'Imagine that. I'm sorry, I never meant to call her a cow; I never meant anything bad . . .'

'That's okay,' the DS assured her. 'We know you didn't. We want to move on now, to Friday night at the party. We've been told that you and Faye Bulloch had an argument there, in the ladies' room.'

'You've been talking to Rae,' she declared. 'That's right, she walked in on it.'

'Who started it?'

'Faye did, as usual. Faye could start a fight in an empty house. She's a thoroughly unpleasant person, with big, cruel, clingy hooks.'

'We've seen a video recording of you, Trudi,' Mann ventured. 'In it you say that you couldn't trust Gino Butler. What was the reason for that?'

'*She* was. Those hooks of hers, they were well and truly into Gino. Anything you told him went straight to her.'

'So you didn't tell him about Leo and Faye's sister getting married?'

'Absolutely not. It's not that I cared about Faye, but I didn't want to cause Leo any grief through her.'

'You did, though, didn't you?' the DI murmured.

Her head bobbed in a small nod and the detectives saw her eyes mist. 'I couldn't help myself. I was in the ladies', and when I came out of the stall she was there, laying on another trowel of make-up. She saw me in the mirror and she said, "Hello, Fatty." The bitch always calls me that. Then she started off on a tirade about my effing boss, and the effing useless lawyer that he'd made her hire, and about Leo and what a C-word he was, and that by hook or by crook she was going to get her hands on half his money. She was more vicious than I'd ever heard her, until I just couldn't take any more of it. I turned on her and I said she was too effing late, because Leo was getting married. That stopped her in her tracks, but only for a second; then she screamed at me, called me a lying C-word. I told her it was true, and that the money would be in the Bulloch family after all, but not her part of it.

'I thought she was going to attack me. I think she would have, but that was when Rae came in and she turned on her and called her something terrible. Rae managed to ignore her completely and went into a stall, and Faye mouthed at me, "Sandra?" and I nodded, and then the artist woman came in, looking angry 'cos she must have heard what Faye called Rae. It dawned on me then what I'd done. I was going to beg Faye to say nothing, but she turned and marched out of there.'

'Did you see her again, back at the function?'

'No, not for at least an hour and a half. I thought she must have gone back to her bungalow to fester. I was terrified that she would confront Leo, but by the time she came back, he had left.'

Provan raised his eyebrows and looked at Mann. She stayed silent, as the implications of her confession dawned on Trudi Pollock, and a look of horror formed on her face.

Fifty-One

It was clear that Faye Bulloch had not been expecting callers. She wore no make-up, and her electric hair was in disorder, pulled back roughly in a ponytail. She was dressed in a grey sweatshirt and matching jogging bottoms; barefoot, she seemed diminished, a smaller, lesser version of the woman they had interviewed a few days before.

She glared at them. 'You might have bloody called,' she complained. 'I was . . .' She faltered as she caught sight of the uniformed woman constable and the tall young man in plain clothes who stood behind Mann and Provan.

'What is this?' she murmured.

'Can we come in, Ms Bulloch?' the DI asked. 'It would be better.'

'Okay,' she said grudgingly, turning her back on them and walking into the house. At a sign from Provan, the junior officers stayed in the hall as the detectives followed her into the kitchen.

"Well?' she demanded, turning to face them with a show of defiance.

'We're here to arrest you, Ms Bulloch,' Mann replied, 'on suspicion of the murder of Leo Speight.'

She paled noticeably but held her ground. 'Bollocks,' she

barked. 'I was in the bungalow at the Blacksmith with my kids when Leo died. I'm calling my sister; she'll sort you two out.'

'Your sister's on compassionate leave, Faye,' Provan told her. 'She's just lost her fiancé, the man she was going away with. You knew that, didn't you?' he added, forestalling a retort as it was formed. 'You found out on Friday evening.'

'That's right,' Mann said. 'Trudi Pollock threw it in your face when you provoked her once too often. You never saw that coming, did you? You never knew that Sandra and Leo were in a relationship. When you found out, we believe that you reacted instantly. You left the party, you left the Blacksmith, you drove down to Leo's house and you laced a carton of almond-flavoured soya milk with poison; the stuff you must have known he drank every night, and through the day, wherever in the world he happened to be.'

'We've got your car on CCTV,' the DS added, 'going there and coming back. Those average speed cameras on the Ayr road arenae just for show.'

'That doesn't prove I was at Leo's,' she protested. 'As it happened, that fat wee bitch Trudi upset me so much that I needed a Librium to calm me down. I'd left them here, so I drove down to get them.'

'That's no' bad off the top of your head,' Provan acknowledged, 'but . . . no use. When was the last time you were in Leo's house?'

'I don't know. Eighteen months ago, two years.'

'I thought you might say that, but it leaves us with a problem. Our chief SOCO – the head man, no' just one of the troops – found a hair in the seal of Leo's fridge. We expected that the DNA test would show it was Sandra's, since she'd been there earlier on last week. It wasnae, though; the DNA he recovered wasnae a match for hers, but it was close. So close that the lab report said it had to have come from a female sibling. When we get you to Glasgow, we're going to take a DNA swab from you, and we know, all of us, what it'll show. Ah think you might need your Librium now, Faye.'

'You can't take me to Glasgow!' she protested. 'My kids are at school; I have to pick them up in half an hour.'

'DC Gowans will do that; plain clothes, so none of the other parents will notice. PC Stone will stay here with them until longer-term care can be arranged.'

'I'm not having Sandra!' she shouted. 'Not her!'

'Do you want them taken by the social workers?' Provan asked.

'Not Sandra!' she hissed.

'Faye,' Mann said quietly, 'you may have to get used to that idea in the long term, but for now there's an alternative. Rae Letts is still at the hotel; she's staying for the funeral. We've spoken to her and she's prepared to come down here and look after Leonard and Jolene, along with her wee one, until a more permanent arrangement can be made. Your children know her. Would you agree to that?'

Bulloch turned and gazed out of the window, looking at the grey waters of the Firth of Clyde as they broke on the beach under a cloudy sky. 'Okay,' she whispered, without looking at them. 'She'll do. Anyone but Sandra.'

'Right,' the DI declared. 'Now you'll be taken to Pitt Street to be questioned under caution. PC Stone will go with you while you pack some clothes. Also you might want to call Moss Lee before we leave.'

'Him? Him that's done bugger-all for me? No, I'll call Gino. It's time I found out how serious he is.'

Fifty-Two

'Is it right?' Gino Butler asked, his incredulity apparent. 'You've arrested Faye for Leo's murder? That's what she said on the phone.'

'Not quite,' Provan corrected him. 'She's been detained on suspicion, to be precise.'

They faced each other across the entrance hall in the Pitt Street building; it was in its death throes as a police office. All of the parking bays outside were occupied by removal vehicles, and a steady stream of men flowed past them, carrying an assortment of furniture bound for shiny new surroundings in Dalmarnock.

'Can I see her?'

'Not right now,' the DS replied. 'She's being processed. Have you retained a lawyer for her like she asked?'

'Yes, a woman called Susannah Himes. She's on her way here; I said I'd meet her. I caught her as she was leaving the High Court. She gave me a message for you: on no account are you to question Faye further until she gets here.'

Provan had heard of Himes; most Scottish detectives had. She possessed a considerable record of successful defences and gloried in the nickname 'the Barracuda'. 'Fuckin' lawyers,' he grunted. 'They think they make the rules. As it happens, we

374

know prisoners' rights as well as they do. We also know what a trial costs, so we're under serious pressure not to fuck it up. The grounds for detention have been put to her, nothing else. Do you want to stick around, Mr Butler, until you can see her? We know you two are involved.'

'I don't think we are now, not if she killed Leo.'

'Aye,' Provan said cheerily. 'I can imagine ye lookin' a wee bit askance at the porridge every time ye had a row. But the way the evidence is lined up, porridge is just a thing Faye'll be doing, for quite a long while.'

'What about the kids?' He looked even more anxious.

'Don't worry about them, arrangements have been made. These youngsters are going to be rich, Gino. If Faye goes away, and that's looking very likely, they're no' going to wind up in a dormitory in a children's home.'

'Bloody right they're not. I won't let that happen to Leo's kids.'

'Good for you.' Provan paused. 'Look, are you stayin' or not? Do ye want to see her?'

Butler sighed. 'No. I don't think that's wise, knowing what she's charged with. I doubt if I could look her in the eye. I will hang around for a word with the lawyer when she arrives, on my own account. Like you said, the Passport Office want to interview me about Gene Alderney. I think I'm in the clear, but you can't be too careful. I've also got to see that book woman again. She's persistent, if nothing else; she's offered me a deal now.'

'Are you going to take it?'

'No. Leo wouldn't have done it, so neither can I. It wouldn't be right.'

The DS left him in reception and trotted up the stairs to the CID office. 'Bulloch's DNA sample's on its way to Gartcosh,'

DC Gowans called out as he crossed the floor on his way to Mann's little room. When he stepped inside, he saw that she had a phone held to her ear. He paused, but she beckoned him to come in.

'At the moment, she says no,' he heard her say, 'and she's adamant about that. But as this progresses, what she wants isn't going to count for too much. It'll be for a sheriff to decide what happens to them, and if you're there and willing, it'll be hard to look past you. Sure. I'll let you know.' She hung up.

'Sandra,' she said. 'I called her and broke the news. She wasn't a hundred per cent surprised, but she was raging. When she calmed down, a bit, she thought about the children. She wants them, permanently. It would be good for her. Like she says, her life's been ripped out from under her. She's lost her man, and in all probability her career; she'll need something to occupy her.'

'Forgive me if I don't shed a tear for her,' Provan growled. 'She's about to inherit Christ knows how many million. Is Faye ready for interview?' he asked. 'Her lawyer'll be here soon. You'll hate this; Butler's hired Himes to defend her.'

'The Barracuda? Ouch! It's just as well our case is watertight.' She reached out and touched wood, just as her desk phone rang once again.

'Detective Inspector Mann?' There was something in Arthur Dorward's opening gambit that made her think of the preliminary chimes of Big Ben. She held her breath and waited for the hour to strike. Unconsciously she grasped the desktop.

'Big plans for tonight?' he asked; still the bells tolled in her head.

'Evening in with my boy. Why?'

'You might need to do a bit of delegation. The lab results on

Leo Speight have just come flooding in. He was poisoned, that's for sure, by something with the same end result as cyanide. What's less certain – sorry, not certain at all – is how.'

Lottie buried her face in her spare hand. 'Bu-gger,' she sighed. She switched the phone on to speaker mode, so that Provan could hear.

'Eloquently put,' the chief SOCO continued, his voice echoing. 'There was no trace of any poison in the carton by his side, none at all. Nor was there any in his stomach contents. They were tested over and over again; that's the main reason why the whole process has taken so long. I've just reported these findings to the fiscal. He's going to order a second autopsy, with another pathologist joining Graeme Bell, whether he likes it or not. Alongside Graeme, the top slicer in Scotland is Sarah Grace, from Edinburgh University, the wife of shh, you know who. She's on maternity leave just now, but the fiscal's sure she'll be up for the challenge. My part in this is over; I've had enough. We've been at the scene twice; there's nothing left there for us to find. It's over to you, gang.'

The line faded to a buzz from the speaker, which died as Mann replaced her phone.

'What the f . . .' she sighed. 'Dan, we're stuffed. We've got that woman down there in detention, thinking she was a stick-on cert for the murder. Now we're back to page one; we're going to have to let her go.'

'No we don't,' he countered.

'Himes will demand it.'

'Himes can demand all she likes. Faye's been detained for questioning, but we don't have to do that tonight. Nor will we. Himes can have as long as she likes wi' her client, she can sleep wi' her for all I care, but we're not going to talk to her until the morning. Right now, Gowans and I are going back down tae Ayr. Arthur might think the seam's exhausted, and he might be right, but I'm going to see if I can hack something else out of it.'

'I'm coming too,' she said.

'No you're not. You're going to pick up Jakey from Vanessa and spend the evening the way you've just told Dorward. You've got a hearing next week and you're not giving those fuckers any more ammunition. Besides,' he added, 'if I have to be an actin' DI, I might as well earn the extra money.'

Fifty-Three

'Where do we start, Sarge?' DC Willie Gowans asked eagerly, standing in the doorway of the house in Kirkhill Road.

Provan enjoyed working with younger subordinates; he had observed over a lengthy career that CID officers who were still at detective constable rank in the first year or two of their thirties were on a downward curve. Age thirty-five, he believed, losses should be cut and the dross returned to uniformed service. Young Gowans was twenty-seven, and he would make the cut; of that his sergeant was sure.

'We find Leo's other stash of soya milk,' he replied. 'He was found in his living area next to the kitchen, wi' a carton of his juice beside him.' He paused. 'Son,' he murmured, 'in my younger days when I was a footballer, I played in midfield and I was always yellin' at my team-mates to take the easy option, to play the simple pass to the guy who was showin' for it, no' tae go for the Hollywood ball right across the park in the hope it might impress any Old Firm scouts that might be watching – no' that any ever were. In this job, the opposite's true. Always look at the obvious, because nine times out of ten that's where the answer lies, but never exclude the long shot altogether. That big fella Skinner, the ex-chief you might have seen around lately; he

379

played Hollywood balls all his career, and he got some crackin' results wi' them. Do you hear what I'm saying to you, Willie?'

'I think so, Sarge; because you found the victim a few feet away from his fridge, you assumed that's where the carton had come from.'

'Spot on. No' just me, mind; the SOCOs did as well. But what none of us knew then was that Leo had been sweating, that he'd been burning off some energy just before he died. Now we do, so let's take a look in the gym.'

He led the way there, finding the key first time from the bunch that he carried. Inside, as he switched on the lights, it occurred to him that the temperature was much lower than on his previous visit, thanks to his turning off the heating. My contribution to savin' the planet, he mused, as a brief, unprompted vision of himself and Lottie in the steam room flashed across his mind.

'When we were here last Saturday,' he said, 'we interviewed Gino Butler in a lounge area.' He pointed to one of the doors at the back of the gym. 'Over there, if I remember right,' he murmured as he walked towards it.

The room was as he and Mann had left it; the TV remote still lay on the U-shaped couch, and in a corner of the room, beside a mineral-water fountain, was something he had seen and disregarded: a small drinks refrigerator. He stepped across and opened it.

'Bingo,' he laughed. It contained a dozen cans of soft drinks, and, as he counted, seven cartons of almond-flavoured soya milk. He took them out, one by one, and checked the 'best before' dates. 'Identical,' he said, showing one to Gowans. 'I'm sure if we look at the one they've been testing, it'll be from the same batch.' His eyes gleamed. 'Right, lad, back to the house.'

They retraced their steps, Gowans struggling to match Provan's unexpected pace. The DS unlocked the big front door and headed for the kitchen, where he swung open the huge American-style fridge. None of the contents had been touched; Gowans wondered how long it would be before they went off, and who would think to clear them, but his sergeant had eyes for only one thing: a single carton of soya milk that sat in a rack in the door.

'Evidence bag, Willie,' he snapped, digging a pair of sterile gloves from a pack in his pocket and putting them on.

'Step one,' he muttered as he secured the carton. 'Like it or not, some lab rat'll be working overtime tonight.' He had not been impressed by Dorward's explanation of the time taken to process the Speight autopsy samples.

'What's step two, Sarge?' Gowans asked.

'Go round the back and hope that they only empty the bins once a fortnight down this way.'

Fifty-Four

There was something indefinably sleek about Susannah Himes that helped Dan Provan understand how she had come by her nickname. He could picture her arrowing through the water, rows of teeth on display as she converged on her chosen prey. Facing her in the interview room, he knew that he was in her sights, but he had no intention of taking evasive action.

'Where's DI Mann?' she demanded. 'I was expecting to see her.'

'She has somewhere else to be,' the DS replied smoothly. 'There's another event taking place in Glasgow this morning that requires her attention.'

Himes' eyes flashed, but a sliver of a smile showed on her face for a second or two. 'That was some stroke you two pulled last night,' she complained. 'I could have had Ms Bulloch home if you hadn't put off interviewing her. From what she told me, your evidence is tenuous at best.'

'You're dreamin' there, Ms Himes,' he laughed. 'We'd have been holdin' her overnight regardless. As it is, I've got some good news for you. The fiscal's decided not to proceed with the murder charge.'

She sat even more upright than before. 'He has? Then what

are we doing here? Release her,' she demanded, 'and let her go home to her children.'

Provan sighed and shook his head. 'Ah, if only life were as uncomplicated as that. Ah havenae got round to the bad news yet. We're holding her in custody pending an appearance before the sheriff this lunchtime. The charge will be attempted murder.'

She switched instantly back into attack mode. 'What kind of stroke are you pulling here, Detective Sergeant?' she snapped. 'Speight is dead. In what possible circumstances could attempted murder be a viable charge?'

'They're weird,' he acknowledged, 'but the charge is viable all right. Last Friday night at Speight's farewell extravaganza at his hotel in Newton Mearns, your client was told something by a Crown witness that drove her into a rage. She was so angry, in fact, that her immediate reaction was to get into her car and drive down to his house. Leo was careless wi' his keys; he'd no idea where they all were, but your client had one of them. We can trace her journey, there and back. We can also put her in the kitchen area, where he died.

'We went there last night and we found in the fridge a carton of his favourite, if fairly disgusting, health drink. He drank two cartons o' the stuff every day, and Faye knew that. She found one in the fridge and she loaded it with a lethal dose of paraquat, a herbicide that she'd found in the garden shed. To emphasise her intent, she actually found four cartons in the fridge, but to make sure he chose the one wi' the poison, she dumped the other three in the dustbin. We found them there last night; from my level of smugness, you can guess that we also found Faye's prints and DNA on all four.'

'I'm sorry,' Himes said quietly. 'She poisoned his drink, but you found the stuff in the fridge. I don't get this. Join the dots for me, please, Sergeant. Was Leo Speight poisoned or was he not?'

'Yes,' Provan retorted, 'he was poisoned . . . only not by your client. Frankly, we don't know how it was done, no' yet, but Faye tried tae kill him sure enough, that we can prove.' He smiled wickedly. 'It wasnae her fault that Leo drank another carton, from another fridge, and not the one that she'd dosed and left for him. Oh aye, she did her damnedest tae poison him, and that's why we're chargin' her. I don't need to interview her again, so we're going straight to court.' He checked his watch. 'That'll be in a couple of hours,' he said. 'You can have as much of that time with her as you like . . . unless you want to catch the first train back to Edinburgh.'

The solicitor winced. 'That sounds like an attractive proposition, but I've started, so I'll finish, like Magnus used to say. Will you oppose bail?'

'That'll be up tae the fiscal,' Provan said, 'but there's another party could be at risk from your client. As long as the bail conditions are tough enough to secure her safety, ye might just swing it.'

He left her alone in the interview room and went back to the CID suite, on its last day as a police facility. As he arrived, he saw his own desk being carried out by two removal men. 'Out wi' the old, eh,' he chuckled, amused by the serendipity of the timing. His mind was filled with light and optimism and thoughts of a new era.

'Come on, Willie,' he called out to Gowans. 'Let's go round to the coffee shop in Sauchiehall Street. We'll only be in the way here.'

'It's our last day here, Sarge,' the DC pointed out.

He shrugged his square shoulders. 'So what, son? I've never been sentimental about buildings.'

They walked downstairs and out into Pitt Street, past the line of furniture vans. As they turned into Glasgow's most famous thoroughfare, a flight of large, long-necked birds flew overhead, seven of them, in single file rather than V formation. Provan thought they were beautiful.

'Are they geese, Sarge?' Gowans asked.

'No, son, they're swans,' Provan replied. Then he laughed spontaneously. 'And if ye listen,' he added, 'ye might even hear them singing.'

Fifty-Five

'Welcome to Glasgow, Professor,' Graeme Bell said to his gowned colleague as he led her into his spotless new autopsy suite.

'Why thank you, Professor,' Sarah Grace replied. 'This is very impressive; it's at least the equal of our facility in Edinburgh.'

The tall pathologist smiled. 'That's central Scottish politics for you; it wouldn't do for either of our cities to have facilities superior to the other, although we did lag behind in Glasgow until this place was built.'

'Tell me about it. When he was a chief constable in Edinburgh, my husband rarely had a good word to say for his colleagues in the west. Then he was appointed to the Strathclyde job and his attitude got adjusted.'

Bell glanced up and to his left. 'I'm glad he could join us for this one too; I thought his story about representing the insurers was just bullshit.'

'It was,' she said, 'but it isn't now. When they heard about the second post-mortem, the company contacted him and asked him to observe and report. We've got quite a crowd up there, in fact. The chief constable and the DCC; also Kirk Dougan, the Glasgow procurator fiscal, if I'm not mistaken. Who's the large lady standing beside him?'

'That's Detective Inspector Lottie Mann; she's well on her way to becoming a legend.'

'Is she indeed?' Grace murmured. 'Bob calls her his female doppelgänger; I can see why. She's formidable.'

'You should see her sidekick. In fact I'm surprised that you can't. They're usually inseparable. It's not like Dan Provan to miss a big event. Speaking of big events, there's a rumour on the pathology grapevine that you did a celebrity autopsy a while back.'

'If I did, Graeme,' she replied discreetly, 'it would be covered by the Official Secrets Act and I could not possibly comment. Let's concentrate on today and give this crowd a show.'

'Yes, let's,' Bell agreed. He walked over to a console and activated audio and video recorders, and also threw a switch that would broadcast their commentary to the viewing gallery.

'I've viewed the recording of the original autopsy, Professor,' Grace began. 'I've read your report and also studied the results of the laboratory analysis of the samples you sent them. I hope we don't have to wait for another week for results following this examination.'

'We won't. I've arranged for any testing we require to be carried out immediately, in this building.'

'That's good,' she said. 'I note that while the presentation, circumstances and specific cause of death, hypoxia, all pointed directly to cyanide poisoning, no traces of the substance were found in the victim, in his stomach or in his blood, where it would normally have been evident. Nor was any found in the carton from which he had been drinking, although the almond smell of the substance was a further pointer to the initial suspicion. What I propose now is that the two of us repeat, detail upon detail, your physical examination and search for an alternative finding. I don't believe that your procedure was flawed. The evidence for your conclusion was so clear that I'd have been of exactly the same view, and proven just as wrong. All we can do here, is do it again.' She looked up at the viewing gallery. 'Be aware,' she told the watchers, 'that this could take some time.'

She pulled her mask over her face, as did her colleague, and they set about their grisly business. Leo Speight was reopened; his musculature, his organs and his brain were re-examined with painstaking thoroughness. The samples taken at the first examination were viewed under a microscope, displayed on screen, and the lab analysis was reviewed. Mostly they worked in silence, but occasionally Grace asked a question, and Bell replied.

After ninety minutes, their work was almost complete. Sarah Grace was about to admit that she was baffled when she came to the last sample taken from the body almost a week before. It was little more than a blue smear.

'What's this?' she asked.

'Oil-based paint,' her colleague told her. 'There was an artist friend of his working at his party. She told the police that they were fooling around, and she put a dab of paint on him. It wasn't relevant, so I set it aside.'

'Yes, I remember now from the recording.' She went back to the autopsy table. 'Graeme, can you show me where you found it?'

'Sure.' He joined her, leaning across the open torso and indicating an area just to the right of the laryngeal prominence, the Adam's apple. 'Right there.'

She moved to the other side of the table, took a magnifying

glass from her pocket and bent over the cadaver, examining the spot. When she was finished, she stood and handed the glass to Bell. 'Take a look, Graeme. Can you confirm that there's a small cut there; looks like a razor nick, probably sustained while shaving. My husband usually calls it a "fuck it!" cut; at least that's what he says when he does it.'

As he did what she asked, she returned to the paint smear, removed the top layer of glass and sniffed.

'I want another blood test run immediately,' she said. 'I also want a chemical analysis of this paint smear. While that's being done, I would like to speak to that artist, wherever she is.'

Fifty-Six

'I've seen something similar to this once before,' Sarah Grace said, 'when I was in general practice in America. A child was brought into my surgery as an emergency, a three-year-old boy in a very bad way, struggling to breathe. At first I thought it was anaphylactic shock, possibly a nut allergy, but when I smelled his breath I got something else. He'd been playing in his father's garage and he had drunk turpentine.'

She paused and looked at her audience, the witnesses to the examination all gathered in Graeme Bell's office.

'This was the same thing, but even more obscure,' she continued. 'Professor Bell and I have just had a discussion with Augusta Cambridge, the artist who was at Mr Speight's event, in his hotel. I'm afraid we left her rather distressed. She told us that when she's at a live event, it's her habit to thin her paints with turpentine. Her brush will be heavy with the stuff. It's been established that, playfully, she dabbed Mr Speight's neck, leaving a smear of paint. When she did so, she landed on a fresh open wound. Detective Inspector Mann, I believe that if you check the victim's personal effects and examine the razor he was using, you will find skin and blood traces on it. Tests have just shown the presence of turpentine in his bloodstream, minute but enough for a man who had an allergy to the stuff, as we reckon he did.'

'That's what killed him?' Mario McGuire gasped. 'An allergy to turps? God, my mother's a painter.'

'What killed him was histotoxic hypoxia,' Sarah countered. 'Tissue poisoning. That's why it was natural to accept the likelihood of cyanide. But hypoxia can be caused by other things. In this case we have a spectacular cocktail; it wasn't only the turpentine that was in play. You see, the paint that Ms Cambridge was using was cobalt blue. For those of you who are unaware, oil paints are essentially pigments in a suspension of oil, thinned in this case by a substance to which the victim was violently allergic. In addition to that, the cobalt blue pigment, which also entered his bloodstream through that razor cut, is extremely toxic.'

'What we're saying,' Professor Bell added, 'is that he was killed by either substance or both. Anything more precise would be speculation.'

'So I can call it accidental death?' Kirk Dougan, the procurator fiscal, asked.

'You're the lawyer,' Sarah replied. 'It's down to you to decide what's an accident, or to a jury if you deem that to be necessary. Speight didn't put that paint on himself. We're not suggesting seriously that you charge Ms Cambridge, because she had no way of knowing that a light-hearted gesture would have such consequences, but . . .'

She looked at her husband. 'She did die at the hands of another, Bob, so your insurer client could be looking at a claim for full value on the policy it so recklessly wrote. If it winds up in court, I'd rather be an expert witness for the claimant than the defender, that's for sure.'

'What a way to go,' Chief Constable Maggie Steele murmured.

'Yup,' Sarah agreed. 'One chance in a hundred thousand, I reckon. But the law of averages isn't called that for nothing. Long shots do come up, time and time again. That's why people gamble. Every time Leo Speight climbed into a boxing ring he was placing a bet, putting his life on the line. Every time each of us gets up in the morning to face the hidden perils of a new day, we do the same thing. Finally Leo lost, but in a way he never imagined.'

Fifty-Seven

There was a confident swagger about Moss Lee as he took his place in the office of Sheriff Rose Romannes, flanked by Scott Mann. He gazed across at his adversary; she was seated a few feet away, on her own.

The door behind them opened and the sheriff entered, followed by her clerk, and by a tall young woman. She was a stranger to the solicitor; he was puzzled, even more so when she seated herself next to Lottie Mann.

'Good morning, everyone,' Sheriff Romannes began cheerfully. 'Mrs Mann, Mr Lee, welcome once more.' She looked at Scott. 'You'll be Mr Mann, I take it.'

He nodded. 'Free at last,' he said. 'Good God Almighty, free at last.'

Lee tensed slightly at his flippancy, tugging his sleeve slightly. The sheriff's smile disappeared. She looked at the newcomer. 'I don't know you.'

'Alexis Skinner, solicitor advocate,' she replied, 'representing Mrs Mann.'

'Mmm,' the judge murmured. 'A solicitor advocate no less. Have you done a child welfare hearing before, Ms Skinner?'

'No, this is my first.'

393

'Then I'll explain proceedings. They're informal – that's why we're here rather than in the courtroom – but not completely. The case is discussed by both sides, arguments are made and countered. I like to keep things non-adversarial, but sometimes that isn't possible. At the close of the hearing I might make suggestions, or I might make an order. If I do that, it's as if it was made in court. Non-compliance can be treated as contempt. Do you understand that?'

She nodded. 'I do. I understand also that witnesses aren't called but that statements can be presented.'

'That's right,' Sheriff Romannes confirmed, 'but it's up to me whether I take any notice of them. Let's proceed. I will begin by saying that I'm concerned that this session is necessary. At the previous hearing I suggested that Mr Mann's parents should be given rights of access to the child, Jake. I accepted a submission, also, that there was nothing about Mr Mann's conviction and prison sentence that should disqualify him as a parent on his release. Now here you are before me, Mr Lee, asking that he be given full custody. Is that not just a bit precipitate?'

'We don't believe so, my lady,' Moss Lee declared, glancing across at Alexis Skinner as if he was trying to assess how much of a threat she presented. 'Last weekend, a crisis developed. The mother, Detective Inspector Mann, became embroiled in a very high-profile homicide investigation; that led immediately to a collapse in the care arrangements that you approved for Jake. As a result, the grandparents, Mr Mann senior and his wife, had to intervene and remove the child to their home, where he was happy and well looked after for the rest of the weekend.

'Mr Mann senior had made arrangements for Jake to be interviewed last Monday for a place at the Glasgow Academy, which clearly would have been in his long-term educational interests. The mother interfered, removing the child, preventing him from keeping that appointment and placing him in the care of an extremely pregnant member of the extended family of the questionable Detective Sergeant Provan, a disreputable, dishevelled gentleman who seems to have a Svengali-like influence over Detective Inspector Mann, and more worryingly over the child at the heart of this matter. That is a situation which the father cannot accept. Mr Scott Mann has his liberty, he is employed by his father on working hours appropriate to a single parent, and he has accommodation that is of a higher standard than that offered by the mother. I submit that the time has come for Jake to be rescued from his unstable environment and given the security he deserves.'

The sheriff nodded as he finished. 'You don't pull your punches, Mr Lee. I have to admit that the scenario you describe gives me cause for concern. Ms Skinner, do you need time to consult with your client and prepare a response? I'm happy to adjourn if you wish.'

'Thank you, my lady,' Alex replied. 'I'm happy to say that I am in a position to rebut Mr Lee's claims, one by one. I'd like to begin by doing something unusual, in response to the character assassination of Acting Detective Inspector Daniel Provan. I'd like to show you a series of photographs, taken yesterday evening, during and after a session at Max's Gym in Glasgow.'

Sheriff Romannes gazed at her, then smiled. 'Let me see. I'm curious.' She took the photographs and studied them; in sequence they featured a middle-aged man, well muscled and tanned, running on a treadmill, operating a cross-trainer and bench-pressing a significant weight; they showed him again, clean shaven and immaculately dressed, standing outside the gym, smiling, with a boy by his side who looked as happy as any child ever did.

Romannes smiled also. 'That being . . .'

'That being the dishevelled, disreputable Detective Sergeant Daniel Provan, who has never come close to failing a fitness test in all his years of police service. The boy is, of course, Jakey Mann, who hardly seems deprived, subdued or in any way at risk.'

She took the images back from the sheriff and drew out several documents, which she laid on the table. 'I know, my lady,' she said, 'that witnesses are not called in this forum, however statements may be lodged and I hope you will examine these. They're precognitions, properly taken by my agent and witnessed. The first is by Mrs Grace Ainslie, who was employed for five years as secretary to Mr Arnold Mann, a post she gave up when she could no longer tolerate his innuendo and casual advances. In her testimony she describes Mr Mann senior's volatile temper, and several physical assaults on junior members of his staff, of both genders. The second and third statements are offered by two people who were Scott Mann's teachers at primary and secondary school. They describe in graphic detail several occasions on which he appeared at school with bruises to his head and body. The fourth is a copy of the disciplinary report prepared on Scott Mann that led to his dismissal from Strathclyde Police Service, on grounds of the abuse of both alcohol and prisoners, and tampering with evidence in criminal investigations. The fifth is a statement by Christine McGlashan, his one-time mistress and co-accused in his criminal trial. She describes his instability, and also acts of violence suffered at his hands. Finally there is an account by my client of the abuse that she herself experienced. These are informal statements at this stage, but every one of those people is willing to give evidence under oath and subject themselves to cross-examination by Mr Lee or anyone else. My lady, I've been investigating these people for less than a week and I've come up with that. Give me another week, and who knows what will surface?'

She passed the documents across the sheriff's desk. 'Finally, my lady,' she continued, 'I would like to address the adequacy of Jakey's present and future care. Vanessa Linares is the partner of Jamie Provan, Acting DI Provan's son; he is an officer in the Scottish Fire and Rescue Service. Ms Linares is not in fact extremely pregnant; she's currently at twenty weeks, and will be in a position to care for the boy for another four months. By that time a long-term arrangement will be in place, one that I am sure will satisfy you. Acting Detective Inspector Provan, after thirty-four years' service as a police officer in and around Glasgow, has decided to retire. He will be a sometime lecturer at the Scottish Police College, but his main retirement occupation will be as carer to Jake Mann.'

She produced one final document from her case and handed it over. 'That is a copy of Acting Detective Inspector Provan's service record. You will see that it contains several commendations for good conduct and a couple for bravery, but not a single disciplinary infraction. My lady, I hope you will read my submissions and will find that Jake Mann could be in no safer place than in his mother's care.'

Fifty-Eight

'Oh Dan, love,' Lottie laughed. 'You should have seen their faces, Scott's and Moss Lee's. Sheriff Romannes adjourned for three hours. When we went back in, she'd read all Alex's reports, and made a few phone calls of her own. She found entirely in my favour; she banned Scott's father from any unsupervised contact with Jakey, and she told Scott that if he ever petitioned her again, he'd lose his own rights of access, which are set from now on at one day every fortnight. That Alex; she is something else.'

'I guessed she might be,' Provan murmured, leaning back on the sofa in her small living room. 'Hey,' he asked quietly, 'what did you call me there?'

'You heard.' She looked at him seriously. 'Dan, are you sure about retiring?'

'Never surer, lass,' he replied. 'A whole new chapter just opened up. With luck, I'll get to read quite a bit.'

'And is that all you want?' She held his gaze. 'You know what I mean.'

'Possibly not,' he admitted after a while. 'But I won't build my hopes up.'

She reached out and touched his cheek, with surprisingly soft fingers for a large hand.

'Maybe you should,' she whispered. 'I swear, these days you look ten years younger.'

Fifty-Nine

'You've viewed it, this film?' Joey Morocco asked.

'Yes,' Skinner replied, 'and Aldorino Moscardinetto's memo to Leo, where he suggested that he saw it as a feature film, not the documentary that Leo had envisaged. I have a copy of what was on the memory stick; all I need is clearance from Leo's heir and I can give it to you.'

'Will you get it?'

'I don't anticipate any problems. Of course,' he continued, 'the story moved on a long way after that. I can add some of the additional material, but it's better if it's properly put together. There's a writer guy I know in Gullane; I've briefed him and he's going to turn the whole thing into a rough screenplay. You were a mate of Aldorino's; I'm sure he'd be pleased, wherever he is, if you could make it all happen.'

The actor smiled, and Skinner knew that he was hooked. 'I'd direct, of course,' Morocco said, 'as well as star. I've been looking to take that step for a while. Mind you, it'll take a bit of funding.'

'I can talk to my colleagues at InterMedia,' Skinner volunteered. 'It is a media company, and given its Italian interests they might kick in some money. If you cast a couple of Spanish actors as well, that would help.'

'Easily done,' Morocco agreed. 'I'm interested, Bob, very interested. Send me what you can when you can. I've got to go now; I have a plane to catch and my taxi's outside.'

Skinner watched his retreating back as he headed for the door of the Balmoral Hotel. He was about to follow him when yet again, inevitably, his phone sounded. Yet again he thought about letting it go to voicemail, but inevitably, he answered.

'Bob,' familiar gruff tones greeted him. Even if his screen had not advised him that Sir James Proud was calling, he would have known his voice whatever the background noise levels.

'Jimmy,' he exclaimed. 'How are you? How's the chemo going?'

'That's fine,' his old chief replied. 'I'm officially in remission. Bob, I'm wondering if you have some time free tonight. The thing is . . . I've got a problem.'